Our Valiant Few

By F. van Wyck Mason

This book is for
CAROLIN and McKENNEY EGERTON
The steadfastness of whose friendship
has been proved so often and in so many ways;
and to the memory of
THOSE SUPREMELY VALIANT SOUTHERNERS
who lost their lives while serving in C.S.S. *Hunley*

Foreword

IN these days of atomic submarines capable of traversing oceans without refueling or surfacing, one becomes better able, perhaps, to appreciate the astounding courage and fortitude of men who fought to volunteer for service aboard a rudimentary submersible which was propelled by hand power and had no reserve of compressed air or even a periscope.

My intention, while preparing this volume, was to learn as much as possible concerning the South's many attempts to break the blockade around Charleston, and about the underwater war waged by the Confederacy; then to attempt to describe these endeavors as accurately as possible. The latter ambition especially proved difficult to fulfill; hardly any descriptions of Mr. H. L. Hunley's "Fish-boat" or accounts of her career agreed on anything: dimensions, dates, or activities. They were, however, unanimous on one point: that C.S.S. *Hunley* sank a Union cruiser and so became the first submarine in history to torpedo an enemy man-of-war.

The author has incorporated what seem to be the most likely dates, events, and descriptions, based on supporting evidence from many widely varying sources.

Great hostility was manifested both in the North and the South towards underwater warfare of any description. Such means of waging war was deemed by many naval officers to be unchivalrous, if not downright cowardly.

Lacking shipyards of any consequence, engineering facilities, and trained shipwrights, the Southern Navy Department perforce turned its attention to marine torpedoes — now termed mines — both contact and electrically fired; torpedo boats; and, finally, to what was at first called a "fish-boat" — a submarine.

vii

In this book, naval vessels belonging to either side are distinguished as such by omitting the article "the" before a ship's name: as, *Palmetto State*. Privately owned vessels such as the *Grey Ghost* retain the article; so, while the submarine is owned by H. L. Hunley — as she was during most of her career — she is called the *Hunley*, but when she is bought and commissioned by the Confederate States Navy she is known as C.S.S. *Hunley*. The names of all blockade-runners, their captains, and their pilots are historic, as well as their accomplishments. The *Grey Ghost* and her company are purely imaginary, but her description belongs to the famous blockade-runner, *Banshee*.

All officers on duty in Charleston and serving aboard Confederate and Union men-of-war were real personages, with the following exceptions: Dabney Seymour, Drummond Mullinix, Peter Burgoyne, and Donald Bryson. It almost goes without saying that the Columbian and Excalibur Companies never existed, any more than the men who speculated through them; but they do portray other companies which existed at the time and operated as described.

The *Charleston Argus* and its staff are entirely fictional, as are the Lambkin, Livesey, Mullinix, Bryson, and Seymour families, and all members thereof. Any families bearing similar names are not to be associated with this book in any manner.

Actually, there was no survivor of C.S.S. *Hunley*'s last plunge, but the names of the rest of the crew are historic and commemorated on a monument to the supremely brave men they were.

My earnest appreciation of invaluable assistance in the preparation of this tale goes to Mr. Robert H. Haynes of the Harvard College Library and his staff, Miss Ruth Coplan and staff of the Enoch Pratt Free Library of Baltimore, and Mrs. James L. Breslove and Miss Jeanne-Louise Hand, my secretaries.

F. van Wyck Mason

"Enfield"
Somerset Bridge
Bermuda

Contents

BOOK I: *Palmetto Squadron*

BOOK II: *Savannah Waters*

BOOK III: *Aide-toi et Dieu T'Aidera*

BOOK ONE

Palmetto Squadron

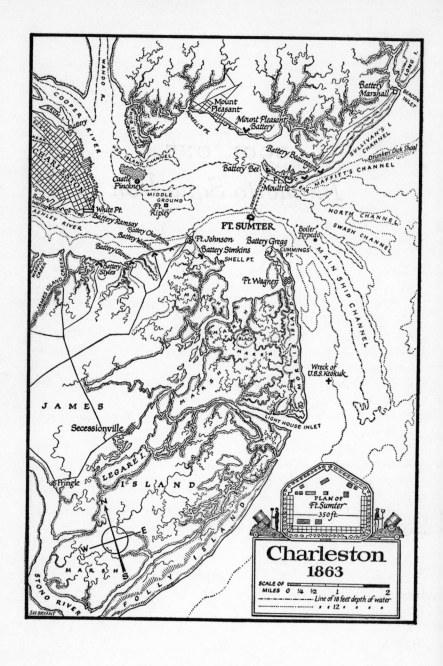

Charleston
1863

PLAN OF
Ft. Sumter
350 ft.

SCALE OF
MILES 0 ¼ ½   1   2
.... Line of 18 feet depth of water
. . . 12 . . .

CHAPTER I **Drunken Dick Shoal**

FOUR men protected by streaming, white-painted oilskins and sou'westers clung to the blockade-runner's flying bridge, tensely watching billow after ragged billow of opaque gray vapor come slipping over a turtleback covering their vessel's sharp ram bow. From time to time fog would eclipse the steamer's small boats, lowered and lashed level with the bulwarks.

A northeast wind, rushing over the Gulf Stream's warm and dark-blue waters, was creating an ever-thickening mist while lashing the Atlantic into choppy, white-crested rollers. As might be expected, this December half-gale blew bitterly cold. Only because a chronometer so indicated were the vessel's officers aware that, ere long, the sun must lift above a horizon lost beyond this baffling, salt-smelling curtain of vapor.

"Hey, Cap'n, we're nearing soundings," bawled the pilot from the wheelhouse. "Feel them swells growin' and draggin'?"

The captain — dark, shoulder-long hair damply asway above his collar — nodded, then clutched the bridge rail as, viciously, the *Grey Ghost* rolled 'way over to port, then pitched like a horse stung by a sandbur lodged beneath its saddle pad.

"Mister Mate, I want quarter-speed," called the pilot, raising reddened eyes from a brass-hooded binnacle.

"Quarter-speed!" the mate bellowed down a speaking tube which found its other end in the engine room.

"Stop yer engines," suddenly commanded the pilot after peering intently into the shifting fog streamers. Over a sudden, shattering roar from the exhaust-pipe valves he yelled through the wheelhouse door: "I need a cast of lead, Captain Bryson, and tell your leadsman to hurry. We've got to look sharp."

3

"As you wish, Mr. Burrus," came the quiet reply.

Once she had commenced to slow, the slender-hulled vessel lost rhythm in concert with the seas, so successive sheets of icy, lacelike spray commenced to soar over the bulwarks and to smother in dripping silver the amorphous outlines of her deck cargo.

While awaiting the leadsman's arrival, Pilot Burrus chanced to glance aft and rapped out an exasperated oath. A great comet's-tail of crimson-gold flame was curling from the sooty lips of the *Grey Ghost*'s two slim funnels.

"Mister Mate, order that damn' lunkhead in your engine room to keep his drafts closed. Lookouts aboard any cruiser within half a mile can spy such a glare, even through a fog like this."

A seaman in dripping white oilskins appeared on the bridge and passed his sounding lead into the pilot's eager hands. Now that the *Grey Ghost*'s outsized paddle wheels had ceased to thresh, a moaning sound, caused by wind among the foreshrouds, became startlingly audible.

"What do you deduce, Mr. Burrus?" presently demanded the runner's master. Fine lines of tension were deepening about a reckless and thin-lipped mouth.

"This here stuff stuck to the tallow is sixteen-fathom sand and showin' black specks," explained the pilot, long body swaying to the vessel's rolling. "Means we've been driven south of our course."

"How far?"

"No telling. We'll fly the blue pigeon again, in — well — mebbe half an hour." Burrus spun over the wheel. "We'll head northwest-by-north for a while. Mr. Mate, ring for half-speed." The pilot bit into a plug of tobacco, nodded to himself. "Yep. Got to pass just north o' that speckled bottom before I dast make the run for Charleston Bar."

The blockade-runner's side wheels had resumed their monotonous beat and spray again was bursting rhythmically over her bows when it became apparent that this fog was growing uneven in density.

At the end of half an hour the pilot wiped away beads of moisture clinging to sparse, sandy-colored chin whiskers. "Reckon we'd better try the lead again, Cap'n."

On this occasion tallow, smeared into the lead's cupped base, displayed only coarse white sand and a trace of blue clay. Immediately Burrus's leathery features relaxed.

"That'll do. I know right where we are; you kin ring for full speed,

4

Mr. Mate. Now all you have to do is pray we don't run slam-bang into some damn' Bluebelly cruiser."

The light by now had so improved that lokouts, lashed to crosstrees on the fore- and mainmasts, became discernible as shapeless black objects swaying, pendulumlike, amid the whirling fog; for, to minimize the *Grey Ghost's* visibility, all topmasts had been sent down. The runner's paddles beat a constantly mounting tempo until the long and narrow craft quivered violently as she drove her ram bow ever deeper into the rising seas.

"Damn this gale to hell and back!" growled the first mate. "Hope we've enough Cardiff coal for another hour's run."

"There's no serious doubt on that score, is there, Mr. Brazenose?" demanded the captain, sharply. "You declared we had plenty."

The mate turned a dripping sou'wester and blinked uncomfortably.

"That's what I figgered in Nassau, sir, but what with our boring into this bloody gale all night, we've consumed a heap of fuel."

The pilot snorted. "You'd better be right! That cheap Belgium coal in your reserve bunkers smokes to beat all hell; by daylight, we can be spotted miles away."

Gradually, the blockade-runner's cargo-cluttered deck became visible until one could make out a dozen men lining the rail to scan the ocean in all directions.

"Well, Mr. Burrus?" came the captain's taut accents. "Do you know where we are, for sure?"

"Aye. We should be bearin' down on Drunken Dick Shoal — provided this here storm ain't played tricks with the tide."

"It'd better not," warned the mate. "Cap'n Bryson, here, ain't paying you no four thousand dollars to pile his ship on a sand bar."

The pilot spat tobacco juice out of the wheelhouse door. "Listen, Mister, if you figger I got any hankering to cool my butt in Fort Warren, or any other Yankee jail, you got another think comin'."

Captain Bryson pulled on tighter a visored cap as he peered into the chill, gray-white vapors rushing by. He drew a deep breath. The next half-hour must decide whether the *Grey Ghost's* million-and-a-half-dollar cargo would reach Charleston or go to the bottom; he entertained no intention of surrendering, no matter what chanced — too many people in Charleston were eager to believe the worst of Raphael Bryson.

An especially furious gust of the northeast magically opened a clear lane through the fog, disclosing, to the anxious men on the *Grey Ghost*'s bridge, a Union blockade ship steaming along, not a quarter of a mile away, and trailing a black streamer of smoke at fight angles to the runner's course. The enemy was a screw-propelled sloop and was close enough for the *Grey Ghost*'s company to count her gun ports and watch the crew gather about a big pivot gun mounted forward.

"Full speed! Quick! For God's sake!" bawled the pilot, cramping the blockade-runner's wheel over to port.

Captain Bryson grinned when, easily and swiftly as a dancer, his sleek little ship spun about, and sped, westward, towards shelter offered by a heavy white bank of fog.

Mr. Brazenose licked bearded lips. "We're in luck, sir, that bulldog ain't spied us, even yet; this sparse top hamper sure helps."

A minute elapsed before the enemy cruiser's lookouts glimpsed the *Grey Ghost*'s fleeting outline, then a bugle shrieked and the steam sloop rounded smartly in pursuit. Spouting Stygian clouds from a squat smokestack, she commenced to close in along a long parallel.

"Damn it," growled Tom Burrus over the paddle wheels' frantic splashings, "yonder's the *Housatonic*, fastest blockader in these waters!"

A Union flag climbed, to stream from the cruiser's signal gaff; it stood out stiff, as though cut out of tin. Next, the man-of-war hoisted a string of varicolored signal flags.

"Well, there it is, Cap'n," grunted the mate. " 'Heave to or take the consequences.' "

"I am as well able to read signals as you, Mr. Brazenose," Bryson remarked, then crossed to the speaking tube. "Enemy ship close astern, Mr. Cameron!" he yelled. "Pour on paraffin — anything that'll burn fast and hot. Tie down your safety valves."

Only instants later, brilliant banderoles of flame burst from the *Grey Ghost*'s funnels and she commenced smoothly to slice the waves at nearly fourteen knots. She rolled sickeningly, though.

"By God, Cap'n, mebbe we'll make it," the pilot cried, ragged beard flowing. "Yore vessel's faster'n any scalded cat."

Soon the fleeing runner's iron fabric began to palpitate, probably because of a too light frame. Like smoke, clouds of spume and lacy spray exploded through openings in the paddle-wheel housings.

On deck, scattered groups of seamen crouched behind the bulwarks for shelter. Some watched the Union bluejacks steadily traversing their

6

piece in line with the fugitive, the rest stared at that glimmering nebulous haven, the fog bank. Now it loomed but a few hundred yards distant.

Across an expanse of white-crested rollers a blinding rose of fire bloomed briefly, then a shell screamed past the bridge, so close that the helmsman, pilot and first officer all ducked. Only Captain Bryson remained erect, though his sodden hair was stirred by the wind of the projectile's passage. His whole attention was concentrated upon this big sloop's stern pivot. If the crew of that piece also missed — then, please God, the fog bank should be reached before either crew could reload.

The Yankee commander must have appreciated the fact that, in a few moments, his quarry could lose herself and, with any luck, escape him, for furious billows of smoke burst from the sloop's funnel.

Captain Bryson's hands tightened on the bridge rail until their knuckles crackled. Only a few seconds of respite, then all would be well.

Through thickening vapors glimmered a second, blinding flash. All hands on deck heard the eerie screech of a passing round shot, followed by a loud *twang!* caused by a wire halyard being severed. It sounded as if some gigantic musician had snapped a string of his harp. The *Grey Ghost's* main gaff came crashing down to dangle, and began to slat wildly against the mast, much as might a man's arm, hanging broken by his side.

Mercifully, the fog bank received the slender, gray fugitive in its dank depths.

"Will the Yankee attempt to follow us?" Bryson's black eyes were boring steadily through the gloom.

"Not if her skipper's in his right mind, he won't," the pilot shouted. "Drunken Dick Shoal lies dead ahead, and his ship draws too much to dast try getting acrost." He grinned. "You can thank them British designers for giving you only eight foot o' draft."

The mate, beard all spangled with moisture, violently shook his head. "Is eight feet all you're allowing on? Hell, man, we draw eight feet, sure enough, but *only* when in ballast!"

The pilot's jaw closed with a click. "Christ A'mighty! What might we be drawing right now?"

"Can't say, for sure."

"Ten foot, maybe?"

"More like eleven, mebbe twelve."

"Why in hell didn't you say so before?"

Captain Bryson bent closer to Tom Burrus. "Never mind that now. Think you can ease us across Drunken Dick?"

"If we're luckier than lucky," the pilot growled. "There's a few places I *might* git you over 'thout grounding."

"Then hold your present course, Mr. Burrus. The fog seems to be thinning."

CHAPTER II "Christmas Gif'"

A DECEMBER northeast gale, screaming over Charleston Harbor, became tinctured by that sour reek peculiar to newly burned buildings and drove dead leaves scurrying madly over Calhoun Street's brick sidewalks. Also it pressed Mrs. Alistair Bryson's gray merino skirt tight about her legs, effectively hinting at their outlines.

Now and then a particularly furious gust whipped about that garment's frayed hem and disclosed ankles which remained shapely despite coarse black cotton stockings. The fabric was lifted sufficiently high to attract the open admiration of a detail from the 1st South Carolina Artillery.

These bearded gunners, India Bryson guessed, must be headed either for Battery Waring, guarding the Ashley River's entrance, or for earthworks thrown up behind Vanderhorst's Wharf to deny an enemy use of the Cooper River.

At the intersection with Pitt Street, the slim, bright-cheeked young woman stepped into a doorway in order more firmly to secure about fashionably sloping shoulders a faded shawl bearing the Bryson clan tartan. While doing so, the girl cast apprehensive glances at the sky, noted that it had become lead-hued and streaked by hurrying, thin gray clouds.

Since a clock in the tower of St. Philip's Church was sounding three, India Bryson calculated that Dorcas Mullinix, her only female friend in this lovely, but persistently aloof, old city, should soon be putting in an appearance. While sauntering towards their rendezvous, India felt the

8

edges of the sidewalk's brick, so thin had grown the soles of once-pretty balmoral boots. She'd bought them nearly three years earlier in Philadelphia. Alistair at the time had teased a bit over their cost but, of late, he'd come to marvel over the way these same balmorals held together.

Philadelphia, Boston, New York! Nowadays, such towns seemed remote as stars in the sky. All the same, she'd never forget the peculiar exhilaration she found in exploring their bustling streets, magnificent shops, restaurants and theaters. Theaters! Momentarily, she closed her eyes, visualizing the wonderful glare caused by gaslights aflare behind tin shields and drawing a radiant boundary between stage and pit.

The girl wrinkled a deliciously short and slightly retroussé nose while attempting to recapture the stimulating odors of grease paint, stale face powder and dust such as pervade dressing rooms the world over. More successfully, India Bryson could recall the rich and exquisitely modulated tones of Mr. Edwin Booth portraying King Lear's anguish, and her own clear voice speaking Cordelia's lines.

Firmly, India warned herself away from such a line of reflection and at the same time wondered why, of late, she so often found herself reliving those glorious days with Mr. Booth's company of players, and that night in Richmond when she'd encountered an exciting and earnest young reporter, striving to establish himself.

After their perhaps too hasty marriage there had been no more footlights for the former Miss Villepigue, no more carefree existence, no more singing or dancing, except rarely and very much in private.

The girl's great dark eyes surveyed a succession of dusty, often cracked and all but empty store windows until she came to a halt before Mr. Hericot's Dry Goods Establishment. She emitted an exasperated sigh.

Lord's mercy! Five dollars now was being asked for a *single* package of needles! She wandered on beneath a succession of wrought-iron balconies draped with leafless wistaria and bougainvillaea vines. What, oh what, could she hope to buy for Alistair's Christmas? So pitifully little merchandise was exposed, and at what prices!

Her gift, of course, ought to be useful; possibly a knitted woolen jerkin or a heavy muffler for use on those mysterious expeditions Alistair kept making to the harbor's outer defenses or among that labyrinth of sounds and marshes which surrounded the city.

Sometimes, such trips would keep the *Argus*'s new managing editor away from home long hours, or even days at a time. From such assign-

9

ments Alistair usually returned bone-weary but showing a satisfied gleam in his eye. Usually, then, the *Argus* would publish some item of news concerning the siege a full day before either the *Mercury* or the *Courier* got around to printing their versions of said event.

Mechanically, India tested a hair net of scarlet chenille securing a chignon of blue-black hair. The girl's eyes widened momentarily on noticing a bolt of brightly colored calamanco cloth, but her interest faded quickly when she read a grimy card resting upon it: ONLY TWENTY-THREE DOLLARS THE YARD — while a pair of man's knitted mittens, stout and warm-looking, could be purchased for a mere fifty!

Gradually, a mirthless smile tightened India's naturally vivid lips. She had added to them a touch of extra brilliance just because she didn't care a picayune what Charleston's bitterly clannish ladies might think about the use of lip rouge. Long ago, she had determined to demonstrate that a female was not necessarily a trollop if, on occasion, she chose to pluck her brows or apply a discreet touch of rouge.

Her awkwardly mended gloves tightened upon a black velvet reticule. Alas, ever since she could remember, she had hated needlework of any sort with an abiding passion. She knew her purse contained exactly fifty Confederate dollars, of which Alistair gently had exacted a promise that she would not part with more than half. By now it appeared that her chances of coming across a suitable gift were slim, especially since Alistair expected her also to purchase the basis for a Christmas dinner out of this pittance.

On peering into a butcher shop's ill-lit window she stifled a moan. On display was but a single scrawny chicken, and that priced at twenty dollars! Bitterly, she thought: And there are still people in this town who insist the Yankee blockade is but an ineffective nuisance.

The girl in the full gray skirts was about to brave the inspection of yet another group of convalescent soldiers when a short, white-haired Negro shuffled up and, after glancing to right and left, knuckled a coachman's crumpled top hat.

He ducked a little bow. " 'Pears like Mistis doan' gre'tly fancy that there fowl?"

When India smiled, all her pointed and tawny features lit. "That, my good Moor, is at least a masterpiece of understatement."

The Negro's rheumy, yellow eyes grew large. "Pah'don, Mistis, mah name ain't 'Moore,' hit's Ambrose."

India suppressed a giggle. "Nevertheless, by any name thou art Moor, even as Othello."

"Yessum, yessum, Ah expec's 'at's Gawd's troof." The Negro peered upwards, carefully. "Mistis, does Ah reckon right you is shoppin' fo' Christmas?"

"You are right; even as the Magi, I do seek a gift suitable for my lord, but also I seek sustenance to grace his less than groaning board." The lightness departed from India's manner. "But enough of jest. Do you know, Ambrose, where I could, perchance, purchase a modest cut of ham?"

Briefly, the bent and diminutive Negro surveyed passers-by; mostly women assisting disabled soldiers. "Ham? Fo' Gawd, Mistis, hit ain't ha'dly possible no mo', not in Charleston." He assumed a conspiratorial manner and further lowered his voice. "But mebbe Ah knows where yo' might fin' a purty sumpin' fo' de gennemun of yo' fancy, real cheap."

India's spirits rose. This might prove to be an extraordinary piece of luck. One heard it whispered that, since the blockade had become effective, not a few fine old families had become faced with ruin. As became their proud tradition, many of these still were making efforts to maintain a front, but the only way they could keep up their pretense was, surreptitiously of course, to part with an ever-increasing number of valuables.

Others lived off an uncertain income derived through the sale of produce secretly fetched in from properties retained in the "back country" to be sold through agents. Never in the world would it do to let society suspect that, in effect, they had become vegetable farmers.

"You read my necessity for a 'purty sumpin' most accurately, Ambrose," she smiled brightly. "Now listen well, O most worthy Moor. I go to meet a friend, and once I come upon her I shall fetch her to a rendezvous in the street behind the college. There I will inspect this gift."

"Yessum. I sho' nuff be behin' de college in half a hour."

The wizened little Negro bobbed another bow, then quickly lost himself among a party of mechanics trudging homewards from work on a great steam ram slowly taking shape in Mr. James Eason's shipyard. Hunched over into their coat collars, the workmen moved silently through the bitter gloom.

It was curious and yet indicative of this city's dogged will that these men, even on the eve of a holiday, had worked overtime to complete a man-of-war still known simply as *Ironclad No. 3*. Probably this devotion was due to the fact that the new ram was felt to be largely a local effort, her cost having been defrayed by the contributions of certain wellborn Charleston ladies. Undoubtedly, this man-of-war would be christened *Charleston* and serve as flagship for what affectionately was known, hereabouts, as the "Palmetto Squadron."

India waved. Mrs. Mullinix's dumpy, black-clad figure was advancing along Calhoun Street, suggestive of a tug breasting a stiff sea. With one hand she held in place a black poke bonnet. A net shopping bag dangled from the other. In Dorcas Mullinix's pink cheeks a not unattractive network of tiny red veins bespoke a girlhood spent among the misty Highlands of Scotland.

" 'Tis a braw breeze, this," she called. "Reminds me of home. How is friend Alistair? As mysterious and occupied as usual?"

"Even more so." India pecked her friend's cold cheek. "Being married to a doctor must be bad enough, but 'tis better by far to remain a widow than wed to a newspaperman!"

Mrs. Mullinix jerked her head towards the jumble of blackened ruins stretching southwards from Calhoun Street. As far as the eye could see, burned structures marred the vista in that direction. Like a grotesque forest swept by fire, chimneys rose above the rubble and windowless, scorched walls groped towards the wind-filled sky.

"Yon's a sore sight to greet the Christmas Day," the widow commented. "And with so many poor people homeless or destitute!"

"There's an equally sad sight in yonder window," India observed. "A box of sulphur matches priced at fifty cents!"

"Fifty cents! The Laird preserve us! They were not half that dear last week." The widow clucked back of her teeth. "Ou, aye. Then I needs must hunt up an auld tinder pistol I've put away."

India brushed a strand of wind-freed sable hair from before her eyes. "How fares Drummie's naval career? Will the captain of the *Chicora* grant his crew Christmas at home?"

"Aye. John Tucker for once is showing a measure of consideration, but Drummond says the captain swears he'll exercise his gun crews 'til they're able to shoot the very buttons off Admiral Du Pont's waistcoat.

" 'Tis well my son fair thrives on hard work," she added, not without quiet satisfaction. "Mr. Payne — the *Chicora*'s principal lieutenant — recently confided to Major Lambkin, Drummie will be posted a probationary lieutenant come the New Year."

"And he's only a lad! Oh, Dorcas, how very proud you must be!" Softly, India clapped mittened hands. "Of him, as of his father."

The widow nodded but her smile faded. How cruel had been Tom Mullinix's fate after long, and far from undistinguished, service afloat! On half-pay and the savings of years, Captain Mullinix, usn (retired), had entered the rice brokerage business and was amassing a modest fortune the day Sumter had been fired upon. Immediately, he'd offered his services to the Confederate States Navy, foreseeing that, willy-nilly, the newborn nation would be forced also to fight upon the sea.

The widow suppressed a sigh while twitching aside her skirts to avoid having them splashed by a passing forage wagon. If Tom had had to die, why couldn't he have fallen, gloriously, in some great, crashing battle, like General Bee at Manassas? Instead, he'd been crushed into an ugly pulp by a falling slab of armor plate while superintending construction of *Palmetto State*. She braced her shoulders and forced herself to smile at the pretty young woman at her side.

"Well, lass, and where shall we seek our Christmas dinner? I hope you've an inspiration, for I'm at my wits end, truly I am. Drummie has the appetite of a dray horse and, so far, I've seen offered only the most miserable kind of food."

Before India could reply, a series of reports, suggestive of a Cyclopean door being slammed in the distance, sounded from the direction of White Point. Pedestrians halted and turned to face the harbor. India counted six shots before the racket died away.

"Yankee ships off Sumter again, no doubt."

"No. Sounds more like Battery Ramsay saluting something or other."

As they set off for the college, Dorcas Mullinix sniffed. "What a childish waste of good powder is all this saluting! Can't those cockerels of the First Carolina show off without shooting their cannons?"

"Apparently not. Poor fellows, they've so little to do, I don't wonder they get bored."

The widow considered her companion's diminutive figure. India walked so lightly, so gracefully, she appeared to be dancing. "And where might Alistair be?"

Deftly, India managed her full skirts around a water-filled hole in the sidewalk. "I've not the least notion. Somebody banged on our door about four o'clock this morning and Alistair just quietly put on his clothes and went out. Reckon I was too sleepy to ask questions. Now let's hurry a bit while I tell you about the mysterious blackamoor who accosted me in Calhoun Street."

Mrs. Mullinix brightened perceptibly. "Oh! So you've been chancy enough to meet a go-between?"

"Let's hope so," India said cheerfully. "Perhaps you'd better let me approach him alone; he's such a frightened little creature he may scuttle away if we both bear down on him."

Despite the great number of black-clad women, crippled soldiers and ragged Negroes begging or selling trifles on street corners, a brave attempt at cheeriness was prevalent in town. In numerous saloons and grogshops the voices of patrons were commencing to rise under the effects of Old London Dock Brandy and Mr. Eggerton's Sugar Mash Whisky — not to mention more liberal potions of a raw bourbon, locally distilled and not inaccurately termed "popskull."

Leathery-faced soldiers on leave, and bearded sailors off the ironclads tied up in the Cooper River, were beginning to tuck sprigs of mistletoe and bright-berried holly into kepis or into the bands of floppy-brimmed hats of woven palmetto fibers dyed brown with walnut juice.

Tatterdemalion and big-eyed pickaninnies pattered, barefooted, from door to door shrilly hawking bunches of mistletoe or perhaps pine boughs decked with shiny brown cones. Not much holly was in evidence; it would have had to be fetched in from points well outside of town.

This afternoon, India observed happily, King Street had come wonderfully alive. Cavalry officers, wearing jaunty ostrich plumes in their hats, and frock-coated civilian riders trotted briskly by among creaking oxcarts and ponderous forage wagons belonging to the Quartermaster's Corps. Often, horseback riders would rein in, salute, then ride along beside a fragile chariot or phaeton, chatting with some bright-eyed girl or stately matron. There also had appeared a surprising number of livery-stable rigs usually occupied by some bronzed young fellow wearing patched and faded uniform, and a fair companion protecting her crinoline from muddy wheels while they sped along calling the season's greetings to various friends.

As India and her companion bent into an increasingly raw wind beating down St. Philip Street, Mrs. Mullinix continually was being saluted and bowed to; but hardly anyone addressed India, beyond an occasional military convalescent recognizing her as that same vivid and gay visitor who had danced so charmingly in various cheerless hospital wards.

"God bless you, lady!" called a one-armed sergeant from across the street. "We ain't never forgot your visit. Merry Christmas to you!"

Disconsolate groups of soldiers on leave slouched about, or leaned against buildings and spat tobacco juice onto the muddy sidewalk. If they were not native Charlestonians there was nothing for them to do, nothing to buy, and nowhere to go save Major Willis's Soldiers' Rest Room, which place long since had become crowded to capacity.

As both women were aware, many a born-and-bred Charleston man was finding himself with no place to go either; so many families had been burned out, or had "refugeed" inland where food was more readily obtainable. Consequently, various warm and well-lighted churches were crowded to capacity.

Bursts of music sounded also from certain small hotels the bars of which were jammed with well-dressed civilians wearing gleaming stovepipe hats and rich, sporty-looking clothes. Most of these wind-burned characters were smoking Havana seegars and ordering drinks for shrill, hard-faced girls wearing bright taffeta dresses gay with Dolly Varden trimmings.

"Blockade-runners," sniffed the widow. "They ought to be ashamed to throw money about like that."

"They ought," India nodded. "But how would we do without them?"

Presently, the ladies entered George Street and commenced following a rusty, cast-iron fence running behind the college. India peered cautiously through rapidly deepening dusk, but detected no sign of the ancient coachman waiting among shadows wrought by a row of deserted and boarded town houses.

"Now out upon it!" India grimaced, through chattering teeth. "Methinks my ancient Ethiop hath cozened me."

"No. Look yonder. Is yon your man?"

"Heah Ah is, Mistis." At the entrance to the drive leading to an abandoned house had appeared a furtive figure which beckoned frantically before merging again with the shadows. India had started casually to cross the street when a trio of familiar figures appeared. They were

Mrs. Robertson, Directress of the Soldiers' Relief Association, the very wealthy and aloof Mrs. Lambkin, and her daughter Serena. Like a squadron of corvettes, the trio bore down, wide skirts swaying opulently over the brick footway and followed by a straggling file of Negro servants bearing willow baskets heavy with purchases.

All three ladies treated the Widow Mullinix to correct, if slightly stiff bows; after all, the late Captain Mullinix *had* been quite as well-born as anybody in town. What a pity Tom had been such a fool as to fall in love with, and marry, a nobody, a plain young governess imported from Scotland by Mr. Bull of Ashley Hall.

Saving for Serena Lambkin, who smiled timidly, India Bryson might not have been visible, so carefully did the older women avert their gaze.

To India's soft, "A pleasant holiday to you, ladies," they returned nothing, only stalked on with shawled shoulders held rigid.

Dorcas's mittened hand came to rest on India's. "Oh, my dear, I'm so sorry, so very sorry. I'd really delight to pull their hair!"

"Serena smiled at me," India reminded her ruefully. "She's really a sweet girl. Tell me, Dorcas, why do so many ladies of this town disapprove of me?"

Dorcas Mullinix cast a sardonic glance after the three shoppers. "They'll never let you forget that you've been on the stage, even the Shakespearean one, or that your husband, who is as well-bred as mine was, has adopted what they, and many others, hold also to be a disreputable profession."

India stared. "Surely you jest! A journalist — disreputable? How wickedly absurd!"

"Of course. Journalists are presumed to lack common decency, the way they pry into people's private affairs, betray confidences, print lies; and — and are said to lead Bohemian — I believe that's the word — if not downright immoral lives."

"Yessum. Hit's all right, Miz' Mullinix, come over. Ah used to ride Marse Tom's race hosses when Ah was young." He cackled thinly. "Never will forget dat time us beat Misto' Rafe Bryson's Moonglow and won five thousan' dolluhs."

"Don't think I'd forget, either. That's a lot of money," laughed India and beckoned her friend.

The widow inquired briskly, "Now then, what have you to offer?"

"Why, Mistis, in dis heah basket Ah's got one big fat hen. Only ten dolluhs."

India gasped. "*Ten dollars!* Oh, Ambrose, that's too much money for me."

"Let me see it." Dorcas pinched the breast of a sizable but still unplucked and undrawn hen. "Big and fat? Humph! This biddy must have hatched during our War with Mexico."

"You's right, Miz' Mullinix, po' Bella weren't 'zactly no spring chicken, but she hain't '*at* old." Aggrieved, Ambrose retreated among the shadows; reappeared carrying a gunny sack from which he pulled by its tail a very limp opossum. "Dis heah fine critter you ladies kin have fo' just five dolluhs."

"Ugh!" India's delicately upturned nose wrinkled itself. "What an ugly beast! A very Caliban amongst animals. Mr. Bryson detests possums; they're so greasy. You have nothing else for sale?"

"No, Mistis, only some triflin' yams and persimmons."

"Any corn meal?" Dorcas queried.

"Laws no, Mistis. Nowadays even feed-cawn fotches thirty dolluhs de bushel."

India's bright nether lip tucked itself between unusually white and regular teeth and she peered carefully through the gloom at this gnomelike creature. "When you first spoke you said something about having a Christmas gift for sale?"

"Yessum." Carefully, Ambrose peered out of the driveway down George Street in both directions and, since there appeared to be no police or provost guards in evidence, he fumbled into a pocket of his shapeless old overcoat.

"Ah done been 'structed sell this — but so's nobody will know about hit."

In a clawlike hand he offered a massive, gold-mounted watch fob supporting a brace of engraved seals; one of jet, the other of carnelian. Triple, swallow-tailed broad ribbons of Lincoln-green grosgrain dangled behind them.

India's heart lifted. "That's a really lovely thing." How well such a fob would look against the brocade waistcoat of Alistair's Sunday suit! "How — how much are you asking for this?"

"Fo' Gawd, Ah don't rightly know. Twenty dolluhs, mebbe?"

The widow sniffed and her straight black brows merged. "You're a shifty old rascal, Ambrose. That fob is worth five times more, and you know it."

"Dat right, Mistis. Doan' seem like even real jewelry bring nothin' like hit used to. Hit's food folk wants these times."

Acidly, Dorcas suggested, "Why don't you offer it to some blockade-runner? He'd have plenty of money."

"Ah dassn't. My Mistis she say, 'Ambrose, you keep away from sech riffraff.' "

India stripped off her clumsily mended glove in order to test the ornament's weight and texture. Yes, its mountings undoubtedly must be gold; the fob was entirely too ponderous to have been fashioned of anything else.

"I — I believe I'll take it," she announced breathlessly. "Yes, I will." How Alistair's eyes would gleam once he unwrapped this opulent bit of jewelry!

Dorcas reminded firmly, "But, India dear, you haven't yet found food for your Christmas dinner."

A rippling laugh escaped the dark-haired girl. "I know it, but oh, I simply *can't* pass up this opportunity."

Eagerly, the old coachman shuffled forward offering a slim object carefully swathed in a ragged silk handkerchief. "Ah got sumpin' else, Mistis — fo' a pretty lady lak you."

"You're not much of a salesman, my worthy Ethiope, to offer a fan on an evening like this." But when India opened it she realized that its silk was adorned by miniatures exquisitely executed in the style of Louis XV. The most delicate imaginable scrollwork decorated the fan's ivory ribs, and rows of wonderfully bright stones had been set into its handle. That one brilliant was missing really didn't matter. "And for this?"

"Surely, you're not going to buy it?" the widow demanded. "What in the world would you do with a fan like that in these times?"

"But it's so very beautiful," India smiled and with a graceful gesture flicked the fan open and winked over its rim at her grim-faced companion. "Alistair can give it to me for Christmas. I must have it. There is so little beauty about in these days."

"Also remember, you sweet, silly idiot, Alistair these days is hard up — to say the least."

"He won't begrudge it me; besides, I'll have saved him the bother of going shopping," India pursued lightly. "How much did you say this is?"

"Ah is supposed to git fifteen dolluhs fo' hit, Mistis," came the uneasy reply.

"There's something queer about all this," the widow commented sharply. "You're positive you came by these things honestly?"

The coachman's yellowish eyes rolled far back in their sockets. "Fo' God, Miz' Mullinix, Ah ain't robbed 'em. No, maum!"

India, bubbling in delight, was forced to conclude by purchasing the possum and a few yams and persimmons for Christmas dinner.

"When Alistair learns about this," sniffed the widow, "I hope he turns you over his knee and warms your pretty bottom. I will wager Alistair is Scotch enough to get hopping mad over such squandering."

India executed a light and whirling dance step or two as they re-entered George Street. "Oh, Dorcas, don't pull such a long mouth. He won't be angry. I'm sure of it. Do you know . . . ? Somehow, I'm certain we're about to have the happiest Christmas ever — blockade or no blockade."

CHAPTER III **The *Grey Ghost***

CAPTAIN McCorkle bent over the pilot boat *Sea Robin*'s huge wheel. "Make her out yet, Mr. Bryson? Yonder, under the lights o' Fort Moultrie."

"Now I do, but for a blockade-runner isn't she quite small?" Alistair Bryson, the *Charleston Argus*'s managing editor, nodded, stared fixedly across the great harbor's misty expanse. Off to port lay Castle Pinckney, while the crumbled or shot-pitted walls of Fort Sumter loomed, blackly stark, to starboard. At the *Sea Robin*'s chuffing approach, huge squadrons of Canada geese raised a strident alarm and reluctantly took flight.

McCorkle bit off a chew. "Ever see a vessel harder to sight?"

"I've not seen her lines before — she's indeed like a phantom."

Deftly, Tim McCorkle steered the pilot boat through a gap in a line of pilings barely protruding above the clay-colored water. Bryson eyed them warily. Those pilings constituted only one of many marine obstructions placed by Major General Beauregard to prevent a sudden bold rush into the harbor by Union men-of-war — as had happened at Port Royal.

Sure enough, three Federal ships, forming the blockaders' inner cordon, could be sighted prowling off Drunken Dick Shoal, their toothpick-thin yards and topmasts asway.

The wind freshened until it began to sigh through the *Sea Robin*'s shrouds, set her smoke-grimed blue-and-white Palmetto Flag to snapping and drew tears from the journalist's deep-set, dark blue eyes.

"Ye'll see her better once she passes under Battery Bee," grunted the pilot boat's captain. "Sure, and there she goes!" Through a pair of battered binoculars Alistair Bryson studied the new arrival with sudden interest. McCorkle had been entirely correct when he'd claimed never to have beheld a blockade-runner quite so hard to distinguish in a half-light. The newspaperman also noticed that her two masts were short, raked sharply aft and devoid of crossyards or topmasts.

Her hull and superstructure had been painted a very light shade of gray. Separated by oversized paddle-wheel housings, two tall and very slim funnels trailed tendrils of grayish, not black, smoke; which meant that she must be using good, clean-burning English coal.

Next, Bryson noted that, to further reduce her silhouette, the runner's small boats, also painted light gray, had been lowered on their davits to a level with the vessel's rails.

"Well, Tim, I reckon we'll soon be boarding one of the first vessels especially designed for running Mr. Lincoln's blockade."

"Where was she built?"

"In England at Leeds' yard; read something about it in the *New York Tribune* last summer."

Alistair's curiosity was piqued still further when he noticed that this curious craft's ram bow was covered by a conical metal hood extending aft from her stem perhaps a quarter of the runner's length; this he estimated to be approximately two hundred feet.

Creating hardly any noise at all, the new arrival commenced to lose speed as soon as she had thrust her bow into Hog Island Channel, with a sureness which argued that some experienced Charleston pilot must be conning her in from the sea.

"Come out on deck, Terry," McCorkle called down the engine

room's speaking tube. "I want yez should see what we've got lyin' to windward."

Presently, the pilot boat's heavily bearded engineer and a pair of black-faced firemen appeared at the rail. They stood shielding their faces against flying spray and watched a British Red Ensign climb to the newcomer's main signal gaff. Then a Confederate flag was broken out at the gray-painted vessel's foretop.

McCorkle wiped moisture from blunt, wind-reddened features. "Ain't she a beauty? Reckon you figure you've your worth o' boat hire this time, Mr. Bryson?" He raised a quizzical brow. "Ye've me fee handy?"

"Not the whole of it, Tim," admitted the journalist, flushing. "I left home half-awake and in such a rush I've fetched along only seventy-five dollars, but my wife has the rest so you'll have the balance as soon as we dock."

"I'll be thanking yez for that, what with tomorrow being Christmas and five young ones acting like angels and lookin' terrible hopeful."

The blockade-runner steamed slowly closer to the waiting pilot boat, then the journalist noticed that sailors, working about her decks, were wearing white coats and white-painted sou'westers.

"Damned if she ain't all iron-built," commented McCorkle, while a deck hand ran out onto the *Sea Robin*'s bow ready to catch a line that soon would come snaking downwards. "And look at the sweet lines to her! I'll bet me plug hat she can run like the Devil from holy watter. Yep. She'll easy outfoot the fastest cruisers the damned Yankees can send this way."

Alistair nodded, then pulled out a sketch pad and pencil. Swiftly he rendered an impression of this beautiful craft's sweeping lines, minimum superstructure, huge paddle boxes, indicated the extreme rake of her funnels and masts. Beneath he wrote: *"Grey Ghost* of Liverpool, December 24, 1862."

Gunners in Battery Bee commenced to fire the customary salute of welcome to an inbound runner and presently Castle Pinckney followed suit. The *Grey Ghost* then repeatedly dipped her colors in acknowledgment. A white veil of steam trailed from the inbound vessel's exhaust pipe indicating that her engines had been stopped but, for quite a while, her bow continued to cleave the yellow-brown water as smoothly as a razor might slice through a chunk of liver.

The *Sea Robin*'s master caught up a battered leather speaking-trumpet. "Heyo, the bridge! Is that Tom Burrus, aboard?"

A figure garbed in a tam-o'-shanter and weather-beaten serge coat thrust a fringe of orange chin whiskers far over the rail.

"Hello yourself, ye dirty Roman Catholic Harp!"

"That's Tom, all right, and the best damned Charleston pilot there is," grinned McCorkle. "I love him like a brother."

"Recognize any of the other men up there?" Alistair queried as he added a few finishing touches to his sketch; long since, he had won local attention through the excellence and accuracy of news sketches, rendered on the spot. Alas, not one newspaper south of Richmond possessed even the most rough-and-ready facilities for reproducing linecuts of newsworthy figures, vessels and events.

He still wondered how his drawing, descriptive of the sinking of the "Stone Fleet" — an unsuccessful attempt on the part of the Federals to block the main channel into Charleston Harbor with dozens of sunken and granite-laden ex-whalers — had ever found its way North, and into reproduction on the pages of *Frank Leslie's Illustrated News*.

It was a continual irritation to note how excellently the work of such staff artists as Thomas Nast and Winslow Homer was being reproduced in *Harper's Magazine* and *Vanity Fair*. He'd met and admired both of these whimsical young fellows during the halcyon days when he had toiled — and writhed — under the acid direction of indefatigable Charles A. Dana of the *New York Tribune* — that worst-hated of Northern newspapers.

While the pilot boat chuffed impudently up to the blockade-runner's sleek side, Bryson became increasingly impressed by the enormous size of the *Grey Ghost*'s steel paddle wheels. Undoubtedly, they had been so designed the better to navigate those shallow sounds of which there were such an abundance along the Confederacy's labyrinthine southeastern waters. . . . A ladder was flung over the *Grey Ghost*'s side and its bottom treads banged hollowly upon the *Sea Robin*'s deck.

Alistair tucked away the sketch pad, shoved the ends of his muffler inside a frayed old overcoat, and swarmed easily up the ladder. He was helped over the rail by a brace of gap-toothed seamen wearing white canvas jumpers.

The boatswain strode forward knuckling his forelock. "Welcome aboard, sir. Captain Bryson's compliments, and will you please come immediately to his cabin?"

Alistair's lively dark eyes flew wide open. "Did you say Captain *Bryson?*"

"Aye, aye, sir. Captain Raphael Bryson commands, and mostly owns, this 'ere vessel."

Excitement quickened the journalist's breathing. Apparently, at long last, he was about to make the acquaintance of his reckless, rakehell first cousin.

Cousin Raphael was the only child of an ambitious uncle who, long years ago, had quitted the original Bryson holdings near Rougelle's Mills, up in Wateree County, for Charleston. Uncle Alexander, so Pa once had told him, had entered the banking business to work so hard and ruthlessly that, very soon, Bryson's Bank began transacting business in a new stone building on Cumberland Street.

He also recalled that Cousin Rafe had been born at the cost of his mother's life, that Uncle Alexander had never remarried and so had devoted his entire attention to the amassing of wealth. As a result, Cousin Rafe had been reared by a succession of governesses and tutors, whom he'd driven to distraction with his arrogance and intransigence. He'd managed to remain at the University of Virginia until, early in his junior year, he had reappeared in Charleston, with a tight-closed mouth and so dangerous a gleam in his eyes that no one felt prompted even mildly to question him.

Alistair's own father, Gordon, meanwhile, had stayed at Rougelle's Mills, whither the first Alistair had conducted his bride, a famous Charleston beauty née Antoinette Proveaux, to take up a soldier's land grant at the close of the War for Independence.

Since arrival in Charleston back in '58, he and India all too often had been regaled by accounts of Rafe's extravagant mode of life, his weird and wonderful practical jokes, his gaming, his passion for race horses and his brazen conduct with the fair sex of no matter what social status.

His excesses and escapades had become especially outrageous following Uncle Alexander's death of yellow fever. To anyone as intelligent as Alistair, it soon became obvious, however, that many of Cousin Rafe's reputed exploits were either wildly exaggerated by the raconteurs, completely untrue, or attributable to some other man.

23

"Captain's cabin, sir," the boatswain announced and saluted smartly.

Alistair paused in the cabin's entrance carefully to survey this almost legendary relative. Still clad in a long, white linen coat, Captain Bryson was smoking a seegar and drinking champagne in company with two remarkably dissimilar individuals. Cousin Rafe, he decided, possessed a typically Bryson countenance: wide at its brow and jaw, high and rather prominent cheekbones and a ruddy complexion. He wore neatly pointed mustaches over a sensitive, yet firm and willful mouth. His cousin's wavy and very dark brown hair was luxuriant, and trimmed so long that it brushed his coat collar. Ruler-straight and rather thick brows almost, but not quite, merged themselves above the bridge of a slender, slightly Roman nose.

In the act of refilling a champagne glass, the *Grey Ghost*'s master became aware of a straight, well-built figure hesitating at his cabin's door. He paused, glass poised, to stare at this wind-reddened apparition in the salt-stained pea jacket.

"Who . . . ?" Then he hurried forward, hand extended. "By God! It's five to one you're Cousin Donald — or is it Cousin Alistair?"

"Well, I'm damned, Rafe —" drawled a tall red-haired young fellow — "and there I've been hoping they'd drowned the rest in your litter — this resemblance is cursed close to astounding."

Alistair smiled, entered the cabin. "You'd win your bet, Cousin Rafe. I'm Alistair."

By the light of a brass lamp swinging easily on gimbals, the blockaderunner's captain, during a long moment, probed his cousin's restless and very dark brown eyes — then made a swift but comprehensive survey of battered, square-toed shoes, crudely patched, well-worn corduroy trousers, and a threadbare pea jacket. Um-m. If Cousin Alistair were married, as his broad gold wedding band suggested, then they must be poverty-poor, or his wife took precious little interest in her husband's appearance.

With a wide, curiously winning smile, Rafe stripped off his white coat and indicated the tallest man in the cabin.

"This is Dabney Seymour, of the Virginia Seymours." All of six feet, the Virginian was built broad in the shoulder and narrow in the hips, and possessed the brightest of bright blue eyes. Sandy-haired and clean-shaven save for luxuriant blond sideburns, he had a rather long face deeply tanned, as if he had recently spent much time under the hot

24

sun. His open good looks, however, were marred by the wide red scar which descended his left cheek in a blazing diagonal.

"Dabney hails from the Virginia Tidewater country," Rafe grinned while pouring yet another glass of champagne. "Try playing poker with him or try to drink him down, if you doubt me."

"I am honored, indeed, sir," the Virginian declared gravely, then bowed without spilling his wine.

Rafe continued: "Dabney's an old friend, a naval engineer who has been gaining experience among the shipbuilders of England for lo these several years. Right now, he is consumed with a patriotic fervor to place his skills at President Davis's disposal."

Alistair considered the tall man with renewed respect. Imagine risking one's life in order to volunteer in the Confederate Navy — a service stupidly neglected and unappreciated since the conflict's outset!

"I'm indeed proud to meet you, sir," declared the journalist. "Flag Officer Ingraham will surely commission an English-trained marine engineer."

"I trust you are correct in that, sir," smiled the scarred man. "You cannot imagine my sensations, just now, on sighting my homeland after so prolonged an exile. I intend to work doubly hard to make up for my delay in arriving to assist our valiant few men-of-war in breaking the blockade."

Alistair fished out a notebook after sharpening the point of a soft pencil. "Do you mind if I make notes? You must have spent considerable time in Bermuda *en route,* or was it in the Bahamas?"

Dabney Seymour smiled easily. "Your cousin is observant, Rafe."

"A newspaperman should be. It was Bermuda?"

"No. Twice I sailed aboard runners out of Nassau; one was chased and shelled by a Yankee cruiser. We were forced to turn back carrying five dead and seven wounded. On my second attempt" — the big Virginian's scar glowed a deeper red — "the runner was captured, and I with it. That was when I acquired this little ornament." He tapped his scar. "They carried me to New York, where I shivered in Fort Lafayette until — well — I managed to escape."

"How, please?" Alistair's pencil was fairly flying.

"I'm afraid that's too long a story to go into, right now," came the cool reply. "I'd like a bit more wine, Mr. Burgoyne."

The individual thus addressed was hatchet-faced, clean-shaven and of very pink complexion. His was a mop of flaming red hair with muttonchop whiskers to match. Of medium build, he was angular as a divider and spoke with the languid accents affected by so many wellborn Englishmen of the day.

"This is Lieutenant the Honorable Peter Burgoyne, of Her Britannic Majesty's Navy," drawled the blockade-runner's captain, while refilling the Virginian's cup.

"It's an honor, sir, to welcome you to the Confederacy," smiled Alistair. "May I publish the purpose of your visit to our country?"

"I would rather that you did not; for the present, at least," the Englishman replied, and his bright blue eyes met the newspaperman's squarely. "Officially, I am now — er — enjoying an indefinite leave. Actually, several fellow officers and I have been sent to observe not only the construction of such vessels as are being built hereabouts, but the orgainization and operation of the Confederate Naval Service as a whole."

Thin lips formed a bland smile. "You see, sir, not only do certain Lords of the Admiralty deem the Southern cause to be just and honorable, but they wish certain of us to obtain — er — practical experience in ironclad warfare, don't you know?"

Alistair inquired, "Has this venture on your part officially been encouraged by your Government?"

The Hororable Peter elevated a quizzical brow. "I must decline to answer that."

"Oh, come now, Peter. We're among friends, at last," said Dabney Seymour. "Tell Mr. Bryson at least something about those ships we are having constructed abroad. Mr. Bryson deserves consideration for having got up early on so raw a morning."

The cry of a sea gull scaling past an open port sounded loud during a brief interval of silence; that, and the dull trampling of feet out on deck.

"Well, sir," the British naval observer commenced through a cloud of fragrant seegar smoke, "I was fortunate enough to be permitted to visit Laird's Shipyard in Liverpool and there, with my own eyes, I saw two men-of-war under construction for your Government. These are to be ironclad, seagoing rams protected by four-and-a-half or five inches of plate armor. Each is to be armed with four nine-inch rifled guns, mounted in two revolving turrets."

"Tell him what their speed's to be," prompted the Virginian. "They'll have to be fast enough to overhaul some very swift cruisers the Unionists have under construction."

"Concerning the speed of these ironclads, I know nothing at all," drawled the Honorable Peter. "But I fancy they have been designed fast and powerful enough to hunt down the best Union ironclads afloat."

"You bring magnificent news, sir! Our readers will be enormously encouraged. How near completion are these men-of-war?"

"About halfway, I daresay; they can't be made ready for commissioning in under ten months," the Englishman replied while wiping wine from a limp red mustache. "My own estimate, y'know."

"Oh, come now, Peter, they'll be ready sooner than that?" Dabney Seymour appeared startled.

"Possibly. Mr. Bullock, the Confederate Naval Agent in England, is most impatient to see these ironclads put to sea."

Faster and faster traveled the journalist's pencil.

Rafe Bryson lifted a hand. "Hold on there, Alistair. Better not get so steamed up."

"Why not? This is wonderful news your English friend is giving. I can promise it will electrify and encourage not only Charleston, but the whole Confederacy." His deep-set eyes glittered. "And the *Argus* will be first to print —"

"But it won't. That's what I was getting at," Rafe said seriously. "Not a single line is to be printed about the building of those seagoing rams."

Dumfounded, the intense, wiry figure glanced up. "And why not, for God's sake?"

"I can answer that," quietly volunteered Dabney Seymour. "The minute Mr. Adams, the Yankee Minister to the Court of St. James's, hears of these vessels, he'll rush to Lord Russell screaming, 'Breach of neutrality!' and threatening war."

Rafe's dark head inclined. He was so tall his hair brushed the deck beams above. "That's no exaggeration. Just before we cleared Liverpool I heard that Mr. Adams already has caught wind of Bullock's rams. All the proof he requires is something like this proposed article to prove that these ironclads *are* being constructed for the Confederacy, and not the Khedive of Egypt — as Laird's is protesting."

An exasperated sigh escaped the journalist. "I expect you're right, but it's damned hard to suppress such good news."

The *Grey Ghost*'s deck commenced gently to vibrate when, under Tim McCorkle's expert piloting, she resumed her progress down Hog Island Channel, paralleling Charleston Harbor's northern shore. The blockade-runner's master pulled on a dark blue overcoat and said: "Let us seek the bridge, gentlemen; I'll confess I've a craving to view my native city. It's been near eight years I've been away."

The pilot's bristle-covered jaw worked harder than ever on a cud of tobacco while he steered past certain flag buoys marking a channel through a pattern of "barrel" torpedoes anchored off Fort Moultrie. Only a few pilots had been informed as to which flags were true guides —the rest served as confusing decoys for a rash enemy seeking to penetrate the inner harbor.

"Sorry, Cap'n," McCorkle grunted presently. "Reckon I'll have to anchor you off Castle Pinckney for a spell. Damn' tide's falling so fast under this wind I daren't risk running you aground."

"Damn! Well, when do we dock and where?" Rafe Bryson demanded.

" 'Twill be late afternoon afore I can dock yer ship to Atlantic Wharf."

"Why not Vanderhorst's?"

McCorkle blinked. "Why, sir, Vanderhorst's was pulled down a year ago, along with the old South Dock. Gin'ral Beauregard has had big batteries thrown up where they used to stand."

"They guard the Cooper River's mouth," Alistair amplified. "Besides, there's plenty of space in port these days, what with only six or eight ships a fortnight making port."

"Aye, sir," McCorkle looked lugubrious. " 'Twill make you sick to view all them great piles of baled cotton, green and rotting on the docks."

A storm must be brewing, Alister reflected while the *Grey Ghost* was nosed cautiously through the torpedo patterns. Restless clouds of lordly canvasbacks and blackheaded ducks kept skimming across the blockade-runner's bow, while over nearby marshes ragged, smokelike clouds of geese and swans kept rising and then settling again.

On Christmas afternoon, the journalist decided, he'd go bag some swans, for all that India complained of eating any more of these succulent and inexpensive waterfowl. Yes. He'd certainly go gunning; any surplus could be sold by Jairus, his copy boy, or sent as Christmas gifts to recruits undergoing instruction at Washington Race Course; the poor fellows out there received so little by way of government rations they'd even fill their cook pots with muskrats or terrapins.

While a rising wind tore at his hair, Alistair glanced to port, noted that today C.S.S. *Palmetto State* was lying at anchor in Fort Sumter's lee. Therefore, C.S.S. *Chicora* must be lying at the Wilmington Line's old wharf.

Tim McCorkle, expertly conning the runner into the inner harbor, was deciding that this vessel was a very pleasurable improvement on those high-sided and clumsy blockade-runners which, at the start of the war, had defied the Union's "soapbox" blockade — so nicknamed because it was enforced by a weird aggregation of converted merchantmen, New York harbor ferryboats and venerable men-of-war retrieved from some shipbreaker's yard.

To the harbor pilot, Captain Bryson's vessel seemed dangerously short in the beam: less than twenty feet, which was all-fired narrow, considering her two hundred feet and more of length. She'd sure roll like a bitch in any sort of sea.

Once his charge had passed Castle Pinckney, McCorkle ordered the *Grey Ghost*'s engines stopped and briefly reversed. Soon an anchor was let go and the long, low-built craft rounded smoothly into the wind. Only then did McCorkle note the presence of two men so very similar in size, feature and coloring that he gaped like a farmer at a side-show. "Holy Mither o' God! I must be drunk!" He collected himself sufficiently to salute the slightly shorter figure wearing a merchant captain's four gold stripes. Then he grinned uncomfortably.

"For sure 'tis the Rascal, himself, and back in Charleston. Och! I'm beggin' yer pardon, sir. I should not have said that last."

The *Grey Ghost*'s master laughed mirthlessly. "So I'm remembered, eh? Well, well, give a dog a bad name . . . Rest easy, Mr. McCorkle, I take no offense."

For some moments Raphael Bryson remained outlined against the lowering sky, staring fixedly upon Charleston. "Well, the old town seems to have suffered hard times since I last saw it. What's become of the Catholic Cathedral and St. Andrew's Hall?"

"Along with a lot of other buildings, they burned down during a great fire we've had," the journalist explained. "The flames cut a swath right across the center of Charleston, all the way from the Cooper to the Ashley."

"How did it start?"

"Some say 'twas set by Yankee spies," McCorkle observed while retying a faded green muffler. "But most believe 'twas caused by some niggers cooking in a vacant lot back o' Russell's machine shop. Sparks from their fire landed in a stack of hay and a fierce gale was blowin' out o' the northeast, so the flames spread quicker'n quick."

Alistair, with one eye watching the progress of a stubby little supply steamer bucking towards Fort Sumter, said, "Our most serious loss was Cameron's Foundry. It burned to the ground along with great stores of cannons, muskets, bayonets and other arms, which we've found damned difficult to replace."

Presently Rafe, long hair whipping in the breeze, turned to regard his cousin. "Tell me, Alistair, is there . . . er . . . should I know anything concerning members of our family or my — former friends?"

"A lot, Rafe, too much to tell you now; you'd better come around to my house tonight."

"Your house? Where is it?"

"It's not really mine. I rent it. It's on Mary Street. The owners refugeed early in the siege."

"I will be touched and honored to do so. Especially do I anticipate meeting Mrs. Bryson. What is her given name?"

"India."

"Lovely! She's from Charleston?"

"No. From Tampa in Florida. Her maiden name was Villepigue."

"Oh, then she's French?" Rafe's fine teeth glimmered. "How very delightful. I know I shall fall in love with her immediately."

"No, India's not exactly French," Alistair corrected, a trifle uneasily. "Her father is from Louisiana. Her mother was born in Toledo, Spain, of a minor noble family. They disinherited her when she ran away with an American sea captain. I expect it was from her that my wife has inherited a passion for dancing and the theater."

Rafe's bold dark eyes crinkled at their corners. "Theater? Then Mrs. Bryson was once a — an actress?"

Alistair looked his cousin full in the face, said evenly: "And a fine one, too. When I first met her she was playing Cordelia in Edwin Booth's Shakesperean Company."

30

"Mrs. Bryson sounds completely fascinating. When shall I have the privilege of paying homage to your lovely bride?"

"Why, instead of tonight, don't you come and share our Christmas dinner? You may find the house a bit cold," Alistair apologized, "but all the same, we'll give you a warm welcome."

"I shall be charmed to accept."

A flurry of snowflakes whirled across the bridge, caused men to readjust their mufflers as the *Grey Ghost*'s engineer blew off the balance of his steam in a twisting white plume.

"You met Mrs. Bryson — where?"

"I'd stopped off in Philadelphia to visit friends. You see, I'd been writing on the *New York Herald* and was going back to Rougelle's Mills on holiday."

"Not *that* dirty Abolitionist rag?"

"I quit the day Fort Sumter was fired upon," came the terse explanation. "But, all the same, it was a fine experience. They really print news up North, not the vaporings of pothouse politicians."

Rafe set foot to the bridge ladder but paused to survey the city — a low outline half a mile distant and dominated by the spires of St. Philip's and St. Michael's Churches.

Memories came flooding back of St. Cecilia Society balls, high-stake card games at the Jockey Club, cocks fighting under gray-bearded live oaks, gay picnics, riding to hounds, fire hunting for deer, jousting and all manner of reckless and less reputable amusements.

Sharpest of all were his recollections of a certain morning when he and hotheaded young George Flood, flushed with vinous rage, had faced each other at twenty paces. Ever so clearly Rafe could hear the wicked hum of George's pistol ball as it grazed his ear; see his enemy's slim body sway, suddenly spin sidewise, then crumple and lie very still with a brilliant stain widening upon the bosom of its elegantly ruffled shirt.

Studiedly casual, the *Grey Ghost*'s master inquired, "Are the Liveseys still at Mulberry Bend? That's near Beaufort, you know."

"No. They evacuated their plantation right after Du Pont's capture of Port Royal; so far, needlessly, it turns out. Ever since, they've been living with cousins."

"Which tells me exactly nothing," smiled Rafe. "The Liveseys must have dozens of cousins."

"Sorry. They're staying with Major St. George Lambkin."

Rafe considered his cousin's strongly modeled features an instant, then asked softly, "Is — er — Miss Julia there?"

"Yes." Alistair suddenly looked exceedingly uncomfortable. "My brother Donald, who at present is courting Miss Serena Lambkin, has met Miss Livesey on several occasions."

"Interesting, and a little awkward, eh? Seeing that we're cousins." Emitting a metallic laugh, he turned aside. "Well, this is luck, being home for Christmas."

Alistair put foot to the bridge ladder, said over his shoulder, "India will be delighted to meet you at long last. By the way, why not bring along your Virginian friend, Seymour? He won't know anyone in town, will he?"

"I think not. We'll be around tomorrow noon, maybe earlier. I'm all impatience to behold this fascinating lady you've been fortunate enough to marry."

CHAPTER IV Manifests and Bills of Lading

WHEN Alistair Bryson reached the deck he found several of the crew clustered in the lee of that metal turtleback which sheltered most of the blockade-runner's bow, and peering through diminishing snow flurries at the town, sprawling so low and dark upon its peninsula. Almost uniformly, the seamen had discarded their white linen jumpers and were passing about a spyglass the better to survey a formidable series of earthworks facing the Cooper.

The *Argus*'s managing editor borrowed the glass and through it learned, to his vast relief, that the *Lady Davis,* a tug customarily chartered by the city's two rival newspapers, lay in her berth; this meant that Charlie Davis of the *Courier* and pompous Ted Ainslee of the *Mercury* must be sleeping off the results of some pre-Christmas bourbon-and-poker party.

With any luck, he'd be able, all by himself, to scan the *Grey Ghost*'s bills of lading and see if she had aboard any of the ink, newsprint and other supplies long since ordered and urgently needed in the *Argus* pressroom. Um. He might also find opportunity to read the British and Bahamian newspapers. Later, he could digest the foreign news and put it to use.

Particularly, he was hoping to discover some copies of the *Index,* a weekly journal subsidized by the Confederate Government and printed in London to disseminate Southern views and news. It also stood to reason that, tomorrow, he might glean further news from his dinner guests. For instance, how was Emperor Louis Napoleon's fine army faring down in Mexico? He was most anxious to ascertain just how firmly the Hapsburg, Maximilian, had seated himself upon the throne; all the South fervently wished him continued success and consequent embarrassment to the government in Washington. Yes, he ought to find out about a lot of things, if only he could provide sufficient liquor to really limber tongues.

Why wouldn't Virginius Roadheaver, the *Argus*'s publisher, look beyond the end of his magnificently roseate nose? Every time he was approached for the payment of even a trifling expense account it touched off a querulous debate.

By this time, India surely must have returned with the ingredients for a fine Christmas dinner. Of course, now she'd have to find more food. He reproached himself for having so precipitately included Cousin Rafe and his friend before learning what delicacies she'd been able to find.

In the blockade-runner's wardroom Alistair encountered his cousin, in company with a Mr. Brazenose — his first mate — and a round little man whose scant hair had been slicked against his skull by a liberal application of Macassar oil. The former proved to be as Scottish as haggis, and wore a fringe of short chin whiskers about lean jaws. The other was seated at a table piled high with all manner of documents.

"This is Mr. Leeming, my supercargo," explained Rafe Bryson. "I've instructed him to show you any bills of lading you'd like to see."

"My thanks, Cousin Rafe, and can I examine the ship's manifest as well?" Alistair hung his cap to a hook and unbuttoned his pea jacket.

"Manifest?" A subtle change became evident in Rafe Bryson's manner. "Sorry. It's confidential."

"I see. Sorry I asked."

33

The supercargo raised watery gray eyes. "Is a Mr. Bunch still Her Majesty's Consular Representative here?"

"He is."

"And does he remain accredited to the United States Government?"

"Damn your impudence!" Angry color flooded the journalist's wind-burned features. "What does it matter? Mr. Bunch represents the Queen of England, which is all that's important."

More tactless a query than Leeming's could hardly have been made in a Southern port. Everyone knew that, because the independence of the Confederate States as yet remained unrecognized by foreign powers, no Consul could be accredited them. It was, then, a bitter paradox that, at the moment, three Consuls, accredited to Washington, were discharging their duties in Charleston: Mr. Robert Bunch, representing the United Kingdom; Señor Muñez Moncada, Her Most Catholic Majesty of Spain; and Baron de St. André, the Emperor of the French. However anomalous their position, these gentlemen had not been in the least deterred from participating, unofficially, in celebrations held in honor of the Southern army's many brilliant victories.

"Mr. Leeming, I fear, is not noted for his tact," grunted Rafe Bryson. "Rest assured, Alistair, our nation *will* be recognized as sovereign the day the Yankee blockade can be proved ineffective. You may be encouraged to hear that, during the past few months, a great many British and Continental shipowners have become strong Southern sympathizers."

"Why?" Alistair looked his incredulity.

"Why, sir," explained Mr. Brazenose, "'tis all on account o' the tyrannical and often illegal treatment the Yankee officers accord neutral vessels. Not to speak o' the shameful way they mistreat the crews o' captured blockade-runners. Aye. I've oft heard it said the Unionists take pleasure in threats of hanging our puir lads for pirates.

"Aye, sir, for a fact, Liverpool, Hull, Glasgow and London are still aboil over the highhanded way the Yankee cruiser, *San Jacinto*, halted and boarded the *Trent* on the high seas, and her flying the British flag."

"Thank you, Mr. Brazenose. This change of heart among foreign shipowners will please our readers. And, Mr. Leeming, may I examine your bills of lading?"

While the *Grey Ghost*'s owner sauntered over to a sideboard and helped himself to a tot of brandy and a sea biscuit, Alistair seated himself and commenced to leaf through the bills.

A frown deepened on the journalist's brow when he noted such ladings as: Rispail Bordeaux Brandy, 100 cases; London Dock Gin, 375 cases; pure magenta watered satin, 350 bolts; Brussels lace, 6 cases; French calfskins, 2 gross; cases of ladies' hats; 6 gross ladies' stays; fancy-colored flannels; ladies' black lace mitts; gentlemen's fur hats — and dozens of bales of striped blue-and-white regatta and fancy summer drill.

He glanced up, beaming. "Ha! Here's what I've been hoping for. I see mention of the newsprint, printer's ink and type fonts Mr. Roadheaver ordered, per the *Ruby*, three months ago; but the quantities seem inaccurate."

"Do they indeed?" snapped the supercargo.

"Yes. I wrote out the list. Where are those rollers for our HOC four-cylinder press?"

Mr. Leeming sniffed. "This is not your order, Mr. Bryson, but supplies consigned to the *Savannah Republican*."

"To hell with the *Republican!* My order was placed months ago, and I've got to have newsprint and ink immediately."

Grinning, Rafe Bryson picked up his cousin's pencil and wrote *Charleston Argus* across the word *Republican*.

"Any newspaper so named can wait a while longer. Mr. Leeming, see to it that our manifest is altered to suit." He laughed, then poured Alistair a tot of brandy. "It's as easy as that."

"But you'll get into trouble —"

"Nonsense. I run this vessel to suit myself. Besides, I can't let down my new-found cousin, now can I?"

Alistair found himself regarding his cousin with positive affection. "How can I thank you, Rafe?"

"Don't try. We're cousins, aren't we? Besides, I've heard the *Argus* is doing our cause a real service; it publishes news, not just the oratory of politicians and windy speeches by myopic patriots."

"That's kindly said. We try to publish the truth, palatable or not — like the better newspapers up North." He might have added, but didn't, that he was largely to be thanked for this policy.

Rapidly, Alistair scanned sheaf after sheaf of bills until he came to the last of them. Then he elevated a quizzical brow. "I wonder," said he slowly, "whether you are aware of a peculiar circumstance concerning this cargo?"

"Can't say as I am. Like everyone else in this business, I transport freight that's light and pays well. What's bothering you?"

"Why, the bulk of your cargo consists of luxuries. Corsets! Brandy! Women's black lace gloves! If you've much freight aboard useful in fighting a war, I haven't noticed it!"

"You're wrong there," Rafe returned drily. "Luxury goods, we are informed by our agents, help to maintain the *esprit de guerre* among our leading families, and pay good dividends as well. Incidentally, I have arms and ammunition in the hold. Not many, but a few. They're listed on a separate invoice."

"It surprises me, Mr. Bryson," sneered the supercargo, "that, after all this time, you don't better understand what risky business it is to run the blockade. Munitions, my dear sir, weigh a lot and so cause a vessel to lie deep in the water; a dangerous thing in crossing a shoal. Moreover, arms show relatively small profits." Noisily, he blew his nose. "Besides, we import goods which have been ordered."

"By whom?"

The question was put so instantly that Leeming replied, "Why, two principal importers are involved on this voyage. They are —"

"Shut up, Leeming!" Rafe's voice was trenchant as a surgeon's scalpel. "Or must I teach you that secrets are to be kept? Here's the arms invoice, Alistair. I fancy you'll discover my cargo contains no more and no less than the customary percentage of munitions of war."

After he had read the list Alistair stared incredulously at the *Grey Ghost's* master. "You call this a 'customary percentage'? Why, last year the *Fingal* landed at Savannah 10,000 Enfield rifles against your — let's see — 500; 1,000,000 cartridges against your 30,000 rounds." He got so mad his voice began to quiver. "She landed in addition 2,000,000 percussion caps, 3000 sabers, 500 revolvers, 1000 carbines and 100,000 cartridges to fit them; she fetched in two large rifled guns as well, and two smaller cannon and 400 barrels of powder. Not three months ago, Captain Bonneau's *Ella and Annie* landed munitions worth a million dollars — gold — on Atlantic Dock."

"A worthy endeavor, no doubt. But pray don't presume to lecture me," warned Rafe; ominous lines suddenly appeared about his mouth. "For your information, 90 per cent of the munitions aboard were purchased for my personal account. I could have trebled my returns had I invested the same sum in liquors or dry goods."

"Then I beg your pardon, Rafe. But don't you also own some of the luxuries?"

"Don't be a fool! Of course, I do," came the harsh response. "I still owe considerable on the purchase of this ship, which may become a total loss every time she dares the blockade. Costs plenty to operate her, too."

"I know well enough what common hands are getting — not to mention pilots at thirty-five hundred dollars the round trip. Still, it makes me sick as a goat to learn about these luxuries when there's such an urgent need for rolling mills and, most of all, marine engines for our ships of war. Our Navy people are starving for boiler iron, let alone rolled armorplate. Our Army lacks even such basic supplies as shoes, uniforms, overcoats, medicines and such, while you blockade runners risk your ships and lives to import fripperies! How *can* you justify that?"

"In one word, 'profits.' " Rafe suddenly seemed unruffled again.

"Isn't this speculation in luxuries siphoning away much of what little gold we still have in the South?"

"I reckon so, but remember that this exported gold serves to support the Confederacy's credit abroad."

"Credit with which to purchase more luxuries."

"Aye, but also to pay for those steam rams building at Laird's — and still others, over in France."

"Tell me, what percentage of this gold is devoted to such purposes?"

Rafe laughed and riffled through a stock of invoices. "Why not inquire of Mr. Menniger, our Secretary of the Treasury, or Navy Secretary Steve Mallory?"

A thuttering roar of steam escaping the exhaust pipes momentarily suspended conversation; when it ended, Alistair heard round English curses rising over the rumbling sounds of cargo already being broken out of the runner's hold.

It was perhaps fortunate that, at this particular moment, Lieutenant the Honorable Peter Burgoyne, RN, should put in an appearance, quietly elegant in frilled shirt, canary-hued waistcoat, gray top hat and blue claw-hammer coat. The sharpness and length of his aquiline profile briefly became silhouetted against a porthole.

"I say," he drawled, "can either of you suggest where I might hope to secure suitable lodgings? I can pay well, incidentally."

Pay well, eh? mused Alistair. The Royal Navy must indeed be generous with its junior officers — but, then, this elegant's income probably was derived from private sources?

Rafe raised a strong, black brow. "If it hasn't burned down, I presume the old Charleston Hotel would be your best bet, Peter. Used to be quite the liveliest spot in town. Good bar. What say, Cousin?"

"The hotel survived the fire, but Mr. Burgoyne won't find accommodation there," Alistair predicted. "Many of General Beauregard's staff officers and their families permanently occupy all but a very few rooms, and those are engaged weeks in advance."

Alistair smiled thinly at this lean, red-haired young Englishman and couldn't make up his mind whether to like him or not — or any Redcoat, for that matter. "You'll doubtless find the sort of accommodation you evidently desire in some handsome private residence."

"Really?" The Britisher pronounced it "rahly." "Why should such people take in boarders?"

"You'll discover many fine homes are occupied only by house-keepers or poor relations — the owners will have refugeed upcountry. If you care to, Mr. Burgoyne, you might stop in at the *Argus*. We keep a list of such places."

"A most excellent suggestion — sir." The Englishman suddenly offered a large cylinder of newspapers secured by string. "As an editor, you might find interest in perusing these copies of the *Times* and *Manchester Guardian*? I say, Rafe, at what time can I go ashore?"

"Early this afternoon," Alistair interjected. "You'll not get over Stickleback Shoal before flood tide."

Mightily relieved that representatives from neither the *Courier* nor the *Mercury* newspapers had as yet put in an appearance, Alistair lingered aboard the blockade-runner and improved the opportunity to inspect this five-hundred-ton craft from stem to stern.

Through skillfully guarded conversations he ascertained that this unprecedented craft was not without serious structural faults. For instance, the *Grey Ghost*'s frame had not been constructed of heavy enough materials; she was too supple, and leaked through her steel plates like a sieve; only constant pumping could keep her holds dry. Further, having been designed to be so very narrow in the beam, she rolled sickeningly, dangerously, in any kind of seaway — like a feverish patient in bed.

He also discovered that, at sea, lookouts were always kept in the crosstrees and were paid a dollar for every sail they reported. Should anyone on deck, however, detect another vessel first, then the men aloft were fined five dollars.

Once the *Grey Ghost* had been smoothly maneuvered into a berth at Atlantic Wharf, quite a large crowd collected to gape at this curious-appearing craft, and to speculate upon the nature of her cargo.

A majority of the onlookers had more than an idle interest in this sleekly unobtrusive new arrival. They were from the crews of two other blockade-runners presently in port. One was the *Ella and Annie;* her captain, handsome, black-bearded Frank Bonneau, was reputed to possess a sixth sense which enabled him to detect the proximity of a Yankee blockader in ample time to steer clear despite storm, fog, or black of night. The other was the equally famous and fortunate *Hattie;* her master had sailed her in and out of Nassau so often that Charleston wags claimed that Harry Libby maintained a packetboat's schedule.

Alistair's sense of bafflement and suspicion mounted steadily when, on exploring the holds, he detected the name of not a single consignee painted on any case, crate or barrel beyond a few large cases marked QUARTERMASTER CORPS, CSA. Otherwise, the only identification on the freight were serial numbers done in varying colors. Um. Why should these importers so jealously conceal their identities?

Bearing his precious bundle of English newspapers under one arm, the journalist at length made his way ashore, and dogtrotted all the way to that dilapidated structure on Charlotte Street which, situated just north of the burned area, housed the *Charleston Argus,* safely distant from Mr. Charles Davis's *Charleston Courier,* on Bay Street, and R. B. Rhett's *Charleston Mercury,* long established on Broad Street.

Although comparatively isolated from its competitors, the *Argus* had the best location, being accessible to such focal news points as the Central Magnetic Telegraph Station, and the South Carolina Railroad and the North Eastern Railroad depots. These advantages, three years earlier, he had been required repeatedly to present to Mr. Road-heaver, before that worthy would consent to move from his site lower down on the peninsula.

As usual, a few loafers, military invalids and soldiers on leave were idling, disinterestedly, before the *Argus's* paste-streaked and paper-patched bulletin board. There wasn't much news; only that the Ladies' Aid Society of Charleston and Major Willis's Rest Room for Soldiers would remain open Christmas Day, and that Federal gunboats had steamed up the Yazoo River to bombard, without success, Confederate positions on Drumgold's Bluff.

As he had fully anticipated, he found none of the staff in the building on Christmas Eve; not even Jairus, his mulatto copy boy. The only tenant of the *Argus* building was an ancient ex-slave charged with keeping cast-iron stoves going in the press and composing rooms.

He found Mr. Roadheaver's grimy office empty, of course, nor was there any indication that either of his two reporters had been present at all that day — not even a recent splash of tobacco juice on the floor.

Annoyance invaded the managing editor — somebody *should* have been present, if only to appreciate the joyous news that the desperately needed newsprint, ink and new type fonts had reached port.

Sighing, Alistair slumped behind his desk in a cold and ill-lighted chamber grandiloquently termed CITY ROOM.

With sanguine hopefulness, he had named each department exactly as they had been in "The Rookery," that equally ancient building in which Charles A. Dana edited the *Tribune* for Horace Greeley. A tired smile flitted over the young journalist's wind-roughened features. Who was it who had couched that wonderful *bon mot* concerning Greeley? "There goes Greeley, a self-made man who worships his creator."

Therefore, upstairs, in the *Argus* building, a visitor would have encountered various doors, marked EDITORIAL OFFICES, COPY ROOM, COMPOSING ROOM, ACCOUNTING ROOM; and, of course, there was the PRESS VAULT.

Downstairs, in the PRESSROOM, stood a six-cylinder Hoe Lightning press, probably the most modern south of Richmond. Alas that, like its competitors, the *Charleston Argus* nowadays had been reduced to a single, badly printed half-sheet which sold for ten cents! And the *Weekly Argus* now cost a quarter.

How the *Tribune's* staff — Joe Stedman, Thomas Bailey Aldrich and the rest — would have derided such pitiful pretentiousness! Why, the *Argus* hadn't even a single private telegraph receiver and its so-called "reference files" were but a sorry, dog-eared and mouse-infested joke.

The managing editor hunched forward; selected a margin trimming to write upon. Paper was growing more precious every day — why, nowadays folks had taken to writing horizontally across their notepaper, then vertically, just as they had during the Revolution.

If only this damned war hadn't broken out! The *Argus*, with its more modern methods of operation, soon would have beaten out its competitors, might even have risen to rival the great *Richmond Examiner* — that arch critic of Jefferson Davis and all his works.

As a series of silvery cloudlets, Alistair's breath vapors lingered about his head while he commenced to draft an article describing the *Grey Ghost*, her special design and construction.

FLEET NEW STEAMER SAFELY REACHES PORT
CAPTAINED BY RAPHAEL BRYSON, FORMER CHARLESTONIAN

That should cause full many an *Argus* subscriber to adjust his spectacles and read every word of what followed. Next, he described the *Grey Ghost's* narrow escape in crossing Drunken Dick Shoal and her encounter with a Union sloop of the outer blockading cordon. Mentally, he composed an encouraging paragraph concerning the munitions she had brought in, but broke off in disgust.

He snorted; glowered unseeingly at the heatless iron stove across the office. French hats! Corsets! Bolts of satin! Cases of cognac! . . . taking up cargo space while Confederate troops shivered, marched on broken shoes and too often fought with flintlocks.

The journalist settled back angrily in his chair, hands plunged into pockets, and asked himself who could be held responsible for squandering the nation's pitifully small supply of gold on such trash? Ah, yes, and what sort of people would speculate in fripperies? Who would buy them on arrival?

A brisk knocking put an end to his speculation. He started up guiltily on recognizing Tim McCorkle. McCorkle swung in, his humorous button of a nose bright and shiny as a ripe cherry and his orange-hued chinwhiskers abristle with the cold.

"And now, me lad, I'll be thanking ye for my boat's hire. 'Tis late, and when I get home Moira McCorkle will be screaming like a hen banshee for money."

"Lord, Tim, I'm dreadfully sorry I've not got it yet. I should have stopped at my house. Here's this much." He produced limp, wrinkled

41

bills in the amount of seventy-five dollars, Richmond money. "If you'll drop in at my house on Mary Street after a bit, you'll get the other twenty-five. My wife has it."

CHAPTER V **Home-coming**

COLONEL Blount Ramsay's pretty little dwelling on Mary Street was really much finer than Alistair Bryson's meager income warranted. His tenancy became possible only because, quite early in the War, old Mrs. Ramsay and her two daughters — all three widowed by Yankee bullets — had retired to Laurel Castle, the family's vast rice plantation upon the Yemassee River. Mrs. Ramsay had deemed it prudent to rent her town house for a pittance rather than lease it to some strange officer, or leave it vacant, to be broken into and pillaged, a fate which had befallen all too many unoccupied residences.

Built of tabby stained to a warm, burnt-orange hue, the Ramsay residence, following an old and fortunate Charleston custom, had been constructed to present only an end to the street. The dwelling was of three stories and had been set far enough back to permit a clump of shiny-leaved magnolias and a single pride of India tree to flourish between it and the street.

On the ground level, as was usual, were the kitchen, storerooms and wine cellar. A set of "welcoming arms" steps mounted to a handsome front door which, in turn, gave access to a hallway off which opened the drawing room, dining room and a small library.

All bedrooms were situated on the third floor. The family had been given to spending the pleasantest hours of spring and autumn on a second-floor balcony which, enclosed by ornate cast-iron grillework, ran across the whole front.

There could be no blinking the fact that the dwelling was far larger than the Brysons needed, hard up as they were, and with never a hand to assist India in keeping house. Still, they enjoyed living there; it was really such a gem of a dwelling, so beautifully designed and tastefully furnished.

By agreement, many rooms were kept locked except for an occasional airing, and, of course, the choicest furniture and bric-a-brac, the family portraits and all the linen and silver had been carried off to Laurel Castle.

The young couple hardly ever used the drawing room. Old Colonel Ramsay's study made an admirable living room. It was much easier to heat, because, of all things, it contained a Franklin stove, brought back long ago from Harvard College by Blount's father.

Alistair's heels rang sharply on the leaf-covered cobbles of a seldom-used driveway. He was grinning broadly. By the Old Harry! It would be fun watching India's reactions when she learned that Raphael Bryson had made port. For years, India, more or less openly, had admitted a penetrating curiosity concerning his wickedly handsome ne'er-do-well cousin. At any rate, whenever Rascal Rafe's name came up she invariably fell silent and listened avidly to all that was said.

By all accounts, Cousin Rafe's escapades had been varied and many; some of them downright scandalous. For example, she knew all about Rafe's open and entirely too intimate affair with a certain wellborn young lady. The resultant duel had left young George Flood stretched dead across a patch of dune grass and Rafe cursing a nasty hole in his shoulder.

A golden rectangle of lamplit windowpanes argued that India must have completed her shopping. Good. He wouldn't have to keep McCorkle waiting. While mounting the front steps he rubbed tentatively a strong and angular jaw darkened by a heavy growth of brownish-black bristles — he'd had no time to shave that morning. Still, India wouldn't mind. In fact, she often admitted enjoying the harsh masculinity of bristles against her skin.

When his hand closed over a doorknob of beautifully fashioned silvered glass, his heart lifted; it always did when he came home to India.

The distinctive light patter made by her feet in descending from the up-stairs living room greeted him when he flung open the door. She sped towards him, wide skirts wildly asway. Her essential fluidity of movement caught and charmed his eye, caused him to ignore the fact that a net of crimson chenille into which she had caught her abundant sable hair had parted here and there.

"Oh, Alistair! Alistair! What a wonderful day this has been!" She fairly hurled herself into his arms, nuzzling his chin and hungrily pressing the softness of her breast against him. Presently, she laced fingers over the nape of his neck.

43

"And what has been so wonderful about it?"

"Oh, darling, I've found us the loveliest, the most beautiful Christmas presents you ever saw."

He terminated a lingering kiss. "India — you've not let yourself get carried away?"

She smothered him again with avid kisses, then looked up, a trifle anxious. "Please don't be angry with me, my heart. Our gifts are so perfectly wonderful."

He fell back a step. "India! You haven't — spent that money I entrusted to you? The twenty-five dollars —"

Her sable lashes fluttered downwards until they silhouetted themselves against the tawny sheen of her cheek. "Your money hasn't been squandered, sweet prince. Besides, it was spent mostly on you, so you needn't glare at me like some maiden-devouring monster!"

"Tell me you're only teasing," he begged desperately. "You still have that twenty-five I told you to save, haven't you? I owe it to Tim McCorkle."

She summoned a wavering pout. "But, darling husband, your gift was so very beautiful I couldn't resist. Wait till you see it. You'll understand."

Dark eyes snapping, he pushed her aside. "No, I won't, you incredible featherbrain. Now, Mistress, just you put on your bonnet and return whatever you bought! I must have twenty-five dollars. Can't you understand? *I must.*"

Her expression crumpled and her chin commenced to quiver. "Oh, Alistair, I would return the gifts if I could. But I just can't." In tragic tones she explained the nature of the transaction. "Oh, dear, I — I'm so — so t-terribly sorry."

"*You're* sorry?" he exclaimed in bitter reproach. "Tim McCorkle's five hungry children were to be fed with that money you've thrown away on a whim."

She swayed towards him, soft bright lips provocatively raised. "I couldn't know that, could I, now? So don't be cross, my precious. It *is* Christmas you know, and — and —"

His hand flickered up, but he checked it just short of a slap. She winced away, really frightened at the black rage in his eyes. "God in Heaven!" he shouted. "Can't you comprehend how very poor we are? You know damned well I need every cent I can lay hands on to keep the *Argus* worth reading."

44

India turned aside and buried her head in the crook of her arm. She began sobbing softly, melodiously. "Oh, what an unkind fate it is to have —"

"For Heaven's sake stop that theatrical nonsense!" He caught her by the arm, shook her a little. "Haven't you a little money hidden somewhere about the house? I *need* twenty-five dollars, I tell you!"

"Alas, no," she wailed and timorously raised piteous, brimming, beautiful, dark blue eyes. "There is but a single dirty old dollar in my reticule."

"Well, then, you can give me that 'beautiful gift' right now. Perhaps Tim can pawn it for what I owe him."

Her eyes flew wide open. "What? You — you'd give Tim *your* Christmas present from me? No, I won't give it to you. You may beat me if you wish, but you shall not see your gift until tomorrow."

The complete absurdity of India's reaction provoked a saving burst of amusement. "Oh, India, India! Will I ever understand you?"

Tear-streaked, her lovely features drew near. "You — you will forgive me?"

He drew a deep breath, then gathered into his embrace the infinitely graceful figure drooping before him. "Why not? Since God has created you devoid of common sense, who am I to criticize His work?" Briefly, he patted her sleek head. "I've invited Cousin Rafe and a Mr. Seymour, for Christmas dinner. He's a Virginian who has come back from England to serve in our Navy so I hope, at least, you've purchased the makings of a fine feast."

Her wail resounded through the cold house, blended with the moaning of a wind among the pride of India tree's bare branches.

She wrenched open the neckline of her gown. "Stab me! You have every reason."

"You needn't become quite so melodramatic, my pet. We can make do with chicken. I know turkey or suckling pig just isn't to be had any more."

Turkey and suckling pig! The very thought of them conjured up glorious memories of "High Feasts" at Rougelle's Mills. Then, house slaves and field hands had risen at dawn to celebrate, to shout "Christmas Gif' "; had fed "high on de hawg" about trestles set up in the yard.

"Damn it, India!" Cold and weary, he was really angry now. "What did you buy?"

"I — I didn't even get a chicken. Only some p-persimmons and a big old p-possum!"

"Possum and persimmons!" he groaned — and Cousin Rafe, by all accounts, was as fine a connoisseur of foods and wines as he was of the fair sex. Oh, no!

CHAPTER VI **Serena Lambkin**

LIKE most of the fine old Colonial mansions occupying the eastern end of town, dapper little Major St. George Lambkin's home on Legaré Street had been constructed during the 1760's in the best Georgian style. Its ceilings were high, its entrance imposing and from its upper two stories a magnificent panoramic view of Charleston's spacious harbor could be enjoyed.

Miss Serena Lambkin and her younger sister, Aurora, therefore were able to watch the squat, ugly little steam ram, *Chicora*, quit a defensive anchorage in Fort Sumter's lee and, trailing a plume of sooty smoke through fitful snow squalls, commence a leisurely progress back to her berth at Mr. Adger's North Wharf.

Pretty soon her sister ship, *Palmetto State*, ought to put out for Sumter, there to lie prepared, on very short notice, to cope with a possible sudden attack on Charleston. Thus far Admiral S. F. Du Pont's blockading squadron — all of wooden construction — perhaps wisely, had declined to offer combat.

Once *Palmetto State* had backed out into a whirling snow flurry which lost her to sight, the young ladies crossed casually to consider their reflections in a tall French pier glass.

Serena wondered: "Oh, dear, how soon will the first of those awful Yankee monitors appear?"

Aurora, incorrigibly pert for a fourteen-year-old young lady, summoned a wise and wicked smile. "Reckon you've time, honey, to put on yo' best basque. Better. Dr. Bryson sure enough will be ringing our doorbell soon's his boat docks!"

"Steam ram, not 'boat,'" Serena corrected mildly. "It's just as easy to call things by their right name. Boats are little things propelled by oars. Any Navy man will tell you so."

The older girl wetted the tips of her middle fingers and with them smoothed wide, narrow brows. If she only dared to darken them just the least bit — like that handsome sister-in-law of Donald's. Her hair was so very blond she knew that, by most lights, she appeared to possess practically no eyebrows whatever. What Serena overlooked, with characteristic modesty, was that her lovely dark brown eyes and the rose triangle formed by a heart-shaped mouth effectively distracted attention from this defect. Further, her hair was the color of spun sugar, lustrous, but not so fine in texture that it could not be trained into fashionable coils, neatly plaited over each ear.

In a gesture of spurious primness, Aurora Lambkin smoothed a lace-trimmed apron. "I'll warrant Mamma gave you fits when she heard Dr. Bryson aimed to come callin' regularly."

Serena smiled tolerantly. "What an incorrigible little Nosy Parker you are."

"Is he comin' to escort you to Christmas Eve service?"

"Well — yes." Serena's pink complexion brightened a trifle, and she hurried on. "Mamma is upset. She's trying so hard to see that we all enjoy an old-fashioned Christmas. Pay no attention to the cross things she says. She doesn't mean them."

Aurora cocked a dark, curly head to one side; seemed puzzled. "Why-for does Cousin" — she pronounced it "Cudd'n" — "Julia look so queer whenever you speak the name of Bryson?"

Serena's glance flitted over to a sewing cabinet bulging with half-completed uniform sleeves, and lingered there. Why did Aurora have to be so noticing — so imaginative? "You must be dreaming it."

"Maybe so," Aurora admitted, inspecting her own darkly piquant, almost elfin, features over her sister's shoulder. She made a little face at herself. "But then why do Cudd'n Julia Livesey have to sit 'round like a sick raincrow ever since she and Cordelia refugeed down from Beaufort?"

" 'Why *does* Cousin Julia,' " corrected Serena, gently. "It's a great pity Madame Dupré should have closed her Academy. I fear you will never learn genteel deportment, and you should, pretty though you are."

The older girl's skirts of brown taffeta whispered back to the French windows facing the harbor. *Br-r-r.* What a perfectly miserable day! A raw wind was still booming, shaking bare tree limbs and hurling lances of snow in from the ocean.

47

She experienced a pang of dull resentment on discovering that, all the same, she could distinguish a number of smoke smudges off Charleston Bar. Oh, those dreadful, inexorable, tireless blockaders! Would they never sail away and allow this once lovely old port to resume the well-bred tenor of its ways?

Serena lingered at the window, seeing but not observing the low outlines of Fort Moultrie — Fort Sullivan during the Revolution. Opposite, across the harbor's mouth, Cummings' Point showed as a brown-black ruler mark upon the water. Near its tip, Battery Wagner, a very powerful defense, warned Mr. Lincoln's wooden warships not to venture close inshore. Set almost midway between these defenses loomed the familiar silhouette of that fort over which all the trouble had commenced. It wasn't precise and pretty any more. Various bombardments had crumbled or blunted many of its salients and shot had pitted the face of its remaining masonry like pale pockmarks.

The slender, blond young woman tilted her head a little to one side, and a smile of reminiscence curved her mouth. How many delightful lawn parties had she not attended on Fort Sumter's parade ground? . . . Even after the fighting had begun.

Wearily, her gaze traversed the wintry landscape; noted, perfunctorily, raw yellow earth marking the presence of batteries thrown up to command the entrance to Wappoo Creek and James Island. There were other emplacements further out among those sere marshes over which dense flocks of waterfowl seemed forever to be wheeling; but she couldn't see them.

The defense nearest the Lambkin mansion, as she well knew, was Battery Waring. It lay not two hundred yards distant and had been constructed from the rubble of an old sugar mill which had stood on Chisholm's Point. The most formidable of Charleston's immediate defenses was Battery Ramsay, an elaborate earthwork thrown up near some crumbling bathhouses on White Point.

Softly humming "The Bonnie Blue Flag," Serena shifted her gaze to the snow-veiled Cooper River. Ah! *Chicora* at last had nosed into her slip, and already her firemen must have banked her boiler fires, because only a wisp of smoke was escaping her single funnel.

Chilled by a draft beating in around the window frame, Serena started to turn away, but paused, intrigued by a glimpse of a most unusual-appearing vessel. Obviously a blockade-runner, fresh in, she was steaming cautiously up the Cooper River's estuary, barely visible because she had been painted a light shade of gray.

"Come here, Aurora. Look. There's the strangest kind of a ship coming in."

"I declare, honey, there's something dashing and maybe a little wicked about her," Aurora cried. "Did you ever see two slimmer smokestacks or shorter masts?"

Serena said she had never seen anything like her before and she'd been studying the harbor every day now for going on three years.

Suddenly, she flung an arm about her sister, squeezed her excitedly. "Oh, Aurora, maybe that's one of those armored cruisers our Government's had built abroad. Donald and Harry Bears were talking about them only last Sunday."

"No. She don't look like a war boat to me. She looks too small and I don't see any cannons about her deck," Aurora said, then wiped away the fog left by her breath on the pane. "Do you?"

"No. But somehow, Aurora, I wouldn't be surprised if that vessel out there isn't somehow — mighty important to us."

"Oh, bosh! You talk like a loony."

"No, I don't," Serena said sharply because, once before, she had experienced equally firm premonitions. Why should she have suffered such a delicious sensation when she had beheld Donald Bryson bowing gravely over her hand? The first thing she noticed was the clearness of small gray eyes, so brilliant behind his spectacles, the sensitivity of a wide, but thin-lipped, mouth.

She recalled inquiring what uniform he was wearing, and he'd told her it was the Confederate States Navy's. She'd blushed, because she'd thought she could recognize any gray uniform.

Their first encounter had been at a great ball Dr. Bull had given at Ashley Plantation in celebration of General Beauregard's ever-glorious rout of the Yankees at Manassas. This dance had taken place so soon after the victory there'd been no time for long lists of casualties to be posted, all edged in black, upon the local newspapers' bulletin boards.

Swiftly, many homes had been shuttered, had displayed mourning wreaths on their door knockers. Later still, the dismal wail of the Dead March sounded in the streets, day after day, until it seemed there would be no end to the number of bodies brought home for burial.

49

Oddly enough, Serena, even now, could recall to the letter, an *In Memoriam* which had appeared in the *Mercury*.

To Captain Paul Hamilton

Go, Soldier, to your glorious rest,
Your truth and valor bearing,
The bravest are the tenderest,
The loving are the daring.

Soberly, Serena Lambkin collected reticule and bonnet, but hesitated over the last pair of white kid gloves in her possession. What more fitting occasion to wear them than to Christmas Eve Services at St. Philip's with Dr. Bryson? Vaguely, she wondered just what magic Papa could have employed to find items so precious.

Passing the room in which reposed her mother, she trod softly. All day, poor dear Mamma had been attempting to conceal — none too well, either — a fear that her ever-courtly husband might not have been able to obtain Christmas leave. After all, St. George must be shouldering heavy responsibilities over there in Fort Moultrie; he came from across the harbor so very irregularly.

A considerable consolation, however, lay in the fact that brother Cato would be back, long enough for Christmas dinner, at least. How wonderful it would be to hear Cato's suddenly deep voice ringing through these chilly halls again.

Indeed, she was achieving distinction these days through having a brother serving in the Navy. Almost every other girl of her set had menfolk serving in the land forces. Would Cato fetch along some gay young fellow officers? She very much hoped so. So many of her friends would be deprived of sweethearts this holiday season.

What a pity, Serena mused while Aurora wandered off down the upper hall humming "Good King Wenceslas," that, because of poor Cousin Julia's unhappy experience with Rafe Bryson, Mamma should so unreasonably condemn everyone bearing the name of Bryson.

Poor Donald! How unlucky for him this dreadful War should have broken out so soon after he had purchased old Dr. Mordecai's practice. Why couldn't Mamma bring herself to say something nice about Dr. Donald? He was good-natured, invariably well-mannered; and he was genuinely patriotic — which was more than could be said concerning his brother, that ubiquitous, seemingly indefatigable and dreadfully outspoken journalist.

What an intense, distracted-appearing individual Alistair Bryson had appeared to be on the few occasions they'd met. Well, maybe he had some excuse? Who wouldn't appear distracted when married to such a bold and scatterbrained Creole hussy? That India was so truly beautiful made the situation no better.

Firmly, Serena knotted her bonnet's ribbons. A pity Doctor Donald could not have sprung from — well — a more affluent family; Heaven knew he was well-enough born. She had learned from Mrs. Heywood, an arbitress of all matters genealogical, that the Clan Bryson had been established in Wateree County back in 1751 by one Gordon; that his son Alistair, in 1776, had come down from the mountains to fight against the British — and surprisingly had won the hand of Antoinette Proveaux, for all that she bore one of the oldest and proudest names in all South Carolina. At the time everybody in Society had deemed it a pity that that brawny young Scot should have borne his pretty young wife back to Rougelle's Mills.

Serena also learned that this rugged Alistair's second son, Alexander, the banker, married well — Sue Ellen Blount, in fact. He had prospered in Charleston and, to his regret, had sired that high-spirited youth who so deserved the sobriquet of Rascal Rafe. Possibly Rafe was a throwback to those wild Highlanders of Ben Mohr who had feuded so bloodily with Clan Ferguson over the centuries?

Maybe Mamma wasn't entirely wrong? With so notorious a cousin and that tactless visionary, Alistair, for a brother, poor Dr. Donald was laboring under no small difficulties with regard to family connections.

A small fire glowed brightly in an attempt to dispel a damp chill pervading Major Lambkin's drawing room, but more of a blaze would be required to overcome the chamber's twelve-foot ceilings and a leakage of cold air through six French doors.

She discovered Cousin Cordelia Livesey lingering before a fireplace distinguished by an elaborate mantel of the finest Italian marble. Serena suppressed a little gasp for, quite shamelessly, the girl had hoisted, high behind her, a skirt of mauve bengaline, hoops and three petticoats, in order to enjoy warmth upon buttocks encased in frilled and liberally beribboned cambric drawers.

"A miserable, raw day, 'Delia."

51

"It certainly is, and I'm *that* put out. I'll just have to wear that tiresome old black velvet cloak *again*." In no great hurry, Cordelia lowered and then pettishly smoothed billowing skirts over straight, pleasingly curved legs. Her eyes sparkled angrily. "Oh, why must those damn' stubborn Yankees keep up their blockade? Why won't they admit that they've lost the war, and let us have new clothes and — and fixings again?"

"How you do run on, 'Delia. You know . . . ? You look extra lovely in that black mantle," smiled Serena. "It's a wonder you can keep your complexion so white and clear on the wretched food we have to offer these days."

Serena flushed, could have bitten off her tongue; she hadn't in the least intended to remind Cordelia that she, Julia and Mrs. Livesey were still on "a little visit," indefinitely prolonged since last July.

They'd appeared without warning from Beaufort, bearing their most precious possessions aboard a ramshackle gundelow. Terror-stricken by the absence of their menfolk, these ladies had abandoned Water Oaks, their magnificent plantation on Harker's Island, upon reading certain exaggerated newspaper reports, and listening to word-of-mouth rumors that Yankee gunboats had entered the Sounds. Lincoln's hirelings were reported to be burning and looting and raping — with official encouragement.

Of course, they and their near neighbors had fled in an access of panic. They didn't know, as the *Argus,* or any other reputable newspaper, could have informed them, that Water Oaks would never be sighted by an enemy vessel for many months to come.

Only after the property had stood silent and deserted for days had a band of runaway slaves plucked up sufficient courage to emerge from the swamps and reconnoiter fearfully a long time before they dared to loot and then set a torch to the stately old "Big House" Allen Livesey had reared in 1798.

Cordelia's narrow foot impatiently patted the floor. "I do hope Harry Bears won't be late. I just hate the way his captain keeps interfering with our appointments."

As if in respect to her plaint, a brisk knocking commenced at the front door. Leander, slow and rheumatic, appeared from the butler's pantry. He muttered dolefully while shuffling over the hall's shining black-and-white marble floor.

"Jest ain't fitten de Lambkins' butler wear ole rags, come Chris'mus Day."

Opposite the drawing room's double door, he paused again to inspect his livery's jacket, and grimaced like a wrinkled old ape. Plainly visible dark spots betrayed that the original six silver buttons recently had been reduced to four. He had losted them monogrammed buttons sometime last month — really had; hadn't sold them privately, like that low-life nigger Buncombe had suggested.

Lieutenant Harry Bears, CSN, today appeared extra smart, consciously proud of a smart, gray-blue and long-skirted uniform tunic recently run in from London. A diamond-shaped design, executed in untarnishable solid gold braid upon each of his cuffs, arose from a single ring and indicated, beyond doubt, that he held a lieutenant's commission in the Regular Naval Establishment.

Smiling, he bowed deep to both ladies. Recent winds had tinted young Bears's wide-jawed face a brilliant red, so his short, blond sideburns and mustaches gleamed silvery by contrast.

"Donald's on his way, Miss Lambkin. Be here, any minute." He winked. "Don's at the barber's this minute gettin' himself trigged out fo' yo' benefit."

"Thank you, Mr. Bears," Serena said and lowered her eyes to conceal a sudden sparkle in them. Cordelia treated her bonnet, gay with a sprig of French flowers, to a final adjustment.

"You two plannin' to attend the Soldiers' Benefit Gala at Mr. D'Arcy's New Year's night? Everyone claims it will be quite an affair."

"I — I'm really not sure," confessed Major Lambkin's big-eyed daughter. "I believe Dr. Bryson plans to spend the day with his brother and sister-in-law."

"Then Donald won't appear," Cordelia predicted coolly. "I'm sure the Alistair Brysons were not invited."

"Then they ought to be. Alistair Bryson's the smartest journalist in town," Bears asserted. "His paper is printin' the only news worth readin' — and believin'." Young Bears's wide features kindled. "Bryson's wife, by the way, is a real peach — a stunner."

Cordelia smiled thinly while securing the tie cords of the black velvet mantle. "Really, now? No doubt, La Fair Bryson entertains your sailors quite as boldly as she does Yankee prisoners and that poor-white riffraff undergoing training out at the Race Course."

53

"Oh, come off it, 'Delia," the lieutenant laughed and readjusted the set of an oblong belt-buckle. It displayed the initials CSN in gold, enclosed in a fat laurel wreath of silver. "Mrs. Bryson does more to cheer up all manner of sad souls than all the long-faced goody-goodies in Charleston lumped together."

"Harry Bears! I do declare you are perfectly outrageous!"

It was nonetheless patent that Cordelia deemed her beau to be anything but outrageous. Smiling at him over her shoulder, she started towards the door, hands tucked into a small ermine muff and looking very pretty in the flowered bonnet.

"We really must leave, else we'll be late at St. Philip's. We shall see you later?"

"Please, 'Delia, let's linger a little while," boomed Bears. "I must give Don some really capital news."

Serena's expression kindled. "Capital news for Dr. Bryson?"

The young fellow picked up a red-topped gray cap with a flat, patent-leather visor, and a five-pointed star within wreath, embroidered on its front.

He lowered his voice; assumed a conspiratorial manner. "You ladies must promise not to breathe a word, but a high-rankin' officer told me that, any hour now, our Palmetto Squadron will steam out and smash the Union blockade so wide open that that baboon up in Washington will wonder what happened.

"Think of it! Everybody will be watchin' what we do. It'll be almighty important. Once the blockade's broken, the English and French navies, sure enough, will start fighting at our side."

"Oh, I hope so, with all my heart." Serena's elation faded swiftly, however. "But haven't you only four warships, while the Yankees keep — Heaven knows how many — here and at Port Royal?"

"That's true enough, Miss Lambkin, but we have two *ironclad* vessels ready for action, manned by well-trained crews, while the Federals keep only wooden ships out yonder. We ought to be able to blow 'em out of the water without sufferin' the least damage to ourselves."

Just as they had, in years gone by, rich, faintly plaintive Negro voices began raising a Christmas carol. Doubtless, they were hoping a window might open and a handful of nuts or candies, or maybe even a few coins, would come scaling down.

The tall young naval officer sniffed audibly on becoming aware of certain savory odors arising from the Lambkin kitchens on the ground floor; undoubtedly tomorrow's High Feast was under preparation.

Serena thought, How wonderful that enough food's been found to fill at least some of those beautiful copper kettles Father imported from France. Too bad, that, last summer, "Cytherea," Papa's plantation house, should have been struck by lightning and burned down. In consequence, the oxcart no longer creaked down Legaré Street, fetching in a pleasing assortment of comestibles.

When the front door's pull-bell jangled again, Serena impulsively started into the hall, but checked her progress in time. How deplorably unladylike. Nonetheless, she lingered, cheeks glowing, at the salon's entrance and pretended to arrange the "watch-spring" stiffening her crinoline into a more perfect circle.

Cordelia slipped an arm through young Bears's and hastily pecked her cousin's cheek, murmuring, "If you don't allow Dr. Bryson to detain you overlong, Harry and I will endeavour to reserve space in our" — she faltered an intsant, then corrected herself — "your pew."

The light of early evening briefly cast into silhouette Medical Lieutenant Donald Bryson's chunky five feet and six inches of height when he entered, cap in hand and scarlet-lined boat cloak bravely aswing. His broad, red-brown features exuded vitality and his eyes leaped with life behind square-lensed spectacles. The physician's light brown hair and short sideburns reflected cheerful flecks of brilliance from the light of a pair of candles flickering on the mantelpiece. He also wore Confederate naval uniform, but it was far from new.

Smiling, he executed an exaggerately formal bow and brushed the floor with his cap. "Miss Lambkin! So delighted to find you at home. May I present my humble respects?"

Laughing lightly, Serena executed a deep court curtsy in acknowledgment ere she held out her hand.

"The season's greeting to you, Dr. Bryson. I trust you find yourself in good health?"

"Excellent, as usual." His voice was deep and strong, yet, somehow, not in the least loud. He dropped his formal manner and took her hands between his, looked steadily into her features and soft, dark brown eyes. "All day I — I've been picturing how you'd appear at this moment, Serena. May I say that you're even more delightful than I'd dared to imagine?"

"You always have been a shameless flatterer." She wanted to add, "Donald," but didn't deem it proper — yet.

He let go her hands and stepped back, suddenly grave of mien.

"I bring news which I'm not sure you'll welcome."

"Oh, I know. Harry Bears was here just now. He told us about your impending attack on the blockade fleet."

Donald Bryson frowned briefly. "It's not that. Harry really shouldn't have mentioned it, but I reckon we're all too free-spoken. Flag Officer Ingraham is rightfully raising Ned about so much careless talk. Some of it's bound to reach enemy ears."

"Then what is this news of yours?"

"It's something — well, something personal."

"What in the world . . . ?"

"You've heard, of course, that a blockade-runner made port today?"

"Better than that. Aurora and I watched her dock; she's painted almost white?"

"That was the *Grey Ghost.*" He drew a slow, worried breath and a subdued note of excitement entered his tone. "Have you heard who is her captain?"

"Really, Doctor, how could I have?"

"He's my cousin, Raphael Bryson."

"Rascal Rafe!" Serena's finger tips flickered up to press hard against her lips and her great eyes flew wide open. "Oh, no! No! Poor Julia. And on Christmas Eve."

"Tell me, Serena, did Rafe really jilt Julia Livesey?"

Serena nodded agitatedly. "Yes, only two days before their wedding was to have taken place. To make it still worse, he ran off with a common overseer's daughter."

CHAPTER VII Noël! Noël! 1862

A SULLEN noise of cannon, firing in the distance, prompted India Bryson reluctantly to awaken, which in itself was curious because, for almost two years now, she'd heard cannonading — usually for futile reasons. The wind had died out, permitting her to identify those evenly spaced, slamming sounds as salutes, rather than shots fired in anger.

Slam! Bang! Bang! . . . Slam! Bang! Bang! The sound suggested some drunken giant trying to close a door on the rim of the world. She felt cold air rush in under the counterpane when, only semiconscious, she roused up. What? Where? Oh, bother! Probably the batteries were saluting another blockade-runner entering Charleston Harbor.

Turning onto her side, she dreamily considered her husband's powerful profile delineated by stars peering through their bedroom's grimy windowpanes.

In wintertime, India usually left open the blinds; she'd found it pleasant to lie abed and watch powdery constellations swing by, bright and remote from this sordid, war-torn planet.

Poor Alistair! What a miserable scene they'd had. Essentially, she'd been to blame; she'd admit it to herself — if to nobody else. No matter what the temptation, she really shouldn't have spent the money he'd entrusted.

Oh, dear. This Christmas Eve had seen Alistair stalking angrily out of the house, to return later, but still so silent and tight-lipped he'd squelched the bright, nonsensical half-apologies trembling on her lips. He'd lugged in a great market basket of food. Where could he have found the money to purchase such items? Oh, dear! She blinked eyes suddenly filled with moisture. Why had she attempted, as a timid peace offering, to present him with a bottle of sherry?

"Where'd you get this?" he'd snapped. "Thought you'd no money."

"Why, Colonel Jefford sent it around. You know, he's the Provost Marshal here in town."

"Yes, but why?"

"I don't know," she'd said. "Unless it was in appreciation of the songs I sang to cheer a train of invalids in the railroad depot."

Restless, she squirmed in the Ramsays' big double bed, wondered where Alistair could have raised money to purchase so fat a hen turkey. Heavens, long ago he had pawned any possession which might fetch a few quick dollars. Whenever a good story loomed in the offing, she knew, Alistair would stoop to any ignominy necessary to hire rigs or charter boats.

57

Why wouldn't that stupid, whisky-soaked Mr. Roadheaver appreciate what a truly superlative job her husband was doing? Who else would have thought to subsidize certain telegraph operators in order that the *Agrus* might first receive important news? Who else was there to thank that the *Argus* had run initial accounts of such great battles as Manassas Junction, Pittsburg Landing, Seven Oaks and Sharpsburg? The *Courier* and *Mercury* hadn't carried the news till many hours afterward.

India sighed, luxuriously stretched lithe limbs and presently dozed off, hearing an old and unhappy query in mind. Whose was the fault that, never in their more than four years of married life, had she become pregnant? Certainly, they both were sufficiently ardent and practiced, by now, to have accomplished her ambition?

Early in the morning, Alistair lugged in a small pine tree, cut during the night, in the back yard of a burned-out and deserted dwelling across the street. He'd no notion what kind of pine it might be, but it was fragrant of some sweet resin. As usual, India proved ingenious in devising ornaments; she produced garlands of popcorn, some dyed pink, strings of scarlet berries and gay little figures and bangles cut out of tinfoil from the lining of an old glove box.

Her *chef d'œuvre* he deemed to be a rather spidery Star of Bethlehem contrived from a sheet of tin. The metal she'd employed was no longer shiny, but, still, it was better than nothing.

India deemed herself rather clever to have purchased, at St. Francis Xavier's Roman Catholic Church, a pair of slender votive tapers. These, cut into convenient lengths, she deftly secured to the Christmas tree branches.

Chattering happily, she and her husband soon completed the trimming and so all that remained to be done was to place their gifts at its base. They both laughed out loud. There were only two small packages wrapped in wrinkled tissue paper and secured by lengths of faded pink ribbon filched from an old petticoat.

Once he had completed shaving and was cleaning his razor he heard her voice, ever thrilling to his ears, singing "Christmas Day in the Morning." Despite generous traces of lather he came pounding downstairs to crush her small, warm body in a joyous embrace.

"Merry Christmas again, my sweetheart." In brave defiance of a chill pervading the house India had donned a thin, Nile green negligée; the silk of which it was fashioned she had purchased in New York at Mr. Wanamaker's wonderful store, four long years ago.

Alistair grinned delightedly. India had plaited her lustrous hair into twin pigtails and had secured tiny sprigs of holly to them with gay red ribbons. So slender and round-eyed did she appear as she hovered about the tree, its candles now brilliantly aglitter, she suggested a lovely child of twelve, rather than an old married woman in her early twenties.

"It's really a lovely tree! Really, my darling, you have the magician's touch." He glanced into the kitchen, saw a fire crackling and table set, brave with a bowl of pine cones and mistletoe. "*Eggs!* Where *did* you find these eggs?"

"Ask me no secrets and I'll tell you no lies!" she laughed softly and patted his cheek. "And just sniff the teapot! Real Lapsang Sochong."

A loud *bang!* in the street caused India to jump and spill her tea.

"That'll be a 'Christmas gun,'" grinned Alistair, "Just like the old days in the back country."

"What are they?"

"Look out and you'll see."

She peered out in time to glimpse a gangling Negro boy about to jump upon and burst a dried and inflated pig's bladder.

"Reckon firecrackers are too hard to come by."

"'Christmas guns' make a louder noise. I used to love to burst them."

A sound of singing came from further down Mary Street. A chorus of lonely and forlorn-appearing soldiers wearing patched and faded gray or brown uniforms were wandering along.

One after another they sang, quite well, too, Christmas carols already old when the last Redcoat had quit Charleston. Windows and doors opened along the street; heads appeared, called "Merry Christmas!" and offered homely little gifts of candy and precious bits of fruitcake wrapped in newspaper.

A second group appeared. To a man they were bony and gaunt and looked out from fiery eyes, black as their shaggy hair. Obviously of Scottish descent, they raised curious, Calvinist hymns. Many of the words sounded quite incomprehensible.

Later appeared a band of Negroes who accompanied themselves on banjoes or guitars and wore sprigs of mistletoe tucked over their ears. When they finished a carol they would crowd around some front door crying, "Christmas gif', good peoples! Christmas gif'!" just as they had before the fighting had begun. They'd not much hope, but an occasional window did go up and a few "shinplasters" would drift into the street to provoke a laughing scramble.

Although it had grown pleasantly warm in the ground floor kitchen and the odor of baking yams sweetened the air, India, nonetheless, looked miserably apprehensive. How painfully inadequate seemed that scrawny hen turkey which, the night before, had appeared almost voluptuously plump. This bird might, if Alistair were clever about his carving, do for four grownups. How lucky that, for some reason, Dr. Donald wouldn't be on hand for "High Feast," but would drop by later.

If only there were wine to offer — even native scuppernong. If only decent wax candles were gracing the festive board, not smelly, dull gray beef-tallow dips. Oh dear, and she so loved to set a pretty table.

India felt better, though, when she fetched in a splint basket of club moss, laurel and mistletoe and deftly arranged them about a beautiful old China punchbowl filled with holly. All the while she chattered gaily, misquoted Shakespeare and kissed Alistair every time he came within range.

During one such caress Alistair remarked, "Someone's putting on a shivaree." Then, to the young Brysons' astonishment, the band music turned into the Ramsay driveway and a dozen-odd musicians in assorted uniforms tramped right up to the front door rendering "Adeste Fideles" with greater enthusiasm than skill.

They were playing a trio of cornets, two French horns and a baritone in addition to a concertina, some banjoes and a single bass drum, which banged away loud enough to set the windows arattle.

"Why, Alistair! How perfectly wonderful! They're serenading us. Who could have sent them?"

Gathering the green negligée about her, India flung open the door, and Alistair gaped; for, swinging along and leading the band with one

60

hand, came Captain Raphael Bryson! A step behind him strode that tall, quiet-voiced Virginian called Dabney Seymour.

"A merry, merry Christmas to you!" they called over the music and, doffing their caps, bowed very deep to the diminutive figure fluttering before the doorway. Behind the musicians four grinning and gaptoothed English seamen straggled along bearing a canvas duffle bag and a couple of baskets from which projected an intriguing number of bottlenecks.

Rafe Bryson's curling, collar-length hair glistened as he called, "Hobbs! That small basket contains rum. Distribute it among yourselves and our musical friends!"

"Merry Christmas, sir, and thank you!"

Hallooing like fox hunters, and waving bottles, musicians and seamen streamed back into Mary Street. The figure in merchant officer's uniform wheeled, grinning broadly, because Alistair had remained in shirt sleeves and still was displaying tide-marks of shaving lather.

The blockade-runner's insouciant grin vanished the instant he glimpsed that lissome, dark-eyed girl dancing excitedly at his cousin's side. How young she looked; so gay and so breath-takingly lovely in that thin dressing gown of shimmering green silk.

So this vital, tawny-complexioned girl had been born India Villepigue in Tampa, and had appeared on the stage?

Well! Well! Rafe "made a leg" in the courtly eighteenth-century style, flicked the ground with a visored cap.

"My humble respects, ma'am," he called up the "welcoming arms" steps, "and the season's greetings."

"And welcome to Charleston, Captain Rafe!" laughed India, as, gown aripple, she descended a step with one slim hand gracefully extended for his salute. "So this is the famous Cousin Rafe?" To herself she said, It's easy to credit what we've heard. There *is* something fascinating and — and dangerous in his expression. Yes, I'll believe he's fought a good many duels and killed poor George Flood.

"Call me 'infamous' and you'll come nearer the mark, if you credit some people," grinned Rafe, quite unabashed. Then, with a flourish, he beckoned forward his companion.

"Mrs. Bryson, may I present Mr. Dabney Seymour? A Virginian, come home to offer his services."

Alistair like this handsome six-footer with the clear and penetrating,

61

bright blue eyes, wide scar and deep, deliberate voice. Said he, "Welcome to Charleston, sir. As a naval officer, I reckon you will find plenty of interest taking place. Please enter, gentlemen," Alistair invited. "I trust you will overlook the chill within, but every bit of coal which finds its way here goes either to our Palmetto Squadron or into some blockade-runner's bunkers."

"The warmth of your welcome suffices," Rafe laughed. "By the bye, I've ordered some sacks of Cardiff coal to be delivered here. Well, fair Cousin," he took India's hand between his and regarded her in subtle appraisal, "since we're doomed to be related, I trust we shall become true friends — and that we'll long remain so." He snapped his fingers. "Hell's fire, Alistair. I forgot, yesterday — any children? I've some toys in one of the baskets."

India's piquant profile flashed when she shook her head once, sharply. "Alas, no. But I've plenty of friends who would go daft with delight over them."

Presently the promised Welsh coal arrived — three wonderful sacks of that clean-burning fuel — and, ere long, cast-iron grates which had not created heat in many a dreary month were glowing about the Ramsay house.

India's soaring excitement expressed itself in a series of breathless little cries of delight while Cousin Rafe's baskets were being emptied onto the living room's lovely, but faded and mouldy-smelling, Aubusson rug.

Improvising joyous dance steps all the while, Alistair's wife sped about fitting pure beeswax candles into various candelabra. Gradually, Colonel Blount Ramsay's lovely little salon came revivified, graciously alive — also the crystal-ornamented dining room with its genuine Sheraton table and chairs.

In addition to brandies, liqueurs of various sorts and a case of champagne, the blockade-runner's captain had brought along a generous selection of sherries, ports and cognacs.

India, thrilled, flung ecstatic arms about her spouse when she perceived the nature of provisions fetched from the *Grey Ghost*. Two great hams; a small, stupidly blinking live green turtle; loops and batons of spicy, red-brown Italian sausage; soft, very smelly cheeses from France; hard ones from Holland, shaped like cannon balls of scarlet.

62

Like huge jewels, pineapples, oranges, limes and lemons soon glowed before the fireplace. The canvas bag in turn disgorged a fat sack of fine white flour, tin boxes of pepper, cloves, cinnamon; even a stone jar of olives and, most exciting of all, a huge box of Parisian bonbons done up with red satin ribbons.

"Lord above!" Alistair indulged in swift and secret calculations, experienced a pang of apprehension. Translated into Confederate currency, Raphael's largesse would fetch, among the secret markets of the South, not a penny less than twenty-five thousand dollars! It wasn't comforting, somehow, to find himself all at once so deeply beholden to this picaresque, if charming, relative.

Mistrusting, as always, his too readable facial reactions, Alistair went out into the yard in search of cold water with which to lace Rafe's excellent, but powerful, French cognac.

He thought, while manipulating the pump handle: It's damned generous of Rafe — too generous, when one considers those poor devils half-starved and freezing on the battlefields of Virginia, of Tennessee and inside Vicksburg.

Fleetingly, the journalist calculated what that twenty-five thousand might have secured in the way of medicines. Um-m. Nowadays quinine, sulphate of morphine and oil of bergamot were bringing one hundred dollars the ounce; calomel and blue mask, twenty; even the most ordinary of surgeons' instruments started at ten thousand dollars the set!

Once the house became warmed up, the two visitors, on India's invitation, cast loose the brass buttons of their tunics. Why the dickens had Rafe elected to wear that sea captain's blue serge? Probably, because to a deplorable degree it resembled a Union uniform. That would be like him. Lieutenant Seymour, however, wore a Confederate naval officer's double-breasted and long-skirted gray coat lacking insignia of any sort.

Throughout a fabulous "High Feast," dished up in midafternoon, India's splendid dark eyes kept straying over to the Christmas tree — about the base of which now reposed not two little packages, but a fascinating collection of parcels. What could they contain? It proved difficult not to confess curiosity, or to squirm in her chair like an impatient small girl.

63

Amid bursts of laughter and hilarious toasts they consumed a magnificent, saddle-colored ham diapered with cloves, garnished by orange slices and basted with a wondrous Madeira sauce concocted by the donor.

Sea-bronzed features flushed, Raphael politely stifled a belch and, at long last, pushed back his chair. "And now, fair Cousin, shall we learn what Saint Nick has brought for a pair of most charming hosts?"

"Oh, yes! Yes! Let's! But first Cousin Rafe, and you, Mr. Seymour." It was entirely typical of India Bryson that she should, somehow, have improvised presents. For the not unattractively scarred Virginian there was a Confederate swordbelt. It was almost new, the gift of an officer grateful on his deathbed. A few very dark bloodstains marred the belt's black leather, but were unnoticeable to the casual eye.

For Alistair's cousin the girl's desperate search had been rewarded by the rediscovery of a long-forgotten theatrical stiletto. Although its hilt was of a florid German silver design set with glass jewels, its blade was surprisingly well-tempered and keen.

Rafe beamed like a small boy, then pecked her lightly on both cheeks. "It's a thing of beauty," he declared, somber eyes asparkle. "I shall gird it on when next we war against the pirates of Barbary."

"Don't laugh," she begged in pretty distress. "This was given me by the great Edwin Booth, himself, the night we closed *Othello.*"

A trifle unsteadily, Rafe bowed, made a wide motion with his right arm. "I crave thy pardon, O fairest of Thespis' daughters. This gift shall ever remain my most precious possession."

"It should," Alistair remarked drily. "Ever since I've known her, India has treasured that gaudy bit of nonsense." Then he turned his attention to the Christmas tree upon which candles now winked in golden cheeriness.

He slipped an arm about his wife's tiny waist and led her forward. "And now, my love, may I behold that mysterious present you bought me?" He almost added, ". . . And provoked our first real fight."

"Merry Christmas, my darling." She kissed him resoundingly. "This fob comes with all my dearest love."

Dabney Seymour watched Rafe peer over his cousin's shoulder. He appeared really impressed by the fine goldsmith's work on the frames securing the pair of signet stones: one of carnelian, the other of jet.

"It is magnificent!" agreed Seymour gravely. "I presume those are family coats of arms engraved upon the seals, Mr. Bryson?"

"Oh, no," India confessed cheerfully. "I have no notion whose they are. But they *are* pretty signets, aren't they?"

"They are," Rafe agreed. "Come, Alistair, snap the fob to your watch. Let's see how the seals appear *in situ*."

Alistair went scarlet to his hair line, then broke into peals of strident laughter. Quite without understanding why, the others joined in until all were breathless.

"Go ahead, snap it on your watch," insisted Rafe.

"T-that's the c-cream of the j-joke," panted the journalist. "You see, I—I pawned my w-watch only yesterday. Had to pay off a debt."

India's warmly golden features froze in an agonized expression. "Oh, you poor dear! So that's where the turkey money . . . ?"

A puzzled frown appeared on the blockade-runner's brow. "*Pawned it!* Why did you, a Bryson, have to pawn anything?"

The newspaperman wiped moisture from his eyes. "I'd my charter boat's captain to pay off. Due to a misunderstanding, India spent the money I'd reserved for him. Since it was impossible to raise the money anywhere else on Christmas Eve—why, I went over to Uncle's."

"Oh, my poor precious!" Bright lips twisted into an anguished line, India flung herself into her husband's arms. "It was all my fault! O dear, and I do love you so very greatly."

Smoothly, Rafe intervened and, grinning, patted India's shoulder. "Cease these vain repinings, O Tragic Muse. Go search beneath yonder tree, and find a little square box."

"Of all weird things!" the journalist burst out when the parcel proved to contain a silver watch less than half as thick as the one he had pawned.

"It should keep good time," drawled the Virginian, speaking for the first time in a long while. "It was manufactured in Switzerland. I have one myself."

More glasses were lifted and there was considerable laughter as India, pretending to be surprised, unwrapped her fan.

"I gave you that?" Alistair burst out.

"Yes, love, and it's just what I wanted."

"But — but what can you want of a fan in midwinter?"

India pressed it to her cheek. "It was so fragile and lovely; besides, it will grow hot again soon enough."

It became Rafe's turn to distribute gifts, which he did graciously, half-mockingly. For India there were items selected from Rafe's private store of "trade goods" as he called them. "They're fripperies calculated to melt obdurate feminine hearts in various ports."

"I fear me," India dimpled, "you seem much too expert in such matters."

"Confound those satin slippers. They're too big, aren't they? Well, no matter, I'm told no lady should ever wear red shoes."

The girl flashed an upward look as she bent, trying on the slippers. "But I'm no lady — according to certain blueblooded dames."

"India!" Alistair's tone was trenchant. "Don't ever say such a thing. You're quite as wellborn and -bred as any nose-in-the-air female mincing along King Street. Never forget that for an instant."

" 'We hold these facts to be self-evident,' " quoted Dabney Seymour. "Why not try on the slippers?"

"Oh, yes! *Yes!* Oh, Alistair, look at those absurd high heels! My feet fairly tingle to dance a jota."

Rafe smiled in lazy amusement. The liquors had induced a whimsical mood. "Then why not yield to your impulse, my dear? Incidentally, if I remember correctly, there's a mantilla in yonder flat box."

To Seymour's pleased surprise his host abruptly abandoned his angry manner, commenced to push aside the salon's furniture while predicting, not without pride: "You've a treat in store. India has studied under the best Gypsy dancers from Seville."

"Capital!" Rafe put down his glass, then executed a couple of light whirling steps. His uniform coat skirts swung wide with the easy strength of his movements. "I'll wager you've a guitar hidden somewhere, my enchanting little hostess?"

"No," Alistair said. "But Charlie Edmund, next door, owns one" — and, hatless, he dashed out.

Seymour then rolled back the Aubusson. He pretended not to notice a generous layer of dust and desiccated insects concealed beneath it.

India had vanished; she reappeared subtly powdered and painted and wearing the scarlet slippers, a wide yellow skirt and a red blouse. She had tucked a lofty Spanish comb into her blue-black hair to support the mantilla.

Rafe's eyes narrowed then, commenced to shine. Here, by God, was the most exciting female he'd beheld in a very long while.

"What a lovely comb," Seymour observed from the corner into which he had retired. "I've never before seen such delicate filagree."

"It was my mother's," the girl explained proudly. "She was Pia Vasquéz from Valencia, in Spain. If only she had taught me more of her language . . . but alas, my parents both wished me brought up in the American manner, and therefore ignorant of things foreign."

"What a great pity," sighed the *Grey Ghost's* master. He stood feet braced well apart, staring, enraptured, across the Ramsays' many-mirrored salon. "Ah, you found castanets — And here's Alistair. Shall I play the guitar?"

"*Pero sí, Señor Capitán.* Here, Alistair, you'll recall the tempo?" She passed him a tambourine, streaming with yellow and red ribbons.

"I'd say your beauty merits a larger audience," commented Lieutenant Seymour while refilling their champagne glasses, "but, Ma'am, you'll never find a more appreciative one."

As a final preparation India lowered a pair of candelabra to the floor before a tall mirror. Effectively it multiplied their flames.

"Careful, dear," Alistair warned. "Keep clear of those flames."

Rafe flexed long and supple fingers before the grate, then commenced, accurately enough, to tune the guitar.

Rafe realized he was feeling finer than Neapolitan silk; wondered whether Cousin Alistair realized what a lucky dog he was to crawl into bed every night with so luscious a piece. Suddenly, he thought of the "jolly girls" he'd known here. Were any of them still about Charleston?

Rafe struck a jangling cord and glanced up from under straight black brows. "Shall it be '*La Habañera,*' *Señora?*"

"*Sí, por favor.*" India's skirts billowed wildly in a ballet dancer's curtsy. She drew herself up, chin elevated, castanets poised above the head.

"*Vamos!*"

The instant the blockade-runner's fingers commenced to fly over the frets India exploded into furious activity. Castanets chattering, rippling and rolling, she swooped, spun, postured, and stamped. Alistair grinned. He was aware, of course, that on various occasions she had danced at soldiers' benefits and in many a malodorous hospital ward.

Never had this girl, this intimate stranger, appeared more exciting, more vital. She stamped, tiny red heels clicking nearly as rapidly as the rattling of her castanets. India's slim body then bent in a series of cape turns which gradually elevated her voluminous petticoats to frothing well above the ankles, then in a violent reverse movement briefly exposed her legs up to the knees.

"Oh, Lord," thought Alistair. "Hope she doesn't get really carried away."

Faster and faster jangled the guitar. Candle flames flickered and twisted madly, created a dancing, golden radiance, emphasizing her skin's tawny luster and that squarish, scarlet oblong formed by parted lips. Her castanets commenced rattling so furiously they sounded like hailstones. Faster, faster. Alistair's anxious eyes remained riveted on his wife — he didn't find comfort in the expression of either Rafe or his big friend, Seymour — nonetheless, he beat an accelerating tempo on his tambourine until India, like a bacchante transported by the expression of her art, rose on tiptoes and, with eyes sensuously half closed, commenced to turn. She whirled while the smother of fabrics attached to her waist lifted higher and higher from the floor.

"India!' Alistair called out, but she seemed not to hear him and continued.

What with the unaccustomed liquor and rich food, the room swayed before Alistair's eyes. He tried to rise but found himself too fascinated, for, amid the billowing froth of his wife's petticoats, now became visible flashes of scarlet garter ribbons and glimpses of silvery skin.

"Olé! Olé!" Rascal Rafe began yelling. He stamped his foot and made of his guitar a maddening accomplice.

Unexpectedly, a woman's voice commented: "What a most unusual dance, my dear. It's Spanish, I presume."

In midturn India faltered, checked herself, then hurriedly smoothed her skirts and came forward, cheeks flaming like poinsettia leaves. The men got to their feet, fumbling guiltily at loosened buttons.

"Why — why, Miss Lambkin! Miss Livesey! This — this is a most unexpected pleasure!"

"That I'll warrant." Cordelia Livesey's voice was painfully cool and

68

precise. "Please forgive us, Mrs. Bryson, I fear we have intruded."

"You — you — you haven't!" burst out India. "Captain Bryson, here, has been g-good enough to p-present us with some of the most d-delicious ch-champagne. You really must try it!"

Cordelia ignored her. She turned, looked the flushed guitarist full in the face and said, icily, "I am sure Raphael Bryson feels entirely at ease — *here*." Then the stately, auburn-haired young woman thrust an arm through that of Lieutenant Bears. "Let us go; we really ought never to have come here."

Almost piteously, India turned to the petite blonde hesitating beside Dr. Donald Bryson's chunky figure. "Won't *you* please stay, Miss Lambkin? Please! We're having such a gay and happy time."

Serena's lovely smile fully disclosed the sheen of her teeth. "Why, I should be charmed to, Mrs. Bryson."

CHAPTER VIII *Charleston Argus*

RHYTHMIC clanking noises, caused by a flat-bed press in operation, beat at Alistair Bryson's aching head with relentless insistence but, pretty soon, today's edition — alas, only fifteen hundred single half-sheets — would be ready for delivery to a waiting handful of newsboys.

Odd to reflect that not even these pitifully few papers could have been printed but for the *Grey Ghost*'s master. A faint grin curved the managing editor's chilled features. Hallelujah! They'd get foaming mad down in Savannah if the *Republican* ever learned what had chanced. His grin broadened when he reflected that, in the supply room, there were being unpacked a dozen fonts of type, as many cases of English printer's ink, type cleaning acids and an imposing pile of newsprint rolls.

Founded in 1858, the *Argus* proudly described itself, on its masthead, as "The Newspaper with a Hundred Eyes," for all that, even in the best of times, Mr. Roadheaver never had simultaneously employed more than five reporters.

Nowadays, only he, and lame old Frank Pollard, remained to obtain, write and edit the news. What a relief that, not for a while yet, would the *Argus* be forced into substituting his reserve of paper hangers' sizing paper for stock — he'd argued the publisher into obtaining a supply against emergencies which inevitably must arise. Competitors were reduced to printing on wallpaper, wrapping paper, in fact paper of any sort which would receive printer's ink.

The managing editor was debating the proper lead for an article descriptive of the *Grey Ghost*'s unique construction when Jairus, his hunchbacked copy boy, shuffled in. A "bright" mulatto of middle age, with a bullet head and pendulous lower lip, Jairus long ago had proved himself far more perceptive and intelligent than his appearance indicated.

"Misto' Bryson, suh? Ah done run down Misto' Mullinix at Adger's Wharf. He downstairs."

"Then don't keep him waiting."

A moment later Drummond Mullinix entered, a slender, freckled youth with eager, tan-colored eyes. Badly wanting a haircut and a shave, he appeared older than his actual eighteen years.

"Heyo, Mr. Bryson," he greeted, grinning from ear to ear. "Hear you-all had a real shivaree over to your place Christmas Day."

"It was, and we did. Won't you take a seat?"

The caller tucked the skirts of a captured blue overcoat about his legs. "Well, suh, what can I do for you?"

"Drummie, recently I've heard talk that our steam rams are about to attack and sink, or drive away, the blockaders."

Passed Midshipman Mullinix jerked a nod. "Well, suh, maybe there's something to it. I hear a lot of talk."

"Please tell me about it," Alistair invited with his breath hovering, halolike, about the hat he neglected to remove. "I really need to know. You're serving aboard the *Palmetto State,* aren't you?"

"No, suh, I'm in the *Chicora*," the youth corrected proudly. "We can shoot rings around the flagship."

"What about this sortie?"

"'Sortie'? Oh, I reckon that's what we call a sally. Well, suh, all I know for sure is that tomorrow we're to fill up our bunkers and magazine and there'll be no shore leave after today."

"Um-m. Sounds like Flag Officer Ingraham does intend to attack the enemy."

"I'm certain-sure of it."

"How so, Drummie?"

The pleasant-faced young fellow turned a little red. "If I tell you, you won't print that I said it? Well, I was stowing charts in our wheelhouse yesterday and I overheard the commodore — that's what we call a flag officer, the other's too long — tell Cap'n Rutledge: 'We will attack them very shortly, so requisition and charge all necessary supplies. Be ready to move on an instant's notice.' Sounds like we're really going out to sink us some Yanks before long, don't it?"

"It does," thoughtfully agreed the journalist. "My sincere thanks, Drum. You may rely upon my discretion. Oh, by the bye, you'll let me know the minute *you* think the attack on the Federals is about to be delivered?"

"Sure will," came the cheerful reply.

"I wish you'd stop at my house. Mrs. Bryson is keeping a bottle of claret for your mother; please convey my affectionate regards as well."

Brows merged, the managing editor returned to the draft of his article on the *Grey Ghost* — and an increasingly unhappy analysis of said vessel's cargo.

He inquired of a clipboard securing exchanges from the *Richmond Examiner*, "Now I wonder why certain importers should want to conceal their names?" Obviously only those indulging in illegal cargoes.

Abruptly his pencil commenced to scrawl:

Who speculates in imports of so dubious a nature that the actual importers are ashamed to stand forth and make themselves known? Why should goods consigned to this port for identification bear only mystical numbers? Could it be that these nameless importers fear that the *Argus* might print the manifests of vessels recently arrived from abroad?

Yes. That hint of scandal should whet a reader's interest. Correspondingly, the *Argus*'s circulation might profit thereby. Once public interest was aroused, it could be further stimulated by details. What of the cargo space pre-empted by French hats, silk stockings, vintage wines and other luxuries so criminally useless to a nation fighting for its life?

> The *Grey Ghost* of Liverpool [he wrote] represents a bold new departure from conventional designs. This swift iron vessel now lies at Atlantic Wharf where she may be inspected at the invitation of her able and most courteous captain.

His pencil hesitated, then traveled jerkily onwards.

> He is Raphael Bryson, formerly a resident of this city. In recent years, he has made London his home. Captain Bryson is the *Grey Ghost's* principal owner and, as we have learned, has had much to do with her design and construction.
>
> It may be of interest to naval architects at present on duty in this port to learn that this new blockade-runner's unladen draft is a scant eight feet, thus enabling her to cross many bars and to utilize a multitude of channels denied to average vessels employed in this patriotic traffic so vital to all our destinies.
>
> Captain Bryson's command, moreover, is completely constructed of iron, the first such vessel ever to enter Charleston Harbor. Her exact speed we are not at liberty to disclose, but are assured it is sufficient to outrun the fleetest Yankee cruiser known to infest our coasts.
>
> Her cargo capacity . . .

The door slammed back to admit a pale, narrow-faced individual clad in a cape shawl and a battered stovepipe hat.

"You the publisher of this heah miserable sheet?" he growled, brandishing a crumpled copy of the *Argus*.

Alistair got quickly to his feet, pushed back his chair for leg room and braced himself. "No, sir. I am its managing editor, and whom have I the honor of addressing?"

"My name, suh, is Peed — Jackson Clay Peed!"

"Indeed? And how can I serve you, Mr. Peed?"

"By ceasing to publish this sort of drivel!" Like a gauntlet Mr. Peed flung the paper onto Alistair's desk.

"To what so-called 'drivel' do you refer, Mr. Peed?" Alistair spoke softly, but was aware of a hot current beginning to eddy down his spine. Not that he was in the least perturbed by the bowie knife jammed into his visitor's belt or on recognizing the outline of a derringer dragging at his waistcoat pocket. Nowadays almost no male ventured abroad completely unarmed.

"This!" the other snapped, planting a grimy forefinger upon a column headed:

THE "GREY GHOST'S" CARGO: WHAT DOES IT INCLUDE?

"What is the nature of your complaint concerning that heading?"

The fellow's truculent, red-rimmed little eyes narrowed. He lowered his voice to a hoarse, tobacco-tinctured whisper. "Certain mighty influential gents around here don't want you should print any more questions about imports. See? They say you better stick to printing speeches, war news, advertisements and poetry."

"No. I don't see. And you can drop your threatening manner, Mr. Peed." The strong angle of Alistair's jutting jaw became more acute. "Who sent you here?"

Mr. Peed glowered and his thin lips flattened themselves. "That's no business of yourn." He summoned a loose smile. "Yo' don't want to stir up no trouble for yo' paper or yo'self, now do you?"

"No sensible man would," Alistair admitted quietly. "I think I understand what you're driving at."

"That's fine. Ah'm mighty pleased. Mah friends tole me, iffen yo' proved sensible, to leave this." A brown envelope generously marked by greasy fingerprints plopped onto the managing editor's inkstained blotter.

Alistair made no effort to pick up the envelope. "And what might be in that?"

The pale man chuckled mirthlessly. "Oh, jest a trifle of cash, mebbe ten thousand, Richmond money. Reckon it'll come in handy. You cain't be sellin' many papers these days; there's more where that come from."

Alistair, returning the envelope to his visitor, said, "Mr. Peed, you may tell your friends the *Argus* can make out all right without this token of their esteem, and, lest you mistake me, I'll tell you that I intend to learn why it's become possible for a selfish few scoundrels to enrich themselves while our fellow citizens are suffering and bravely

73

dying for their country. This newspaper will continue to investigate traffic in luxuries and, in due course, will print its findings."

The gaunt man stared, then licked colorless, scarlike lips. He dropped his hand to his waistcoat's level. "Like hell you will! Just remember, Mister, Ah came to yo' politelike, but since yo' ain't bein' agreeable . . . Well" — his voice took on a grating note — "Ah 'm warnin' you, keep on bein' nosy over them imports and neither you, nor this lyin' sheet, will last longer than a pine splinter in hell!"

Alistair commenced briskly to cast loose his jacket's buttons. "You annoy me, Mr. Peed."

"Don't try to hurt me, else I'll sho'ly shoot you down," he rasped and produced the derringer. "Me and mah friends don't aim to take no sass off no snot-nose cuckold —"

The black-haired editor's body stiffened as if pierced by some knife's point. "Cuckold!"

"Sho' now," sneered Peed. "Ain't you surprised? Only the whole town knows that furrin actress you married will tumble with any officer who's young and handsome."

Before the other could cock his weapon, Alistair Bryson had vaulted the desk and clamped hands over Peed's hairy throat. Once his derringer had thudded onto the floor he shook the other with such violence that his hat flew off and his head was snapped, pendulumlike, from shoulder to shoulder. When the visitor ceased to struggle, Alistair frog-marched Mr. Peed out into the hall, kicked him downstairs and finally heaved him, sprawling, out onto the sidewalk, thereby startling buggy horses tethered to the *Argus*'s well-gnawed hitching rail.

"Stay out of my sight, you scum," warned the newspaperman in a soft, deadly voice. "I'll surely kill you if I meet you again."

Massaging the knuckles of one hand against the palm of its fellow, he climbed, panting gently, to his office, and was not astonished to find Mr. Virginius Roadheaver. His fat cheeks, veined in scarlet, were quivering in anxiety and his bulbous nose shone a brighter shade of rose than usual.

"What the hell's been going on here, Bryson?" he rumbled. "More trouble with the creditors?"

"No." Alistair fought to speak calmly. "I merely expelled a swine who threatened the paper, then made a disparaging remark concerning my wife."

Roadheaver's tiny, white-lashed blue eyes narrowed. "Did he now? Funny, I've been meaning to talk with you about her."

"At the moment it would be extremely unwise to discuss Mrs. Bryson."

The publisher goggled a little, then, belly jiggling beneath a food-stained waistcoat of black velours, he waddled over to use a wide-mouthed cuspidor. "Very well. I suppose the matter can wait. How did that fellow threaten us?"

Succinctly Alistair explained; was relieved to watch Mr. Road-heaver's shiny double chin commence to glow like the wattles of an angry turkey cock.

"What! He tried to bribe us from our duty to the public?"

"He did."

"Then you were quite right, Bryson, in throwing him out. Not all the wealth of this fair Southland shall ever tempt Virginius Road-heaver into suppressing a single syllable of the truth!"

"Then, I take it, I'm to continue an investigation of importations from abroad?"

"By God, sir, you are!" roared the publisher. "I cannot tolerate that our brave lads in the field should go wanting while greedy wor-shipers of Mammon reap a golden harvest." He paused, looked brightly about. "Say, Bryson, that's not a bad line. I'll use it in my next editorial."

"I certainly would, sir. That's a most telling phrase. Very neatly put. By the bye, what did you think of the copy for that story on the *Grey Ghost?*"

"Ah-humph! Afraid I haven't had time to peruse it, but I am sure it displays your usual accurate observation and penetrating in-sight." The publisher spat out his chew of tobacco and wiped away brown stains on the back of a hand.

"Mr. Roadheaver?"

"Yes?"

"Will you write me a draft to cover some expense money I've advanced? You probably aren't aware of it, but the *Argus* owes me not an inconsiderable balance."

"*Tchk-tchk!*" Pain manifested itself in his rubicund features. "Of course, I didn't know, my boy. Go draw your due from the cashier at once."

"I've already seen him. He claims his ready cash amounts to just two hundred dollars — Carolina currency."

"Only two hundred, Carolina?" In his agitation Mr. Roadheaver fell to picking at hairs sprouting from his nostrils. "Harumph! Well, well, Bryson, that's unfortunate. Most unfortunate. I'll see what can be done, so don't concern yourself. Within a few days you'll be paid every penny the paper owes you — maybe in greenbacks." He clapped Alistair on the back in jovial fashion. "No more worrying now, my lad. And now I am off to take coffee with General Beauregard, that paladin, that unrecognized Napoleon of our embattled Confederacy."

Alistair sighed. Things must be even worse than he'd suspected. God knew when he'd get paid even a part of the debt. "Mind if I devote a short column to Captain Gray's new appointment?"

"Gray? Who the devil is Captain Gray?"

"Matthew Gray has been here a month or more with our Navy's Torpedo Service. Now he's to be head of a new organization called the Naval Submarine Battery."

Mr. Roadheaver's fat shoulders wriggled under a claw-hammer coat of snuff-brown serge. "He'll be important?"

"He'll rank next to Flag Officer Ingraham."

"What's *he* do?"

"Oh, he only commands the Naval Station here." Enthusiasm entered the journalist's voice. "I predict that Captain Gray will accomplish more towards keeping our harbor free of the Yankee fleet than anyone else."

"Then go ahead. Puff him all you please. You seldom are mistaken in such matters." The publisher from his coattail produced a flat brown bottle. "Damn' cold in here. Here. Try a swig of popskull. It isn't much — still, it's better than pinetop."

CHAPTER IX Her Britannic Majesty's Consul

LIEUTENANT the Honorable Peter Burgoyne, RN, wearing expensively cut civilian clothes, paused in front of Her Britannic

76

Majesty's Consulate and ran disapproving eyes over faded yellow paint scaling from its grimly unimaginative façade of cement-coated tabby. A pair of snaky and forlorn-appearing pride of India trees flanked the entrance and poised clusters of weathered brown berries against an unseasonably brilliant blue sky. A manservant, unmistakably English, answered his ring, read his card, then gravely ushered him into a small and untastefully furnished waiting room.

"Mr. Bunch, sir, is occupied for the moment." The servant's manner was deferential; after all, was not this gentleman not only an officer of Her Majesty's Navy but an "Honorable" as well? "Mr. Peake, the Vice-Consul, however, will be pleased to converse with you, sir, until Mr. Bunch is at liberty."

Lieutenant Burgoyne made no immediate reply, only stroked curly, dark red muttonchop whiskers while surveying his surroundings with deceptive casualness. He found it amazing to reflect that from these rather shabby premises emanated the bulk of the Foreign Office's knowledge concerning the true state of affairs within the Southern Confederacy.

"My business, my good man, concerns Mr. Bunch," he drawled. "However, I shall be pleased to speak with Mr. Peake."

To his surprise the Vice-Consul appeared to be a Tenniel-cartoon Yankee, characterized as he was by a nose as pointed and sharp as a cleaver and an angular, deeply cleft chin. He suffered from a terrifying squint, and his voice was characterized by a nasal twang which could only have originated somewhere north of the Merrimack River.

He smiled bleakly. "Yes, Mr. Burgoyne, your suspicions are entirely correct. I am indeed Yankee-bred, though, years ago, I became a true-blue Southerner by conviction." The Vice-Consul's steel-colored, gimlet eyes bored into his caller's bright blue ones until at length a faint smile curved his slash of a mouth. "You see, sir, I have been employed in this consulate ever since 1854 and, if I may say so, I'm better acquainted with and know about more Carolinians and Georgians than most native sons. You are here, sir, on a diplomatic mission?"

The Englishman frowned a little, then seated himself upon a horse-hair-covered chair and crossed long legs elegantly garbed in fawn-colored pantaloons. "Is that really a legitimate concern of yours, Mr. Peake?"

"Probably not," admitted the Vice-Consul. "I didn't aim to appear nosy, Mr. Burgoyne. I was just wondering whether I might be of service, you being so new in town."

"You might, at that. Is there a tailor worthy of the name remaining in this miserable, half-burned city?"

"You'll not find one to suit your taste, sir. You see, Jefford Hutchins returned to London last year, claiming he couldn't make a living any more — the local gentry have grown too poor — mostly."

The Honorable Peter languidly elevated an auburn eyebrow. " 'Mostly,' I believe you said?"

The Vice-Consul nodded, lowered his voice. "There are, here in Charleston, some who are making their 'tarnal fortunes these days; speculators in blockade-running stocks — importers and such."

"So? How very interestin'," drawled the wiry young elegant. "Tell me, Mr. Peake, in your opinion, do the Confederates stand any chance of smashing the Union's blockade by the use of such iron-clad monstrosities as I've seen in the Cooper River?"

Mr. Peake tugged briefly at his reddish, beaklike nose, summoned a wary expression. "Shouldn't wonder, sir, but you, being a naval officer, might foretell that a sight better than I. Mebbe you don't know that the Federal cruisers out yonder, without exception, are of wooden construction?"

Following a discreet knock a door opened and the manservant reappeared to usher the caller into a high-ceilinged room dominated by a lithograph portrait of Queen Victoria and a somewhat smaller likeness of the Prince Consort, yet draped in dusty crêpe. Mr. Bunch's office, Peter Burgoyne noted with approval, seemed scrupulously clean. His desk fairly gleamed and its brass inkwell and other ornaments glistened with polish.

Her Majesty's Consul was tall, bald, and bland of expression as he offered his hand. "May I say 'Welcome to Charleston,' sir? I trust the lodgings we engaged proved adequate?"

"For the moment. How did you know I was coming here?"

"Through a communication received per H.M.S. *Petrel*. She made port last week."

"Ah. Really decent of you to receive me so promptly." It was obvious to Lieutenant the Honorable Peter Burgoyne that already he had been identified as the younger son of an earl; Mr. Bunch, therefore was diffident concerning his position. As a mere lieutenant serving in the Royal Navy, Burgoyne's rank would be rated by any *chef de protocol* as well below that of any of Her Majesty's Consuls. Socially speaking, however, Mr. Bunch — although obviously a gentleman of breeding and poise — would undoubtedly have found himself yielding precedence at any state function. Burgoyne compromised, therefore, by adopting a polite yet subtly patronizing air while unlocking a pigskin dispatch case and producing from it a long envelope bearing the Admiralty's impressive seal done in dark blue wax.

In no great hurry, Mr. Bunch donned a pair of square-lensed steel spectacles, unfolded and commenced to read the enclosures. Meanwhile the caller, attracted by a trampling of hoofs and the cadence of marching feet, wandered over to a window facing the harbor. He was in time to witness the appearance of an officer astride a thin, but magnificently conformed, thoroughbred. The black-bearded cavalier below was riding with graceful ease, but his tunic looked deplorably shabby and ill-pressed. Buttons were lacking from the double row descending its breast.

Swinging smartly along in his wake, marched a column of infantry. They were wearing almost every imaginable variety of garment. Burgoyne noted that, under freshly cleaned crossbelts, some men wore the ruins of those gay uniforms in which socially elect militia companies had marched off to war; others were garbed in serviceable captured blue uniform jackets disguised by the addition of bright red cuffs and collars.

The majority, however, wore checkered shirts under shapeless gray blouses and trousers of homespun dyed butternut-brown. As to their footgear . . . ! The toes actually had been worn out of some of their boots and many soles flapped loose to every stride. Their headgear ranged from militia shakos and kepis to slouch hats of felt or flat, broad-brimmed sombreros of woven palmetto fibers.

How loosely and easily they marched. Their movements were completely devoid of that stiff precision characteristic of European troops. The muskets they shouldered were sloped at a uniform angle, however, and looked well cared for.

Presently, there rumbled into sight a big *fourgon* drawn by four horses; next a mule-pulled quartermaster's forage wagon; then an unpainted two-wheeled farm cart and other nondescript vehicles. It did not escape the tall Englishman's perception that harness, worn by the draft animals below, often had been spliced with wire and that, in many instances, rope had been substituted for leather.

This rattling, jolting column of empty wagons was escorted by what Burgoyne guessed must be Home Guards; there was not a trace of spit-and-polish about them. For the most part, these soldiers were bent but rangey graybeards and fresh-faced boys. Nevertheless, a unanimous determination seemed to characterize their expressions.

Turning, the Honorable Peter noted that Mr. Bunch had removed his spectacles, and, thoughtfully, was tapping his teeth with them.

"Apparently, Sir Alexander Milne desires me to facilitate posting you aboard one of the Rebel — er — Confederate ironclads — in the capacity of an observer, I believe."

Burgoyne abandoned his bored manner, replied briskly, "Precisely. Other officers of Her Majesty's Navy have been dispatched to Wilmington and other ports for similar duty. Their Lordships of the Admiralty are most anxious, y'know, to learn everything possible concerning ironclads in action."

The younger man's high forehead glistened when he bent forward and still further lowered his voice. "You are aware, no doubt, that we have a certain number of such under construction. Can't let the French outdistance us, you know, and their *Gloire* is quite formidable. Sir Alexander believes there is no substitute for practical experience, so my colleagues and I are expected to observe the armament, gunnery and other capacities of ironclads in action."

Said he with a wry smile, "An equal number of us have been designated to observe the Union Navy's monitors."

Judicially, Mr. Bunch pursed full and shiny lips. "May I inquire how many such gentlemen are now observing the Federal Navy?"

Burgoyne flushed to the roots of his dark red hair. "So far, none, I fear. Appears that a Mr. Welles, the American Secretary for Marine Affairs, views the presence of British officers aboard Federal ships with suspicion."

The Consul's hand crept absently up to massage a round, pink-white chin. "However, because of the terrible defeat of their forces before Fredericksburg, and with a commerce raider, the *Alabama*, sinking Union ships within two hundred miles of New York, I fancy the Government in Washington can be made to listen to reason."

The naval officer stood very straight. "In my regard, sir, do you anticipate difficulties?"

Mr. Bunch deliberated. "No. I can think of no reason to deter me from presenting you to Flag Officer Ingraham. He commands the Naval Station here and is a personal friend. Although President Davis at the moment is reported bitter over Lord Russell's failure officially to receive Mr. James Mason, his Commissioner in London, I don't believe we will encounter many objections in securing an observer's appointment. These Southerners are avid for attention from Europe."

"I see. How many ironclads do the Secessionists have in commission here?"

"The *Palmetto State*, and the *Chicora*. A still more powerful ram, to be called the *Charleston*, is incomplete." Mr. Bunch tested the point of a paper knife on a finger tip, then looked up and smiled. "Before long you will meet the *Palmetto State*'s captain, Commander John Rutledge. It is important that you should make friends with him; the Rutledges are among the first families of South Carolina."

"Indeed?" drawled Burgoyne. "I presume Rutledge 'chaws' tobacco like all the rest?"

Mr. Bunch's sloping shoulders straightened themselves and a touch of asperity sharpened his voice. "Mr. Burgoyne, may I earnestly suggest that, until you observe for yourself how well-bred Carolinians deport themselves, you refrain from voicing such untactful comments?"

The Englishman stared and his lean features stiffened. "I already have had some experience with the so-called Southern aristocracy, Mr. Bunch. Just before I departed, I attended a dinner at Stafford House at which James Mason, the Confederate Commissioner, and some of his colleagues were present. The fellow acted like an incredible boor and had the voice of an amorous bull. As for tact — Ah, well. However, you may rest assured, Mr. Bunch, that while I speak frankly in your Consulate, I would not do so elsewhere."

He arose, donned his pearl-gray top hat. "When you have arranged an interview with this Ingraham pray inform me at once."

"I will do so, sir. Flag Officer Ingraham is much occupied these days." The Consul cast a quick glance at his office door before adding, "I have been reliably informed that, very soon, an attempt to break the blockade will be made. Incidentally, Commodore Ingraham also is descended from a distinguished South Carolina family. Does his name, by any chance, bear any significance for you?"

"No. Should it?" Burgoyne picked up gloves and an ivory-topped walking stick.

"Possibly. Duncan Ingraham's grandfather was an officer in the *Bonhomme Richard* when she was — er — lucky enough to capture H.M.S. *Serapis* off Scarborough Head."

Then, indeed, did the Honorable Peter's complexion flame until it was almost of a hue with his sideburns. Few officers of the Royal Navy cared to be reminded of that epic engagement, or of John Paul Jones's "We have not yet begun to fight!"

Stiffly, the caller bowed. Gad! How he loathed these clever, exasperatingly well-informed and polite civil servants. Somehow, they made a chap feel almost callow, fearfully ignorant. "I thank you for the reminder, sir. Good day." On the threshold, however, the naval officer's erect figure hesitated. "Mr. Bunch, what about this chap, Mr. Peake? Suggests a thoroughgoing Yankee."

"He is one, but married to an Englishwoman of good family. She comes from Lincolnshire, I believe, a place called Scopwick. Her maiden name was Parker, Hope Parker. For your information, sir, Mr. Peake has dwelt in Charleston since a very young man. To this Consulate his understanding of the South in general, and Carolinians in particular, has proved invaluable — to say the least."

CHAPTER X **At Adger's North Wharf**

LIFE in Charleston grew more monotonous than ever for the vast majority of its inhabitants. There was little to relieve the uncomfortable tedium of existence: no horse races any more, no cotillions, no plays at the Dock Street Theater — only a hastily arranged cock- or dogfight, now and then. Depressing, too, was that vista of countless cotton bales rotting, green, yellow and black, upon docks long vacant. Months ago the flood of bales had overflowed every available warehouse. Whole weeks passed when nothing of consequence occurred beyond the publication of long, long casualty lists and the funerals that resulted.

Because there was little else to do, a throng composed of unemployed mechanics, homeless Negroes and off-duty soldiers and seamen collected upon nearby wharfs and loading ramps to watch the *Grey Ghost* discharge her cargo.

On the Cooper's tan-gray surface drifted a few rowboats and sailing skiffs occupied by roustabouts who, lacking employment, had taken to fishing or trapping wild fowl to keep alive.

Together with that tall and devotedly patriotic Virginian, Dabney Seymour, Medical Lieutenant Donald Bryson occupied chairs placed atop *Palmetto State*'s rust-red casemate. From such an elevation they were able to obtain a fine view of all that might transpire over on Adger's North Wharf. There, the gray-white blockade-runner lay tied up.

"Reckon they'll soon commence hoisting out munitions," predicted the physician. "They must have unloaded everything else. Yes. I'm right. See? There's an Army wagon train coming down Tradd Street."

The sandy-haired Virginian nodded and continued to study the craft he had boarded three days earlier in Nassau as if he never before had seen her, or the British red ensign curling lazily from her jack staff.

Movement to open a route for the wagons began among shrill youngsters, women in wide skirts and poke bonnets, military loafers, ragged free Negroes and much better dressed slaves.

"Look over there," suddenly drawled Seymour. "Can it be that we are about to be honored with a touch of high rank?"

A brief, glittering column of gray-clad horsemen was trotting smartly along East Bay Street in the direction of Adger's North Wharf.

"That little fellow in the blue-gray uniform with all that gold braid on his sleeves is Major General Beauregard," Donald informed him. "He commands the whole Southeastern District."

Dabney Seymour caught up a pair of field glasses and descried a short individual whose pointed imperial beard and spike mustaches showed up sharp as pencil marks against olive-hued features. Beneath the little General's scarlet-topped kepi, plentiful hair showed gray-white, but his vivid black eyes seemed lively.

"Riding at Beauregard's left is Brigadier General J. J. Raines. He's a fine engineer out of the Old Army. He's immediately responsible for Charleston's defense."

While Beauregard and his staff were dismounting, the blockade-runner thrice dipped her colors in salute.

Donald found no difficulty in recognizing his cousin's erect, blue-clad figure descending a gangway onto the wharf, but the distance was too great to permit his hearing what was being said before Captain Raphael Bryson escorted the District Commander to his bridge.

Presently the leading wagon rumbled out over the water until its driver pulled up opposite the blockade-runner's forward cargo boom. The other wagons lined up behind, and the crowd surged forward yelling, "Hurry up! Hoist out them guns!" . . . "Break out a powder kag. I need to shoot some Yankees!"

A resounding shout sent dirty-gray-white gulls flapping away in fright when, at length, a cargo boom jerkily elevated a gun limber, spinning lazily, into the daylight. The crowd's excitement swelled even louder when a cannon barrel swung starkly silhouetted against the wintry sky.

"Hurray! Hurray! That'll soon blow plenty Bluebellies to hell!" The *fourgon* wagon received the gun's barrel and its carriage, wheels and limber, then turned and drove off the wharf. The next wagon in line moved forward to receive two small fieldpieces and some cases of shot to fit it.

The blockade-runner next discharged a quartet of howitzers. Real shouts arose when the crowd recognized, dangling from the whip, some cases of muskets.

"Rifles! Them's what we-uns need!" shrilled a lanky youth and waved his hat. "I'm sure fixin' to enlist tomorrow."

Six wagons had been loaded when, abruptly, activity ceased although the column of waiting transport vehicles still stretched back to the entrance to Tradd Street.

"Quit loafin'," someone shouted. "Unload the rest!"

A foreman swaggered to the blockage-runner's rail, cupped his hands and yelled: "Ain't no 'rest'! That's all. Best git fer home."

Incredulous, Donald glanced at his companion. "Can those be *all* the munitions you brought in?"

"Looks like it," the Virginian admitted somberly. "Remember, I was only a passenger."

84

"Well, let's go below. I feel I need a drink."

"Good. I was about to impose on you to show me over your vessel. I've never been aboard an ironclad and I'll confess I'm deeply curious to see what she's like."

They descended a wooden ladder temporarily affixed to the exterior of *Palmetto State*'s casemate aft of an armored pilothouse rising but two feet above the carapace's top.

By dint of patient questioning the Virginian ascertained that *Palmetto State* was one hundred and fifty feet in overall length; had a beam of thirty-five feet and a draft of twelve. Her armor, he was told, was stout, consisting as it did of a double layer of two-inch iron plates bolted to backing of solid oak nearly two feet thick. The ram's construction, Donald Bryson said, had been supervised by Mr. James M. Eason; he also had built *Chicora*.

"Since by training I'm a civil engineer, I don't know as much about ordnance as I ought," Seymour confessed as their heels rang along the ram's dim, neatly cluttered gun deck. It was so low a tall man continually must bend over to avoid bashing his head against deck beams supporting the casemate's iron roof. "For example, I've no notion what the caliber of these guns might be."

The thick-bodied young physician chuckled. "You're overlooking the fact that I, too, am no gunnery officer. However," he patted the dully gleaming breech of a long-snouted cannon, "I do know that our Number One piece here is a nine-inch smoothbore; so is our stern gun."

"Nine inches, eh? Doesn't sound too imposing." Dabney hesitated. "Er, aren't some types of cannon described by poundage? 'Sixty pound, thirty-two pound' and so on?"

Donald Bryson looked his surprise. "You really don't understand much about ordnance, Mr. Seymour, and that's a fact. 'Inches' refers to the diameter of the bore of a cannon's tube. 'Pounds' refers to the weight of the largest solid projectile a piece can fire."

"Sorry to appear so dense, but I do want to learn. What about these — these side guns?"

"All four of our broadside pieces," Donald expatiated, "are banded and rifled thirty-two-pounders."

The doctor rattled on as they threaded a course among the gun carriages and stepped over their slides. In neatly arranged patterns, shifting and training tackles coiled like disciplined brown serpents beside the transoms; while levers, rammers and sponge staffs stood in their racks, straight and stiff as crack troops on parade.

By daylight, inadequately beating through cracks around the gun-port covers, the patently fascinated Virginian numbered *Palmetto State's* side battery as six guns.

A soft, sibilant sound caused by steam leaking from some ill-fitted connection blended agreeably with the eternal chuckling whisper of the current along the ram's bottom, but this subtle symphony became drowned by the ringing clang and scrape of some stoker's shovel suddenly at work below.

Except for a tiny galley amidships and a half dozen cots placed between the guns — evidently for the convenience of a guard detail — there seemed to be no provision for a crew to subsist on board. Clearly, *Palmetto State* had not been designed as a seagoing man-of-war.

"They mayn't look so smart," Donald was saying, "but it's some-thing to watch our gun crews at drill. Captain Rutledge has really taught them to shoot — as our Yankee friends outside the bar will soon discover."

"Soon?" The Virginian raised quizzical, sandy blond brows. "Then you're expecting to go into action shortly?"

"Yes. For example, today's *Courier* predicts — and I do wish they hadn't — that the blockade will be ended almost any hour. The writer promised that this vessel and the *Chicora* will steam out and quickly smash Admiral Du Pont's wooden ships to splinters." He led up a dully resounding companionway into the ram's cramped but heavily armored wheelhouse and bent to squint out of an eye-slit. "I imagine his prediction is accurate enough."

"Why, Doctor?"

Donald hesitated an instant. "Commodore Ingraham has received intelligence that several Yankee monitors have started South."

"Monitors?" the Virginian burst out. "Why, I thought they had only one such vessel! The one that fought the *Merrimac* to a draw in Hampton Roads."

"Oh, no. Last summer the Federals built at least six more like the one you speak of, or so our agents up North report."

"Then the term 'monitor' has become applied to any craft bearing a revolving turret?"

86

"That's right. You can see now why our Naval Command needs to break the blockade before any monitors appear in these waters." Donald led into a tiny cubicle. "Now this is what I laughingly call the *Palmetto State*'s cockpit. My operating table, sir." With a wave of a broad hand he indicated an ordinary kitchen table covered with red-and-white-checked oilcloth. From its edges dangled four broad, leather straps. "Yonder stands my surgeon's chest. It doesn't contain much except sutures, surgical needles, saws, forceps and a few old scalpels." He sighed and looked miserable. "I'd been hoping some good English instruments might come in aboard the *Grey Ghost.*"

"There weren't any?"

"Not a one."

The Officer of the Deck appeared and was introduced as Lieutenant John Payne. He was short, quick of movement, and had penetrating gray eyes that seemed never to be at rest. Obviously, he was pleased to escape boredom and so led down a lantern-lit engine room in which a pair of boilers hissed comfortably. It reeked of coal gas and oil and the body odors of the two blackened and sweat-bathed stokers on duty.

"This engine isn't much," Payne explained. "Came out of the *James Gray*, a tugboat, so you can't expect it to do more than give a vessel of this tonnage steerageway. Engines are the major problem in both of our rams."

"About guns and such I'm stupid as the brutes that perish. But marine engines are something else." Dabney Seymour's expression brightened and, stooping, he examined the builders' name plate, then looked at a series of gauges. "Um-m. English. Built by Johnston's, some time back. Now I'd guess this is a low-pressure pivot-acting engine; that its cylinders will be about thirty inches in diameter, and its pistons have a stroke of twenty inches?"

Lieutenant Payne uttered a cry of delight. "By God, sir, you're entirely correct on all points. Someone with such experience is needed at the Naval Station. You've been ordered down by Richmond?"

"No. I came in on the *Grey Ghost*. I've been working in England. God knows, I want to do what I can." Seymour straightened until his visored cap brushed the engine room's ceiling. "Your designers really must be hard-put to ask a weak little engine like this to drive an ironclad."

87

Beneath a grease-marked gray blouse, Lieutenant Payne shrugged. "Needs must when the Devil drives."

"How fast can you steam?"

"No better than five knots, even in slack water."

Seymour looked aghast. "Is that really so? Why, that's just crawling. Is the other ram any faster?"

"Don't know, for sure, but I've heard her speed's about the same and she, too, draws twelve feet. Lucky our armor's thick enough to stop anything the Yankees can throw at us."

Dr. Donald Bryson, glancing at the big Virginian's long, scarred features, noted the depth of his concentration. Obviously, the engineer was eager, as quickly as possible, to absorb any and all cogent facts concerning the vessels in which he yearned to serve.

Lieutenant Payne led the way aloft, drawled over his shoulder, "You can see at a glance these rams are designed for inshore duty. They'd founder in even half a gale in the Atlantic." He summoned a wry smile. "I presume you've noticed, Mr. Seymour, that this steam ram carries davits for only one small-boat?"

"I was wondering. Your crew numbers . . . ?"

"Over a hundred men and officers, so, if anything goes really wrong, it means Davy Jones for most of us."

At the Widow Barrow's drab but cleanly boardinghouse, Dabney Seymour nodded pleasantly to fellow guests assembled to partake of a none too hearty midday meal, but went on to his room on the third floor. From it he enjoyed a remarkably comprehensive prospect of the waterfront.

Um-m. Down yonder lay the vessel he had just visited, an ugly red-brown oblong. How small *Palmetto State* seemed under the lazy tendril of smoke mounting from her single funnel. After securing his door, the Virginian knelt to unlock a brassbound sea chest and to remove from its oaken depths a slim black volume equipped with a lock.

Without even bothering to remove his cap, the marine engineer seated himself and commenced neatly to record what he'd learned. By long experience, he'd discovered that the sooner such mechanical information was set down, the less the chance of error; in this projected affiliation he didn't want to make mistakes — not after coming all the way out from England.

88

After locking his notebook, Seymour selected a sheet of notepaper the heading of which read "Cammell, Laird & Company, Ltd., Marine Engineers and Shipbuilders, Birkenhead," then drafted a letter to the Honorable Stephen R. Mallory, applying for a lieutenant's commission in the Engineering Branch of the Confederate States Navy.

Lips pursed in concentration, he listed his qualifications and experience as modestly as possible. Finally, in an attempt to lend weight to his application, he noted certain deficiencies obvious in *Palmetto State*'s machinery and what might be done about them.

He concluded by recommending, very respectfully, that the Honorable Secretary's Department consider the possible development of torpedo boats. Such deadly little craft, designed to operate partially submerged, already were being experimented with by both the French and British Navies. In Seymour's opinion, these vessels did not need to be expensive and could quickly be constructed as a possible solution to the threat posed by the armored, seagoing monitors under construction up North.

CHAPTER XI Sewing Circle

IN Major St. George Lambkin's drawing room, three young ladies sat sewing before a small and smoky fire. Their full skirts had been arranged tightly about their ankles, not so much in response to a sense of modesty as to keep warm. Petticoats of challis or French flannel were simply not to be had these days, except by the ladies of a few still wealthy families.

Everyone was saying that Major Lambkin must be uncommonly clever about the management of his affairs, especially since he was on duty in Richmond so much of the time. That courteously grave little aristocrat — he stood but five feet three inches in height — somehow had managed to keep his income intact.

On this, the fifth day after Christmas, shirttail-sized black messenger boys scampered importantly among the handful of mansions yet occupied by their owners, to General Beauregard's and other headquarters, and to the Confederate States Navy's bleak offices in the Customs House.

Mr. Armand D'Arcy, the invitations stated, was planning to welcome the New Year with a gala arranged for the Benefit of the Soldiers' Relief Association, following an eggnog party at the home of Captain and Mrs. F. D. Lee.

Cordelia Livesey bent her shining head to bite off a thread. "I declare, I 'most can't wait till Thursday! Everybody who is anybody is planning to attend the gala. I declare my feet simply itch to dance again." She glanced across at Serena busily assembling unsewn sections of gray uniform upon a long Louis XV marble-topped table. Unassembled pieces littered the drawing room's gleaming floor; sleeves here, backs and collars there. Little Aurora was biting her lips in concentration, and sewing clumsily.

Busy with buttonholes was Betty Flood, Charleston's reigning belle. Society agreed, almost without dissent, that in all the tidewater country one couldn't expect to come across a lovelier young lady. Her complexion was that of rose petals and she had deliciously fugitive dimples and luxuriantly long hair in the best romantic tradition. Just like one of Sir Walter Scott's romantic heroines, Betty could recognize the precise moment to fetch a sad sigh, when to appear shocked and when to flutter.

Serena gazed mildly at Julia Livesey's empty chair. Why was she being so deplorably tardy?

Betty drawled: "Reckon we oughtn't to waste fine stitching on such wretched cloth. Most likely it'll come apart in a hurry, so let's save eyesight for good material off a blockade-runner."

Cordelia nodded. "Maybe you're right. Besides, Mamma says it's best to stitch four uniforms halfway right than one done up in style."

Serena glanced at Cordelia. "Coz, did you go to view the *Grey Ghost?* Wish I'd had time, but there was so much to attend to about the house."

"I sho'ly did, and — and — what do you think? *That* woman was on the bridge chatting with General Beauregard and Rascal Rafe, bold as brass."

For several moments the only sounds in this cool drawing room came from the snipping shears.

Serena lowered her work, said softly, "Always remember the old adage, Aurora, 'A singed cat mayn't be as bad as it looks.' "

"All the same I think it's utterly shameless the way she encourages that rapscallion, that rake, Rafe, to dance attendance on her. Especially after the awful thing he did to poor dear Julia."

Aurora's lustrous gray eyes rounded themselves until they suggested those of a startled kitten.

"What's a rake?"

"Back in England during the Regency, certain noblemen acted so wild and reckless they were called 'rakehells,' I mean, Hades," Cordelia informed with some asperity. "Reckon Rascal Rafe pitted more chickens than any blood of his age around Baltimore, Richmond or Savannah, when he wasn't getting — er — intoxicated or throwing away his papa's money at some gambling table."

"Oh-h. He sounds romantic," Aurora gurgled.

"He's more than just romantic," Serena said soberly. "He wounded poor Willie Haycox so badly in a duel he has never walked since. Later he killed —"

"Whom did he — kill?" gasped Serena's younger sister.

Betty Flood's gaze dropped as she cried, bitterly: "My cousin, George. Rafe laughed and took his time in shooting George down after he had missed."

"But he stood for George's bullet," Serena reminded her, relieved that the conversation had veered away from Julia. This wasn't exactly the moment for Aurora to be told that Alexander Bryson's reckless son had seduced and had run away abroad with the pretty, silly wife of the Livesey's overseer, only a few days before he was to have married her Cousin Julia. Her sister might just as well also remain in ignorance of the fact that Cordelia's twin, Joseph, had sworn to shoot Raphael Bryson the instant he came up with that scoundrel. Of those present, only Cordelia was aware that Julia, one delirious moonlit evening, had permitted her fiancé certain intimacies properly reserved for married people; and had confessed as much during an unusually hysterical outburst of shame and grief.

So Cordelia understood better than anyone else why, ever since the *Grey Ghost's* arrival in port, her elder sister had remained quietly aloof from any social gathering.

Betty Flood burst out, "Villains like Rascal Rafe ought to be forever excluded from the society of decent people!"

Serena's winged brows slightly arched themselves. "Isn't such talk un-Christian? After all, Rafe did that wrong a long while ago. Probably he has repented and has adopted sober ways. After all, the Brysons *are* an old, established Carolina family."

The Flood girl said sharply, "I'm sure *I* don't want to see him again, no matter how reformed he may be."

"But I do," Aurora said softly. "He sounds simply fascinatin'."

"Honey, let's not talk any more about him," Serena pleaded. "It was, sure enough, a sad, bad business; but after all, isn't it over and done with?"

"Not for Joe, it isn't," snapped Cordelia. "He still hates Rafe like the Devil's own."

The young women started at a sudden loud knocking at the door. "Captain Bryson am callin', Miss Serena," the butler's thin voice quavered.

"*Captain Bryson!*" Cordelia jumped up, cheeks flaming. "You may inform him that we are not at home."

"If that is so, Miss Livesey, you must have returned at amazing speed." Raphael, clad in a merchant officer's blue uniform, loomed tall in the doorway. Its gold-plated buttons flashed like sparks from beneath a blacksmith's hammer. The atmosphere became electric when to each of the ladies he then offered a sedate bow; only little Aurora arose and bobbed a curtsy.

Completely self-assured, the *Grey Ghost's* captain summoned a curiously winning smile, and addressed Serena. "It occurred to me, Miss Lambkin, that possibly you and your charming guests might welcome a few pairs of French ballroom slippers I've brought? I trust you will honor me by accepting them."

Cordelia arose with chin lifted and lips flattened. "Thank you, Captain Bryson! I wouldn't dream of accepting any gift from such as you."

"Nor I," came Betty Flood's icy accents. "I presume that, not being a gentleman, sir, you are unaware that you are intruding?"

"Am I, indeed?" laughed the figure in blue, not in the least affronted.

Aurora's skirts swayed forward over scattered uniform parts. "You can speak fo' yo'self, Betty Flood, but my onliest pair of dancin' slippers look simply disgraceful."

"Thank you, Miss . . . ?"

"This is my sister, Aurora." Serena smiled and advanced. "This is Captain Bryson."

Nothing could have been more unconcernedly graceful than the way Rafe raised her fingers to his lips, then went out into the hall to return with a number of slim packages wrapped in tissue paper. He presented each of the Lambkin ladies with one, then, bronzed features aglow, he went over to Cordelia seated, marble-faced and rigid, on her chair. "If you don't care to accept this trifling gift won't you please bestow it on someone who would?"

"Sir, I regret that —" She broke off short, aware that skirts were rustling at the drawing room's door.

"Julia!" she called sharply. "Don't come in!" But Julia Livesey's tall, magnificently proportioned figure already had swept inside.

"I'm sorry to be so tardy," she commenced, "but I —" When she saw the caller she halted so abruptly that her skirts of mulberry challis frothed about her legs.

Serena watched her cousin's large, light gray eyes widen, then close tight shut, to expel vision of him. Then the eyes reopened and she stared as if under the influence of mesmerism. A taut silence descended over the drawing room and persisted until, with a low cry, Serena hurried over to her cousin. "Julia, I'm so sorry this has happened."

The two central figures paid not the least attention, simply gazed on each other as if nothing else existed in all the world.

Numbly, Julia was telling herself: He's handsomer than ever. And that fascinating gleam of recklessness still shines in his eyes. There's new strength, humor in the lines about his mouth — but that touch of cruelty . . . it is still there. Raphael Bryson's hair, tiny goatee and sideburns were still of a brown so deep as to approach black. Above his flat, small ears shone tiny patches of silver.

Everyone present heard Julia draw an incredibly long breath before she said in frozen accents, "And how do you do, Captain?"

"Julia. I — I —" When, all at once, he grasped her hands she smiled woodenly but made no effort to free them. "Oh, Julia. There are so many things I must tell you — explain —"

Gently, Julia withdrew her fingers from his grasp. "Captain Bryson, I fear that I have no interest in anything you might have to say."

Cordelia stepped forward, eyes and pink mouth hard with hate. "It is only fair to warn you, sir, that our brother, Joseph, has taken oath to kill you — as you so richly deserve."

An amused laugh escaped the supple, blue-clad figure. "Now that's no news at all, Miss Livesey. A dozen people have told me as much. If, after all these years, your brother still intends to pursue his intent, I shall, of course, place myself at his disposal.

"And now, ladies, my humble service to you." Rafe bowed; then, after depositing the rest of his parcels upon the nearest chair, strode lightly from Major Lambkin's drawing room leaving it peopled by figures, motionless as those in some wax museum.

CHAPTER XII **Torpedo Bureau**

OCCUPYING a high-ceilinged, fly-specked and dingy office in the former United States Customs House, Flag Officer Duncan Nathaniel Ingraham stood, lost in thought, before a window upon the dirty panes of which someone had used his finger to trace a lopsided heart and the initials J.L.H. Half-turning, he threw into profile shaggy, jutting brows, a bristling forelock and features craggy as those Highlands his ancestors had left before the War for Independence.

Alistair Bryson watched the Station Commandant's hands clasp themselves behind a ramrod-straight back. Without facing him, Ingraham asked, "Well, sir, and how can I be of service to you?"

"I have requested this interview, sir, because among clippings recently received from the *Mobile Register* was one which I believe might interest you."

"And what is it about?"

"Well, sir, it described the launching of a craft described as a 'submarine boat.'"

Ingraham's heavy brows merged as, sharply, he considered his caller. "A submarine boat?"

"The article says it is called 'the American Diver' in Mobile," the journalist continued eagerly. "Great things are expected of Mr. Hunley's invention. It is expected to attack an enemy while it is *completely submerged!*"

94

"The *Argus* will do well to waste no time or space on such nonsense," he snapped. "Sounds like another newfangled marine monstrosity Matt Maury chooses to encourage."

When Flag Officer Ingraham strode back to his desk, two large and two small stars, on shoulder straps framed in gold thread, gleamed dully as did long diamonds of gold braid on his cuffs. Three rings of the same material encircled his forearms.

"Exactly what does the clipping say about this 'American Diver'?"

Aware of this harsh-featured individual's intent regard, Alistair read:

> This marvelous craft was designed and paid for by Mr. Horace L. Hunley, a merchant of this city. Formerly he conducted a cotton brokerage business in New Orleans.

"So that Hunley crackpot is at it again?"

"Obviously you've heard of him before, sir."

"Only that last year he importuned the Navy Department in general, and Secretary Mallory in particular, to distraction with pleas for recognition and assistance. Mr. Hunley, sir, has had no experience whatever as a marine architect. There is no ground for these wild claims and predictions he advances. In my opinion, Hunley is a humbug — a dangerous and deluded amateur."

"I see, sir. It says here that Mr. Hunley last attempted, at his own expense, to construct a submersible. It was uncompleted when the Yankees captured New Orleans, so his initial invention had to be pushed into the Mississippi."

Moodily, Ingraham picked up a paper knife, fingered it. "And so that zany has started all over again?"

"Yes, sir. The article states that this 'diver,' by some called a 'fish-boat,' has been designed to attack an enemy while fully submerged."

"And how is she supposed to hurt an enemy? By ramming?"

"No, sir. This fish-boat, if I understand correctly, is to dive under her objective whilst towing a torpedo on a length of line. This torpedo is supposed to swim nearer the surface and to explode on contact. In your opinion, sir, is such a maneuver possible?"

The Flag Officer's deeply lined cheeks became suffused. "No! God never destined man to fight like a monster under the sea. Torpedoes and mines, sir, are cowardly weapons — the Devil's own inventions."

He glared from beneath shaggy, iron-gray brows. "Such warfare is utterly dishonorable — like shooting a man from ambush." His anger mounted until his big voice made the office resound. "Torpedoes, submarine bombs and such are abominations in the sight of every self-respecting naval officer, North or South! Never will I countenance cowardly infernal machines which can blow human beings into Eternity without granting them the least opportunity of preparing themselves to meet their Maker."

Flag Officer Ingraham took an agitated turn across his chart-hung office, and so angrily that a fat tiger cat, drowsing behind a potbellied stove, raised his head and opened one wary eye in a manner ridiculously suggestive of a drunken man who, reposing in a gutter, recognizes the approach of a police constable.

Hurriedly, the journalist scribbled notes on Ingraham's remarks. He wasn't particularly astonished at the Flag Officer's comments; similar sentiments often had been expressed by such professional naval men as Commanders John Rutledge and John R. Tucker as well as many captured Union naval officers.

Relentlessly, he pursued his interview. "What if this 'American Diver' should prove practical? Could vessels of this type, not being affected by fire from the enemy, sink sufficient ships to break the blockade?"

"They might, *if* they can perform as claimed — which any well-trained naval engineer will doubt."

Flag Officer Ingraham continued to flex the paper knife between powerful, brown-splotched hands. "Does that clipping offer any further information? I need to know all I can concerning it, and the claims raised for it."

"Yes, sir. It was constructed at Mobile in Park & Lyons' boatyard from designs prepared by a Mr. Horace L. Hunley and his partners, Messers McClintock and Watson. She is reported to be of wood sheathed in boiler iron, thirty-five feet in length and having a diameter of about six feet. She is screw-propelled —"

"Bah!" snorted Ingraham. "Tell me, sir, how it is possible for a steam engine to operate under water? Her fires would drown and her crew suffocate. This is a floating coffin Hunley has designed; a complete absurdity, on the face of it!"

"Perhaps this submersible is to be otherwise propelled."

"How then?"

"I'm afraid I don't know. The article says nothing on the subject." The tomcat arose and sidled over to strop itself delicately against Alistair's leg. "Then, sir, you place no confidence in such a fish-boat's ability to sink enemy ships?"

"No. If the Yankee blockade is to be broken — *and it will be broken!* — that will be accomplished by ships fighting on the surface as they always have done, by armored rams like the *Chicora, Palmetto State* and the *Atlanta* we're building down in Savannah. A fleet of steam rams, faster and better-constructed than those we now possess, is the only answer to our problem."

"Our *Virginia,* sir," growled the Flag Officer, "demonstrated on Hampton Roads that wooden ships, even powerful modern ones like the *Congress* and the *Cumberland,* cannot hope to prevail against an ironclad enemy."

On long legs, Duncan Ingraham strode over to a huge map of Charleston Harbor displaying in red the positions of various batteries, forts and marine obstructions. Alistair wished, but did not dare, to inquire what manner of defenses were indicated by rows of cabalistic-appearing red crosses, blue dots, green circles and so on.

"When, sir, do you propose to attack the blocking fleet?" the *Argus's* managing editor was inquiring when Commander John R. Rutledge entered, accompanied by a short, dark-complexioned officer. Alistair recognized him as Lieutenant Commander John R. Tucker.

"These gentlemen," Ingraham remarked acidly, "can reassure the *Argus* that we need to employ no fish-boats or other infernal machines to break the blockade."

Smiling, Rutledge held out his hand, inquired, "Aren't you Bryson, the editor of the *Argus,* whose brother is serving as my medical officer?"

"Yes. Donald frequently has mentioned the excellency of the discipline and training maintained by you aboard the flagship."

Commander Tucker's bright black eyes sparkled while he undid hooks securing a gray, scarlet-lined boat-cloak. "In that case permit me, sir, to offer congratulations to Mr. Roadheaver's courageous editorial denouncing the disgraceful nature of cargoes currently being imported." He addressed the Naval Station Commandant. "Would you believe it, sir, the *Wild Dayrell* made port last night carrying but six cases of muskets and a few barrels of powder?"

"Aye, I'll credit that," Duncan Ingraham said and his strong face fell into weary lines. "Does it not seem incredible, Mr. Bryson, that certain

Southerners can be so lost to decency that they will speculate with the lives of patriots to amass a fortune?"

"Then, sir —" the newspaperman retrieved a round, rusty-black hat — "you are willing to be quoted as deeming the fish-boat to be worthless as a weapon of warfare?"

"It's worthless — it's inhuman! Please inform Mr. Roadheaver that he may publish my opinion. Good day, Mr. Bryson. Come, gentlemen, we have much to do in final preparation for . . ." He fell silent and delved into a portfolio marked "Secret."

No sooner had the newspaperman disappeared than there strode into the Station Commandant's office a waspish, thin-faced officer wearing an odd-shade naval uniform and accompanied by Dabney Seymour, the scarred Virginian.

An atmosphere of antagonism immediately manifested itself. "Well, what is it, Captain Gray?"

"Sir," Captain M. M. Gray, Chief of Submarine Defenses, held himself rigidly erect: "I have here a telegram from the Navy Department requesting that an engineer lieutenant's commission be issued to Mr. Seymour, here. He is an expert marine engineer, having enjoyed considerable training and experience among various British shipbuilding concerns."

Ingraham's beetling brows climbed a trifle. "There should be no difficulty over that. I can use a trained engineer on this station. God knows those feeble scrapheaps we use for engines need every possible care."

"No doubt, sir, but Mr. Seymour desires to enter the Torpedo and Submarine Battery Service."

All three officers looked their disgust. "Does he, indeed?" rasped Commander Tucker. "In that case why doesn't Mr. Seymour apply for a commission in the Army — to General Raines?"

"Your pardon, gentlemen," broke in the Virginian's soft voice. "Captain Gray has omitted to mention that I will gladly devote all the time you desire in caring for the steam ram's engines. If I held an Army commission such a service would be impossible, would it not?"

"It would. Um-m." Ingraham's fingers in passing over his chin caused a soft, rasping sound. "In that case, I agree to commissioning Mr. Seymour in our Torpedo and Submarine Battery Service."

CHAPTER XIII

In Charleston Jail

INDIA BRYSON gave a defiant toss of her head. "I don't care a rap what people say, Rafe. Those poor people starving in the City Jail *aren't* devils incarnate! They're every bit as human as our own poor boys imprisoned in Fort Wadsworth and even worse places."

Captain Raphael Bryson nodded, glanced over his shoulder at members of his crew lugging a pair of heavy laundry baskets. One, however, carried only a guitar.

" 'The quality of mercy is not strained,' " smilingly quoted the *Grey Ghost's* owner. "Strange though it seems in a patriotic Southron, I approve most heartily your desire to inject even a brief ray of sunshine into the drab existence of our captives."

He directed a quick glance at India striding briskly along with color high in her golden cheeks. "You're aware, of course, my dear, that when people learn of our visiting the Yankees tongues will wag more viciously than ever?"

"Aren't we both accustomed to that?" With a quick, birdlike motion India peered up at her companion from under a rain-spattered velvet bonnet. "It won't bother me, if it doesn't you."

The outlines of Charleston Jail presently loomed through the drizzle, forbidding, stark and cold. At its entrance an unshaven officer halted, then in a surly fashion, admitted the little group. He punctuated his remarks by squirting tobacco juice at a spittoon in a corner of the jailer's office.

"Sure, I reckon you can go in," he drawled. "Though what you want with them damn' Bluebellies is beyond me."

A sour reek, generated by human bodies too long unwashed, the nauseating, acid stench of excrement and other filth, beat through the heavy door of iron bars. Before it slouched a pair of guards, slovenly graybeards mostly, wearing civilian garments. Save for the dirty white crossbelts, cartridge boxes and the ancient bayoneted flintlock muskets they supported, one never would have taken these haggard oldsters for soldiers. Tears sprang to India's eyes when she noticed that someone had tied a scraggly holly branch above that grim portal they guarded.

"Willy" — the Officer of the Guard turned to a plump individual wearing a sergeant's stripes and carrying a bunch of keys at his belt — "Jest you go rout out Major Whittaker."

"Whittakuh, suh?"

"Yes. He's the Yankees' senior officer."

The unshaven officer on duty cast a morose glance at a clothesbasket which, on being deposited, gave off a cheery clink, as of many bottles. "Say, Mister, you shorely ain't aimin' to bestow them there vittles on a pack o' wuthless Yankees?"

"I certainly do aim to, Major," Rafe replied.

How clean and handsome he looks against this sordid background, India was thinking — and felt her heart beat quicker against her ribs.

"It's one hell of a fine patriot you are!" snapped the officer. "Me and my boys could use such stuff ever so easy."

"Must I remind you, Major, that these passes have been duly signed by the Provost Marshal, and that this is my property with which I have the right to do as I please?"

"Well, reckon I can't stop you, at that, but it just ain't fitten to give such vittles to Yankees." The fellow's eyes shone like shards of bottle glass set in old leather when India, in the Superintendent's office, removed her damp mantle of green grenadine and hung it on a rusty nail. The young woman's lithe, perfectly proportioned body was bright in a basque of red satin tied loose over a low-cut blouse of white. A flaring, many-flounced skirt of yellow silk adorned by scarlet velvet poppies flared like a burst of sunlight in the fetid half-light. From her reticule India produced a Spanish comb and a mantilla.

The dirty officer's hairy jaw sagged. "What air you fixin' to do, ma'am, in a rig like that?"

The provocative curve of India's vivid lips widened. "Why, sir, I intend to dance for your prisoners and perhaps sing a little, if they'd enjoy it."

"Reckon they will, all right. Many of 'em ain't sighted a female woman in a year or more."

The plump sergeant exposed big yellow teeth in a half-leer. "Say, ain't you the same actress" — he put a world of meaning in the appellation — "what danced for them recruits out to the race track last month?"

Rafe caught the fellow by his food-stained blouse, used deadly calm accents. "This *lady* has often entertained our forces. Don't you forget the 'lady' part of it."

The hollow sound of feet advancing over stone flooring sounded beyond bars worn shiny at waist height from a continual application of hands. Between two Home Guards, mere smooth-faced boys, appeared a straight, well-set-up and yellow-bearded individual. He wore his filthy blue tunic as if it were a dress uniform, for all that only dangling threads remained to mark the position of several buttons. A once-white shirt also lacked buttons as well as collar.

"You sent for me?" The captive major's sunken and gray-tinged features expressed a veiled contempt of this slovenly, tobacco-stained jailer. When he noticed India a trembling, filthy hand crept up to button his shirt's neckband.

"Reckon so. This yere *lady,*" he emphasized in such a tone that color streamed back into Rafe's tanned features, "aims to try to amuse yore fellers awhile. Dunno why."

The prisoner's red-rimmed and lackluster blue eyes widened and his lips drew back from gums turning black with scurvy. "Dear me, a miracle come to pass. Someone in this moth-eaten Citadel of Sedition contemplates a kindly gesture towards blood-drinking Northern barbarians."

Rafe offered the scarecrow in blue — he was an artilleryman by his red pipings — a muscular, hairy hand. "I'm Captain Bryson, sir, commanding the blockade-runner *Grey Ghost*. This lady is Mrs. Alistair Bryson. In honor of the Christmas season she has volunteered to sing and dance for you and your fellow prisoners."

As if upon an apparition from another planet, the Northerner gaped at India's crisp loveliness. "I, sir, am Major Richard Whittaker of the 3rd Rhode Island Volunteer Artillery.

"This —" he hesitated, and jerked a stiff bow — "is a most unexpected surprise, ma'am. Please excuse my appearance. One half-inch water pipe must serve the needs of above three hundred men, and we have received no parcels from home since late last summer."

In thoughtful silence Rafe and the guitar player followed India's gay outline into a fetid, sour-smelling miasma which seemed to reach out from the cells to affront their senses. Presently they entered the jail's mess hall. Dining tables occupied only one end of this long and dimly lit chamber, for, lining the three other walls, were ranged untidy piles of pine straw, long ago fragrant and clean. Now these piles were occupied by half-dressed figures that lay motionless or sat weakly propped against the wall; figures which might have populated Dante's Inferno.

Most of these emaciated and vacant-eyed inmates were infantrymen but, here and there, a soiled cavalry or an artillery uniform was recognizable. Also present were a goodly number of sailors in filthy jumpers and baggy, dark-blue trousers.

Of all ages, the enlisted men possessed only one attribute in common: a weariness of expression and slowness of motion; they all scratched continually at ribby bodies often revealed by a lack of shirt or underwear.

To serve as a stage, a brace of sturdy tables had been pushed against a whitewashed greasy wall marred by numberless obscene drawings and inscriptions done in charcoal. India shivered. How utterly incredible that humans deliberately would reduce fellow human beings to so bestial a state! Some of the sick didn't even raise their heads, just lay there staring blankly at the cobweb-infested ceiling high above.

Ranged before the stage already stood a dense throng. Prisoners from the other cell blocks came filing in to further poison the already stinking atmosphere with the fluttering of their rags. When India's red bolero and yellow skirt advanced a path was opened through the audience.

"God!" a voice called out. "I'd plumb forgot people ever could be so clean!"

Rafe, striding along in the little performer's wake, occupied himself by trying not to hold his nose against the mephitic atmosphere and in attempting to remain unshaken by the sight of so many hideous, festering sores and pus-yellowed bandages. God, what stark hopelessness showed in the sunken eyes following his course — it approached stupor. These poor devils couldn't have consumed a real meal in weeks — months, more probably.

By some freak of the weather, just as India stepped from a bench onto the tables, the rain clouds parted and loosed a long slant of yellow radiance grimly barred in black. With the effectiveness of a spotlight the sunbeam set the colors of the entertainer's costume aglow, touched the gold filigree on her comb with fire and effectively revealed those soft curves trembling beneath her blouse.

Never a coarse comment was raised. Many of the men — especially the younger ones — forgot to scratch, looked as if they were dreaming.

Of squalor and dirt India Bryson had encountered a sufficiency in certain training camps and hospitals these past months, but she'd seen nothing even faintly rivaling this abysmal misery.

Hurriedly, she motioned forward her guitar player. Meanwhile Major Whittaker was seating himself among a handful of dedicated officers who had elected to share their men's misfortune.

Opening a huge, spangled fan, India stepped to the platform's edge and queried in a clear, carrying voice: "What shall I sing for you, boys?"

Since most of the men seemed to want "The Girl I Left Behind Me," she flashed a wide white smile and began to sing.

When, at length, her lilting voice died away, tears had drawn clean lines down many a lined and dirt-grayed countenance.

CHAPTER XIV Crumbacker's Warehouse

A COPY of a dispatch received by the Quartermaster General, Richmond, Virginia, read:

VICKSBURG, MISSISSIPPI

FAILURE TO SECURE DECISIVE VICTORY AT CHICKASAW BLUFFS ATTRIBUT-ABLE TO CRITICAL SHORTAGE SHOES, SMALL ARMS, AMMUNITION. WHEN ENEMY RETREATED ONLY THREE ROUNDS PER MAN AMMUNITION RE-MAINED TO 42ND GEORGIA, 51ST TENNESSEE, 50TH TENNESSEE. BOW-MAN'S MISSISSIPPI ARTILLERY, TUMIN'S TEXAS BATTERY HAVE NO AMMU-NITION WHATEVER.

CANNOT CONTINUE MUCH LONGER SUPPLYING OUR FORCES FROM CAPTURED SUPPLIES. ENEMY ENJOYS ABUNDANCE. WE HAVE NOTHING.

SETH M. BARTON
BRIG. GEN., CSA

From the third floor of that mouldy building in which the *Charleston Argus* was published, Alistair Bryson could obtain an excellent view of the wharves, warehouses and batteries lining the Cooper River's south bank.

Yonder, clumps of slim, rust-coated funnels rose among weather-beaten pilothouses: above this fleet, slowly dying since 1861, rotten stays, shrouds and halyards swayed in the slightest breeze like pennants.

Near at hand lay that dry dock in which the great ram to be christened *Charleston,* the city's pride, was taking shape despite a desperate shortage of materials and skilled shipwrights. Beyond her, minor naval vessels lay, somnolent, in their slips: *General Clinch, Ettiwan, Sumter, Chesterfield, Lady Davis* and others — all converted tugs or steamers.

Beyond these naval vessels could be discerned the sharply raked masts and funnels of the four blockade-runners presently in port. He recognized them all: *Lynx,* Captain Craig; *Fanny,* Captain Henry Howard; *Grey Ghost;* then, furthest away, *Wild Dayrell* fresh in from Nassau.

Alistair groped for a bandanna handkerchief to dry a suddenly runny nose. He hoped he'd sounded convincing in pleading urgent work at the *Argus* to avoid witnessing India's performance at the jail. Long and unhappily familiar with the conditions prevalent there, he simply wouldn't endure its sights and smells unless duty required it.

Rafe, he reckoned, was growing pretty exasperated over the non-arrival of enough English coal to drive the *Grey Ghost* past those ships so tirelessly prowling the Atlantic. One Blue screen cruised just beyond Charleston Bar, the other some twenty-five miles farther offshore.

Now that today's edition had been put to bed, the *Argus's* staff had departed save for printer's devils sorting body type from pie boxes in the composing room.

Alistair resettled a faded shawl-cape over his shoulders. Br-r-r! Why did an unheated room always feel so much colder than the out of doors? At the end of India's Christmas gift, he pulled out the watch Rafe had presented.

Um-m. Four o'clock. Jairus should soon be back. He'd sent the hunchback to loaf among the cotton bales piled hill-high upon Brown's Wharf. He'd been instructed to observe the delivery of freight into Eli Crumbacker's big, weather-beaten brick warehouse and to note its nature as far as he was able.

Certain of the *Grey Ghost's* cargo cases, those identified by numbers

104

only, he himself had watched being hauled to the Northeast Railroad depot and manhandled onto cars boarded for Richmond.

The light now was fading so rapidly the journalist descended to the ground floor and was heading for the pressroom when Jairus's twisted figure appeared, silent as a ghost, from among shadows reeking of job ink and type cleaner.

"Sorry Ah'm late, suh, but Ah come so directly's Ah could."

"You found out what I wanted?"

Beckoning, the copy boy edged around a row of type stands and retreated behind a big job press. "Misto Bryson, dis afternoon dey was fo' drayloads' numbahed crates drive over to Misto Crumbackuh's wa'house."

"How were they numbered?" He peered steadily through the gloom.

"Sixty-t'ree an' eighteen." The hunchback obviously was proud of his ability to read, and even to figure a little.

"Good." Alistair delved into plaid pantaloons, then counted out several limp examples of South Carolina currency. "That's fine work, Jairus. Did you note any marked twelve, forty-two or seventy-four?"

"Yassuh, but dey done been unloaded over to Wilcox & Hervey's place."

"Keep your eyes skinned and try to find out from the stevedores whether any cargo marked like that came in on the *Wild Dayrell*."

The copy boy hesitated; rolled anxious, yellowish eyes. "Misto Bryson, iffen Ah wuz you Ah wouldn' nohow go foolin' round Misto Crumbackuh's wa'house."

"Why not?"

"Ah noticed plenty mean-looking stranger-men hangin' round de dock. Dey got plenty knives and guns hung all over deyseves. An' round Wilcox's, dey's fellas what knows de inside of de jail house mighty well."

So Crumbacker's warehouse would appear to be under guard? Why? Obviously because something must be kept hidden there from public inspection. Um-m. What person or persons were encouraging this nefarious traffic?

In his office, the journalist settled at his desk, steepled fingers over his nose and, lost in thought, watched gray breath-vapors eddy about them, delicate and ephemeral. The consignees undoubtedly must be known to the late Major Crumbacker's manager, one Jed Turner who, until the fighting began, had been the notoriously brutal head overseer on a nearby rice plantation.

Turner's account books, together with certain possibly informative manifests and bills of lading, it stood to reason, would be kept in the warehouse's office.

Darkness had descended to conceal the burned district, but a distinctive reek as of charred timbers and decomposing plaster was strong in the air when Alistair Bryson emerged upon silent and shadow-ruled Charlotte Street and struck off for the waterfront.

Whew — the wind cut like a sickle, chilled him; but not so much as the realization that he was actually on his way to commit a felony; in Carolina, the act of breaking and entering another's property after sundown did not count as simple robbery. *Felony!* Pulses quickened, he stepped across the street to avoid a group of female slaves chattering loudly as they shuffled along, balancing huge bundles of kindling on turbaned heads.

Crumbacker's big, three-story brick warehouse he knew to be situated at the end of Pritchard Street and fronting a long dock. A good thing so raw a wind was blowing in from the sea; excepting for occasional provost guards, hardly anyone was abroad.

He hoped no one noticed the studious scrutiny he gave to Major Crumbacker's property and its environs. Once he had assured himself nobody was loitering among the shadows of various adjacent alleys or doorways, he drew a deep, deep breath, then marched boldly across the street and tried a door which promised to give access to the second floor. To his joyous relief a big iron knob turned, the lock clucked, then the ill-painted door swung inwards.

Immediately, he realized that, at the foot of a staircase leading upwards, someone had left burning a kerosene lamp. Because of a cracked and long-unwashed chimney it was giving off a very poor light.

"Anybody around?"

When he heard no one reply Alistair closed the door behind him, took care to slip its bolt into place. Um-m. This lamp, surely, must mean that, somewhere about this dim and rat-infested structure, a watchman would be on duty. He found him snoring peacefully upon a cotton bale in the receiving room with mouth sagging blackly open and sparse white beard stabbing at the ceiling. All about, in grotesque, geometrical patterns, loomed mounds of casks, chests and cases. Propped against the bale's coarse netting a double-barreled shotgun — an antique flintlock — stood cocked, ready for instant use.

"You awake, Mister?" the journalist called in a low voice. All the reply he got was a steady, rasping noise made by rats gnawing at a wooden case — which must have contained food; that, and a soft *lap-lapping* of the tide about pilings supporting Crumbacker's Wharf.

A long instant's intent inspection decided Alistair that this watchman really was sleeping, not just indulging in a surreptitious cat nap, so he caught up the lantern and tiptoed over to a pile of freight. There, he examined a number of lightly built wooden cases bearing the number 63 or 18, crudely done in black, and the legend "per *Grey Ghost*, Liverpool."

To his sharp chagrin not even a single case had been opened that he might examine its contents. When, gingerly, he tried lifting one, it proved to be so very light it must have contained dry goods — corsets, perhaps, or French bonnets? Certainly, local customs inspectors had been in no great hurry to examine these importations. Why? *Why? WHY?*

For a space the prowler held his light before a row of barrels that smelt of brandy and other spiritis. All bore the anme *M. Fournier et Fils, Bordeaux* and were marked with the number 63.

Obviously, to open these cases would be impossible, so the newspaper-man's only remaining recourse was to find invoices covering this shipment. What a pity so much of this mysterious, and thus far unidentifiable, cargo should already have gone rattling off towards Richmond!

At the foot of a well-worn stairs leading to the second floor the prowler paused and, for a long while, listened intently. When he heard only the watchman's rattling snores, Alistair restored the lantern to its former position after igniting a candle from its flame. Shielding his taper with his hat, he climbed upstairs to find the accounting room door closed, but unlocked; heavy window shutters of sheet-iron had been shut and barred into position.

The intruder commenced to tremble gently and, although the atmosphere in here was dank, perspiration sprang out across his forehead. Now, irretrievably, he was about to risk his personal honor — public disgrace, a prison term, even. Nonetheless he approached the nearest bookkeeper's desk. There were four of them: marked A–G, the next H–N, and so on. If *only* he had some idea of the name, or names, under which the consignees, known only by numerals, were transacting business, he'd know where to begin.

"Well, here goes," he breathed; commenced to tug at the first desk's drawer and found it locked; he selected from beside a sheet-iron stove a small poker and used it as a jimmy. He had to exert considerable pressure before the wood gave and caused a staccato *crack!* which, in his imagination, sounded loud as a pistol shot. God above! The whole front of the drawer had broken off and clattered onto the floor.

Heart in mouth, the journalist froze, listened. Unseeing, his gaze roved over dingy walls hung with the yellowed and fly-blown prints advertising various steamships. Reassured, he reached into the drawer, but his hand shook so violently that the papers he found rustled in his grasp like dead leaves in a wind.

Exasperation filled him when he recognized only manifests used aboard such blockade-runners as *Night Hawk, Hattie, Emilie,* and *St. Pierre.* These, he knew, had made port weeks earlier. Nothing concerning *Wild Dayrell* or *Grey Ghost* . . .

Hurriedly, the newspaperman replaced the invoices and managed to jam the drawer's broken front back into position.

Lips compressed, he thought hard, then cursed himself for not having foreseen that, in all probability, the damaging invoices would not be kept within reach of ordinary clerks and other employees. Um-m. What about the manager's office across the hall?

Again the intruder employed his poker to force a big roll-top desk's two drawers. In one of them reposed several fat bundles of Confederate and Carolina State currency secured by lengths of dirty cotton twine; also a Navy Colt revolver and a scattering of loose cartridges.

In the second drawer he found a single-sheet newspaper, neatly folded, and was gripping a fat brown envelope bearing broken red wax seals when, with unmistakable clarity, he heard not one but several sets of footsteps ascending the stairs.

Instantly, he snuffed the candle, stuffed envelope and paper into his jacket's inner pocket, then crouched in rigid expectancy beside the roll-top desk.

"I tell you I saw a light!"

"The hell you did. You bin hittin' that popskull too hard."

At least three men were out there. With poker held ready, Alistair

Bryson tiptoed over to the door and hoped to remain at least momentarily concealed behind its panels when it swung open.

"Joe's right, b'Gawd. Someone *has* been here. I smell candle smoke. You . . ."

There was nothing else to do. Alistair pushed the door away from him so violently as to send one man reeling across the office, then brought his poker down hard on an arm clawing in his direction. Its owner screamed and fell back, leaving a clear path to the corridor. Here loomed a figure, appearing gigantic in the uncertain light. Again Alistair lashed out, then bounded down the stairs although someone below was shouting to know what was wrong. Alistair pivoted on a newel post and leaped towards the aged watchman who, with shotgun leveled, was attempting to block the warehouse's Laurent Street exit.

Bending low, the fugitive raced by him; a double door giving on to Crumbacker's Wharf stood partially open. He was dodging towards it among stacks of freight when the watchman yelped, "Hi, there! Stop else I'll shoot! Stop!"

Then it was as if some Cyclopean hornet had stung his shoulder. The fugitive staggered and fell onto his knees. Subconsciously, he knew his trousers' knees had been ripped wide open. Sounded the clatter of many feet descending from the office, breathless shouts and yells.

"That way! Out on the pier!" The watchman's thin voice was screeching. "Can't git far. Must ha' hit him. Git him! Git him!"

Somehow, Alistair lurched out onto the dock to which, fortunately, no vessel lay tied up. With his foremost pursuers less than seventy feet behind, the journalist, thinking fast, pretended to stagger, and then tumbled heavily over the dock's edge and the Cooper's black waters closed over his head like a smothering, icy hood.

CHAPTER XV **Apparition**

IN Colonel Ramsay's living room a pair of those beautiful beeswax candles presented by Rafe Bryson on Christmas Day burned with a clear, bright flame, not at all like the smoky tallow dips customarily in use; a few lumps of precious cannel coal sputtered warmly in a grate. The guests, invited by India for liqueurs and coffee, clustered about the fireplace. Elsewhere, it was pretty cold in this high-ceilinged parlor.

Passed Midshipman Drummond Mullinix sank onto his heels to extend chapped hands towards the dancing flames, blissfully unaware of his mother's prideful glances.

Lieutenant Dabney Seymour, CSN, was offering a cuff for his hostess's admiration. Upon it glittered a hoop of bright gold braid, below the Navy's identifying lozenge.

Drummond stood up, grinning. "Say, it's sure fine you got your commission signed so quick, Mister Seymour. You'll be able to go along when we attack the Yankee cruisers."

"Thank you, Mr. Mullinix, believe me, I am all impatience to turn my poor ability towards whipping the enemy." The scarred Virginian turned to Medical Lieutenant Bryson. "In your opinion, Donald, when will we make this move? It's been hanging fire much too long."

"Depends on when we can bunker some decent coal; at least that's what Cap'n Rutledge says."

Young Mullinix laughed. "My Pa used to say that North Carolina coal is a lot like most politicians — generates plenty of smoke but no useful fire."

From the far corner in which he was sipping armagnac, Lieutenant the Honorable Peter Burgoyne spoke unexpectedly. "That was well put. I have scarce been able to comprehend some of the speeches and editorials I read in your newspapers."

The lean figure bowed stiffly in India's direction. "I do not refer to the *Argus*, ma'am. Your husband's newspaper is an anomaly among such purveyors of prejudice and ignorance as the *Richmond Examiner* and the *Savannah Republican*."

The Englishman inquired crisply of Donald Bryson, "And when do you think you will try conclusions with the Unionists?"

"Soon as the weather's right. Oh, by the way, how fare your ambitions towards becoming an observer?"

Burgoyne summoned an enigmatic half-smile. "Well enough. I hear I'm to be posted to duty aboard a steam ram under construction in some city called Savannah. Where is that, may I ask?"

"A little over a hundred miles south of here," smiled Donald. "The ram you're headed for will be the *Atlanta.* I've heard the Navy Department expects great things of her."

"Indeed?"

"She's supposed to be much faster than any ironclad we now have in commission. You see, before being remodeled, she was the fast blockade-runner, *Fingal.*"

The Honorable Peter ceased toying with his fob's seals and asked, "And what is to be her weight of armor?"

Donald flushed embarrassedly. "I really don't know, Mr. Burgoyne. Besides, that's secret."

A snorting laugh escaped Dabney Seymour while he put down his glass. "Then it's a shining wonder! You can hear about every other military secret discussed in any tavern."

"Yes. Is it not amazing? Especially since I've heard this port fairly swarms with Union sympathizers." The English naval officer then sauntered over to where India brightly presided over a tray of refreshments.

"One hears, Mrs. Bryson, that your performance before the Union prisoners was a great success. Yours was a very Christian act — and no doubt lovely to watch."

India arose, swept him an airy curtsy. "Why, thank you, sir, but I fear those poor devils were so starved for amusement they'd have applauded a one-legged clog dancer. They presented me with this." From a corner cupboard she produced a gray-painted ship model some eighteen inches in length.

"Why, India, what a curious vessel," observed Mrs. Mullinix. "What in the world is it modeled on?"

"An ironclad of theirs called the *Monitor,*" her son explained.

"I see the builder has added a pair of extra guns to her turret," commented Seymour. "Or am I in error? The *Illustrated London News'* artist pictured the *Monitor* as mounting only two pieces of ordnance. Am I correct, Peter?"

"You are. I have heard similar ironclads are building up North. Can this be so?"

Donald looked his surprise. "Why, yes. Three or four certainly have been completed. Yesterday, the Commodore received a telegram from Mr. Mallory verifying the report."

"Who might Mr. Mallory be?" the English officer queried as he warmed long legs before the fire. In tartan pantaloons, bottle-green claw-hammer coat, waistcoat of yellow satin, he cut a fine figure.

"Mr. Stephen B. Mallory, sir," Donald supplied, "is our Secretary of the Navy. Everyone on the Station claims he's accomplishing miracles for the service despite Mr. Davis's indifference and the hostility of several Cabinet members. Apparently, we're soon to have a real Navy."

"So your President takes small interest in naval affairs?"

"We have to fight for every yard of wire," the midshipman stated solemnly.

"What kind of wire?" Engineer Lieutenant Seymour queried. "Telegraph wire?"

"No sir, waterproof wire. It's used in firing electrical torpedoes — like the boiler type."

"And what, may I ask, might a boiler-torpedo be?"

Flattered by such obvious attention, young Mullinix hitched forward, the buttons on his short shell-jacket winking red-gold by the firelight. "Why, sir, it's nothin' more than a boiler off an old locomotive that's been waterproofed and crammed full of gunpowder."

"Oh, Drummie!" India clapped hands in brisk enthusiasm. "And how is this machine made to — to go off?"

"Well, now, Mis' India, I don't know for sure," admitted young Mullinix. "But I heard someone say there's something called an 'electric wet battery' kept on shore connected to wires which lead out to the boiler torpedo. When a Yankee warship passes over it, all you have to do is to throw a switch then, *bango!* a whole parcel of Bluebellies go flying through the air, like popcorn out of a popper."

"How very interesting," drawled the big Virginian. "I should like to inspect one."

"God send we can find use for such," said Donald Bryson. "When is Rafe coming in?"

Despite herself, color crept out over India's smooth cheeks. "I really don't know just when to expect him. Now, if you'll all make yourselves comfortable I'll go put some water on to heat for a toddy — the wind is growing raw." Petticoats whispering, Alistair's wife sped from the room with a tread so light as to be barely audible.

"You have actually been aboard the famous *Warrior*, Mr. Burgoyne?" demanded young Mullinix.

"Why, yes, on several occasions."

Only Donald Bryson heard a brief but sibilant hiss in the pantry, so he arose quietly, saying that he would go help his sister-in-law.

He discovered India, her black eyes rounded by shock. She beckoned dazedly. "Thank God, it's you. Come quickly, Donald, and for God's sake be quiet!" She turned; led the way to the ground floor. Before the kitchen's great iron stove upon which a kettle hissed comfortably, lay sprawled a bedraggled, muddied figure amid a widening puddle of dirty water streaked with bright red blood.

"God almighty! It's Alistair!" Bending low, the physician conducted a hurried examination and quickly traced the source of hemorrhage to three round holes punched through fabric covering his brother's left shoulder blade.

"He's been shot . . . with buckshot, at first guess," he announced in an anxious undertone. Then, bending low, he put his mouth to the other's ear, muttered, "Can you hear me? Just flex a finger if you can."

"Oh, Donald, it's no use. He's quite unconscious," softly wailed India. Characteristically, she wasted no time and already had procured a towel and a basin of steaming water with which she wiped, as best she might, a layer of foul black scum from the victim's face and hands.

Donald straightened and his eyes behind his spectacles were steady and sure. He spoke crisply. "Do just as I say. Return to your guests and for Heaven's sake act as though nothing's happened. I'll mix the toddies and decide what's to be done about Alistair."

CHAPTER XVI **The Crusader**

MEDICAL Lieutenant Bryson made his manners to his hostess and departed in advance of the other guests, ostensibly on his way back to duty, but actually to circle around to the Ramsay kitchen and let himself in. He lifted the journalist onto a long pine settee once utilized by house slaves. Alistair, although ghastly pale, meanwhile had regained a degree of consciousness and was moaning, mumbling unintelligibly.

113

"And now, Bunk—" Donald employed Alistair's childhood nickname; even for brothers they had been uncommonly close — "let's see how badly they've winged you."

While Donald was peeling off his brother's muddied jacket and blood-drenched shirt, India could be heard merrily bidding her guests Godspeed. What an actress! Who would have guessed that her husband lay bleeding and helpless below stairs?

"Good-by, Dorcas, you must bring Drummie again soon. Hear? . . . Good night, Mr. Burgoyne. Good luck on your Savannah assignment."

Unfortunately, Lieutenant Seymour was disposed to linger; the voices upstairs droned on.

"Care to tell me more how this happened, Bunk?"

In short, labored sentences, punctuated by involuntary gasps of pain, Alistair gave an account of the night's doings.

The physician's broad red features contracted. "You *are* in a mess, and that's a fact. Lord! Father'd turn over in his grave if ever a son of his was brought to trial for felony."

"Aye. But I had to examine — those manifests."

"Did you discover significant information?"

"Don't know — yet," Alistair wheezed, and winced when his brother's finger tips commenced to explore a set of ragged holes in his shoulder. "Might find something useful — envelope — it's in — coat pocket?"

"Yes. There's a newspaper, too. Everything soaked."

"Be very careful, Don."

"I will, seeing's you risked your life and reputation for them."

"How bad am I hurt?"

"I believe you have been lucky, Bunk. Whoever shot at you was swinging hard to the left, so you've only taken what looks like three small buckshot in your shoulder. However, I am afraid the balls are driven in too deep for me to probe for right now."

Once Donald had swabbed away the gore and grime from three perfectly round and purple-red punctures, he noted with satisfaction that they almost ceased to bleed. Perhaps this was due to contact with cold salt water?

"You're lucky you were wearing a heavy jacket," Donald told him. "Else those buckshot would have penetrated much deeper. Seems your shoulder blade hasn't been fractured, so you'll soon be well — *if* morbidity doesn't set in. Frankly, we doctors don't fancy deep wounds with dirt in them."

Dabney Seymour must have taken his leave at long last for India came rushing down to the kitchen, great-eyed with anxiety, and threw herself onto her knees beside her husband and passionately pressed his livid lips. "Oh, my darling — are you all right? Donald, how — how bad off is he?"

"Better than I'd dared hope. No bones fractured and, of course, no severed arteries. But he's been cruelly hurt, all the same."

"Oh, Alistair! My darling Alistair!" Again the girl held her mouth to his chilled lips. Faugh! How this mud clinging to his trousers stank. "However did this happen? Footpads?"

Alistair managed the ghost of a grin. "No, dear. Got caught committing a felony."

"Felony?" The girl's anguished gaze flashed up to Donald, grimly scrubbing off mud and blood at the kitchen sink. "Oh, Alistair! This is scarcely a time for jest. Why? What?"

"I'm not jesting. Oh — h!" The patient locked his teeth to stop a scream. For want of other antiseptics, Donald, from a small sponge, had begun to drip brandy into the shot holes. Vigorously, he then kneaded the discolored flesh surrounding each shot wound.

"But this — this felony?" India persisted.

"Wanted — examine some invoices — Crumbacker's warehouse."

"Yes, my darling, but I still don't understand."

"Wanted to learn which of our local patriots — wasting cargo space — should be importing only munitions."

"Stop talking, both of you!" ordered the physician. "India, go fetch lint and plenty bandages. You've some?"

"I've been preparing some for the Soldiers' Relief."

Alistair caught at his brother's wrist. "Please, Don, please fix me up so's I can go — *Argus* tomorrow. Must pretend nothing's happened — mustn't be suspected."

"That's impossible. Aside from your hurts, you've swallowed enough foul water to make a goat sick; unless I miss my guess you'll soon be running a fine fever."

"Nevertheless — must observe normal routine — just in case —"

"In case of what?" came India's query. *"You weren't recognized?"*

"Don't think so. Jumped from behind — office door very suddenly, corridor was dark."

"What about that watchman?" Donald demanded as, firmly, he knotted an outer bandage in place. "He get a look at you?"

"Possibly. But he's old and the light was poor. We'll have to trust to luck."

CHAPTER XVII *Bahamas Gazette*

TO suppress evidence of pains stabbing fiercely, irregularly, at his shoulder called for all of Alistair Bryson's resolution. The buckshot were still there, penetrated too deeply to be removed without enlarging the points of entry beyond all hope of concealment. Nonetheless, the *Argus's* managing editor wrote the lead for a story received via the magnetic telegraph concerning a gunboat action recently fought in the vicinity of Vicksburg.

His office door banged open so suddenly he started and the resultant pain almost made him faint; then Mr. Roadheaver, more red of face than usual, blustered in. Alistair's heart sank on recognizing the publisher's companion as the white-bearded watchman in Crumbacker's warehouse!

"Bryson, I want Mr. Summers, here, to describe an attempted robbery last night. You write up such things better than most."

It proved no easy matter for that drawn-faced figure behind the desk to summon an easy smile and shake hands. His breath faltered. The old fellow's rheumy, red-rimmed eyes had widened a little, and his tobacco-stained chin quivered as he stared upon the editor's figure, blackly outlined against the office's dirty windowpanes.

"Come see me when you've finished with Mr. Summers." Mr. Roadheaver directed a parabola of tobacco juice towards a cuspidor, but missed. "I need to talk to you."

"Funniest thing, Misto' Bryson," the ancient quavered as he dropped onto a cane-bottomed chair and spread knobby, freckled hands over patches covering his knees. "Danged if you don't look the very spit of a fellow I'm fixin' to tell you about."

"What an odd coincidence."

"Yep. But ye cain't be him."

"Why so?" Somehow Alistair managed an amused half-smile while struggling to keep down near-panic. Good God, what if this old man had come to recognize him?

"Cause I winged the robber good. Yes, *suh!* He almost fell down and we found his blood all over the floor. Heh! Heh!" Summers whacked his thigh several times in ghoulish satisfaction. "Reckon, though, he drownded when he fell off our wharf. His cap floated ashore."

"Shouldn't wonder but your man's crab food, right now. Suppose you tell me just what happened?"

The old man complied. "Wisht I could ha' got a better look at him, but he came a-boilin' down them steps like the Old Nick was snappin' at his ass. Besides, my lantern weren't nohow clean. Well, seems like the robber was after something in our office — broke open some desks searchin'."

Biting lips against pain gnawing at his shoulder, Alistair wrote down the old man's deposition; meanwhile he attempted to find reassurance; certainly, he didn't like the sly way the watchman kept squinting at him.

"Did he make off with anything of value?"

Summers pulled out a plug, cut off a piece of tobacco and conveyed it to his mouth on his jackknife's blade. He didn't have a tooth in his head, it seemed. "That there's the funny part of it, Mister. 'Pears like he didn't break in to steal no goods. Just papers, so Misto' Turner thinks."

"What kind of papers?"

Summers's bony shoulders rose under a shawl coat. "Dunno. They must have been valuable, though. Misto' Turner's raging mad. He's offerin' five hundred dollars, Richmond money, for information leadin' to the robber's arrest dead or alive. Wouldn't mind earnin' it my ownself. Nosiree, I wouldn't. Not in these blamed hard times."

The old man arose jerkily and circled behind Alistair's desk, to stand blinking down at the editor's scribbled notes.

"Everything there, Mr. Summers?"

"Yep, reckon ye've got it all writ down fair and true. Spelt my name right, too!"

"Thank you for coming in, Mr. Summers."

"Nice knowin' ye. Real nice. Me, I always read the *Argus.*"

Before Alistair could anticipate his intent the watchman suddenly slapped him on the back and provoked so searing a barb of pain that the room spun about his head amid a shower of fiery splinters. He uttered a strangled gasp.

"So long, Mister."

"No need to knock my wind out," he choked.

"Don't get shirty, Mister," mumbled the visitor. "I only meant to act friendlylike. Be seein' you later, I reckon." And he shuffled out, thin, yellow-white hair swaying over a greasy coat collar.

Only when the oldster's tread had died away on the stairs did Alistair dare to wipe from his forehead a sudden sheen of cold sweat. God above, how almost insufferable was this pain. Had his gasp been noticed? Just what had Summers implied by that "Be seein' you later"?

He needed to rest, to pull himself together. He did so, then started in search of Virginius Roadheaver, but halted abruptly. Was it imagination, or *had* that slap started blood trickling from his wounds?

A hurried inspection of his coat indicated that, probably, no blood was seeping into sight. Better go see Mr. Roadheaver and find out what might be bothering the publisher.

To his relieved astonishment Mr. Roadheaver only observed, "I've just heard about a gala to be held New Year's night at Mr. D'Arcy's home."

"What's the occasion?"

"It's to benefit Confederate prisoners held in the North. A very worthy cause, Bryson. Very. I expect you and your wife will attend?"

"No. We're not going."

"I wish you would."

"Need I remind you, sir, that social events are no responsibility of mine?"

"True, enough, my boy." Nervously, the publisher batted fat-lidded and blood-injected eyes. " 'Tisn't for that reason I reckon you'd better go."

"Why then?"

"If I tell you, you won't get all steamed up?"

"I won't. Why do you want us to go?"

"If you attended together it would slow down idle gossip concerning" — Mr. Roadheaver drew back a little — "your wife and a certain block-ade-runner captain."

A brittle laugh escaped the journalist. "Gossip about . . . them?

That's sheer and utter nonsense. Raphael Bryson's my first cousin, so he has the run of my house."

"I understand that, all right, but some other folks don't," the publisher averred and embarrassedly picked his nose.

Conscious now of a sharper ache than that lancing his shoulder, Alistair nodded in frozen fashion. "Very well, we'll attend. Thank you for your tact."

Steel talons, as of invisible harpies, clawed the managing editor's back when, after bolting the office door, he eased off his coat and discovered that the bleeding had been insufficient to saturate the compress and, apparently, had stopped. Damn that senile fool, Summers. All at once he wondered. Had that slap on the back been merely an expression of joviality, or had it been in the nature of a test? Um-m. The old night-watchman's manner had been anything but jolly.

Downstairs sounded the *clank-clank* of presses being started. Nowadays the ponderous flywheels motivating them no longer were turned by steam. A quartet of stalwart slaves easily could grind out the daily edition — less than fifteen hundred copies of late.

Voices sounded loud in the composing room. Obviously, holiday liquor was being circulated. He wished he dared join in the celebration but didn't dare to — his head already was swimming, and the ache of his wound all but intolerable.

Accordingly, the journalist unlocked a small cast-iron safe and from it extracted the newspaper and envelope discovered at Crumbacker's.

Sweating hard and breathing a little heavily, he smoothed out and studied a water-stained copy of the *Bahamas Gazette* and, to his sharp surprise, noted it to be dated many weeks earlier: October 3, 1862.

Why, he asked of himself, should so old a newspaper have been thus carefully locked away?

It was difficult to ignore the pain rising in his shoulder, but he forced himself to consider its every printed word. The publishers reported that a Major Huse, Purchasing Agent for the Confederate Government in the Bahamas, was offering cotton for sale and only at 200 per cent increase over wharfside price in Charleston; that Isaac Campbell & Company — a shady firm if ever there was one — had on hand plenty of Virginia tobacco for sale to any one willing to meet their price.

It required a determined effort, but he forced himself to analyze advertisements for all sorts of liquors, millinery, fancy dry goods, and women's apparel, evidently in great demand in the Confederate States.

A brief editorial attracted, and held, his attention. Its writer, with evident confidence, predicted the happy effect of the Army of the Potomac's sanguinary defeat before Fredericksburg upon the price of Confederate Government bonds in London and Paris.

Although Alistair reread every line of the *Gazette* with painstaking care, he detected nothing which even remotely could indicate the identity of consignees indicated by the numbers 18, 62, 12, 42 and 74. Yet, he insisted to himself, this newspaper *must* have some connection with the mystery, else why should this outdated isue have been pinned to those damaging manifests?

Exasperated, he flung himself back in his chair and experienced excruciating pain. Lord! How could such unimportant-appearing little wounds hurt so much?

To ward off a sudden, alarming faintness, he took from a desk drawer a small flask containing brandy bestowed by Rafe. A deep swallow warmed him and lifted his spirits sufficiently to encourage him into examining an envelope marked, "Crumbacker & Co., Shipping Agents." From it he removed six bills of lading made out in a precise British script.

Presently he hunched forward, lips forming a soundless whistle. God's glory! Small wonder these consignees, whoever they might be, had deemed it discreet to remain anonymous! Listed here, he found several dozen cases of French corsets, silk hose and dancing slippers; hundreds of bolts of Italian silk, India muslin; several gross of ladies' black lace mitts and Bedouin wrappers.

Another bill of lading mentioned "Dolly Varden" trimming for dresses, Prunella shoes, balmoral boots, chenille hair nets, Zouave jackets, chemisettes, camisoles, corset covers and other mysterious items evidently intended for female wear or adornment. Still another firm had imported a wide selection of perfumes, pomades, rouge, linen handkerchiefs, bracelets, lockets, rings, necklaces and combs.

Angrily, Alistair stared at the pile of papers curling before him. "Silk turban bonnets!" he growled. "Jockey hats with Garibaldi feathers and Congress gaiters." For those poor wretches shivering on the Peninsula of Virginia and penned up in Vicksburg?

His fingers quivered when he saw listed, on the last invoice, Eau de

Vie de Danzig, brocaded waistcoats and gentlemen's green paletot coats trimmed in astrakhan.

Of choice champagnes, liqueurs and brandies, a hundred and more cases had been imported, not to mention generous consignments of Old London Dock gin, burgundy, port, Malaga and armagnac.

Carefully he re-examined each and every document and nowhere found mention of mens' woolen underwear, Dutch blanket coats, military cloth, goods, shirts, campaign hats, boots and shoes — or medicines.

For some moments he debated his next move, then perceived that, being in possession of so detailed a description of these items, he might readily work backwards once such goods were put up for auction in Bee Block — as were most blockade-run cargoes.

Alistair shivered violently and, when his teeth commenced to chatter, swallowed some more of Rafe's brandy. But it didn't seem to do much good this time. Perhaps he'd write Mr. Roadheaver's next editorial at home?

CHAPTER XVIII Our Captive Friends Will Benefit

CAPTAIN Bryson descended lightly from a hired carriage which, not long ago, had served the Manigault family, and ascended the now familiar "welcoming arms" steps to find India waiting in the library, radiant and wearing a most effective emerald-green shawl of Chinese silk. A candelabrum, flickering before a mirror, bathed the girl's darkly vivacious features in a golden effulgence and heightened the color on her lips.

Smiling, she swayed towards him with hands extended. "Oh, Rafe, how handsome you are! And what a perfectly lovely dress suit."

She was telling no less than the truth. His opera cloak, lined in bright blue satin, had slipped back on its tie-cords to expose rows of crisp frills descending his shirtfront, and large pearl studs. His dress-suit coat was of plum-colored French velvet. A Windsor tie, although knotted with seeming negligence, nonetheless had been most effectively arranged.

She barely saw Rafe's eyes sparkle before he bent to kiss her fingers;

but delicious darts of excitement, mingled with apprehension, penetrated her being.

"From the beginning, India, I have deemed you surpassingly lovely, but I swear that, until this moment, I haven't appreciated the true glory of a loveliness which is yours, and yours alone, my dear."

Heart beating like the wings of a bird newly imprisoned, India acknowledged his observation with a ballerina's curtsy; lowered her shining dark head almost to the parquet floor.

"Mil gracias, señor!" Then she looked up, laughing, a little breathlessly, quite unaware that her gown's bosom had swayed sufficiently to more than hint at the symmetrical swellings it had been designed to conceal.

Rafe directed a quick glance about the room, then swept her bright form into his arms and kissed her on the mouth. India yielded a long moment, even arched towards him a little, but then pushed him back with surprising strength.

"I suppose we really *are* kissing cousins, Rafe," she admitted, smiling, "so I shan't chide you — this time." Turning aside, she caught up white kid gloves from the hall table and went over to pat a stray curl into place before a mirror.

Boldly handsome features still flushed, Rafe retied his cloak's tasseled cords. "Where is Alistair?"

"Oh, that tiresome sot he works for sent him a note a little while ago, saying a matter has come up only Alistair can cope with. He promised to join us at the Benefit, first minute he's able."

"What foul luck! Why's he so damn' conscientious? Shall we go? I've a carriage for the whole evening." He grinned. "Believe it or not, for once, its pair don't resemble crow baits." At the same time he was thinking: This should be fun; she's a most accomplished coquette. *I will and I won't* — and all that. Well, lovely India, let us see what we shall see.

While assisting her into a cloak of rust-red grosgrain, he experimented by brushing his lips over fragrant ringlets nodding above the nape of her neck. Good! She made no objection, but if she were aware of his caress she gave no indication of it.

The street before the D'Arcy mansion already was choked by all sorts of vehicles, by people arriving on horseback and by couples on foot. Adding to the congestion was a throng of off-duty military, curious Negroes and envious folk who had not been invited.

Those in the street could hear a thrilling, if cacophonous, tuning of violins, English horns and violas, and harpists striking tentative arpeggios.

The night, unseasonably warm, was silvering the D'Arcy mansion's long-unpainted white façade into glamorous beauty with the light of a kindly three-quarter moon.

Warmth, light and gaiety prevailed in Mr. D'Arcy's Louis XV ballroom as it had not since the fighting began. Holly and mistletoe graced sconces and chandeliers of gleaming crystal, and festoons of laurel looped the grand staircase.

Wandering about, regardless of outmoded finery, the old city's gentility bowed, curtsied and kissed one another sedately. Uniforms of all sorts and conditions moved everywhere; not a few of the wearers in addition wore empty sleeves, slings, or bandages freshly applied for this occasion.

Mrs. Ida Hamilton, rapturously reporting this festivity for the *Mercury,* made hurried notes:

> Among the patrons of this memorable gathering were many of the fairest and the bravest of our most distinguished families: Pringles, Jamisons, Ancrums, Middletons, Huguenenins, Lambkins, Liveseys, Williams, Adgers . . .

Mrs. Hamilton glanced at the entrance and, before she knew what she was doing, she had included the name "Bryson" because she was gazing into the sardonic features of Alexander Bryson's son.

Miss Julia Livesey was among the first to notice India pause, scintillating and shapely as ever, at the ballroom's entrance to watch laughing couples whirl past. To fight off a sudden enervating breathlessness, Julia steadied herself against a chairback. Merciful Heavens! Why should the very sight of Raphael Bryson direct fiery currents into her neck and bosom?

As from a distance, she overheard some woman immediately behind her say: "I told you she'd not stay away. She's much too bold and common for sensitivity."

"Birds of a feather!" hissed her companion. "See? She's being escorted by Raphael Bryson, her cousin-in-law."

" — And latest conquest, so they say."

A snowy-headed gentleman with the profile of an aged hawk growled: "By Jupiter, that sure enough *is* Rafe! What a monumental gall the rascal has to dare to show his face before Charleston society."

"Pray God, Joe Livesey doesn't come here," whispered Betty Flood, who had arrived in the Lambkin carriage. "He's in town on leave; did you know?"

Julia averted her head and turned quickly. "Betty dear, do you mind escorting me into the conservatory? I fear I'm feeling a little faint."

Fortunately the musicians selected that particular moment to strike up a lively schottische to set dozens of eager young couples in motion, huge, bouffant skirts to billowing and gold-buttoned uniform coattails to flying. The dancers kept calling greetings and chattering, as do people suddenly enjoying release from an interminable succession of dull and uneventful, if anxious days. Many were greeting old friends not seen in many a sad moon. Others called queries and compliments.

Obviously, the presence of so prepossessing a couple as India and Rafe attracted immediate attention. Hundreds of eyes followed their movements as, with supreme ease, they executed a number of complicated steps.

Seldom had India experienced such exhilaration on a dancing floor. She felt lighter and lighter as, magically, cares, doubts and disappointments melted to music, to the rhythm in their bodies, to the sturdy pressure of Rafe's arms and hands. What if her gown had been new four years ago? There were older styles in evidence. Few other young women were wearing fresh artificial flowers — another gift of Rafe's — in their hair. Best of all, her ballroom slippers were unmistakably new, and of the latest Parisian style.

Not a few dancers performed only simple steps, the better to observe darkly this insouciant, bronzed reprobate in the elegant evening clothes. Not in nearly a decade had most of those present laid eyes upon him. Now he was guiding his lithe young partner about the floor expertly avoiding awkward or self-occupied couples, apparently all unaware of the quiet furore prevailing in Mr. D'Arcy's ballroom.

Medical Lieutenant Bryson and Miss Serena Lambkin lingered over a cut-glass bowl of claret punch before returning to the dancing floor.

Serena gasped: "The Lord help us! There's Rafe yonder."

"Blast that arrogant fool!" groaned Donald. "Why should *he*, of all people, beau India, tonight of all nights?"

"Why is it so unfortunate tonight?"

"India was supposed to attend this affair *with her husband,* in order to quell a lot of vicious gossip that's being spread. Now God knows what won't be said." He peered anxiously about the great, many-mirrored room. "See Alistair anywhere?"

"No, I don't," Serena replied in a hushed voice. "I fear a most unpleasant scene may soon take place."

From behind steel-rimmed spectacles Donald's bright brown eyes probed hers.

"Julia's brother, Joe Livesey, is known to be on his way here."

Donald stiffened. "I don't see him."

"I don't think he has arrived yet. He told Julia he intended first to stop in at the Trenholms' party." Her lovely, softly pink features contracted. "For Heaven's sake, Donald, tell Rafe he must, he simply *must* depart immediately. Take his place with India."

"I will. But you don't know my precious cousin. He'll not listen."

A throng of dancers twirling to the strains of the "Prairie Flower Waltz" rendered progress across the ballroom difficult, so by the time Donald had returned Serena to the company of her mother and her irascible gamecock of a father — very stiff of bearing and imposing in a brand-new gray uniform and scarlet sash — he found India drifting, feather-light, about the floor on the arm of straight-backed and red-faced Peter Burgoyne.

Of either cousin or brother there was no trace. Alistair must still be scribbling in his office, while Rafe was entering Mr. D'Arcy's conservatory. The blockade-runner had noted Julia disappear through its door. Presently he discovered that statuesque young lady taking refuge on a settee in a palm-screened bay window.

"Julia," he called in a low voice which, nonetheless, penetrated that hubbub beyond the conservatory's glass doors.

"Yes, Rafe?" Full, rose-hued skirts rustled softly when she arose, stood uncertainly.

"Surely, Julia, you aren't going to be afraid, now that I've returned?"

"You have been a very long while in coming back to me," she countered unsteadily. Great and luminous as a night-prowling cat's, her eyes considered him. "Why, oh why, Rafe, did you — do what you did?"

"For the life of me I really can't tell you." His powerful, cruelly fine features loomed nearer. "I must have been insane so to betray the gentlest, purest and most adorable of women." Rafe took cool hands that remained limp in his grasp. "I can only swear — if it will soften your just wrath — that never, for one moment, have I ceased to regret my abominable conduct. Many times I have commenced letters abjectly begging your forgiveness but they were never completed, they failed so miserably to express the depth of my contrition or to describe the tortures of my conscience."

"I, too," murmured Julia Livesey in a small, quivering voice, "have suffered tortures — those of humiliation, abandonment and fear. Oh, how I loved you, Raphael; you'll never understand how deeply. So gladly I gave you my soul and myself."

She watched his arms part in the old, familiar gesture. "Then come to me, darling. We can begin again. Can't you see? I crave, I need your love to lend purpose to my existence."

"Do you — Rafe?" The oval of her face, faintly illumined by moonlight beating through the conservatory's glass roof, revealed the gradual creation of a rapturous expression as she stepped into his embrace.

Their lips met and clung, hungry and vibrant, but for only an instant, then Julia wrenched free. On the far side of the potted palms a voice, thickened by liquor, suddenly was declaring, "All we need is some decent rifles and we'll clear those damn' Bluebellies off Stono Island in no time."

Rafe caught her close again. "Julia, I must — see you — alone. Now."

She struggled silently a moment; then, recalling the futility of escaping his hold, pressed softly fragrant fingers over his lips. "Let me go! People will see."

"Then we must leave," he whispered fiercely. "I *will* talk to you. I won't wait. Understand?"

"But Rafe — please — please —"

"Listen to me, my dearest. I have a closed carriage waiting. We can ride around in it until we've said what must be said."

"I can't, Rafe, I can't! Don't you understand? I still love you, but I — I simply *can't* resume."

"We can and we shall," he declared fiercely. "I'll bring my carriage to the servants' entrance. Meet me there."

Julia shivered and averted her face while pushing herself free. "No, I will not. I won't leave this house with you!"

126

Had Henry Bears been not so rapturously in love he might have noticed anxious lines sketched about Cordelia's pretty pink mouth — shaped so much like a cupid's bow — but he could hear her whisper, "Oh, Henry, where *can* Julia have disappeared to? Lord's sake! Betty Flood and I have searched everywhere. She just isn't here any more."

Not at all concerned, Lieutenant Bears patted his partner's hand. "She's gone home. After all, it's not strange. She must have heard that Rascal Rafe's present."

"But is he? I haven't noticed him in quite a while. Have you, honey?"

"Come to think of it, no, and that's what bothers me most." Cordelia stared straight into Henry's broad, reddish features. "You've no notion of what outrageous deeds that — that wretch is capable." She acknowledged the bow of an elderly gentleman wearing a Home Guard uniform, then smiled brightly. "Has Cousin Joe Livesey appeared yet?"

"Apparently not; he must be enjoying Mr. Trenholm's hospitality."

To a martial ruffle of drumbeats, Pierre Gustave Toutant Beauregard, Major General csa, appeared to make a brief plea for generous donations.

"Our prisoners in enemy hands need help," said he. "The Northerners are feeding or housing their captives at all well."

Once ringing cheers for the suave and ever-picturesque "Napoleon of the South" had faded, a wounded officer, drawn and gray of countenance, announced that one of the city's most distinguished soldier-citizens would make a further appeal.

Serena's softly blue eyes brightened as, proudly, she watched her father's short and erect figure stride to the cleared center of the dancing floor. Major Lambkin presented a most soldierly appearance in his uniform, that of the 1st South Carolina Regular Artillery. A double row of gilt buttons descending his double-breasted tunic, glowed as if incandescent, and a wide scarlet sash, secured by his swordbelt, flashed bravely.

The little Major's features were tanned and finely modeled and, by the use of wax, he had trained his mustaches and goatee into very sharp points, imitating the mode set by Louis Napoleon. Never a trace of gray was visible amid abundant black hair which curled down to his collar of scarlet velvet.

Everyone appeared expectant: Major Lambkin's oratory was known to excel in a city which always had prided herself upon the eloquence of her sons.

". . . I therefore appeal to you all!" The speaker's voice soared to a conclusion. "Open not only your hearts but also your pocketbooks for the benefit of gallant Southrons suffering cruelly in the cause of freedom and independence."

Turning, Serena's father smiled at the District Commander — then, as an experienced public speaker, lowered his voice to sharpen his audience's attention.

"I hope that General Beauregard, here, will mention at least one of three bitter surprises we have in store for our blockading friends. As for my part, I can only promise that, as surely as the sun will rise tomorrow, our beloved city soon again will be as open to foreign commerce as she was in 1861!"

An undertone of excited conjecture swelled in the great, crystal-hung ballroom. Everybody, of course, knew that, at almost any hour now, *Chicora* and *Palmetto State* would sally out to sink and drive away Abe Lincoln's pesky wooden gunboats. But what of the other weapons so exasperatingly hinted at?

General Beauregard beckoned, then, and spoke swiftly, softly, into Major Lambkin's ear, whereupon that eloquent gentleman was seen to color as, reluctantly, he nodded several times and quickly brought his peroration to a conclusion.

At this moment Lieutenant Joseph Livesey, CSA, appeared arm-in-arm with two fellow-officers from Captain W. L. Trenholm's Battery of Flying Artillery.

Obviously, all three must have been addressing themselves to Mr. Trenholm's excellent sour mash bourbon with more earnestness than discretion.

Captain Raphael Bryson's closed carriage, after rasping and clattering along Rutledge Street's cobbled surface, proceeded much more smoothly once that thoroughfare became a rutted dirt road leading inland and paralleling the South Carolina Railway's right-of-way. An odor of mouldy upholstery, unique to hired carriages, was unusually pungent in this vehicle; its windows and lamps rattled loosely.

By bright moonlight, Julia Livesey found little difficulty in studying Rafe's well-remembered profile. She thought it appeared sharper and harder than that of the handsome young firebrand who'd come acourting to Mulberry Bend. Try as she would, somehow she couldn't bring herself to remove her hand from his or to object when, smoothly, he slipped a sinewy arm about her.

She did, however, assuage her conscience by protesting: "This is a mad thing to do; you're being utterly outrageous again. Rafe, where are you taking me? I — you — mustn't."

"Of course we're being outrageous, my love." His sideburns tickled when he bent to kiss her. "But isn't this unexpected sortie delightful?"

"Oh yes, yes! But Rafe — this really isn't being sensible. You must have hypnotized me into driving about like this. I must be mad."

"Mad?" he mocked. "I quite agree. *We* are mad — madly in love. And this moment is precious because it came so unexpectedly."

"Unexpectedly?" Among the shadows Julia's dark eyes widened and she laughed a little while the carriage rolled on through the moonlight. "Rafe, you haven't changed one little bit! Do you really expect me to believe that you had this carriage waiting — just by accident? Or . . ." She paused, then, hating herself, purred on, "Or hadn't you originally intended to take that fascinating Mrs. Bryson for a drive by moonlight?"

"By God, you act jealous, you wonderful girl." His exultant laughter drowned out the soft *clip-clop* of the horses' hoofs.

While, fervently, he kissed Julia's mouth, eyes and throat, the carriage's body rocked gently; occasionally, yellow-red lights in some house drifted by.

Sighing, Julia finally pushed him away, but allowed the warm fragrance of her head to ride upon his shoulder.

"What of India — and you?" she asked huskily. "There's beginning to be talk."

"There will always be talk about me and any attractive young woman I'm seen with," he assured her gravely. "As for tonight, I happened to escort India because, at the last minute, Cousin Alistair's publisher summoned him to the *Argus*."

"How convenient. And you were only too happy to oblige?"

"I'll not deny that. India makes a delightful companion. She is sweet, and intelligent, and has a generous disposition; but rest assured, my darling, she's no more to me than a charming and vivacious companion. Incidentally, she's very admiring of you."

Julia emitted a small sigh of relief, then sat up and dabbed first at her hair, then a row of black velvet bows decorating the front of her rose-hued ball gown.

"Won't you please instruct your coachman to turn back, Rafe?"

"Turn back? No. Not yet. It's been far too long since I've listened to the music of your voice or savored the sweetness of your mouth."

Gently inexorable, his arms enfolded her even more ardently than before, bent her back on the seat until the moon silvered the anxious rapture of her expression and sheen of her bosom.

"No, Rafe, no. I beg of you. Don't! Never should I ever have met you alone."

"Oh, Julia, Julia! I'm starved for the touch of you," he whispered, his breath warming, moistening her ear. She recognized his aura, that all but forgotten blend of tobacco, pomade, cognac and of his essential masculinity.

"Don't, Rafe! You mustn't!"

With one hand he held her imprisoned, while the other strayed importunate, impatient, expert. His lips bruised hers in so savage an ardency that she struggled for breath — and determination to cry out. Instead, her body went slack, then became animated with response.

Through frosty moonlight the carriage rolled, swaying easily out a sandy road lined by tall pines standing straight as the pillars of some Gothic church.

"Ah-h, to have found my lost darling again. How very soft and warm you are — your skin so very smooth — I'd forgotten."

"Oh, Rafe! This — is evil — wicked. After all these years I — I can't bear such ecstasy —"

"You love me still?"

"I never have loved anyone saving you, my darling. Ah — h-h. Please! Hold me, touch me as you used to. Yes — that's it. You can never guess how many nights I've cried myself to sleep envisioning you holding some lovely foreign woman like this. Did you ever pity that pathetic, inexperienced girl from the Tidewater — who couldn't sufficiently arouse you?"

"Don't say such things, Julia!" he whispered fiercely. "Believe me, my beloved, despite the wiles you imagine foreign women to possess, I have never truly loved anyone saving you."

Her hands crept up to press the back of his neck. "Hold me, Raphael. Ah-h — my sweetheart — swear, as you hope for redemption, that you'll never again abandon me."

"I swear it, Julia," he panted. "Truly I do — I never make the same mistake twice."

Silence descended, violated only by the smothered impact of hoofs striking sandy soil.

"Rafe, darling, when shall I see you next?" Julia murmured while restoring hoops and petticoats to order.

"Whenever and wherever you like, and publicly, I hope."

"Oh, no! That would be unwise, for the present at least. Have you any idea how many people still feel about you here in town? You've enemies by the dozen, I'm afraid."

His dominant features loomed near, eager. "Suppose I lease a cottage somewhere on the edge of town? They say there are a plenty of them. I can use a *pied-à-terre,* since I shall keep on blockade-running until — or unless — something happens."

"No! No, Rafe!" wailed Julia, hurriedly retying certain velvet bows. "That would be too risky. Everyone would hear of it in no time. Besides, are you not due to sail very soon?" Her eyes probed whitely through the gloom.

"I had expected to," admitted the blockade-runner's captain, "but only this morning my engineer reports that our propeller shaft gaskets must be repaired. Apparently, my *Grey Ghost* took a worse pounding than I suspected when we crossed Drunken Dick Shoal." He straightened his cravat, spoke urgently. "Then, if the cottage notion isn't feasible, suppose you slip aboard, late in the evening? I'll send a carriage for you to wherever you say. There's really small risk involved."

"Much as I adore you, I wouldn't dare!" came Julia's frightened voice. "I will not expose my family and the Lambkins to further scandal. Surely, you'll agree?"

Rafe's arms tightened about her so relentlessly that an exudation of warm and fragrant air from beneath her clothing swirled upwards. "I'll agree to nothing that keeps you from me. Julia, darling, I'll dispatch this same carriage to the bandstand in White Point park. It will arrive at eight and wait an hour, my precious. And I'll be awaiting you, oh, so hungrily, aboard my ship."

"But — but, Rafe — really I — I couldn't man —" She was jolted into silence when the carriage wheels dropped suddenly into a deep rut and banged their foreheads so shrewdly together that tiny vivid lights swam before their eyes.

"You'll come?"

"I won't promise," she faltered. "But I'll try; so kiss me again, Rafe, and promise on your honor that we will be wed as soon as the *Grey Ghost* reaches Nassau. You'll really have to, this time —"

"That is what I intend, sweet silly," came the easy reply.

CHAPTER XIX Lieut. Joseph Livesey, CSA

WHEN Alistair Bryson at last located his cousin the latter was so innocently helping himself to a goblet of punch that angry lights leaped into the journalist's haggard eyes. "What the devil have you been up to? Didn't you promise to look out for India?"

"I did," came the unruffled admission.

"Well, she tells me you've not been seen here, let alone near her, since you arrived!"

"Oh, I've been about," Rafe treated his cousin to a friendly smile. "Besides, India has more gentlemen admirers than you or I ever imagined. It's small wonder; she's the prettiest girl present, by a long sea mile."

Alistair caught the other's sleeve and spoke in grim earnestness. "Save your breath and listen to me. You must leave this place immediately."

"That's an amusing notion. Why?"

"You know Joseph Livesey, don't you?"

"Ah, yes. He was a hot-tempered, ill-mannered pup, if ever there was one." What a nuisance he was at Mulberry Bend.

Anxious lines deepened about Alistair's mouth as he drew Raphael into an alcove. "Well, he's no longer a small boy. For years, he's told everyone he's going to call you out on Julia's account. Joe's looking for you this very minute — so, for all our sakes, clear out, will you?"

Rafe's strong, slightly uneven teeth flashed. "Thanks for your solicitude, dear Cousin, but I find this gala most diverting, so many old acquaintances — and critics; besides, the music pleases me and I intend claiming the next polka with your lovely wife." In the act of turning away Rafe checked himself, eyes narrowed. "Are you all right, Alistair? You've no color and otherwise look as if you'd been pulled through a knothole."

"You imagine things, I'm well enough," lied Alistair, vaguely aware that his features had begun to glisten with a sudden clammy perspiration. Brother Donald's prediction had proved entirely accurate. The buckshot holes in his back had turned purplish-red, dreadfully swollen, and were suppurating freely enough to cause a gagging stench every time the dressings were renewed. How much he would have preferred to stay at home! However, the necessity of dancing with his wife could not be denied; not after Mr. Roadheaver's all too pointed comments.

"Reckon I haven't been sleeping well, Rafe."

"Who could, with India under the same roof!"

Splashes of scarlet suddenly streaked the editor's cheek bones, relieved his leaden complexion. "Take care, Rafe! Such remarks definitely are out of order."

Alistair swayed suddenly, lurched towards an open window. God's mercy. His back felt afire from shoulders to waist. Nearby candle flames wavered in his vision. When Drummond Mullinix danced by, pink and perspiring, with a lovely dark girl in his arms, he saw a double image of them. He also forgot about tipsy Joe Livesey and his politely murderous manner.

Weakly, he beckoned Rafe. "Please — find India. You were right. I — I am not feeling at all well; in fact, I'm damn' sick."

Genuinely concerned, Rafe guided his cousin to a settee. "I'm going to summon a physician. Just now saw Dr. Lynch."

"No! Don't do that! Get Donald if he's still here. No one else."

"All right. Just stay here and try not to faint. I'll be back in a moment."

Without apologies, the *Grey Ghost*'s captain shouldered aside dancing couples until he spied Donald Bryson across the ballroom. He looked none too pleased at being even momentarily parted from Serena, but followed Rafe to a corner.

"What's wrong?"

"Alistair's been taken sick in the card room. He looks deathly. What's wrong?"

Donald blinked behind his glasses. "I've not the least idea. Ah, here's India. Look after Serena, you two."

Rafe summoned a bland smile as India's yellow skirt and Chinese shawl gleamed while Serena was borne off to participate in a quadrille. "Ah, Cousin India, how very fortuitous! I trust I'm in time to claim you for this dance."

"Where *have* you been all this time?" she snapped. "I'd never dreamed you could be so ungallant."

Raphael Bryson opened his mouth to reply but a whole constellation of white-hot stars exploded before his eyes. Coldly raging, he spun about and found himself confronting a tall, straight and black-haired young lieutenant. Deadly lights played in his intense gray-blue eyes.

"Must I introduce myself, Mr. Bryson, or do you recall who I am?" he demanded, employing the overly careful enunciation of a drunken man, suddenly sobered.

"I remember you well enough." Rafe was icily calm as, deliberately, he rubbed his tingling cheek. "I reckon you're Joe Livesey, that insufferable puppy who used to spy on me at Mulberry Bend."

Although the musicians struck up a quadrille, no one paid the least attention.

Rafe became conscious of Dabney Seymour, the scarred Virginian, at his side, looking tall and solemn in his new naval uniform. "Do I correctly presume, Captain Bryson, that you may require the services of a second?"

CHAPTER XX **On the Sandspit**

THE morning was unbelievably still, the air clammy, like that in some vast and empty necropolis. It had grown so cold during the night that skims of fragile ice had formed among dead reeds fringing the Ashley River's banks. Indeed, it was so quiet Dabney Seymour distinctly caught the chuckle of mallards and the squeaking of widgeons feeding in a great yellow-brown marsh across this silver and black river.

Upstream, and barely visible in this uncertain pearl-gray light, a long, flat sandspit thrust like a probing forefinger into the current in the direction of a sunken steamboat's snag-draped pilothouse. The wreck, lifted dark and shapeless above tide, looked as black as a charcoal smudge marring a sheet of clean gray paper. In all directions the horizon seemed to lie but a stone's throw distant.

At the former race track, become an Army preparation camp, sounded the thin, hysterical playing of fifes and a dry rattle of drums beating the reveille.

Nearer at hand, roosters commenced to crow and dogs halfheartedly to yap about some colored man's shack of pine slabs.

Over the soft snuffling of Raphael Bryson's mount could be heard a sibilant whistling caused by the wings of myriad invisible waterfowl speeding out to broad water. Soon the sun would lift above water oaks towering blackly along the shore.

Because current and sandspit were so nearly of a hue, four figures silhouetted in long black cloaks seemed to stand up on the water.

"It appears we should grant Master Livesey full marks for promptness," Rafe Bryson smiled over his shoulder; characteristically, perhaps, he still was wearing his generously frilled dress shirt, evening clothes and cape.

"Shall we dismount?" Seymour suggested quietly. "We can secure our nags to that snag by the water's edge."

Saddle horses already tethered to the roots of an overturned tree swung their heads and sharpened ears in curiosity. When one of them snorted, gray vapors from its nostrils hung low over rippled sand left bare by an ebbing tide.

As the two tall figures started out onto the sandspit they found no difficulty in recognizing young Livesey; he was so much slighter than his companions.

Seymour produced a small and battered silver flask. "Care for a sip of brandy before we join them?"

"Why not? It seems it will prove a lovely morning, but it *is* a bit on the cool side."

Footprints already on the sandspit showed up distinct and black as if etched in ink. Ridgelets of disturbed sand assumed a faint pinkish tint as the dawn brightened.

Lieutenant Joseph Livesey of the Flying Artillery, watching the steady approach of these two cloaked figures, found it necessary to clench his jaw to silence a sudden chattering. Well, there came the man he intended killing. And he *would* kill him. Was not he himself conceded to be the prettiest pistol shot in the whole battalion? Besides, he had the right on his side. Yes. Of course he'd shoot down Rascal Rafe for the unmitigated blackguard he'd proved himself. Joe really couldn't recall how many fist fights he'd had over some real or fancied innuendoes concerning Julia's unhappy love affair. Such a hot tide of hatred welled up that he commenced to tremble gently. Damn! He wished the strong black *café royale* he had gulped a while back would accomplish more towards dispelling a queasy sensation at the pit of his stomach.

Nervously, he watched fatherly old Dr. Lynch, off duty from Fort Sumter, open worn leather saddlebags and methodically lay out bandages, tampons, sponges, instruments and medicaments upon a cloak spread wide over the sand.

Joe directed a glance at Tim Clasby, another lieutenant in Battery B, and saw that Tim was standing rigid as if he were undergoing inspection on some parade ground. Was Tim recalling that this deadly calm and faintly smiling individual advancing along the sandspit had killed George Flood? That, on another occasion, his bullet had nicked Willie Haycox's spine and crippled him for life?

An attenuated line of geese appeared flapping down the Ashley low over the glassy surface. Their discordant gaggling cries sounded loud as if they were flying with gunshot.

The president, a Colonel Phoebus, looked very young to have attained so exalted a rank. He talked thickly, as if he had a bad cold. "Dr. Lynch and I already have paced off twenty yards and have drawn two lines in the sand over which neither principal must advance. Is that understood?" He glanced first at Tim Clasby, then at Dabney Seymour.

"I shall call out 'One, two, three,' " he announced. "The principals may fire *at any time after* the count, but he must stand and receive his opponent's shot. Do I make myself clear, gentlemen?"

"Quite," Seymour said softly.

"Correct, Mr. Clasby?"

"Correct, sir."

"It is my duty to —" the president broke off to blow his nose resoundingly — "to ask you to endeavor to effect a reconciliation between your principals. Do you deem such a reconciliation possible, Mr. Clasby?"

"No, sir. Joe — Mr. Livesey, I mean — sure aims to kill yonder skunk."

Outraged, Colonel Phoebus's voice rang out over the silver-hued river and sandspit. "Modify your language, sir. This is an affair between gentlemen, not guttersnipes. And what do you say, Mr. Seymour?"

The big Virginian's scarred features relaxed. "Captain Bryson, I believe, is prepared to consider an apology."

"Sir, Mr. Livesey insists on fighting." Clasby's voice sounded quite small and flat amid this gray immensity. "He aims to kill this fellow who trifled with poor Miss Julia's affections."

"Very well," snuffled the president. "Shall we proceed?"

Phoebus removed from under his arm a silver-bound case of French dueling pistols; slender, wickedly beautiful, teak-handled affairs with set-triggers. They must be of recent manufacture, since both were equipped with percussion-cap locks rather than flints.

"As the challenged party you may take your choice of weapons, Mr. Seymour. It really doesn't matter, both pistols are exactly alike."

Big brass spurs on young Clasby's jackboots clinked gently when he about-faced and stalked back to his principal and presented the pistol, butt first. Then he moved to the left some ten feet, but still on a line with Joseph Livesey. Scowling, the artilleryman jerked from its holster a Navy Colt and cocked it.

The master of the *Grey Ghost* meanwhile removed his cloak and folded it neatly before placing a tall stovepipe hat upon it. Next he removed his evening coat. How white-frothed the frills of his shirtfront above a black cummerbund!

Pale as death, but no longer shaking, Joe Livesey watched his opponent's almost insultingly deliberate preparations and reminded himself that, when the time came, he must remember evenly to squeeze the pistol's butt with his whole hand and not jerk at its trigger and so depress the weapon's barrel.

Isolated, the figure of Dr. Lynch stood waiting quietly to one side. Already, he had turned back his cuffs.

"Make ready!" called Colonel Phoebus after clearing his throat.

Joe Livesey turned, presenting his right side to his enemy, stood with slim legs showing the Artillery's bright red stripe descending his breeches' leg. Distinctly he caught the *cluck!* of Dabney Seymour's pistol as he, like young Clasby, prepared to shoot either duelist who might fire before the word. Despite himself, Joe Livesey swayed a trifle, and a sudden realization of the sky's immensity came home. He saw himself and his enemy as tiny, dramatic figures occupying the center of a vast and lonely stage.

"One!" Colonel Phoebus's hoarse voice rang out over the waters' lazy lapping against the sand.

Unhurriedly, Lieutenant Joseph Livesey, csa, raised his pistol to the vertical in line with his profile.

"Two!" Why should a flight of redheaded ducks choose this precise moment to go skimming by right over the sandbar?

"Three!"

Quickly, yet evenly, Julia's twin lowered his pistol at arm's length, glimpsed Raphael Bryson's supple silhouette and squeezed with his whole hand. Orange-red flame flared in his face, then pungent smoke fumes stung his nostrils. His arm was jarred by the recoil, and a staccato report reverberated along the riverbank.

Because this morning was so very windless, smoke from Joe's shot hung motionless a long moment, effectively screening his enemy.

An icy barb of incredulity pierced him when the gray-white fumes parted sufficiently to reveal Rascal Rafe. He was still standing as he had last been seen, with cocked pistol held at the perpendicular. At such a range how could Joe have missed?

Now it seemed as if some giant's hands commenced to wring Joe's bowels as a washerwoman wrings out a towel. He knew now that he, not Raphael Bryson, was going to die; be shot down and die, just like poor George Flood.

It was with a curious sense of unbelief that he watched Rascal Rafe gradually lower his pistol's barrel until that deadly bright little ring presented by its muzzle formed a perfect "O." What would be his sensations when the bullet crashed into him? Would it hurt much? Or would his consciousness be snuffed out swiftly, painlessly?

"Shoot, sir," called the president. "To delay thus is cruel — inhuman. For God's sake, shoot!"

"Thank you, sir. I believe I will," Rafe said. Then, turning and without seeming to aim, he fired at a snag drifting down towards Charleston Harbor. His bullet struck the wood squarely, causing a dull *ta-chunk*.

CHAPTER XXI Valley of the Shadow

ALTHOUGH they didn't admit it even to one another, neither Dr. Lynch nor Medical Lieutenant Bryson for several days believed that the *Argus*'s editor could possibly survive. The harbor's foul waters had generated so virulent an infection that a network of angry dark red lines spread all over Alistair's back and the wounded shoulder swelled until, as Jairus put it, "Hit sho' looked lak a smoked ham."

The journalist undoubtedly would have perished, despite his wife's ceaseless care, but for certain precious drugs Rafe Bryson had fetched from the *Grey Ghost*'s medical stores.

The patient lingered a long while in semiconscious state; at times raved about blockade-runners, speculators and over the wrongness of slavery; on other occasions he recalled those halcyon days on the *New York Tribune;* but most of all he babbled about his wife. How he first had beheld her in the role of Cordelia, how he had courted her, had followed her company down to Washington and Richmond.

He experienced febrile hallucinations that he was editing the South's greatest newspaper. Why, it belonged to the Associated Press, maintained special correspondents in every European capital, and published the news days ahead of any other competitor.

Weaving grotesque courses through his delirium were familiar figures: Rafe, Roadheaver, Lieutenant the Honorable Peter Burgoyne, General Beauregard and, strangely enough, Dabney Seymour, who was so insatiably curious about everything. In one especially tortured hallucination he was forced, helpless, to watch his wife, wholly nude, performing the *hodeadah* — that lascivious Caribbean dance — upon the foredeck of a vast blockade-runner running bulwark-deep, bearing a cargo of furs, champagne, French corsets, and balmoral boots. Applauding wildly were Virginius Roadheaver and that grizzled old watchman who had shot him, and so must be held responsible for this shameless scene.

Then he would mumble and moan until someone applied ice-cold compresses to his face and wrists.

Despite the wholehearted disapproval of her family, Serena Lambkin often came to relieve India when, fatigued beyond endurance, she was forced to seek repose.

To India's great surprise, Cordelia Livesey from time to time appeared, pretty and petite as a drawing out of *Godey's Lady's Book*. As a rule she brought a basket of delicacies unsuitable for so ill a person as Alistair. Obviously, Cordelia's real interest was not in the invalid's condition, but rather in ascertaining what might be going on outside the sickroom in the Ramsay house.

She even made a pretense of being civil to Rafe on the rare occasions she encountered him. Serena explained this as gratitude over the rascal's forbearance on that dawn-lit point of sand, which was all the more remarkable because Joe Livesey's bullet actually had broken the skin of Rafe's foreshoulder and so had ruined his new dress coat.

Julia now appeared like a woman transformed. Self-confident, almost gay, she was tireless in soliciting from the ladies of her acquaintance funds destined to complete the great ram, C.S.S. *Charleston*.

Rafe cared not a hoot about the matter of his recent *beau geste* and only laughed tolerantly when several gentlemen who, previously, had stared into space at his approach, now nodded and murmured, "Good day to you, sir."

Alistair's fever finally broke, he became able to sit up and listened fretfully to India's reading of the *Argus*. "Good God, how badly can a man write? Frank Pollard could make an account of the Crucifixion sound tedious."

When a measure of strength returned, the invalid would, for hours on end, study that soiled and wrinkled copy of the *Bahamas Gazette* found in Crumbacker's warehouse. Over and over, he read and analyzed its every printed word. If only he had had some experience in cryptography! He debated presenting his problem to shrewd Major Shelly, General Beauregard's Intelligence Officer, but decided against it because Jairus slunk up to the back door one afternoon and begged to address his employer in private.

"Boss, Ah's mighty rejoiceful you didn't go to Shut-Eye Town fo' keeps. Ah done pray plenty fervent."

"Thank you, Jairus. You undoubtedly pulled me through."

"Nossuh, Ah reckon not, but yo' best ack mighty keerful when you gits up and about." The hunchback's slate-gray features had contracted.

"What do you mean?"

"Dey's certain peoples 'round dis town keeps speckerlatin' howcome you git dem holes in yo' back."

"Nonsense! It's known I fell on an iron rake. Nobody knows what's really wrong with me."

The mulatto's close-cropped bullet head swayed in negation. "Nossuh. Dey's a heap mo' knows yo' wuz hurt by de business end of a shotgun."

"How did the news get out?"

"Dunno, Misto Bryson," the hunchback replied anxiously. "But hits sho'ly all ovah town. Folks claim you done been seen ambulatin' 'round Crumbacker's war'house night of de robbery. An' dat old watchman *he* say fo' sure it was somebody mighty lak you, or yo' spit and image, he done shot at."

From Jairus the invalid also ascertained that only a few blockade-runners still were contriving to sift through the Yankees' recently tightened double cordon of cruisers. Further, he reported that a fleet of Union ironclads — How many? Six, maybe seven — had arrived safely at nearby Port Royal. Everybody figured that once these monitors got refitted they'd surely attempt to subdue the harbor forts and capture the city.

"Oh, God," groaned Alistair. "Here I lie like some damned, weanling puppy while someone's *got* to discover the truth."

Towards the end of January, 1863, Alistair's tough, Highland ancestry asserted itself; he ate more, tottered over to a chair by the window and read avidly every newspaper he could obtain. Especially, he scanned those published in Richmond, and devoted most time to a scrutiny of advertisements offering for sale blockade goods or shares in various companies concerned with that trade. The Columbian Importing Company, headed by a Brigadier General Rackley, seemed to offer the most nutrious food for thought.

In mobcap and apron, India was preparing Alistair's gruel in the kitchen when a familiar double knock sounded at the back door. It was Rafe, bearing, as usual, a basket of supplies. He pulled off his sea captain's cap and, for a wonder, his chilled lips only pecked India's cheek as he announced smilingly, "I located a three-rib roast. Only hope it isn't mule meat."

India clapped gleeful hands. "Oh, Rafe, how ever did you manage? Oh, you poor dear, you look half frozen!"

"I am! There's a mean northwest wind blowing," Rafe admitted, and went over to hang his sodden boat cloak beside the stove. "Rode clear out to Fenwick's to get this meat." He considered her, colorfully neat, even in her house clothes.

"You rode all that just to find beef for Alistair?"

"But, of course, dearest Cousin. May I claim a reward?"

The girl's face lit and her lively dark eyes swept slowly up to melt his. "Oh, yes! Yes! But for your generosity and the drugs you've brought, Alistair surely would have died. You saved him, or so Donald maintains. So I guess I'd better kiss you, Cousin Rafe," she cried lightly. "And with all my heart, which will be easy, because, next to Alistair, I love you best. How wrong people have been about you! You're really so sweet and thoughtful. I — I'd like to scratch the eyes out of certain supposedly well-bred ladies who go about hinting that you and Julia — are —"

In the act of warming his hands above the stove Rafe paused — demanded curiously, "And just what do these dear ladies whisper?"

India flushed and looked aside. "Of course it's nonsense, sheer nonsense, but, well, they claim that Julia has forgiven you and that — that you meet each other — *alone!* Of all the silly gossip!"

He laughed easily and shrugged. "As you say, it's nonsense! And now, Cousin dear, my reward?"

India's slim figure swayed forward and her head tilted back offering

142

the rich redness of her mouth. Easily, he lifted her so that not even the tips of her toes touched the floor.

When he relaxed his embrace he held her face framed between his hands. "Dear little India! Can you not sense the depth of my feelings?"

"Of course. Nobody in the world could be more thoughtful, more unselfish. Now let me down." She kissed him again, lightly on either cheek, and her long lashes descended in time to veil a sudden warmth in her eyes.

"Am I not fortunate to have married into so wonderful a family — Alistair, Donald and you?"

"Undoubtedly," he grinned. "By the way, how is Alistair getting along?"

"He's been mending wonderfully well; but I fear he's had a poor day."

"Sorry to hear it. Any explanation?"

"Jairus, that clever copy boy from the *Argus,* called. He must have brought disquieting news. Will you go upstairs and see Alistair?"

"I wish that I could," he told her, and resettled his collar. "But I really must get back to my ship. At long last we're about to sail; engine's repaired, Welsh coal in the bunker. I have only to await word that our Friends in Blue out there have scattered in pursuit, or that a storm is brewing."

She was bent over the stove when he approached and, from behind, gently cupped hands over breasts riding softly, firmly beneath a band of muslin. He kissed the nape of her neck. "And so, my sweet, bid Alistair good afternoon for me."

India turned and her arms slipped quickly about his neck. "Oh, Rafe, I shall feel so forlorn after you sail. You have been such a — a tower of strength to us. You'll return soon?"

He ignored the question and a slow smile widened his mouth. "Will you indeed feel forlorn?"

"But of course."

"Then, perhaps," he murmured, "you need not —"

Her winged brows elevated themselves a trifle. "I need not feel forlorn. What can you mean?"

"I leave you to conjecture, dearest Cousin," he laughed softly and, retrieving his cloak, quietly departed.

CHAPTER XXII

Battery Waring

GUN crews of the Ninth Volunteer Artillery on duty in Battery Waring, having suffered the tedium of yet another simulated loading and firing exercise, dispersed about the emplacement in search of shelter while waiting for their relief to appear. Wearing shawls or a weird assortment of cloaks and overcoats, they looked tired, cold and enormously bored — as if they were recovering from a tremendous drunk.

The day was gray and raw because a sharp northwest wind was blowing. Dabney Seymour deplored its violence while striding down Legaré street in the direction of White Point Gardens, which lay at the tip of the long, low peninsula upon which Charleston had grown.

Formerly, White Point Gardens had been a lovely little park — in which lovers strolled of a moonlit evening — but now about its bandstand stood only jagged tree stumps. Long ago, once beautiful trees had been hacked down by gun crews.

The Yankee blockaders had been remarkably unlucky of late; seldom had so many blockade-runners become able to slip by them.

What colorful names these vessels had: *Hebe, Night Hawk, Banshee, Will o' the Wisp, Lynx,* and the fabulously fortunate *Venus,* owned by a Captain Lionel Goldschmid, a shrewd and courageous English Jew. At least two thirds of the runners showed British flags, the rest either South Carolina's blue-and-white Palmetto Flag or the Stars and Bars.

Most of the ornate cast-iron benches facing the Ashley showed great patches of rust through once-white paint, and the Point seemed deserted save for Negro vagrants sleeping with knees drawn up under their chins.

With the breeze whipping the skirt of his gray uniform overcoat, Dabney proceeded along the embankment until he came upon a lanky figure who sat whittling, with legs crossed, engaged in mournful contemplation of the harbor. The only movement out there was caused by little flags flown on buoys set to mark the position of torpedoes, nets and other underwater obstructions. Everybody in town knew that most of these markers were misleading; only a few highranking officers were aware which floats marked a pattern of real torpedoes, and which indicated dummies.

Lieutenant Seymour stared out at the faded flags and lamented that, as *Palmetto State's* assistant engineer, he hadn't been privileged to learn which flags marked the real defense. But he would, once his transfer to the Submarine Battery had been approved.

The crunching of Seymour's boots along a gravel walk prompted the solitary lounger to rise and nod.

"A good day to you, sir."

"Good? It's hardly that, now is it, Mr. Peake?"

"Guess not. Now what brought you down here on this miserable afternoon?"

He smiled, dropped onto the bench beside the Vice-Consul and offered a case of seegars. "Only an attempt to expel engine-room fumes from my lungs. With all these runners in port shouldn't wonder but you must be pretty busy at Her Majesty's Consulate?"

"Why?"

"Most of these runners are of British registry."

"We're plenty busy, and that's a fact."

"I hope they brought good news."

The Vice-Counsul's faded gray eyes narrowed as he plunged hands deep into his pockets. "Well, now, if you're hoping to hear that Lord Russell's finally formally received the Confederate Commissioners, you're to be disappointed. But you can take heart over something, sir. 'Tis reliably reported that the seagoing ironclads building at Lairds' are nearing completion. I hear one ram's to be named *Stonewall Jackson*."

"Capital!" Seymour observed. "If only she could be on hand tomorrow."

"Tomorrow, Mr. Seymour?" Elisha Peake's craggy, parchment-hued features tightened. "They — Commodore Ingraham — really ain't going out to try breaking the blockade?"

The scarred Virginian laughed shortly, produced a match and vainly attempted to light his seegar. "No wonder you appear incredulous, my friend. We've had so many false alarms; too many. But this time I believe we've been given a genuine alert."

"Why so?"

"I can't get a light here. Suppose we step over yonder."

In the lee of a rough shed sheltering ammunition for Battery Waring, the pair halted.

"That's mighty good news, sir, but what makes you so certain-sure?"

The taller figure delayed response until he got his smoke well alight. "Well, for one thing, I notice that the *Grey Ghost* and a good many other outward-bound blockade-runners are loading in a hurry and are keeping their crews aboard."

"So she really intends to try breaking out? Figgered she never would, what with her captain so pleased to be home."

Seymour and his companion emerged from the shed's lee, strolled past the breeches of the tall, wheeled cannon and, after returning a number of salutes, peered out over the harbor. Nothing at all could be seen of the blockaders save for a few faint streaks of smoke, low on the horizon.

At long last the artillerymen's relief appeared, to be greeted by raucous cries of "Where the hell you been?" "Damn nice of you to come at all." "Drink up all yer likker, or what?"

"Naow, I don't aim to appear disbelieving," drawled the Vice-Consul. "But does anything else make you sure your rams really are making ready to steam out?"

"For one thing, all officers and men serving in the *Chicora* as well as the *Palmetto State* have been ordered to report aboard by six o'clock tonight."

Mr. Peake spat tobacco juice and his Adam's apple jerked nervously. "Thought they'd no living quarters aboard them rams."

"That's right. There aren't any," Seymour said. "Reckon we'll just have to seek rest where it isn't. Another thing which makes me believe we're going out is that our poor little coal bunkers have been filled — with good coal for a change. Then, again, fresh ammunition is being charged."

"Well, now, do tell," drawled Elisha Peake and thoughtfully scratched at a long and angular chin. " 'Bout when do you calculate you folks might get on the move?"

"Sometime during the night is my guess. We're so slow we want to be very close to the enemy come daylight."

Energetically, Mr. Peake blew his nose. "Congratulations, Mr. Seymour. It's a good thing you're going to make your effort before them new monitors show up."

"Monitors on their way here? Where did you hear that?" Seymour demanded sharply.

"Now, Mr. Seymour," the Vice-Counsul tipped a ponderous wink, "you'd be astonished to learn how well Her Majesty's Navy keeps itself informed. Yep, heard tell some monitors, better than the one that fought the *Merrimac* — by the way, she went down in a gale off Hatteras, not long ago — are layin' in Hampton Roads this minute."

"How many?"

"Some report four — others, six."

A soft whistle escaped the towering figure in blue-gray. "That's most alarming. Thank God, they'll not be on hand tomorrow."

"Expect you'll most likely run out on the morning ebb?"

"Why?"

"Well, water'll be low and old Du Pont's pilots will have to look alive or run themselves aground."

Seymour grinned. "Your reasoning is sound, Mr. Peake. Pray present my kind regards to Mr. Burgoyne. Seen him recently?"

"No," drawled the Vice-Consul and again blew his nose on a faded red bandanna. "Heard tell he went down to Savannah t'other day to inspect the ram you're building down there on the hull of a blockade-runner. 'Fact, this *Atlanta* — that's what we hear she'll be named — might be got ready to fight by early spring."

"Let's hope she's everything her designers predict." Dabney arose briskly, pulled his flat-visored cap on tighter. "Well, reckon I'd better bid you good day and get back to my ship."

Mr. Peake nodded and offered a long and bony hand. "It's been real nice bumping into you like this. Real pleasant. Should you run short of rum or tobacco, Friend Seymour, remember we've always a-plenty over to the Consulate. Feel free to stop in, any time."

Mr. Peake reseated himself and watched *Palmetto State*'s assistant engineer become lost to sight down East Battery Street. Only then did the Vice-Consul arise and hurriedly seek a jerry-built fisherman's shack canting above the Ashley's highwater mark. On its side in misshapen white letters had been daubed: S. BAGNOLD. FRESH FISH, ORSTERS & CRABES.

Elisha Peake did not bother to knock but boldly pushed open a loosely constructed board door, whereupon a muscular Negro roused blinking, but alert, from a bed of rags in a corner. "Yassuh, yassuh? Got some mighty fine orsters, fresh as — Ho! Hit's you, Misto' Peake!"

"Yes, it is. Wake up, Saul and get your gear together," ordered the Vice-Consul sharply. "You're going night-fishing off Cummings' Point."

The fisherman's little eyes ringed themselves in yellow. "Tonight, Boss? No-suh. Ah cain't nowise do dat — not wid so mean a wind blowin'! Listen. It do shake dis cabin like a terrier dawg."

"Nevertheless you'll go, because there's fifty dollars — greenbacks — in it. Now listen carefully. When you meet their picket boats, tell the officer in command that both rams for sure will come out on the ebb just before dawn tomorrow. Understand?"

Doubtfully, Saul scratched grayish fuzz on his bullet head.

"Oh, mah soul! Ah sho'd admire to earn that money, Boss, but mah boat's so leetle and dat wind's mekkin' up worser all de time."

"Very well," growled the Vice-Consul, "I'll make it seventy-five dollars. You'll chance it?"

Saul Bagnold's teeth gleamed in his shack's recesses. "Sho' will, Boss, iffen Ah have to carry dat boat on mah back."

CHAPTER XXIII **The Palmetto Squadron Departs**

THE few steeple clocks still functioning in and about Charleston were disputing the precise hour of 11 P.M., January 30, 1863, when the Confederate States Ship *Palmetto State* commenced slowly to back out of her slip. Fountains of jewel-like sparks gushed from her squat funnel, then cascaded down to wink out on the water or upon her flat deck and casemate's top.

Despite the hour, a little crowd of civilians had assembled to watch Commodore Duncan Ingraham's command depart on its all-important mission. "God grant them victory!" . . . "Sink those damned cruisers out there!" . . . from people tight-lipped and anxious, one heard voices saying . . . "Dear Lord, protect my man these next few hours."

Chicora's propeller also commenced to churn, and little flame tongues licked brightly over the lip of her chimney. Those on shore could hear the labored hiss and pound of her engine turning over. Already the naval steam tenders *Clinch, Ettiwan* and *Chesterfield* — all armed side-wheelers — had backed out and were waiting on the river, invisible because of a silvery mist which had arisen now that the previously fierce wind abruptly had died out.

Quite distinctly, the chilled and silent watchers could recognize the rasp of a stoker's coal scoop over iron footplates; that, and a hoarse, rhythmic coughing caused by steam escaping from various exhaust pipes.

The crowd coughed, too, when a puff of wind drove *Palmetto State*'s smoke into their faces.

Once the flagship had ceased to back and drifted, motionless, on the ebbing tide, a low cheer broke out. "Blow them damn' Blue-bellies back to Hell where they come from!" "Show 'em we can build and fight ships, too!"

Half-seen through the gloom as low, blunt outlines, the rams, to a mad clanging of engine-room bells, gathered forward speed; gradually, their running lights became dim, haloed by haze, and soon they were lost to sight altogether.

Passed Midshipman Drummond Mullinix, recently promoted to duty aboard *Palmetto State*, Commodore Ingraham's flagship, sternly suppressed a desire to yawn continuously. Odd, ever since he'd been a small boy deep excitement had always manifested itself in this embarrassing manner. He sat on a shot-locker, fingers laced over knees and, for the thousandth time, considered the dully gleaming chaces and breechplate of the ram's Number One gun — a ponderous, eighty-pound Brooke rifle. How he loved that sleek engine of destruction — from her muzzle sight to her chace!

"At last!" he exulted to himself. "At last we're going to prove we're just as good sailors as those damned old nigger lovers. By Grabs, they'll soon learn to respect us."

The youth rubbed a liberally freckled nose and grinned. What might

Aurora Livesey be doing right now — if she weren't sleeping? Did he dare suppose she might be thinking of him, aboard the flagship? Maybe.

Wasn't Aurora just the prettiest, sweetest girl *ever*? So inexpressibly dainty, so natural, yet so ladylike and aloof. Yes, sir, today he'd so bear himself that Aurora Livesey might be proud to admit, ever so casually: "Drummond Mullinix? Why, yes, he's a very good friend of mine. Wasn't it wonderful the way he distinguished himself when we broke the Yankee blockade?"

More briefly his thoughts became centered upon his mother. Although he couldn't be sure of it, he felt strangely certain that she had been somewhere in that little crowd waving the flagship farewell. Poor Ma! She certainly had struggled hard not to let folks even guess how hard Pa's death had hit her, any more than she'd whined over a failing income which had necessitated her taking in sewing. He was mighty proud of Pa's memory, too. He'd died for his country just as much as if he'd fallen on some battlefield, instead of being crushed under a piece of armor plate.

Gazing along the gun deck, dimly lit by a scattering of battle lanterns, he noted members of various gun crews lying or squatting about their pieces. Most of these gaunt and bearded fellows were looking mighty solemn now; only a few halfheartedly were playing seven-up or faro. The ram's engine throbbed and squished on and on, her deck vibrating gently to each turn of the big, eight-foot propeller.

Taut, but affecting a convincingly easy manner, Lieutenants Porcher, Shryock and and the rest circulated about the gun deck, mechanically and needlessly checking racks of rammers, spongers, the wetting of fire screens, the disposition of vent drills, fuse wrenches, gunlocks and such. The young men cracked jokes but, all the same, they were grave under it all. They looked much older.

Below, in the engine room, Dabney Seymour had stripped to an oil-smeared undershirt and pants. He streamed sweat while, in company with Chief Engineer Jordan, they tested bearings and listened with apprehension to the machinery's varied noises. The engine, to their practiced ears, didn't sound easy or smooth-running at all. Instead, it was straining, hissing and chattering — which was not surprising. After all, it *had* come out of a tugboat and never had been designed to push so many tons of wood and iron through the water.

The towering assistant engineer cast a somber eye at the boiler pressure gauges, then sharply reminded the two oilers of their duty to keep the piston tracks well lubricated.

That no light might serve to alert the enemy all the flagship's gunport covers were kept closed, so only Flag Officer Ingraham, Captain Rutledge and their bearded pilots, Gladden and Johnson, could see anything at all outside the ram's hull; and they could just glimpse *Chicora*'s running lights as she steamed through strata of fog haunting the harbor's dead-calm waters.

Those in the flagship's pilothouse could only guess that *Ettiwan, General Clinch* and *Chesterfield* were following *Chicora*, perhaps dangerously close; squattering noises caused by their paddles sounded disturbingly audible.

Thus, at a sluggish five knots an hour, the Palmetto Squadron, in line ahead, steamed past Castle Pinckney, then lost headway to permit a guard-boat to lead them along a lane through lines of nets, torpedo fields and other obstructions. The crews held their breath, nervously eyed one another; these devilish contraptions had the dangerous faculty of going adrift. Only last week, the *Spindrift*, a blockade-runner, had had her bottom blown out by a torpedo which had parted from its mooring.

About two of the morning the flagship's lanterns signaled her consorts to anchor, Chief Pilot Gladden being of the opinion that the tide had not risen sufficiently to insure safe passage over Charleston Bar. After all, *Palmetto State* drew fourteen feet and *Chicora* twelve.

Medical Lieutenant Bryson could not recall a night so unearthly still. Those aboard distinctly heard the "All's well" of sentries in various shore batteries. Just to occupy himself, he once more examined his supply of medicines, tourniquets, compresses and splints, laid out beside the kitchen table upon which he would be expected to operate. Lovingly he fingered his instruments of fine Sheffield steel. The sawdust scattered on the deck lay thick and even. Ready at hand were the big lanterns he would have to use in this gloomy cubicle; also a row of wooden tubs into which might be tossed amputated limbs.

Once *Palmetto State* had dropped anchor and the hissing throb of her engine had faded, the young physician decided to make a circuit of the gun deck and smiled on seeing a very young shotman nervously oiling an already dripping gunlock.

Certain of the crew were pretending to sleep on the deck, but their effort was a transparent failure; the atmosphere was too stiflingly hot and full of coal gas.

How many of these bearded or fresh young faces were destined to assume the ashen hue of death before today's sun went down? How many? There could be no knowing. Perhaps he might lie among them? A chill trickled the length of Donald's spine on recalling accounts of the ghastly mutilations a single shell could cause. It didn't help any to reflect that the enemy gunners, admittedly, were terribly proficient.

Flag Officer Ingraham, his neat gray tunic for once open at the throat, said, "Captain Rutledge, do you mind once more repeating your estimate of the enemy's probable strength?"

"Aye, aye, sir. At sundown last night our picket boats sighted nine vessels in the enemy's inner cordon: the *Memphis*, reportedly, is their flagship, she's a fast former blockade-runner, screw-propelled; the *Mercedita* — a barkentine-rigged propeller. The *Quaker City* —"

"What's her armament?"

"Sorry, sir, we have not yet been informed. She has just appeared on the station. Then there is the *Keystone State*, a schooner-rigged side-wheeler. Her armament consists of —" frowning, he flipped over a well-worn notebook's leaves, held it to the binnacle's light — "one one-hundred-and-fifty-pounder Dahlgren rifle; six eight-inch smoothbores and two thirty-pound rifles."

Rutledge then went on to describe the United States Ships *Stettin, Ottawa, Unadilla, Augusta* and, most powerful of all, *Housatonic*, a new steam sloop which a deserter had reported as mounting a Parrott rifled gun of heavy caliber; three thirty-pound Parrott rifles; a nine-inch Dahlgren smoothbore and some smaller pieces.

"That makes the odds against us heavy indeed. I wouldn't fancy them at all if the enemy had any ironclads out there."

"That's very true, sir," agreed Rutledge, a pleasant, strikingly handsome individual. "But I'm sure you haven't overlooked one point, sir."

Ingraham's heavy iron gray brows merged above cavernous eyes. He spoke impatiently. "Every one of the enemy has the foot of us by at least three knots. I know, how well I know. Why, in God's name, can't

152

those people up in Richmond force these rascally blockade-runners to import modern engines for us?"

CHAPTER XXIV U.S.S. *Mercedita* [1]

AT four of the morning signal lanterns, briefly displayed on the flagship's stern, instructed the Palmetto Squadron to raise anchor and get under way, for now the tide was high over that same bar which, in 1776, had caused King George III's captains so much grief.

Everyone aboard felt the bar sucking at *Chicora*'s keel and heard the rushing whisper of sand along her bottom as the false dawn threw Fort Moultrie into blurred silhouette.

"There's one of 'em!" suddenly cried a stunted little pilot named Aldert. "See her? No, yander. She's that blur off the starboard quarter."

"Damned if *I* kin see anything in this damned murk," growled Second Pilot Payne. "You must be imagining things, Jim."

"No, I hain't. Come a minute more, you'll spy her, too."

By some vagary of the weather, all of a sudden, not one, but three, vessels hove dimly into sight. One, the breathless men on the wheelhouse thought to be a big, screw-driven barkentine; the other two were smaller; probably schooner-rigged side-wheelers. The light was so poor no one could be certain about what he saw.

"Steer two points to starboard, if you please, Mr. Aldert," Captain Tucker ordered in a conversational tone.

"Aye, aye, sir." Obediently, he spun his wheel which was entirely too small for so ponderous a ship, therefore the ram answered her helm only very sluggishly.

"Look!" burst out Lieutenant Glassell, his voice taut. "Look at the flagship! She, too, has sighted the enemy."

A volcano of sparks, gushing from *Palmetto State*'s stumpy funnel, was about all that marked her position while she drove through the glassy waters towards the big barkentine at the top of her pitiful speed. The enemy ship, apparently, had yet not taken alarm. She lay motionless and broadside on.

"Looks like we're fixing to ram, sir," observed Henry Bears in a hoarse undertone.

The dawn mist had parted so abruptly that *Palmetto State* had been able to approach, quite unobserved, to within two hundred yards of the Union ship.

Over the clanking of *Chicora*'s engine, Captain Tucker and his officers heard the sudden, hysterical screaming of a bugle aboard the barkentine. It was too late to give effective alarm because *Palmetto State*'s heavy iron beak was surging straight at her.

An errant finger of mist interposed, so that was all *Chicora* saw of the impending action. This was just as well, because they now had business of their own.

Within the steaming, hot casemate, Lieutenant Porcher was growling, "These cussed gunports *have* been cut too small. We won't be able to traverse or elevate our guns efficiently. You'll see. Told Eason so, when he was building her."

"Wish to God this fog would clear off, it's thicker out there than a Dutchman's head!" Due to the increasing heat within *Palmetto State*'s casemate, even elegantly dressed Lieutenant Shryock stripped to his shirt sleeves before he went to squint along the barrel of Number Two gun.

"Stand ready! Enemy in sight," an excited voice called down the pilothouse companionway.

Gunners assigned to *Palmetto State*'s First Division suffered at their stations about the ram's great forward gun. Loaders, shotmen, tacklemen and trainers alike strained their vision and swore while trying to penetrate a wall of gray mist shifting beyond the rifle's muzzle. Although Passed Midshipman Mullinix's pulses began to throb, he resolved to preserve a cool exterior and set an example for the rest of Number One gun's crew. All the same, he couldn't help flicking away a film of sweat forming on his forehead. This not being able to see out was the very devil! How far away was this enemy ship? What might be her rig and armament?

The youth glanced sidewise at the row of round shot waiting, deadly and black, within the hempen rings which prevented their rolling about. He hoped he wasn't looking half as anxious and scared as some of the men nearby. Some were swearing softly, monotonously, meaninglessly. To a man their naked, hairy bodies glistened with sweat clear down to their belts. Still, nothing could be seen beyond the gunport; a deep voice, quivering with tension, called down from aloft: "Stand by to ram!"

"There she is!" the second pointer of Number One gun yelped. "I see her! Christ! She's big as a barn!" In his capacity as gun captain, Drummond, his mouth gone dry as a bone, squinted past the Brooke's muzzle. Then his heart leaped like a shot deer. Yonder, dimly visible through the whirling vapors, loomed a ship's black-painted side! He made out shroud futtocks, next a gunport, then a small-boat swinging to its davits; finally the red-painted muzzles of three great cannon stared at him like sightless Cyclopean eyes. Suppose one of them let go? Icy currents raced down Drummond's back and into his toes.

"Hold hard, all hands!" Officers were shouting along the gun deck.

The Widow Mullinix's son grabbed hold of a training tackle's bight and froze onto it so hard he felt hempen fibers drive into his palms. Now *Palmetto State*'s engines were straining at their best speed and the ram's whole hull throbbed and complained. Round-eyed, the midshipman watched that black wall of wood loom closer and closer. No longer could he see the Yankee's small-boat; the gunport's top prevented that; now those cannon muzzles appeared near enough to touch. God! An overwhelming urge to urinate seized him. Glancing about, he saw a dark rivulet meandering away from an old handspike man.

A terrific, breath-halting crash was followed by the grinding snarl of wood being shattered and a sharp crackle of riven timbers as the ram drove her beak deep, deep into the barkentine's side. Great waves surged over *Palmetto State*'s flat, iron bow, gushed through the Number One's port and momentarily flooded the gun deck. Gunners careless about their hand holds were flung flat and drenched. All manner of loose gear clattered as if a tool chest had been dropped. Meanwhile the flagship's engines faltered, then stopped altogether.

Blond Lieutenant Porcher — eyes grown enormous in his whisker-framed face — cupped hands, yelled, "Number One gun, *fire!*"

Over a yammering raised by terrified human beings aboard the stricken vessel, Mullinix gulped and steadied himself against the recoil slide. He tried to shout, "Stations, Number One! Stand clear!" but his voice sounded thin and scared as he cocked the gunlock. Gripping the tarry lanyard, he ran back. A single strong jerk upon it provoked an infernal glare briefly to illuminate the entire gun deck. It revealed in the minutest detail the crudely finished timbers supporting the ram's armor.

During an instant Number One gun's crew swayed as if in drink, semi-dazed at their posts. Someone quavered, "Mah Gowd! Ah'm deef! Ah cain't hear nuthin!"

"Run in!" Drummond's voice blared unexpectedly, loud as a trumpet. "Come on, Barker, and you, Anderson, hump yourselves! What have you drilled for all this time?"

Tackle-men sprang into action, heaved until the great gun, already recoiled to the hurters on its tracks, were hauled clear of its much too restricting port.

Just as a sponge rammer was plunged down the eighty-pounder's reeking throat, a second explosion made the casemate resound like a beaten gong. This report was not staccato. Beyond the gunports soul-shaking cries and tortured shrieks arose above a sibilant, screaming roar.

"We've busted her boiler!" a voice exulted. "Damn' Yanks cain't escape."

Young Mullinix, peering through the momentarily vacant gunport, received impressions of a vast, jagged hole out of which spurted furious, woolly billows of steam and clouds of swirling gray-brown gun smoke.

To their last hour the men serving in *Palmetto State*'s casemate would be haunted by a hideous clamor raised by luckless wretches as they died, scalded — literally skinned alive — by steam from the punctured boilers.

"Ah-h Christ! Somebody kill me — quick!"

"Help! Help! Oh, God, my eyes. I can't see!"

"Oh-h-skin's stripped clean off my arms!"

Signal rockets hissed up, jewel-bright, from the enemy's quarter-deck. Those in *Palmetto State*'s wheelhouse glimpsed a swarm of naked, half-dressed seamen obviously just routed from their hammocks rush, panic-stricken, about the barkentine's slanting deck. The weight of the Confederate's beak had pulled her enemy over onto her port beam.

Flag Officer Ingraham's harsh voice could be heard. "What ship is that?"

"U.S.S. *Mercedita,* Captain Stellwagen!"

"Do you surrender?"

"Yes!" called a hoarse voice. "For God's sake don't hurt us further!"

"Who is speaking?"

"Lieutenant Abbott, sir. For God's sake, stand by. We're sinking fast."

"Then strike your flag and send a boat."

Only when the Stars and Stripes, half-seen, had come fluttering down did Captain Rutledge direct the ram's engine reversed. Below, Dabney Seymour was hoping against hope that it had not broken down.

On the Union vessel's quarter-deck appeared a figure, ludicrous and pathetic-looking in a flannel nightshirt and sleep-twisted gray hair.

"I am Captain Stellwagen. To whom am I surrendering?"

When he was told, the distraught Northerner bade his boat's crew to hurry. More steam was roaring up through various hatches and companionways. A cry was raised that water had risen to the engine footings.

"Do you and your crew give parole yourselves not to fight again against the Confederate States until properly exchanged?" Rutledge shouted.

"I do ! I do!" yelled Captain Stellwagen. "What's wrong with our boat, Mr. Abbott?"

A coxswain answered him. "Plug's missing from her bottom, sir. We can't stay afloat."

"Then you must wait for our tenders," Captain Rutledge shouted.

Capriciously, the mist closed in again as, with a pillar of sooty smoke pouring from her funnel, *Palmetto State* backed off through a litter of broken planking, smashed timbers and other debris.

The flagship's engine wheezed like a tired old man climbing a staircase, but responded, so Dabney heaved a sigh of relief and used his wrist to wipe away a coating of coal dust.

Up in the wheelhouse taut, jubilant men peered through the baffling half-light. They sobered instantly. In response to *Mercedita*'s rockets no less than seven Federal men-of-war were in sight. Their firemen must be piling on coal, so dense was the smoke they raised while converging upon U.S.S. *Mercedita,* lying dead in the water and listing so far to port that her yards and topmasts were reflected in the glassy sea.

Straight at the ugly, gray-brown ram streamed two big paddlewheelers, obviously converted merchantmen; *Palmetto State*'s gun crews grinned and licked their lips in expectation. Wooden ships. They'd sure enough get blown to Kingdom-come when they came in range. More distant, cruised a small screw sloop which, by her rakish lines, must be a captured blockade-runner taken, like so many others, into the Union service. Far away and just rounding Cummings' Point loomed the sinister silhouette of U.S.S. *Housatonic*, the only real warship on duty with the inner cordon.

On C.S.S. *Ettiwan's* flying bridge, Alistair Bryson, still weak and pallid, while watching the action develop made a series of hurried sketches and diagrams, rejoicing that an off-duty harbor pilot, cursing at his elbow, could identify most of those tiny, hurrying black vessels. He was aware, therefore, that in from the sea were rushing *Quaker City* and *Keystone State,* both side-wheel schooners. *Unadilla* was the smallest enemy, except for *Memphis,* another former blockade-runner.

Alistair's pencil flashed back and forth diagramming courses and positions, noting corresponding time, for all that he was so dead-tired and hungry and that giddiness was threatening. He'd have given a lot just to rest for a spell but, indubitably, it would soon be proved whether a pair of ironclads could sink or drive into flight Admiral Du Pont's swarming blockaders.

Using a pair of borrowed binoculars, the journalist found no difficulty in recognizing *Chicora*. Flying a big Stars and Bars flag, she lay to starboard far away and firing steadily at a tall steam schooner. Breathless, he watched gray-white puffs of smoke spurt, one after the other, from the ram's broadside guns. Gun smoke drifted also about *Keystone State;* and brief, silvery geysers spouted from the glassy water about *Chicora*.

The Confederate gunnery must have been superior for, as that infuriating mist recommenced to obscure the roadstead, those aboard *Ettiwan* watched the Yankee paddle-wheeler abruptly veer from her course. She then lost headway and great billows of smoke commenced to pour from her amidships.

"Hot damn! That's two damn' blockaders out of action," crowed *Ettiwan's* pilot. "Wonder why the *Palmetto State*'s leaving her prize?"

"By those signals," drawled a sallow lieutenant commanding the tender, "Cap'n Rutledge wants the *Clinch* to secure the prize. He's nearest by far. Reckon we might run down and see if we cain't find the *Chicora* and oblige her the same way."

Accordingly, *Ettiwan's* helm was ground over and sent her nosing into an errant bank of fog.

"Damn this mist to hell and back," raged Pilot West.

"Think you can find the *Palmetto State's* prize?" Alistair demanded, haggard eyes flickering up from his notebook.

"Pray God. It'll be like searching for a pin on a sand dune."

CHAPTER XXV **U.S.S.** *Mercedita* [2]

CHICORA'S first shot was fired at 5:45 A.M., the morning of January 31, 1863. Lieutenant Henry Bears, the ram's gunnery officer, a methodical young man, entered that fact in her log. Her objective was a smallish steam schooner, steaming head on, and still half a mile distant. Seconds after *Chicora's* port broadside roared, sections of the Union vessel's bulwarks and top hamper could be seen flying like kindling under some Titan's ax.

To Lieutenant Glassell it was sheer delight to note how smartly *Chicora's* guns were being served: proved that Johnny Tucker's endless drills hadn't been wasted.

Under the thudding reports of her battery the ram's carapace reverberated until its iron sides echoed fit to agonize a man's eardrums. There being no wind, the red-faced gunners couldn't see to shoot; lazy billows of rotten-smelling powder fumes, hanging low, mingled with patches of baffling sea mist, effectively isolating her from her quarry.

Just before the visibility became nil, *Chicora's* crew caught a glimpse of their enemy, still moving, but down by the head and expelling great clouds of smoke and steam through her main hatch.

"So much for one, sir." Lieutenant Glassell smiled at Captain Tucker. "How shall we proceed?"

"Mr. Glassell, order full speed. Pilot, steer four points to port. I hope I noted a side-wheeler approaching."

When the vagrant mist thinned once more, a subdued cheer arose in *Chicora's* pilothouse. A big side-wheeler *was* running in with steam up and guns manned. Promptly, *Chicora* veered to starboard that her nine-inchers in broadside might be brought to bear. The enemy's side blossomed smoke and roundshot screeched by, missing *Chicora's* carapace by a few feet. Lieutenant Bears and several others in the wheel-house looked embarrassed because they had ducked, involuntarily, of course.

Twice *Chicora's* broadside thundered, effectively raking *Keystone State* — a big, converted merchantman. An instant later a puff of wind whisked away tendrils of fog to reveal no less than three other blockaders steering in *Chicora's* direction.

A shrill yell reverberated through the ram's gun deck. A shell from Number Two gun had burst squarely over *Keystone State's* port paddle-wheel housing, knocking it into a jagged mess. Spouting smoke and flame, the Federal cruiser wallowed on the sea.

"That got her, sir," panted Glassell, "She's ours. Why don't she strike? She's helpless."

Henry Bears grabbed Rutledge's arm. "Look, sir, look! Yonder's the flagship!"

Lumbering down from the north came *Palmetto State,* trailing a funereal band of smoke low over the slate-hued waters. Before long the flagship also opened fire. It didn't take long. Hammered by terribly precise gunnery from both Rebel rams, *Keystone State* had no choice but to haul down her colors.

"Sir! Shall we run alongside and take possession?"

Sharply, Captain Tucker shook his head. "Not yet, Mr. Glassell. The enemy can't escape with a smashed paddle wheel. I intend to drive away yonder would-be rescuers."

Two fast steam brigs were bearing down. Tentatively, they were identified as U.S.S. *Stettin* and *Ottawa.* No call yet to be concerned about *Housatonic,* still two miles distant, at the very least.

The ram's starboard battery for the first time was afforded opportunity to prove the value of their training. With extraordinary rapidity they sent shot splashing about the Union warships until they stood to starboard, then turned tail and ran back out to sea at top speed.

"Huh! Goddamn' Abolitionists hain't got no stomach. Watch them skedaddle!"

Although John Tucker implored Hugh Clarke, *Chicora's* chief engineer, to coax a little more speed from his engine, the sluggish ram could in no wise close in.

Yet again the fog veiled sea and sky, so *Chicora* wasted an hour in exploring successive barriers of shimmering gray-white vapors. Once she blundered upon a barkentine looming big as a hill, and found time to deliver a broadside ere the apparition became lost to sight.

By eight o'clock the mists finally cleared away, exposing sandy coastline, great harbor and fortifications alike — and brought bitter disappointment to the Palmetto Squadron.

Off to seaward could be described U.S.S. *Mercedita,* being towed to safety by *Housatonic; Keystone State,* relying on her remaining paddle wheel, limping away behind a screen of consorts. In all probability she would get back for refitting at Port Royal, barring the advent of foul weather.

An attempted pursuit would prove futile. The Confederate commanders knew that. Their vessels lacked speed and fuel to recapture their prizes. All the same they smiled, slapped each other on the back; for the first time since the blockade had been initiated, early in '62, not an undamaged Union ship was anywhere to be observed!

Palmetto State and *Chicora* dropped anchor behind the bar in Swash Channel while the tenders steered for the city with crews mouthing blasphemies because the fog had conspired to prevent their taking possession of the surrendered Yankee vessels.

To a triumphant tooting of her whistle, *Ettiwan* was about to enter the Cooper River when Alistair Bryson, hovering on the brink of collapse, noted *General Clinch* losing headway and, in dull curiosity, watched her lower a smallboat. Why? When *Ettiwan* plowed by, its crew was pulling a human body from the water.

"Mind steering a bit closer, Mr. Chew?" Alistair begged. "Might pick up an item of news."

Ettiwan's captain obliged and steered close. A crew member hollered through cupped hands. "A Yank, or one of we-uns?"

"Hell, no. Hit's only a nigger fisherman name of Saul," shouted back the smallboat's coxwain. "Must have been out in last night's storm."

Ettiwan's pilot squirted tobacco juice off the end of the bridge. "Funny Saul'd go fishin' when it was blowin' so hard. He wasn't no fool."

CHAPTER XXVI **The Consuls**

BY noon after the disappearance of the blockade fleet, Charleston's waterfront was black with people. Everybody wanted to know what had happened. How many Yankee ships had been sunk? How many captured? Had the blockaders really been driven away?

Alistair, on the verge of collapse, but rejoicing over his crammed sketchbook, unsteadily descended *Ettiwan's* gangplank even before it had been fully secured. The first person he recognized was the generously bewhiskered and outwardly impassive British Consul.

People milling about within earshot stopped talking to gaze hopefully at that journalist's pinch-face and badly wrinkled clothes. "What's happened out there?" "Whole Yankee fleet's been sunk, I hear." Voices began calling further back in the throng.

"Is the Union fleet dispersed — beaten?"

"It would appear so, Mr. Bunch," Alistair replied in an undertone. "When we recrossed the bar not a Yankee vessel was to be sighted, anywhere; not even through a telescope."

Mr. Bunch stepped closer and also lowered his voice. "Can you give me the net, the practical results of this action? How many Union ships were sunk or captured and by whom — that sort of thing?"

"Not at present," Alistair shook a head which seemed ready to float away from his shoulders. "Forgive me, sir, but I really must hurry to my office. Anybody off the *Ettiwan* can satisfy your queries. They saw just as much as I."

Someone in the crowd had overheard the words ". . . Not a Yankee ship in sight," and repeated them, evoking shrill Rebel yells and cries of "Hosannah!" "Hurrah!" "Jubilee day is here!" "Hear that? Not a Yankee ship's in sight." "Our rams have sunk the whole Bluebelly fleet!" "Blockade's broken for sure!" "We can trade again!"

162

Louder, ever louder, sounded all along the waterfront the exultant cheering. "Blockade's broken! Jubilee! Jubilee!"

It came as no surprise to Alistair that, as he dogtrotted heavily towards the *Argus*'s building, he should glimpse the French Consul, white-bearded and distinguished-appearing Baron de St. André, restlessly occupying a handsome new landau near the foot of Tradd Street. Well might the diplomat appear excited! If, indeed, the Union's stranglehold on Charleston had been truly broken, then the diplomatic repercussions must be beyond immediate calculation.

Somewhere down near White Point Gardens a battery suddenly commenced to fire salutes, then in rapid succession other batteries, even over on James Island and distant Cummings' Point, followed suit until the racket became so deafening and continuous that chargers ridden by General Beauregard and his staff snorted, reared and caracoled as if in battle, while clattering along Bay Street towards the waterfront.

The Commanding General, obviously, was in a high state of excitement. The Creole's expressive and large, bright-black eyes fairly sparkled and unusual patches of color were darkening his swarthy cheeks. Ever popular, the "Napoleon of the South" was being cheered to the echo by the crowd.

The boys and youthful soldiers now appeared, running along the streets and shouting: "Blockade's been busted wide open! Hurray!"

In their wake shutters swung back and windows banged up to shouts of, "Blockade's broken for sure?"

"Yep. Bluebellies hev really skedaddled."

Breathless, his head really swimming now, Alistair swayed into the *Argus* building gasping, "Thompson! Peters! Sewall! Where in hell are you! Come here. Quick! Quick!" But for answer he received only silence. Everyone, with the exception of Jairus, it appeared, had gone to hear about the great victory at sea. "By God! Just wouldn't those sorry dogs desert at a moment like this?"

Trembling violently, the managing editor dropped behind his desk, snatched up a pencil and commenced shakily to write.

THE BLOCKADE ENDS! — he decided on for a two-column leader — *UNION FLEET ROUTED*. Then, below: OUR RAMS WIN GLORIOUS VICTORY AGAINST GREAT ODDS. TWO ENEMY VESSELS TAKEN!

In his ears swelled the din of varied forms of rejoicing: church bells clanged and detachments of troops fired *feux-de-joie* in various squares and parks. Down the street sounded the hysterical braying of impromptu bands.

Drawing on his will power to the fullest, Alistair consulted his notes and diagrams then, with quivering fingers — he had not eaten all day — drove his pencil on and on. Oh, God, if only his staff hadn't deserted *en masse!* What a useless pack of misfits! No newspaperman worthy of the designation would not long since have come pelting back.

Jairus shuffled in to answer his jangling of a hand bell. "Carry this directly over to the telegraph office and tell Mr. Belknap I want this secretly dispatched to the *Richmond Whig*. On your way, don't let anybody see it — no matter what. Understand? Then see if you can find some of the staff."

"Yessuh, Boss. Ah'll find 'em and send 'em home, iffen dey ain't too daid drunk." Jairus hesitated, yellowish eyes concerned. "Boss, you look mighty hongry and ailing. Cain't I fetch you a little snack?"

"Damn it, no! Get over to the telegraph office as fast as you can run!"

Towards evening the celebrations grew wilder. Bonfires flamed on many street corners, horsemen galloped about firing revolvers into the air and screaming like wildcats skinned alive. A few publicans, overcome by the general excitement, for a while offered free drinks; flags, mostly South Carolina's, fluttered on every available flagstaff or dangled over beautiful, cast-iron balcony railings.

Most colored folk, meantime, slunk quietly along side streets. They dared not refuse to join in the whistling and dancing when confronted by the exhilarated citizens, but it was obvious that they were downcast — the great majority of them. The hand of Pharaoh had been strengthened.

Alistair sought the dirty composing room, reeking of cleaning acids and benzine, and himself prepared the leaders. Alas, there no longer was available beautiful eighteen-pica capital letters, hand carved from laurel or baywood; such were not to be found. Since no staff member appeared, he set leaders and sub-headlines; then he repaired to a type stand, but found that he could work only slowly; his vision was growing

164

cloudy and a long while had elapsed since last he'd handled a printer's tweezers and composing stick.

Gradually, the body of the account took shape. God above! Why hadn't a single damned printer returned to help set perhaps the most significant news in two years — Bull Run, Antietam, and Fredericksburg not excepted? Doggedly, he unlocked and ripped out the edition's lead column, rearranged the chase afterwards, then sought the lead cutter and himself trimmed rules for border and edges. Next he selected the proper riglets and awkwardly evened his type with a rubber mallet. Finally he locked the chase frames and almost smiled. By God, he was going to see an edition on the street tonight — the same day as the victory.

The hunchbacked mulatto returned after a while, sweating and anxious-eyed. "Misto' Bryson, I — I done hunted everywheres an' found some ob our people."

"Good. Hope they hurry," grunted the editor and drew a wide smear of ink across his cheek when he brushed away beads of cold sweat.

"Sorry, suh, but dey all say dey gwine celebrate till tomorrow maw'in'. Dey just wouldn't listen to me. Dis yere town is done gone crazy." From a fold of old newsprint he produced a soggy-looking bread and cheese sandwich. "Better eat dis, Boss, iffen you don't aim to cave in."

"Thanks, I expect you're right." He munched mechanically but had to struggle to down each mouthful. "We'll have to go to press on the Number Two flat-bed. Is there ink in its fountain?"

"Yessuh, Boss. Dey's aplenty."

"All right. Start turning the flywheel."

This flat-bed Campbell was very old, but remained the only press suitable for so shorthanded an operation. Jairus lugged over a stack of clean half-sheets and dumped them onto the feeding table and, grunting under the effort, set in motion a heavy iron flywheel which motivated the machinery. The journalist then fed sheets into the mechanism and noted with relief that, when the wooden fingers had flipped over the printed pages, the resultant impressions looked even as they slid out onto the tray.

He had run off some five hundred copies when Pollard, his principal reporter, appeared, ginger-hued whiskers streaming and wildly excited.

"Mr. Bryson! I've just been down the harbor aboard the *Petrel* —

that British corvette — along with Mr. Bunch," he panted and mopped scarlet features. "The other foreign consuls chartered tugs."

"Great work, Pollard. I feared you were off just celebrating."

"Oh, no, sir. Not with news like this in the air. Know what? Mr. Muñoz, the Spanish Consul, and the French one, just now have announced officially that they consider the blockade to have been broken!"

"My God, that *is* news! What decided them?"

"Why, they sailed 'way out beyond Cummings' Point and didn't even sight the smoke of a Yankee gunboat! I've been told General Beauregard and Commodore Ingraham have sent a dispatch to President Davis solemnly declaring the port of Charleston is open. A proclamation to that effect's to be published in the morning. By God! What a glorious day. Do you mind?" He seized Alistair's ink-smeared hand and pumped it vigorously.

"It will be a still more glorious day," wearily observed the managing editor, "once we've collected some newsboys and got this edition on sale."

CHAPTER XXVII **Divers Dispatches**

IN Richmond, the Honorable Judah P. Benjamin, Secretary of State for the Confederate States of America, settled his short and corpulent body back in a black leather swivel chair, the springs of which protested a little under his weight.

The Secretary sat with arms relaxed along his chair's arms, plump features more waxily pallid than ever, thus seen by lamplight. Thoughtfully, he caressed a prominent and fleshy nose, the shape of which left no doubt about his ancestry. Full lids sagged over his intense and slightly protruberant black eyes.

With the other hand he fiddled absently at a louis d'or gleaming opulently from a thick gold watch chain. Like a miniature cable, it traversed a waistcoat of pearl-gray silk.

A sound of running feet along a corridor leading to his office caused

Mr. Secretary Benjamin to straighten up and lose his somnolent attitude.

"Mr. Benjamin! Mr. Benjamin, sir!" A code clerk burst in, short, straw-colored chin whiskers aquiver. "That rumor received by the *Whig* must be founded on fact."

"Rumor? What rumor? Stop babbling, man, and make sense!"

"It concerns a telegram, great news, forwarded by the *Charleston Argus!*" The code clerk thrust forward a telegraph form. "Please read this, sir."

"Bah! The newspapers are all unreliable." Deliberately, Judah Benjamin opened a case, settled square-lensed, gold-rimmed spectacles in place. Leaning slightly forward, he read:

HEADQUARTERS, LAND AND NAVAL FORCES, CHARLESTON, S. C.
January 31st, 1863

At about five o'clock this morning, the Confederate States naval force on this station attacked the United States blockading fleet off the harbor of the city of Charleston, and sunk, dispersed, or drove off and out of sight for the time the entire hostile fleet.

Therefore we, the undersigned, commanders respectively of the Confederate States naval and land forces in this quarter, do hereby formally declare the blockade by the United States of said city of Charleston, S. C., to be raised by a superior force of the Confederate States from and after this 31st day of January, S. D., 1863.

G. T. BEAUREGARD
General Commanding

D. N. INGRAHAM
Flag Officer Commanding Naval Forces in South Carolina

Official: THOMAS JORDAN
Chief of Staff

The Secretary's expression kindled. "What a truly magnificent achievement!" he said slowly, after rereading the message. "Let us pray this report is accurate — every glorious word of it. In Europe what a profound impression this will make! Sit down, Mr. Haskell, and make note that I order General Beauregard's dispatch to be forwarded to every foreign consul within our jurisdiction." He steepled hands under a dimpled little chin. "Tomorrow, you will cause this dispatch, also, to reach them."

DEPARTMENT OF STATE, RICHMOND
January 31st, 1863

HONORABLE SIR:

I am instructed by the President of the Confederate States of America to inform you that this government has received an official dispatch signed by General Beauregard and Flag Officer Ingraham, commanding the naval forces of the Confederacy on the coast of South Carolina, unequivocally stating that the blockade of the harbor of Charleston has been broken by the complete dispersion and disappearance of the blockading squadron in consequence of a successful attack made upon it by our ironclad rams.

You are doubtless aware that, by the Law of Nations, a blockade when thus broken by superior force, ceases to exist, and cannot be subsequently enforced, unless established *de novo,* with adequate forces and after due notice to Neutral Powers. It has been deemed proper to give you the information herein contained for the guidance of such vessels of your Nation as may choose to carry on commerce with the now open port of Charleston.

Respectfully, your obedient servant,

J. P. BENJAMIN
Secretary of State

The Secretary scarcely had concluded dictating when another messenger burst in.

"Mr. Secretary! I have here a telegram from the Spanish Consul at Charleston verifying General Beauregard's every claim. Señor Muñoz states that, in company with the Baron de St. André, he surveyed the Roads and sighted no Union vessel, even with the aid of binoculars."

"Good. Good. Good! That will lend authority to announcements to be forwarded to Paris and Madrid." He paused, little eyes beady beneath sleepy-appearing lids. A few wrinkles channeled the smooth white expanse of his forehead. "And what does Her Britannic Majesty's Consul have to say in this regard?"

"It appears, sir, that although this Department has, as yet, received no communication from him, Mr. Bunch went out to sea aboard

H.M.S. *Petrel* and came to the same conclusion; there are no longer blockade ships operating off Charleston!"

By the amber radiance created by a green-shaded desk lamp, a smile could be seen to widen over the Secretary of State's pudgy countenance as he heaved himself erect. "Well, gentlemen, this certainly is most welcome news; the best since our victory at Fredericksburg. I must inform Mr. Davis at once. Haskell, you may notify representatives of the press to assemble here in an hour's time."

CHAPTER XXVIII **Captain's Cabin**

DARKNESS had fallen, so, through his cabin's porthole, Raphael Bryson could glimpse the leaping glare of bonfires revealing stark chimneys that marked the site of burned buildings. Raucous outbursts of revelry, around taverns lining the waterfront, evoked a faint grin. They sure were whooping it up ashore, and no mistake about it. Wasn't every day the South scored a great naval victory. Maybe this hysteria was justified, but should so much precious powder be wasted in useless salutes? Remote batteries still were firing minute guns.

Damn! With so many people crowding the streets was there any chance of Julia's finding her way aboard? It was not likely, much as he hated to admit the probability.

"The poor, deluded fools!" he muttered, then went over to uncork a bottle of cognac. "Why make such racket until it's been proved the Yankees really *have* called quits? Flamboyant as he is, whatever could have prompted Gustave Beauregard to authorize such a proclamation? Surely, an officer of his experience shouldn't have deluded himself into imagining that anything more than a minor naval action had been won."

Rafe poured out a jigger of Courvoisier, but didn't drink, only held and warmed the glass while his thoughts raced on. "And what does this so-called victory prove?" he asked himself. "Only what's been known quite a long time. That wooden ships, no matter how heavily armed, can't stand up to ironclads." His free hand strayed up to tug at his neat black goatee. "Wonder how long will be required to bring home the fact that our ironclads are so infernally slow the enemy need only circle at safe range until bad weather breaks or the ram's fuel gives out?"

Heavy, dark brown brows merged, he rang for his steward. "Atkins, is my private gangway properly rigged?"

"Aye, aye, sir."

"And no men on deck, saving the lookout on our stern?"

"Aye, aye, sir."

"Good! And all supplies arrived aboard? Stowed?"

"Aye, aye, sir. We can sail the minute you're so minded, sir."

Well, he wasn't so minded, not while even the least possibility remained that Julia might reappear, silent as a wraith and beautiful as a goddess, to share this cabin's cozy warmth for tonight.

"Atkins, pass the word for Mr. Brazenose to hold all hands aboard as they return."

"Aye, aye, sir."

Irritably Rafe sipped at the fragrant, mahogany-hued liqueur, then commenced pacing back and forth. He heard the ship's bell sound. Damn those prancing idiots on shore! Here it was nine o'clock and no Julia. Surprisingly, he found himself growing taut with expectancy, to catch the first whisper of skirts along the deck. How sensuous a pleasure to press her close, then, the cabin lamp turned low, to explore, to undo the fragrant intricacies of her garments. Unbelievable though it appeared, he must be coming really to love Julia. Outwardly, that young woman seemed the coolly aloof and charmingly reserved aristocrat, yet, all in an instant, she could become transformed into a tumultuous, ardent creature shamelessly avid for love.

No longer able to endure such suspense, Rafe stepped out onto his flying bridge to scan shadows sketched across the blockade-runner's narrow deck, and then the wharf. Like any delighted schoolboy, he started on realizing that a shawl-muffled female figure was flitting towards the forward gangplank.

A furious disappointment seized him: that wasn't Julia down there! The woman below walked stooped over, and wore a bandanna knotted about her head. Moreover, her skirts sagged unevenly towards the left. Damnation! This must be a servant bearing some message from the Lambkin residence, for the shapeless figure hesitated not at all, but crossed the gangplank and commenced silently to ascend the bridge ladder.

The *Grey Ghost*'s master stepped back into his cabin — and, in seething disappointment, was pouring a second cognac when the brass-bound door swung quickly open.

"Rafe! My own darling! Rafe!"

The leanly powerful figure's jaw sagged ludicrously. Julia Livesey had stuffed enough material under some servant's plain brown house-gown completely to distort the proportions of her own magnificent figure; a yellow cotton handkerchief concealed her lustrous tresses and her fair complexion had been darkened by an uneven application of burnt cork.

Every sense stirred by Julia's unique, subtly erotic aura, he embraced her so fiercely as to make her cry out, then go limp in his arms.

"Take care, my beloved," she warned breathlessly, "else you'll streak my disguise, and I must return as I came. The crowds have gone quite mad. I can't stay long."

He shot the door bolt, then took Julia's hands and stood back to gaze hungrily upon the grotesque figure she made. "Do you know? I rather fancy you like this. They say *mulatas* make the liveliest sort of bedfellows."

"Oh-h! You're wicked to say such a thing — but I like it, too."

While, deftly, he released a cheap brass brooch securing the shawl, her black gloved hands briefly framed his features; then she stood on tiptoe to kiss him and left a dark smudge. "Oh, Rafe! Wasn't I foolhardy beyond all description to come here — tonight of all times? Still, I simply had to be with you to celebrate the victory."

Presently she stepped from a pool of garments lying on the cabin's floor, blackened face a preposterous contrast to the pallid sheen presented by the rest of her body.

"Darling," came Julia's drowsy voice, "when will you be sailing?"

Rafe grinned, propped himself up on a pillow and pushed a damp lock of hair from his eyes. "In about three days' time."

"Oh, dearest, why must you wait so long? I heard the *Grey Ghost* was ready to sail at any hour."

"Nevertheless, we still lack certain supplies, my pet," he told her indolently.

171

"I can scarce wait," she whispered in his ear. "I have everything I plan to take along all packed and ready, so I can appear aboard within thirty minutes of the time your message reaches me. You will send Abrahams, won't you?"

"Naturally. He's known about the Lambkin place and keeps a close mouth, so I've heard."

Long since it had been discovered that Abrahams, at present employed aboard the *Grey Ghost* as an assistant engineer, for quite a while before hostilities broke out had worked aboard Mr. Horatio Livesey's line of coastal steamers. Julia, one evening, had recognized him loafing along the waterfront and had even recalled his captaining a small steamer which, on occasion, had transported gay parties to picnics on some little islands below Beaufort.

"Don't fret, my precious. I'll send word by Abrahams the instant we're ready."

CHAPTER XXIX **Back Copy**

THE Weird Sisters, it would seem, continued to smile upon beleaguered Charleston for, right after the blockade had been declared lifted, *Isaac Smith,* a fine new Federal gunboat, was ambushed and captured in the Stono River after a brisk little battle and her company of one hundred and sixty-five disconsolate souls imprisoned in Charleston's hopelessly overcrowded jail.

Immediately, Naval Headquarters announced that the prize would be refitted quickly and commissioned under the name of *Stono,* a prediction so pleasing to the *Argus's* managing editor that, personally, he wrote the account.

He still glowed under Virginius Roadheaver's praise for having sent that dispatch so promptly to Richmond. The *Argus's* prestige had never been higher. In fact, the publisher took occasion to celebrate the twin victories with such bibulous enthusiasm that he failed to appear in his office for two whole days.

Alistair would have been feeling happier than in a long while, save for one thing: his continued inability to extract that information which must be concealed somewhere in that back copy of the *Bahamas Gazette*. Why else had this newspaper been clipped to the incriminating manifests and secured from casual inspection?

After producing a key and unlocking the small safe in a corner of his office, Alistair yet again commenced to analyze, from every possible angle, articles, editorials and advertisements he was beginning to know by heart.

An errant shaft of sunlight, surprisingly brilliant and warm for a winter's day, lanced through grimy panes to illumine the crumpled and water-stained sheet under inspection. The journalist's attention wandered, came to rest upon the *Gazette*'s shadow projected across his desk's top. Here and there, within its sable oblong, showed a scattering of tiny pinpoints of light! When, his heart soaring, he wheeled about and held the newspaper at right angles to the sunbeam *myriad more minute bright dots became visible.*

Breathless, he then pressed the *Gazette* tight against a windowpane and almost whooped in his excitement. Whole lines of glowing little spots now had sprung into existence. These punctures, he reasoned, couldn't possibly be of an accidental nature because they appeared in parallel lines.

Recollections of Crumbacker's returned in graphic clarity: the desk drawer's splintering, that sudden sound of feet on the stairs, the watchman's startled eyes and the flash of his shotgun, and the pain. Oh, yes. The pain.

"By God, I wonder, I wonder!" The newspaperman kept the little newspaper held to the light, and penciled a ring about each glowing pinpoint; then he reversed the quarter sheet and recircled all the dots. Perspiring gently, and all at once feeling nowhere near so fatigued, Alistair smoothed the *Gazette* on his desk, promptly to discover that each perforation had been made just above a certain letter, not below, or to either side of it. When copying the succession of marked letters on the front page's side they spelt nothing; but when he reversed the sheet and copied the circled letters, they immediately made sense.

Some indicated letters appeared in advertisements, others in items of news, or even in funeral notices, or "in memoriams." When he had noted all the indicated letters he read:

TOMESSERSCRUMBACKERANDCOMPANYCASESNUMBEREDSIXTYTHREE
EIGHTEENINDICATEMERCHANDISECONSIGNEDTOMESSERSATRIEGLERAW
WASSONSTGLAMBKINCHARLESTONOPERATINGASEXCALIBURTRADING

Only a few more moments were required to subdivide this message into intelligible words. Then indeed did air come hissing into Alistair's lungs.

TO MESSERS CRUMBACKER AND COMPANY CASES NUMBERED SIXTY-THREE, EIGHTEEN INDICATE MERCHANDISE CONSIGNED TO MESSERS A. T. RIEGLER, A. W. WASSON, ST. G LAMBKIN, CHARLESTON OPERATING AS EX-CALIBUR TRADING.

Lambkin? There was only one family of that name in the city. God Almighty! Serena's father, the renowned orator and patriot, must be a callous speculator!

Another paragraph materialized. When properly spaced and punctuated it read:

NUMBERS TWELVE, FORTY-TWO, SEVENTY-FOUR INDICATE FREIGHT DES-TINED ACCOUNT MESSERS W. Z. RACKLEY, T. J. FISHPAW, L. N. BRUGH OPERATING AS COLUMBIAN IMPORT COMPANY, RICHMOND.

Dizzy with excitement, the journalist sagged suddenly in his chair. Well, here was positive proof that he hadn't been barking up the wrong tree that night in Crumbacker's. God in Heaven! What a tempest was going to blow once it became known that such men as Brigadier General William Z. Rackley, Judge August Riegler, Senator T. J. Fishpaw, Major Isaac N. Brugh — a famous Lincoln-hating orator — not to mention Major St. George Lambkin, that devoted patriot and pillar of Charleston society, were implicated. Imagine these distinguished gentlemen quietly amassing great wealth through the importation of goods useless to the defense of a nation fighting for its life.

Alistair sensed himself to be profoundly elated — and a little frightened, too. Dare the *Argus* expose to obloquy the names of men so prominent? Dark and deep-set eyes brooding, the editor sat staring across the office and recalling those seemingly endless lists of casualties he'd ordered posted on the bulletin boards or the muffled sobs, shrill, anguished wails testifying that still another woman knew she must now face life alone. . . . How many battles and skirmishes had been need-lessly lost through the want of munitions and basic equipment? How many brave men had perished in agony, lacking even elementary med-ical supplies?

A deep, deep breath so expanded Alistair's chest that those slowly healing holes in his shoulder began to itch and burn like fiery mouths. He arose, went over to the window and stood there long enough to reach a decision. He would set the article himself; it would be brief and factual. He would not editorialize at all. Let his readers draw their own conclusions.

CHAPTER XXX **Departure of the *Grey Ghost***

THAT joyous, delirious sense of liberation which had swept the city proved, alas, to be as ephemeral as that buoyant exhilaration which accompanies the drinking of too much champagne; and, *en masse*, Charlestonians suffered an identical depression by consequence. Scarcely thirty hours after "the *Mercedita* affair," as the action was being termed, cruisers appeared, to resume their relentless prowling off Charleston Bar — albeit more warily.

It was significant, too, that grim old Rear-Admiral Du Pont, in Port Royal, had assigned to this duty only swift, heavily armed vessels, surely capable of outrunning the Confederate ironclads.

As Dabney Seymour privately observed, captains of wooden ships would find no reason for closing in; they had merely to cruise out of gunshot until the rams exhausted their fuel, or were forced to retire through the advent of heavy weather.

Sadly, posters reproducing General Beauregard's and Flag Officer Ingraham's proclamation were ripped down; now little laughter sounded in streets and taverns. All the same only a few people admitted to a sense of hopelessness. Everyone else felt sure that, eventually, a way could be found permanently to drive away those tenacious Blue cruisers.

Dorcas Mullinix and her good friend Mrs. Bentley, chairwoman of the Soldier's Beneficial Association, decided that since they were passing so near to the Brysons', they might call and hear Alistair's eye-witness account of that hollow victory beyond the bar.

"Poor Drummie is so cast down that neither surrendered Yankee ship was secured and brought in," the widow was remarking as, briskly, they turned into Mary Street. "His ship's company now talk only about the day the *Charleston* will be ready. She's bigger, you know, Addie, and that nice Dabney Seymour says she's designed to be much faster than either of our present rams. Surely, she'll be able to drive away the enemy."

"I am sure she will," declared Mrs. Bentley, primly resettling her bonnet. A sharp-faced, nervous-mannered little woman, she suggested nothing so much as a hen sparrow. "Only last night I was conversing with Captain Gray of the Submarine Defense and *he* spoke of another scheme to reopen the port.

"He mentioned our Navy's building a lot of rafts mounting a number of torpedoes. These are in addition to the torpedo boats we hear so many rumors about. Frankly, Dorcas, I don't know much about those new boats," Mrs. Bentley admitted, "but they do sound formidable. Maybe *they* will be able to drive the Yankees from our shores."

"Torpedo boats? Yes, certainly, those must be the 'Davids' Drummie was talking about." Mrs. Mullinix managed full gray skirts over a mud puddle. "He says Lieutenant Glassell knows what he's about, says they'll do the trick."

In unison two ladies' lace-trimmed bonnets inclined towards an acquaintance across the street.

"This is indeed sweet of you, Addie," the widow smiled, "finally to give in and call on Mrs. Bryson. She's really a dear child, and always cheerful, and so generous with her talents. I fear she has been much misunderstood."

Mrs. Bentley's thin shoulders squared themselves a trifle. "It's only because I've known you so long, Dorcas Mullinix, and respect your great understanding of human nature that I'm about to call upon an *actress!*"

"Now, now, Addie, actress or not, I assure you that she is a fine woman. Frivolous though India Bryson may appear on occasion, none is more steadfastly devoted to her husband — and to the Cause."

They entered Colonel Ramsay's brown-cobbled driveway and, collecting skirts, ascended the "welcoming arms" stairway and paused at

176

its marble landing. Mrs. Mullinix's hand was closing over a bell knob of silvered glass when Mrs. Bentley uttered a sibilant gasp and her fingers closed over the widow's wrist with convulsive strength.

"Don't ring!" she whispered fiercely.

"Why not?"

"Just look through this window!" The afternoon sun was shining brilliantly into a small sitting room situated to the right of the front door, creating a merciless radiance which revealed, to the last detail, a man and woman swaying in close embrace near the center of the room.

"Merciful Heavens!" choked Dorcas Mullinix — for, beyond question, India Bryson was nude to the waist and writhing amid a flurry of disordered garments within the muscular arms of Rascal Rafe. The widow remained rooted in horror just long enough to reassure herself that, indeed, she was seeing what she believed she saw.

The two inside must have glimpsed those bonnet-framed faces, for India began hurriedly to pull material over her breasts once the surprised couple had sprung apart.

"Why, Rafe! What an unexpected pleasure!" Smilingly, India stepped back from her front door. "Isn't it the most glorious afternoon?"

"Yes. The best I think I have ever known." When, after closing the front door, he kissed her lips, India didn't think too much about it. After all, Rafe had kissed her thus before, and usually in Alistair's presence; but now she noted Rafe's heightened color — also that, for the first time in many days, he was garbed in his merchant officer's dark blue uniform.

"Well, darling," he chuckled, "at last I have come to claim you. The *Grey Ghost* sails at sundown."

India's fringed and luminous dark eyes slowly rounded while her smile faded. " 'Claim me'? Whatever are you talking about? Are you joking?"

"Of course not, you adorable sweet simpleton. Surely you've been anticipating this moment as impatiently as I." Without ceasing to clasp her tight and, stimulated by her struggles, he kissed her mouth repeatedly. "I came the instant I made sure that Alistair's at Fort Beauregard and won't return until late tonight."

"Let me go!" Furious, India placed hands against his chest and

177

pushed with all her strength. It was to no avail. "Can you be drunk?"

"Naturally not! I'm taking you away from this dull, moldering place to Nassau, England — all over this great and wonderful world."

India flinched violently away, and again attempted to break free. "You must have lost your mind, Rafe!"

"Oh, no I haven't. But if you wish to play the coy damsel a bit" — he laughed a little wildly — "why, I'll indulge your histrionic talents because I know how truly you love me."

"But I don't love you — not that way. Please let go, you hurt me."

"What a great actress! You sound almost convincing, but I've read the love in your eyes a hundred times and felt it in the way you meet my gaze and my lips. It's been torture not to have taken you to bed long since."

Seriously frightened now, India commenced to twist violently within his grasp. A seam of her bodice parted, made a small, snarling sound. Then some buttons clattered upon the parquet floor. "Let me go," she panted. "For God's sake be honest, Rafe! Have I ever said anything to make you think I might desert Alistair?"

"Maybe not your lips, but your eyes and this glorious body of yours have told me as much."

"But, that's wrong! All wrong," wailed India when dislodged hairpins released her waist-long hair into a sable waterfall. "Oh, please! Please! Let me go!"

"When I release you, you'll go pack; you won't need much. We can replenish your wardrobe in Nassau." Eyes intense and gorged, he spoke in urgent undertones. "Can't you understand, India? I must, and will, have you — I need you so."

In desperation she hammered small fists upon his broad blue chest. In the excesses of her terror she began to hiss protests in Spanish. "Váya! Rélajamé! I loathe you! Que clase de pechero! Puerco! Now I know why you are called as you are."

For so slight a person, India, because of her dancing, proved uncommonly strong. Frantically, her supple young body twisted this way and that, but he gripped her bodice and camisole's top — as usual she had disdained the use of a corset while at home — he laughed louder, more wickedly triumphant when, bit by bit, her upper clothing gave way until her shoulders gleamed bare.

"God, what a *tigrita* — what a superb actress! No, don't keep on trying to pull away, I am not letting you go!"

"But you will, *malvado!*" She spat into his eyes and lunged sidewise to a snarl of violently ripped fabrics. Cool air rushed over rose-pointed contours suddenly exposed. But still she could not quite break free, so they reeled and spun across the floor in a grotesque sort of polka.

"You never were more maddeningly seductive," he panted, then crushed her so effectively that her arms became immobilized between her naked bosom and the cruelly hard buttons on his tunic.

The girl's features then became contorted into what might have passed for a lascivious smile. India cramped her head aside from his questing lips, cried in a shaking voice, "Alistair will kill you!"

"Other men have sworn to do the same, yet, somehow, I'm still all of a piece. And now, dearest India, have we had enough of this play acting?" Peering into her suffused and hair-streaked features, he read a new and terrified expression.

"*Señor Dios!* People at the window!"

His head snapped about, and, sure enough, two bonneted heads were clearly to be recognized.

"Blast them to hell!"

Instantly, he let her go and set about reordering his uniform while, sobbing hysterically, India strove to gather up the tattered fabrics into a covering.

Dizzied as if she had executed a series of pirouettes much too fast, India realized that Dorcas Mullinix, her one steadfast friend, had looked in upon this outrageous scene.

To the weeping girl's utter astonishment Rafe appeared inordinately pleased. "Now that those dear ladies have detected us in *flagrante delicto*," he chuckled, "you will *have* to sail with me. You will, won't you?"

India shuddered, swayed a little. "Oh, yes. I've no choice. I will, I'll join you tonight, but I must come by myself."

"That's my girl! You must be aboard by eight sharp," he directed and kissed her gently. "I daren't miss the tide, not with those damn' Yankee cruisers prowling offshore again."

"I'll be on time — the theater teaches one that." She smiled tremulously. "Now, in pity's name, leave at once!"

"How wonderful it will be to quit this gossip-ridden city." He slapped her playfully on the rear, then, retrieving his cap, descended lightly to the street.

CHAPTER XXXI Drunken Dick Shoal Again

SELDOM had First Officer Brazenose observed his captain quite so morose as when the *Grey Ghost* commenced to steam quietly across Charleston Harbor.

Something, or, as Mr. Brazenose more correctly conjectured, someone, must have crossed Captain Bryson in no minor fashion. Nothing, of course, but some frill could be responsible for this dangerous delay in getting under way. Why, the runner actually hadn't been backed out of her slip until Pilot Makin, flatly and profanely, had refused to dawdle a moment longer, if the runner were not to postpone her departure another twenty-four hours.

"Damn' tide waits for no man — or woman," he'd growled.

Eagerly, Mr. Brazenose snuffed a faint whiff of salt air fresh in from the Atlantic. He rejoiced. He'd a bellyful of Charleston, hoped to God next time the Cap'n would head into Wilmington or Galveston, maybe. The first twinges of apprehension tugged at his mouth's corners. Before long the *Grey Ghost* would begin feeling her way through the inner cordon. Out yonder cannon were waiting, big guns which, in a twinkle, could cripple a ship or snuff out a fellow's life but it would be finer than silk, mused the first officer, to cruise emerald-hued waters again, to tie up once more under the Bahamas' warm sun and to taste fresh fruit, and liquor which wasn't raw corn whisky.

Mr. Brazenose was impatient, also, to learn what his privately owned cotton might bring. Maybe fifty pounds sterling the bale? It wasn't impossible — prices had been soaring when the *Grey Ghost* had cleared Fort William Point. If so, he'd net a profit of nearly 400 per cent and he would be well on his way towards affluence.

Raphael Bryson remained at the starboard end of the flying bridge; he still could not credit having been so mistaken. Who'd ever have dreamed India would be such an utter idiot to linger where, inevitably, she must undergo the worst sort of public scorn and degradation?

In short, angry strides he patrolled the bridge with collar raised against a brisk night wind. Moodily, he watched the dim loom of Castle Pinckney appear off to port. There was only one bright fact to dwell on: weather conditions were made to order. There was no fog, yet the sky was so heavily overcast by low, fast-moving clouds that not a single star was visible.

"Show yer recognition signals," the pilot's hoarse voice ordered from the wheelhouse. The quartermaster then hoisted four lanterns which would apprise gunners in Battery Bee and Forts Moultrie and Beauregard that this darkly speeding vessel was off on a friendly errand. Blue, yellow, blue and red, the lights jiggled gaily to the beat of the great paddle wheels.

Rafe strode over to the pilothouse and instructed Mr. Brazenose to call him the moment the ship entered Sullivan's Channel and, in baffled resentment, sought his cabin. While removing his cloak he noted, without interest, that crackers and cheese already had been set out by his steward. With a wry smile he noted two glasses and a bottle of champagne chilling in its bucket of precious ice.

He was lighting a seegar when a subtle noise behind him caused him to whirl about. The door of his clothes closet had opened just a crack. "Is it all safe to come out?"

"Who the devil's in there . . . ?" His voice faded when in the closet sounded a rustling as of silken petticoats and slim fingers slipped around the door's edge. The blockade-runner's heart soared like a buck deer clearing a windfall. India! India was in there. He hadn't been wrong after all!

Had a derelict torpedo struck his ship Rafe could not have been more stunned than when that closet door swung open. Characteristically his recovery was superb, instantaneous.

He rushed forward, beaming, feverishly impatient to take the apparition into his arms.

"Welcome aboard, Julia, darling. I hope it wasn't too infernally stuffy in there."

"Oh, Rafe! My dearly beloved, Rafe," she whispered. "I declare I most fainted with delight when Abrahams came to fetch me; I told him to, the minute you were ready to sail."

181

It would have required a person far more astute than Julia Livesey ever to have suspected Raphael Bryson of having taken no part in the dispatching of Abrahams.

Timidly, her fingers arose and stroked his crisp, dark brown sideburns. "Oh, Raphael, darling, I'm going to make you the most devoted, faithful and adoring wife any man has ever had. Just you wait and see."

CHAPTER XXXII **Explosion**

AS a rule the *Charleston Argus*, like its rivals, the *Courier* and the *Mercury*, appeared upon the streets around seven of the morning. Then ragged little Negroes would scamper about town distributing the edition to regular subscribers; others would wander the streets shrilly hawking their supply; the rest would depart to peddle copies around various brothels, hotels, barracks, and taverns.

On reaching his office, Alistair noted, to his mild surprise, that Jairus must have tidied up his desk. The papers on it had been neatly stacked, but in an unfamiliar sequence. The editor seated himself and tried to decide whether it served the best interests of military security to describe, in detail, alterations being made to the recently captured *Isaac P. Smith*. But he couldn't. His mind kept reverting to one question: how soon would various interested parties hear about a certain close-set and inconspicuously situated article?

Nervously, the editor picked up his current edition, dated February 3, 1863, and reread the article.

QUESTIONABLE IMPORTATIONS

It has come to the attention of this publication that much valuable space aboard blockade-runners for some time arriving in this port has been pre-empted by freight consignments of a nature which can contribute less than nothing to the successful prosecution of our War for Independence.

The *Argus* has ascertained that two importing firms are particularly remiss in this more than questionable traffic.

Instead of arms, ammunition, munitions, clothing, boots and medicines, the Excalibur Trading Company of this City, and the Columbian Importing Company of Richmond, are importing huge shipments of ladies' finery, hats, fancy liquors, costly materials and luxury goods of every description.

It will, no doubt, come as an unpleasant surprise for our readers to learn the names of the principal shareholders in these companies. The *Argus* prints these names solely in the hope that these gentlemen will see the error of their ways and in the future will desist from such unpatriotic activities.

Alistair drew a deep breath and noted that his ink-spotted hands had begun to shake so much as to cause edges of the copy to rattle softly.

The principal shareholders in the Excalibur Trading Company are Judge August T. Riegler, Mr. Archer Wasson and Major St. George Lambkin.

He let the sheet fall and sat back, lips pursed. Um-m. And just how would Brother Donald react to this summary exposure of his fiancée's father? *Semper Veritas* was the motto appearing on the *Argus* masthead: "Always the truth." To steady himself, Alistair continued reading and drew another deep breath.

The Columbian Import Company of Richmond, we learn, is headed by Brigadier General Paul Rackley, Senator T. T. Fishpaw and Major I. N. Brough of the Sanitary Corps' Headquarters.

Well, there it was. God alone knew what now would come of it. He glanced at the watch Rafe had presented and a whimsical smile curved his lips. Then he scanned its fob — that Christmas gift of India's. Um-m. Time indicated was 8:45.

"Well, here it comes," he muttered. A brittle clattering of hurrying hoofs on cobbles drew near.

His supposition proved entirely correct, for, glancing below, he recognized Judge Riegler's glossy green-and-black phaeton being pulled up below.

183

The Judge descended with an alacrity which belied his advanced years; then, purple-faced, followed an enormous belly across the sidewalk.

The phaeton barely had pulled away before a pair of horsemen turned into narrow little Charlotte Street at a gallop. Um-m. These riders would be the Honorable Archer Wasson, accompanied by his eldest son and partner. Once they had secured their mounts to the newspaper's well-gnawed hitching rail their outraged voices rang loud.

Jairus appeared, yellowish eyes round in alarm.

"Misto' Bryson, suh! Misto' Bryson! Misto' Roadheavuh want you. Bettah come down direckly. He mighty wrathful."

Alistair smiled wanly. "Very well. The condemned man did not eat a hearty breakfast."

"What dat, suh?"

Alistair drew himself up and, squaring his shoulders, thought hard about those thousands of needlessly ill-armed and hungry men shivering and dying in the field.

The publisher sat behind his desk, his three fat chins gone a sickly shade of grayish-pink. Confronting him stood Judge Riegler and Archer Wasson and his son.

"Who conceived this abominable, lying article?" roared Mr. Roadheaver.

"I did, sir."

"How dared you print such a — a monstrous calumny?"

"Because the facts contained in it are true," replied Alistair coldly. "I would have submitted it for your approval yesterday, sir, but you — er — were indisposed." He'd been drunker than usual, all day.

"Then you are not in the custom, Mr. Roadheaver, of allowing your employees to publish such accusatory articles on their own responsibility?" The Judge's little eyes narrowed, shone threateningly metallic.

"Indeed not, Your Honor," babbled Virginius Roadheaver. "I — I really don't know what to say."

Mr. Wasson, a sallow, flat-faced fellow grown arrogant through the rapid accumulation of great wealth, shook his fist under the publisher's colorful nose. "Well, you'd damn' well better *find* something to say. As publisher, you're responsible for what appears in this pitiful rag of yours, so it's you my son and I are going to sue for every penny you own."

184

His tirade was interrupted by the arrival of a sheep-faced lawyer who said he was representing Major Lambkin.

"You will presently be made to discover, Mr. Roadheaver," said he, glaring about, "that in this state there are severe laws against libel."

In a paroxysm of despair Roadheaver waved plump hands until the dirty edges of his cuffs appeared. "Gentlemen! Gentlemen! You must believe that I'm as miserably unhappy over this unfortunate article as are any of you. I — I'll publish an extra bearing an immediate retraction and any apology you gentlemen may dictate."

Cheeks gone crimson as an angry turkeycock's wattles, the big-bellied publisher bore down upon his editor. "You, you miserable idiot! How dared you slander these upright and deeply patriotic gentlemen?"

"I wrote only the truth," Alistair insisted steadily, and became conscious of a curious buzzing sensation in his finger tips. A sense of impending menace lay in the baleful stare of the only man who thus far had voiced no threats, nor had even spoken, for that matter.

"Since you claim to have written only the truth," Major Lambkin's lawyer was purring, "you surely must have proof of allegations so serious?"

Mr. Roadheaver gripped Alistair by the lapels. A terrible fear shone in his bloodshot little eyes as he shouted, "Do you have real proof?"

"Certainly, sir. Otherwise I should not have felt justified in printing the accusation."

Judge Riegler, who, as some political enemy had said, "wore the noble profile of a decadent Roman emperor," glanced briefly, questioningly, in the younger Mr. Wasson's direction, then, receiving an inscrutable smile, diverted his attention to what Major Lambkin's lawyer was saying.

"I demand to see your proof at once."

"If you gentlemen will accompany me, I will produce the evidence. It will prove conclusive, rest assured of that."

The whole group followed Alistair upstairs to his bleak little office.

The voices of newsboys hawking the now celebrated edition sounded shrill and somewhat taunting as the editor, very pale and drawn of expression, produced the brass key to his safe, knelt and presently swung back its door.

When Alistair peered within, it seemed as if some tough had brought a blackjack down on the back of his neck. The pigeonhole in which he had preserved the incriminating manifests and the *Bahamas Gazette* was devoid of contents.

Aware of angry attention, Alistair fumbled faster and faster through the safe and, bathed in chill perspiration, ended by raking a shapeless mass of papers onto the gritty floor.

"Well?" growled Mr. Roadheaver, "And where is this 'conclusive' evidence of yours? You'd better find it in a hurry."

The kneeling figure exhaled sharply. "But I locked them in there last night!"

"*What* was supposed to be in there?" coldly demanded Mr. Wasson, Senior.

"Manifests from the *Grey Ghost* and the *Wild Dayrell!*" Alistair burst out wildly, then stood up. "Those manifests, sir, showed only code numbers to describe the contents of certain cases and barrels. With them was a Bahamian newspaper which, again in code, named the consignees —" He swung to confront this semicircle of hot-eyed men.

"I wish I could, but I cannot, congratulate you, sir, upon a most consummate bit of play acting," observed Judge Riegler, suddenly mopping his brow. "You almost had me convinced you'd evidence of some sort to back up your calumnies."

"They were stolen during the night," Alistair insisted hotly. "I tell you, I *had* proof."

"That's nonsense, my dear young man, and you know it," bleated the sheep-faced lawyer. "Mr. Roadheaver, do you see how irresponsible your employee has proved himself? I think you had better retain counsel and prepare to defend yourself against a suit for libel."

The younger Wasson was big, plainly dressed, and had an Indianlike look about him — high cheekbones, coppery complexion and straight black hair. Lips flattened over large white teeth, he stepped forward. "To hell with libel suits, Pa. This paper's got no money to satisfy a verdict. It's been skating on the rim of bankruptcy a long while. *I* aim to take judgment out of this damn young liar's hide."

"Shut your mouth, Paul!" his father snapped, all at once ominously calm and self-confident. "Don't know how you feel, August, but Mr. Bryson's charges are too absurd to be dignified by a horsewhipping." He

186

turned to Judge Riegler. "I propose to do nothing further in this matter except demand that this misguided fool be discharged."

The publisher fairly babbled assurance. "Collect your things, Bryson, and clear out. Don't you ever put foot on these premises again!" Piteously, he rolled his eyes. "Now I — I trust you other gentlemen will be as generous as Mr. Wasson and won't sue — if I publish an immediate apology?"

"Ha-hum!" Major Lambkin's lawyer left off fraying a long gray goatee, spoke precisely. "Of course I cannot certainly express my client's views on the subject, but I believe he would be inclined not to prosecute if this fellow is made to leave Charleston at once; so precipitate a departure would be tantamount to a confession of guilt."

"And that, sir, is exactly why I refuse to run away," came the journalist's level tones. "What I wrote is the truth, plain and simple. Since Mr. Roadheaver has discharged me, for which I cannot blame him, perhaps it is just as well, since I shall not swerve from my efforts to prove my assertions."

"You, sir," observed the younger Wasson with a thin smile, "are either a very brave man — or a foolhardy idiot; we shall soon learn which. Come, Pa, let's get down to the warehouse."

CHAPTER XXXIII **Bad News**

INDIA Bryson wrung out a pair of her husband's long woolen drawers and hung them to dry over the kitchen stove. She moved in a numbed misery which had gripped her since the preceding afternoon. So far, Alistair could not have been told, but certainly he must learn ere long. She was beginning to think that she should have explained straight away what had chanced, even if the *Grey Ghost* had sailed and it was therefore impossible to obtain Raphael's corroboration.

That Mrs. Bently must have disseminated the scandalous news with speed she deduced through the stony stares with which her bows were received by certain women who, when she had ventured out to make necessary purchases, had looked completely through her.

Frowning, she commenced to rub a chemise upon the washboard. It isn't fair! she thought in futile rebellion. Why, oh why, had her callers chosen that one, ambiguous instant to peer in? Had they arrived five minutes earlier or five minutes later, there could have been no possibility of misconstruing the situation. Oh, dear!

Footsteps were sounding along the driveway. She dried her hands, hoped against hope Dorcas might be calling to grant her the opportunity of offering some explanation. But Alistair strode in, haggard of expression. His usually erect shoulders were sagging and his deep-set eyes burning as if under a recurrence of fever.

"Why, darling, whatever in the world are you doing home at this hour?" India faltered. Obviously he had been given some garbled tale of her being seen, seminude, in Rafe's embrace.

In the doorway he paused and, using the back of his hand, pushed a strand of hair from his forehead. "India, I fear I bring very bad news. I have just been discharged from the *Argus*."

"Oh, how dreadful for you, my poor darling!" she quavered, struggling in violent crosscurrents of relief and anxiety. "How could that drunkard, that odious Mr. Roadheaver, do such a thing? And after all you've done for his newspaper. What in the world happened?"

After dipping up a cup of water and drinking thirstily, he sank onto a sagging cane-bottomed chair and, in a dull monotone, related the whole story — from the time his suspicions concerning the luxury goods had been aroused, to the moment of his summary dismissal.

"I should have suspected something was wrong when I found my desk had been disturbed during the night. I wonder which one hired the thief." He summoned a bitter smile. "Thief? That's rich. *I'm* a thief, and hoist by my own petard!"

"Oh, Alistair, how awful! How could anybody have got the key to your safe?"

"Oh, it's a simple affair and would require a competent locksmith no time at all to open. Of course, I should never have left the evidence there. I fear you've married a colossal imbecile."

"Oh, my dear!" she raised great, vital dark eyes and ran over to put arms about him. "Always remember that I deem whatever you do to be only honorable and right."

188

He kissed her in profound gratitude, felt a measure of his despair depart. "Thank you, India dear. Now let me decide what had best be done."

They sat in miserable silence for a while, India gently stroking his unruly black hair.

"Done? Surely you don't intend to remain in Charleston?"

"I do."

"But those men and their friends are all powerful; they know that you printed the truth about them." Fiercely, she clung to him. "They won't dare let you live to prove it. We must leave. I'll go start packing at once."

"No. I'm not going to scuttle off with my tail between my legs."

After a while India admitted the futility of further argument; not for nothing was Alistair Bryson descended from a long line of Scots, stubbornly loyal to their convictions.

"What kind of position can you find? No newspaper here will hire you."

"Possibly I'll apply for work at Theodore Stoney's shipyard."

India's taut expression lessened. "Isn't that where those torpedo boats are under construction — the ones called 'Davids'?"

"Exactly. I intend to apply for a job as a draftsman — I once studied mechanical drawing, as well as free hand."

"I'm sure Mr. Stoney will give you an opportunity." She brightened. "Are these boats called 'Davids' because they are so little and the Yankee ships so big?"

"David and Goliath, eh? Now that's a reasonable supposition, but, actually, they're named after an inventor named David Bushnell. During the Revolution, he experimented with a torpedo boat which attacked a British payship in the East River and, I think, sank her. I'll go apply for the job after dinner — no use wasting time."

"Oh, Alistair, I do admire you! It takes so much quiet courage to do what you've done."

"Where's Dorcas keeping herself?" Using a penknife, Alistair sliced a sliver from a hard heel of a cheese. "She hasn't dropped in for quite some time."

"Why — why," India drew a quivering breath and looked hard at him, but he kept his attention on his food. "I was going to tell you something in that connection." Her heart surged. Now! Now was the moment. She had drawn breath to start her account when a furious hammering sounded on the front door.

"I'll go see who it is. Don't let the stew scorch." India sped upstairs.

"Where is Alistair?" By those three words alone, Alistair knew his brother must be in one of his fortunately rare cold rages.

"Why — why, whatever is wrong?" India quivered. "Do come down to the kitchen, Donald, and warm up."

"Don't need to warm up, you — you *creature!* I'm boiling mad." The doctor must have brushed India aside, for he clattered down the kitchen steps making more noise than a troop of cavalry.

His mouth full, the journalist nodded amiably. "How are things going aboard the rams?"

"To hell with the rams! What does this mean?" Eyes furiously aglitter behind his spectacles, Donald brandished a copy of the *Argus* before his brother's face. "Why — how dare you defame Serena's father like this?"

The elder brother pushed aside his plate and spoke in an icy voice. "Calm down. I haven't libeled him or anyone else named in that article. Now hear me out."

"I won't calm down, you blithering, blundering idiot!" roared the physician. "You've turned Serena's family against me! She's just broken our engagement."

"Oh, Donald. Believe that I'm dreadfully sorry."

"A damned lot of good being sorry will do! After two days' duty down the harbor, what do I come back to but *this!* How could you do this to your own brother? Have I ever done you a disservice?"

Alistair placed a hand on his brother's gray shoulder only to have it violently shrugged away. "Please listen. I didn't do this to harm *you*. I worried terribly over the possible consequences for you."

The shorter man's round face loomed a furious hue which made his light brown sideburns seem almost blond.

"I'll bet you did!"

"You understand me well enough to know that I'd never have printed such a story if I weren't convinced of the facts; that it is my paper's solemn duty to make them known. Maybe something can be done to discourage speculators like these."

"I only know that I've a self-satisfied prig for a brother. I'm sorry we're related. Don't ever call me 'brother' again."

India's skirts rustled as she ran up to him and seized his arm. "Please, Donald! For God's sake don't say such terrible things. You knew about the proof he found at Crumbacker's. Didn't you yourself remove that envelope and the Bahamas newspaper from Alistair's coat?"

But Donald Bryson was far too angry to pay attention; he twisted free of her grasp, snarling, "And who may you be, you brazen slut, to advise me what to do? You! Whose name is being sniggered over at every bar in town!"

The girl blanched tragically, her voice dulled. "No! Please let me tell — explain."

Alistair's voice was incisive as one of the doctor's own scalpels. "Answer me, Donald! What the hell do you mean by calling my wife a 'slut'?"

Features working like those of an epileptic, the younger brother swung to confront the gaunt, pale-faced figure. "You make a perfect pair! You and your precious trollop of a wife!"

"You're evidently out of your head but, by God, you'd better mind your tongue!"

"Why should I, you great, blind fool! You, whose wife was seen dancing, half-naked, with Rascal Rafe?"

White-hot lights seemed to explode, to hurl splinters through Alistair's brain. "India!" His agonized gaze encompassed her. "What does he mean, dancing naked?"

"Please! Please!" wailed the girl. "As you hope for God's mercy, let me explain! Things weren't as they seemed. I swear it! *Nombre de Dios*, I do! Dorcas misunderstood —"

"Be still!" Alistair swayed, shaken by the recollection of countless innuendoes, sly sniggers and veiled illusions. He hadn't paid them the least attention, not one of them, yet there was Donald calling India a whore to her face, and she looking guilty as Jezebel and sniveling for a chance to explain. If it hadn't been Rascal Rafe he might have listened, but the fellow was far too accomplished a seducer.

"What's that old saying? Where there's smoke?" He laughed stridently. "Very well, you two. You've managed the killing of my love for you to perfection. I hope you're proud of yourselves. I'm going out," he announced in a strangled voice. "I must breathe clean air."

"Oh, Alistair! No! First you must listen to me!" But he stormed past her and vanished through the barren, winter-killed garden. Quickly he became lost to sight down the alley.

CHAPTER XXXIV The Freightyard

WITHOUT purpose, the *Argus's* ex-managing editor strayed, hatless and glassy-eyed, along Meeting Street in the general direction of the South Carolina Railroad's passenger depot. The possibility of taking a train somewhere haunted the back of his mind. He had money, for, unexpectedly, Mr. Roadheaver had paid him every penny of back debts and wages to date. The bills he had tucked between the pages of that little sketchbook he always carried in a hip pocket, carefully secured by a band of elastic.

He ignored, alike, salutations and hostile regards. Since the day was dark and rainy, he must have presented a curious appearance, shuffling along with uncovered head and lacking either coat or shawl.

The driver of an Army forage wagon cursed viciously when Alistair stepped unheeding into its path, but he paid no attention, any more than to hungry curs which, denned in burned houses, snapped at his heels.

"Slut!" . . . "Trollop!" Donald's accusations clanged incessantly, maddeningly, in his brain. How many times had he not doggedly assured himself that India never had been deliberately indiscreet, let alone faithless. In his eyes she had remained a bright, vivacious creature, possessed of unbounded vitality and so charmingly devoid of many restraints.

The street's inch-deep cold mud squelched drearily under his boots as they carried him north along King Street, under the peeling signs of shops and taverns. How could Rafe, rogue though he undoubtedly was, be so utterly lost to decency as to seduce India in his own cousin's home? He wanted to feel outraged but couldn't for the moment, only sick, weary and so terribly alone.

Through a fine, slanting rain, reverberated the clang of the locomotive's bell and sounds of martial music. To his surprise he was plodding into the city side of the South Carolina Railroad's freightyard. Glancing disinterestedly to his left, he noted a troop train preparing to pull out, bearing more offerings to the cannon growling, far away, to the north and west.

On various car platforms, young soldiers clowned as usual and shouted ribald jests at a small crowd standing about in the rain beneath dripping umbrellas. Under the umbrellas lingered a scattering of drawn-faced women in damp and muddied skirts. Quite a few were crying right out loud; they'd been here like this before. To see off these replacements a trio of officers was present. They sat their horses uncomfortably with water dripping in thin, silvery trickles from rubber ponchos and broad-brimmed hats.

Already the musicians of a sodden military band were hoisting their instruments preparatory to marching away. The drums had no resonance left in them; only thumped dully, like a wet dog's tail on the floor.

Twice, thrice the locomotive's whistle tooted, then a great cloud of smoke was regurgitated by its bell-shaped funnel, coupling links banged and, at a snail's pace, the troop train jerked into motion. The little crowd tried to cheer but only sounded disconsolate.

Alistair halted, rubbed water from his brows and wondered: Maybe there's the answer; perhaps I should enlist? Yet he doubted that he would. To fight for States' Rights and Southern Independence was commendable, yet the idea of perpetuating the institution of slavery remained utterly repugnant. Possibly he might obtain employment on some newspaper out West, the *Memphis Avalanche,* the *Columbus Guardian* or, even more feasibly, on the *Mobile Register?* He'd known Forsythe, the *Register's* editor, in New York. Why not go West? He had his severance pay and still was wearing his watch and its rich fob. He intended to pawn it, straight away, and rid himself of this reminder of India.

He scarcely knew that the muddy road his feet were following now wound among tall stacks of cotton bales. Some had lain there so long that weeds were sprouting from their upper sides. Others had big, black rotten holes eaten into them. Like yellow buttes, piles of raw railroad ties, telegraph poles and rough-sawed planking loomed in the distance.

Dimly aware that the wind now was biting through his jacket and that rain had begun to seep down his back he sought the lee of a scales shed and lingered there. What about India? Despite her brazen shamelessness, was it right to storm off, leaving her destitute?

If only a steady, truthful woman like Dorcas Mullinix's testimony hadn't been involved! Surely, *she* could have been trusted to interpret a dubious situation to her old friend's favor?

Alistair became aware of a solid-looking man advancing through the pelting rain. He was wearing a Federal soldier's military cape over civilian clothes and a broad-brimmed hat pulled low over his brows.

The other halted a few feet distant, then observed in a hoarse, low-pitched voice, "I reckon, Mr. Bryson, you'd better come with me for a stroll."

A revolver's muzzle peeped through the cloak's front. "Don't argue."

"What do you want of me?" A painful breathlessness seized the sodden hatless figure. He stared stupidly upon the apparition.

"You'll learn later." The fellow's alert black eyes glittered with reptilian brilliance. "Walk three paces ahead of me, Mister, and turn when I tell you. Make a sudden move or swerve aside and you'll get shot down like the yellow dog you are."

There was no choice but to move off in the direction indicated by the stranger. In dead silence the two squelched along between piles of firewood for locomotives, wet heaps of military supplies, then through a park of *fourgon* wagons and artillery limbers awaiting shipment.

A dull fear manifested itself. What was going to be done to him?

Eventually their route followed a lonely puddle-dotted country road which wound in a southerly direction until swamps closed in from both sides. Brown and yellow cattails, reeds and other marsh grasses shivered under the wind's violence and a few stray gulls wheeled by. For Alistair it would have been useless to call out. Due to the inclemency of the weather the few rude cabins they passed were tight-shuttered and there was no one anywhere to be seen except a few miserable-looking Negroes hunting muskrats in the distance.

Eventually the Ashley's yellow-gray waters glistened, lead-hued,

194

beyond a line of great live oaks; from their boughs long beards of Spanish moss swayed gravely in the wind. Then the prisoner noticed a group of figures waiting in the lee of a tumbled-down boat shed, and a bilious taste welled into his mouth.

"Those men are waiting to kill me. I must get away, somehow! India needs money —"

Desperately but without turning his head he examined his surroundings. It was no good. The marsh came right up to this miserable road.

"Good work, Doggett," greeted the tallest of the waiting men. There were three of them, all carrying shotguns which they shielded from the rain under a variety of coats. "He offer to fight?"

"Naw. Like most blackmailers, he's a yellow cur. . . . Came along like a little lamb, didn't you?" sneered the captor. . . . "Boat ready?"

"Yep."

A four-oared wherry lay tied up to a wharf from which rice long ago had been loaded aboard ocean-going sailships. The rusting ruins of the rice mill which had husked the grain and flailed it loomed, an ugly blemish, on the river's bank.

Icy claws dug keep into his bowels as Alistair burst out, "Please! What do you gentlemen want? What's this all about?"

"Over on the island you'll find out," grated a chunky, red-bearded fellow called Charlie. "But first, here's a little present from the Excalibur Trading Company."

A smashing blow on the jaw made Alistair's teeth rattle, sent him lurching crazily across the rutted road towards another stranger who promptly kicked him so savagely on the shin that he lurched within reach of another tormentor. This one drove his shotgun's butt into the wild-eyed prisoner's stomach and dropped him, writhing, onto the mud.

Dizzy and bleeding from his mouth, the *Argus*'s ex-managing editor was half-beaten, half-hauled out over a rotting wharf, then dropped into icy water slopping about on the wherry's bottom.

"Think anybody seen you?" queried another abductor answering to the sobriquet of Cherokee.

"Couple of niggers, maybe; they'd know better than to open their yaps."

Alistair, lying dazed on the bottom, watched his captor plunk himself in the stern and grab the tiller. What a broad, vicious face was his, all seamed with scars left by some disease.

"You fixin' to take this skunk to Sibley's?"

"Yep. We can work uninterrupted out there."

Sibley? Dimly, the name penetrated Alistair's misery. Then he remembered a once-palatial plantation house. It had been destroyed by fire some time before the war, and was situated upon an island a little way up the Ashley. So that was where he was going to see the end of his days?

CHAPTER XXXV On Sibley's Island

THE roof of the Sibley mansion's spacious brick cookhouse had mostly fallen in but one end still stood, clothed in shadow. Great iron stoves rusting there no longer gave off succulent odors, only an acrid reek of cow dung, rat turds and bat droppings. Rays from a single smoky lantern only faintly illuminated four rough figures busying themselves with a man who swung, triced by the hands, from one of a row of hooks let into a massive roof ceiling. In the old days clusters of game, haunches of venison, innumerable brown hams and sides of bacon had dangled from those hooks.

Since it had been stripped to the waist, the suspended figure glimmered yellow-white and revolved because the *Argus*'s ex-managing editor's toes barely grazed the rubble-littered ground.

The man called Cherokee held the lantern close to the attenuated body. "This yere's sure 'nuff the feller Summers shot at that night."

"What you mean?"

"See these yere scabs on his back? Naught but buckshot will make wounds so round. He's the whoreson stole them manifests, all right."

Doggett grabbed the prisoner's ear and twisted it hard. "Now you'd best speak up. Who paid you to write them lies you printed?"

"Those weren't lies," Alistair said faintly.

Doggett twisted harder.

Silence, despite rending pain.

"Who sent you to Crumbacker's?" rasped Cherokee, puffing hard on a seegar. "Answer me true else you'll get this where 'twon't feel extry comfortable. Talk, damn you."

The inquisitor's feral eyes reflected crimson pinpoints as he puffed harder on his seegar, then held its glowing end over Alistair's navel.

"Swear before God — no one else — anything to do with — investigation," moaned the prisoner. "Oh God, let me down, my arms hurt so."

"Bastard's lying," snapped Doggett. "Jam that butt into his belly-button."

An augur of incandescent steel bored into the captive, spraying molten sparks of agony. Moaning, Alistair tried to kick out, but the effort was without effect; the pain resultant in his wrists was too great. A violent revulsion against his fate gripped him.

"Speak up. Who else was in this plot?"

"No one. Oh-h! Stop, please stop."

"Roadheaver know about it?"

"No! Nothing. For God's sake stop." A thin scream was torn from his lungs, then a tendril of smoke smelling like scorched beef swirled up into his nostrils and caused him to vomit weakly. "I was all alone!" he choked.

Anguished, eternal ages elapsed ere the charred weed went out and was removed.

"Then, whyfor'd you shove yer dirty nose into business that ain't none of yours?" growled a voice the victim was too confused to identify.

"Isn't right our soldiers should die — for want of weapons. Oh-h — as you hope for Christ's mercy, let me down — please! Please. I can't stand any more. Can't tell you anything — would if I could."

"That's a damn' lie!" yelled Doggett's harsh voice. "Somebody was payin' you. Major was certain sure of it."

"He's wrong, wrong." Alistair's arms were sheathed in agony, their muscles became red-hot wires, their joints intolerable, throbbing receptacles of pain. "Only — did what — thought right."

By the dim lantern's light the inquisition continued while flaming pinwheels whirred, now bright now dim, in his eyeballs. Unseen knife-points dug into the journalist's back, cut searing, shallow designs about his torso that released hot rivulets that swiftly soaked his trousers and dripped onto the dirty flooring.

How horrible to die here in this fetid cellar. So an end was coming to everything: hopes, joys, ambitions, sorrows? Voices, no longer intelligible, kept beating upon his fading consciousness. The burning and cutting graduated into a torment too acute to be endured, and he dangled stupefied, a hideous red-and-white hulk.

"By Jesus, ain't he the stubbornest mule?" grunted Cherokee, wiping sweat from his cheek.

"Maybe he wasn't lying," the man Doggett ventured. "Maybe he *was* all alone."

"Yep, or he sure 'nuff would have squealed when that seegar warmed his balls."

"Well," came a query from Charlie, "what do we do now?"

"Reckon we'll finish him off. Cain't leave him to blab," the speaker broke into a cackling laugh. "He knows us by sight, too damn' well."

"What say we make it a spo'ting matter?" suggested Cherokee. "Let's chuck him into the river and see who can pot him before he sinks."

The man Doggett shook his head. "To hell with that. Gators are all wintering now, you halfwit. Besides Mr. Wasson said to take no chances. He don't want no corpse come drifing down river."

"Well, then, what you aim to do? Damn' if I'm goin' gravediggin'. Hit's onlucky."

"Buried people can get dug up," Doggett said, cleaning his knife against his boot sole. "We'll lug him out back of the stables and shoot him — the vultures this time of year are mighty hongry."

Cursing nervously, the torturers hauled their victim's limp and sanguinary figure back out into the rain and flung it deep into a bed of dried sorghum stalks. A single shot sounded. Alistair's body jerked convulsively under the bullet's impact, then shuddered gently and finally lay still.

BOOK TWO
Savannah Waters

CHAPTER 1 Railroad South

FOR Lieutenant the Honorable Peter Burgoyne, RN, his trip from Charleston to Savannah would remain forever engraved in his memory as the nadir of his travels. In later years not even the dusty discomfort of Indian bullock carts or the malodorous lurching of camels across the Sudan would even approximate the annoyances suffered during this brief but seemingly interminable trip.

When a coatless and unshaven trainman informed him that, before very long, the train was due to reach its destination he almost forgot himself and smiled at the saturnine Army contractor who shared his wooden bench. But he didn't quite; from a corner of his mouth the fellow was dribbling brown tobacco juice down the front of a filthy hickory shirt.

Although law forbade any Southern railroad trains to proceed in excess of ten miles per hour — it having become necessary to conserve irreplaceable rolling stock — the locomotive seldom clanked along faster than at half that speed.

To the weary, dirty, and disgusted Briton — dust actually had dulled the lustre of his dull red muttonchop whiskers — the locomotive forever seemed to be stopping to replenish either its water or its fuel supply; the wood it burned must have been green, indeed, so often did the engine halt simply in order to accumulate sufficient pressure to proceed.

About halfway to Savannah the train's weary progress further was slowed because to it had been coupled a trio of boxcars jam-packed with shaggy, half-uniformed troops homeward bound on furlough. These tough veterans, hard-faced and incredibly quick-tempered, sang, fought and drank almost without interruption, but curiously enough, never intentionally offered offense to any female passenger.

201

Although the Honorable Peter thought he had seen some savage specimens roaming Charleston's streets he found he had not, by any means,
encountered the worst of the rabble recruited from the swamps and
forests of this ghostly, beautiful coastline. Never a man aboard failed
to wear jammed into his belt at least one long-bladed sheath knife
or a hand gun of some sort.

Most of these casual troops were surprisingly young, thin, sallow and
wore lank shocks of hair falling like manes down to their collars. Not a
few had been wounded. All of them were filthy as to clothes and person
and bragged all the time about what horrible things they had done to
those Yankee sons-of-bitches; and would do when their furlough was up.
Without exception, they chewed tobacco all the time, but then so did
the few decently dressed civilians.

It astonished the Englishman that a plethora of jewelry, most of it
obviously imitation, was worn by both sexes. Their clothes might be
threadbare and patched but, inevitably, heavy rings, watch chains, ear-
rings, necklaces and brooches were much in evidence.

Mile after mile the train had rattled through the bottom lands where
sullen little fires smoldered among clumps of jack pines or flared brightly
among stunted-looking palmettoes. At such times air in the cars would
grow blue with smoke and set people to coughing and wishing the water
supply had not given out.

On the afternoon of the first day the local was sidetracked to permit
the passage of some northbound train. It must have broken down for,
hour after hour, the southbound train remained motionless, its engine
panting tiredly. Before the other train's headlight appeared, the sun had
sunk and owls were commencing to hoot in a nearby forest.

Sleep was impossible. All the cars of this train were so cruelly overcrowded that people crouched on their luggage in the aisles and on the
platforms and didn't try to visit the malodorous privies. After Yemassee
Junction, not even standing room was available, so those who could
scrambled up onto the coach roofs to huddle there, trying to bat out
sparks which kept raining down.

Peter Burgoyne yearned for the swift, clean and silent cars back
home, especially when a farmer suddenly became carsick and vomited all
over the man in the hickory shirt.

Gagging, Burgoyne attempted resolutely to dwell on such delightful
subjects as sea duty aboard H.M.S. *Courageous,* yachting off Cowes

and the Côte d'Azur, punting at Henley and bracing, early-morning gallops about Oakleigh Towers, the family estate.

Despite his personal unhappiness, Peter experienced a deep compassion for the females aboard for all that, obviously, they belonged to the lower classes. They were so poorly dressed and usually held a squalling infant, which of course had to be fed from time to time. With lank hair veiling gaunt faces, they would, undaunted, pull out a leathery breast and feed their young.

A single bit of good fortune befell Viscount Oakleigh's second son when his train took an hour to change engines at a hamlet called Ridgeville. There most of the passengers detrained to stretch their legs and make hurried ablutions at a horse trough or to purchase food from Negro women offering cold yams and soggy chicken pies for sale.

Grown wise in the ways of Southern travel, Peter was among the first to regain his seat, and was thankful that someone had swept out at least a part of the accumulated litter. A tall, spruce young man clad in Confederate States naval uniform appeared. He looked freshly shaven, and his linen was so spotless he made the newly washed Briton feel like a chimney sweep after work.

"Do you mind sharing your seat with me, sir?" the stranger inquired, giving a soft salute.

"Most certainly not. It will be a real pleasure," Peter was astonished at himself. Really, now. Never before had he admitted it might be pleasant to sit beside a stranger — and an American at that.

The officer, a lieutenant by the small gold stars adorning his shoulder straps, easily heaved a carpetbag up onto the rack, then, turning, he smiled broadly and offered his hand.

"I am Lieutenant Hamilton Dalton, sir, Confederate States Navy; at your service. I am traveling to join my ship in Savannah."

Lieutenant Dalton might have been thirty; his long face was characterized by an alert, almost wary, expression. There were, however, humorous lines about the corners of eyes hooded by heavy black brows.

"How very interesting," Burgoyne drawled. Then, because the other seemed so patently to expect it, he introduced himself.

"Oh, so you're a British naval officer? Well, well, that's fine. You've quite a Navy over there, we hear."

Burgoyne reddened to his hat's brim and his bright blue eyes took on a frosty look. "Er, one might safely say as much."

"Are you, too, headed for Savannah?" Dalton put cap and overcoat beside the carpetbag and seated himself, after undoing his tunic's buttons.

"Yes. Hardly know what to expect, though."

"Used to be a very busy port. It's still a pretty place. Founded by the Spanish, I think, and very old. Acquainted with anybody there?"

The Englishman shook his dark red head. "No. I've only letters of introduction from a friend in Charleston."

"Charleston?" Lieutenant Dalton's wary expression softened. "In the old days I used to attend the St. Cecilia balls there. Who wrote the letters for you?"

Silently damning the fellow's friendly curiosity, Peter produced a pair of sweat-dampened envelopes.

"Oh, yes. I know Judge Riegler. They used to call him the 'Hanging Judge.' And who's it addressed to?"

Deeper resentment commenced to smolder in Peter and he might have been rude, except that he was coming to understand that only a genuine desire to be of assistance as a rule prompted apparently impertinent questions.

"Why, I believe one is addressed to a gentleman named Willents, the other to a Captain Reynolds Seymour." He forced himself to encourage further conversation. "Do you happen to be acquainted with Captain Seymour?"

"No. I hail from Wilmington — that's up in North Carolina," Dalton explained, politely. "I've only visited Savannah a few times."

To his own surprise, the Honorable Peter found himself divulging that he was expected to lodge with the Seymour family until such time as he might find quarters aboard a seagoing ram which was reported to be nearing completion. He was to serve aboard her as an official observer.

"Seagoing ram? Why, she's got to be the *Atlanta*." Enthusiasm entered the North Carolinian's manner. "Say, isn't this queer? *I'm* supposed to report aboard her, too; soon's I reach Savannah. Doubt if we'll be able to, though."

"Why not?"

"Well . . ." Dalton produced a well-charred briar pipe and commenced methodically to load it. "Yesterday, at the Charleston Naval Station, I heard that the *Atlanta* won't be ready for action for a good many weeks."

"The deuce you say! Why didn't they tell me so?" Burgoyne felt both irritated and chagrined. Lord knew he didn't relish the prospect of idling about a dilapidated Southern port for several weeks. "In Charleston, everyone I spoke to said she's ready for commissioning; that's why I'm on this wretched train."

Dalton nodded sympathy. "Isn't that just like the Navy Department? All the same, you won't regret waiting. Savannah's really fine and folks there are right hospitable — make a man feel right at home."

"I fancy so," sighed Peter, envisioning endless platters of fried chicken and fritters, or ham and collard greens. "What about the *Atlanta*? I know very little of her."

"She'll be a first-class ironclad, more heavily armored and much faster than any ram we've built — so far. She'll cruise at ten knots, or so the brothers Tift expect." Dalton grimaced. "Small use in trying to fight Yankees if you can only crawl. They discovered that through the *Mercedita* action."

"Quite right. Would you — er, care for an apple?" The Honorable Peter asked. What in the world had happened? Here he was not only conversing with a stranger but actually offering him food. However, very likely he would be seeing a lot more of this shrewd, clear-eyed lieutenant.

"As you say, Mr. Dalton, greater speed is essential to the success of your naval vessels. I observed your *Chicora* and *Palmetto State* in their valiant, but largely fruitless, action."

The other sat up excitedly. "Did you? Did you now! Would you — mind giving me your impressions, sir? They are sure to be constructive."

"The Confederate ships were skillfully maneuvered and their gunnery was most precise." The Englishman's shiny, red features formed a taut smile. "In fact I venture that few crews of Her Majesty's Navy could have bettered the marksmanship displayed by your rams."

Over a leisurely warning from the locomotive's bell, Dalton asked slowly, "Did the Yankees *really* lose three ships? Our newspapers exaggerate so damned often."

"Hardly. As nearly as Her Majesty's Consul could ascertain, one enemy ship *may* have gone down in the fog, but the *Mercedita* and the *Keystone State*, although badly hurt, got clean away."

A sigh escaped Peter's companion. "I feared as much." His shaggy black brows merged. "Have you any practical comments or suggestions?"

"Yes. The casemates of future ships of this type," came the crisp reply,

205

"might better be designed with a sharper angle of slope. Again, the gunports on your rams are entirely too small. They are not sufficiently spacious to permit proper elevation or traverse; all your gunnery officers complained about it."

Dalton nodded abstractedly. "Such a defect won't be present in the *Atlanta*. I'm sure it won't. From all I hear we're to fight at last on an efficient man-of-war."

"Let us hope as much. Of what will her battery consist?" No one would have guessed how studiously, albeit casually, Her Majesty's naval observer was framing his queries, or the care with which he was noting the replies.

"She's supposed to mount only eight guns in all, but each piece is modern and very powerful." He fetched out a scrap of paper and on his knees sketched a deck plan. "Note how the casement is rounded, well out, at either end."

"For what purpose, may I inquire?" The young Englishman was at pains to seem only politely interested.

"Why, sir, don't you see? The design allows the *Atlanta*'s forward and after guns to be fired in broadside, as well as ahead or astern!"

"Hum. Deucedly ingenious," the Englishman admitted and, knitting reddish brows, treated the rendering to a careful scrutiny while the whistle shrieked and the train bumped into motion. "Must remember this."

The North Carolinian then went on to describe other innovations; explained that this new ram was being constructed from the hull of a fabulously successful blockade-runner, the *Fingal*. Reputedly she possessed extra fine, flowing lines. Certainly the Tift brothers must have profited from errors perpetrated in building such ill-fated rams as *Louisiana* and *Mississippi*.

" 'Twill prove a great day for our Country, sir, when a commissioning pennant is hoisted above the *Atlanta* — a turn in the tide of our naval fortunes," Dalton predicted.

Peter slightly inclined his head, peered out of a cracked and grimy window at a row of shirttail pickaninnies standing, white-eyed before a row of tumbled-down log cabins. They began waving and jumping crazily up and down as the train rattled by.

"Why so fervent, Mr. Dalton?" queried the Briton, fingering his jaw.

"Don't know as I should mention it, sir, but our agents in the North report that a flotilla of monitors recently cleared Newport News, southward bound."

"Indeed? I confess I am more than a little curious to watch this type in action. Remarkable concept, the revolving turret, eh, Mr. Dalton? The Admiralty may experiment with such, but not if your *Atlanta* can defeat the monitors."

"She surely will! I'll stake a year's pay on it!"

The forest of swamp gums, persimmons and towering live oaks, impartially festooned with ghostly streamers of Spanish moss, retreated from the right-of-way, exposing to view small and forlorn fields in which bolls of unpicked cotton glistened among clumps of weeds.

From the manner in which his fellow passengers commenced to squirm on their seats and to collect their belongings, the Honorable Peter deduced that this hideous journey, at last, must be nearing its conclusion.

What sort of persons might be Captain and Mrs. Reynolds Seymour? Were they of the fading cotton-and-rice aristocracy, or would they belong to the middle class, dogged in their struggles to survive slave competition and entrenched wealth?

The Seymours, he hoped, would prove to be members of the middle class. Around Charleston his position had become downright awkward, if not embarrassing. No sooner had it become known that his father was a viscount than society had fawned, had conspired to bring him into the company of eligible daughters.

To his amused astonishment, a few powerful planters privately had invited his opinion as to whether some member of Britain's Royal House might be persuaded someday to rule over the Southland? As President Davis' popularity faded, the idea became more frequently advanced. It should prove illuminating to learn whether the fires of Secession burned in Savannah as hotly as in Charleston.

What was it Major Lambkin had said when he learned of the Englishman's destination? Something like, "You mustn't expect too much from Georgians, sir. After all, most of *their* ancestors were either redemptioners or transported criminals."

CHAPTER II

Beau Rivage

OBSERVANT English travelers — that peripatetic journalist, W. W. Russell, among them — had written that, along the Savannah River immediately above the city of that name, were situated an impressive number of manor houses, termed "great houses" by the natives. Lieutenant the Honorable Peter Burgoyne found that there had been no exaggeration in that respect. Along the banks and on every peninsula and bend arose a stately mansion, often at the top of a series of terraces. But most of these houses had grown weather-beaten and neglected during the past three years.

Captain Reynolds Seymour's Beau Rivage alone still shone, white and pristine, against a dark background of mighty water oaks, shiny magnolias and graceful cedars.

In the flower beds of Beau Rivage early flowers bloomed just as brightly as they had when "Ole Mistis" McGoffin had been there, tenderly supervising their care. Between these estates shimmered giant rectangles formed by banks enclosing the rice fields. Nowadays, most of these fields served only as a lush haven for dense flocks of wintering waterfowl.

The boat slip of Beau Rivage also had been kept up, so, to all intents and purposes, the handsome old plantation house had suffered not a whit because of the war, or because "Ole Mistis" had gone peacefully to her grave nearly a year ago.

Senator McGoffin, white-haired and still straight as any ruler, remained among the living, but had failed to recover from the shock of his beloved's demise. Nowadays the Senator wandered, vacant-eyed and palsied, about his precious estate, so senile that, frequently, he confused the identity of very old friends and even forgot his house slaves' names.

A guest familiar with the table set at Beau Rivage in antebellum days, however, would have detected subtle changes. No longer was offered quite so wide a selection of wines or so many varieties of food, yet, by comparison to repasts served on neighboring plantations, the Seymours' fare was little short of Lucullan.

208

For example, at Drake's plantation, situated a mile or so upstream, two thirds of the great house had been closed up with only a skeleton staff of superannuated servants attending the wants of old Mr. and Mrs. Drake, outwardly unbroken, but proudly mourning twin sons slain in a trifling skirmish among the mountains of what the Yankees now were calling the Free State of West Virginia.

Manigault's, on the river's far side, had been entirely closed. Only a "white trash" caretaker and his slattern of a wife occupied the fine old house in order to scare away marauders or limit depredations committed constantly by an ever increasing swarm of runaway slaves, deserters and starving small farmers.

Fortunately for Sylvia McGoffin Seymour, her father remained unaware that, in and about Savannah, bitter rumors were circulating concerning eye-taking young Reynolds Seymour sauntering about town in the uniform of a nebulous unit called "the Cape Chatham Fencibles."

Certain it was that these Fencibles had never done guard duty, let alone seen action. Why, its handful of members drilled but twice a month and then got drunk afterwards. Nor did Seymour's exquisitely dressed and lovely young bride escape captious gossip, for all that she'd been born and reared at Beau Rivage.

Before the war, as all polite society was aware, that lovely young heiress called Sylvia McGoffin had been widely courted until, quite inexplicably, she had decided upon a penniless young Virginian, a marine architect by the name of Irad Seymour, and had gone off to live in Baltimore — and poverty. They also heard in Savannah that, once war had broken out, this same Seymour had done rather well in the Navy Department. In fact, at the time of his death by accident, he had become a commander, assigned to Chief Naval Engineer Williamson's office in Richmond.

What tightened mouths and knitted brows upon many a shadowed porch in Savannah was the fact that although Sylvia looked mournfully lovely in her widow's weeds, she had worn them less than three months, and had consoled herself by marrying Irad's dashing and much younger brother, Reynolds.

So the Hodgsons, Lockes, Bartows, Wards and Manigaults and many others who, every morning, fearfully scanned casualty lists appearing in the *Republican*, were given bitterly to quoting Hamlet: "the funeral baked meats did coldly furnish forth the marriage tables."

Genteel Savannah, however, remained at least outwardly civil, and bowed politely whenever the handsome young Captain and his bride drove about town in freshly varnished green-and-black chariotee. After all, wasn't it better to remain on the safe side of a man known to have powerful political connections in Richmond? . . . Besides, my dear, I hear that the Seymour family, up in Virginia — they live right near Norfolk you know — is an ancient and a distinguished one. . . . Have you really? Well I've heard that certain doubts attended the unheralded arrival here of Reynolds Seymour. That must have been back in 1860, I believe. Anyhow, it's got about that this young fellow departed from the University of Virginia in a hurry — a matter of a card game and too many aces. Of course, it mightn't be true at all. . . .

Nonetheless the fact remained for all to witness that, although lacking any connections whatever, that darkly handsome and beautifully mannered young man quickly had ingratiated himself with the city's social, political and commercial leaders.

Attended by quite a bit of fanfare, tactless to say the least in these times, the beauteous Sylvia and her new husband had returned to occupy Beau Rivage late in 1862.

Could you believe it? They brought no less than three freightcars filled with expensive household goods from Richmond — in spite of the terrible congestion on our railways. . . . Yes, and did you know that, only a day or so later, *another* two freightcars brought that chariotee and those beautiful black carriage horses they use?

It's abominably selfish to keep such useful beasts for private use. Long ago they should have been turned over to the cavalry or flying artillery — just as we did. . . .

So spoke ladies over delicate cups containing not a brew from China but the steepings of dried raspberry leaves.

If Sylvia Seymour failed to furnish a sufficient subject for speculation there always remained her husband. . . . My dear, it's said that Reynolds's conduct in Richmond and Charleston is just short of scandalous! Why, he riots about those places just as he used to around here the first year of the war. And do *you* know he still calls — late at night, of course — upon that Creole hussy on Milledge Street? You'd think Sylvia would find out. . . . That's the shocking part of it. She has. She knows all about that — that creature's existence. Jenny told me so. Why doesn't she do something about it? I really can't comprehend. Lydia McGoffin would turn over in her grave if she knew that her daughter doesn't seem to notice Reynolds's long and mysterious absences.

Why, sometimes a whole fortnight passes without her knowing his whereabouts. Well, my dear, *wherever* he goes he always comes home with a mightily well-stuffed wallet. So Julius tells me. What do you think? . . . It's very likely so, Parthenia. Fred's raging. This parvenu pays all his accounts either in gold or with Yankee greenbacks, so it's only natural, Fred says, that all manner of speculative propositions are offered him so he's making money hand over fist. . . . (Wistfully.) I wish we could export even a little of our rice. Tom says it'll spoil soon as the weather warms.

Peter Burgoyne couldn't know it, but, about the time of his arrival in town, a certain envious tolerance was being accorded the Seymours. The war seemed to be progressing favorably, what with the great victories won on land this year.

There'd be sea victories, too, pretty soon. In a few weeks the great new *Atlanta,* pride of all Georgia, would steam down-river and disperse those Blue cruisers hovering among the Sounds. Even sooner, the Buzzard State would make another bid for glory. *Nashville,* a powerful and well-armed privateer, was about to elude the blockade. Once at sea she would become a commerce raider, a fit consort for *Sumter, Florida* and the breath-takingly successful *Alabama.* Recently the last had been sinking Yankee ships within two hundred miles of New York, thereby throwing that polygot metropolis into a shaking panic.

Seldom of late had the vast dining room of Beau Rivage appeared so splendid. On sideboard and table Georgian silver glowed with a blue-white luster. Two graceful wine coolers of a rare Directoire pattern exposed the necks of heavily beaded champagne bottles plunged deep in ice. The napery could not have been more spotless or costly. For a center-piece a profusion of tropical fruits — worth their weight in gold — tumbled out of a huge silver Horn of Plenty. The long table was reputed to be the product of Mr. Sheraton's personal skill and its lustrous mahogany's surface unerringly reflected candle flames supported by elaborate crystal candeleabra.

"To welcome you to our home, Mr. Burgoyne, is a rare pleasure," the hostess murmured, large and sherry-hued eyes languidly, but narrowly, surveying this ruddy-faced sailor of the Queen. "Alas, I fear that we, in this embattled Nation, must suffer by comparison to those comforts to which you are accustomed."

"Why, ma'am, at Eton we were taught that 'comparisons are odious,' but not in this case. Nowhere in Oakleigh Towers could be boasted a table half so — so sumptuous."

From the head of the table, Reynolds Seymour raised a slender goblet of brandy and water. He looked very handsome in that uniform prescribed for an officer of the Cape Chatham Fencibles. Of dark green, its tunic was adorned by silver epaulettes and buttons securing a plastron of claret-colored silk.

The host bowed in his armchair. "You are most flattering, sir; however, I'll bet your wines are choicer." By candlelight Reynolds's dark and too sensitive features glowed with an irrepressible vitality. Curly and plentiful brown hair and mustaches glistened with a recent application of Macassar oil.

"Every wine I have thus far tasted seems excellent," Peter mumbled. "But, of course, I'm a sailor, and no connoisseur."

"Let's invite my brother-in-law's opinion of the Médoc," Sylvia suggested in her slightly husky but musical voice. "I fear the commission merchant we bought it from is none too reputable."

Following his hostess's eye, the Briton, almost for the first time noticed that, across the table, was seated a big, wide-jawed, sandy-haired officer wearing a well-pressed and neatly patched gray-blue uniform. Peter soon found himself marveling that two men, so completely dissimilar in every physical respect as Samuel and Reynolds Seymour, could be even distantly related.

Lieutenant-Commander Samuel Seymour's deeply tanned and good-humored features relaxed. "All I can say, my dear Sylvia, is that I'd be very happy to go right on drinking wines even half so delicious.

"What do you say, Louise?" he demanded of his petite, vivacious and olive-skinned young wife, who had been Louise de Bienville Cottier of La Rue Conti, in New Orleans.

Delicately Samuel Seymour's wife lifted her glass and held it to a candle's flame, permitting its rich ruby hues to be better appreciated. "I think, *mon cœur,* this Pontet-Canet would have earned even Papa's approval."

SKETCH BOOK

1862 - 1864

Drawings made in and around Charleston S.C.

Property of Alistair Bryson

India ready
to dance

King Cotton

Winning the War

Raphael Bryson

Adger's Wharf

"De Roustabouts
am here, Suh."

"Farewell my Love!"

A Congressman

De Deacon

White gold

Christmas morning at Major Lamkin's 1862

Christmas Eve
43 Mary St. 1862

Shivaree

"A Real Firecater"

"Jairus" in a hurry

Vendue at Bee's Block

Pocotaglio R.R. yard
Charleston

Gen'l Beauregard
inspects the 1st S.C. Inf. (reg.)

Mr. Roadheaver
"Editorial policy"

"Skip mah Lou"

collapsible
Smokestack

Water Line

Rudder

Torpedo Boom   Torpedo

David N⁰ 2
1863

Sergeant Berry Benson
Co. H. 1st S.C. Infantry

Apprentice Pilot

Captain Frank N. Bonneau

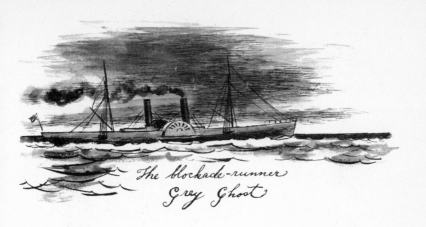

The blockade-runner
Grey Ghost

The Battery
Charleston. 1863

Chase at Sea

A real Buckaroo

J. J. Remegan

Unloading the Hunley

Flag officer Duncan Ingraham
Con. States Navy at Charleston

Keg Torpedo

Ironclads attacking Fort Sumter

Torpedoing of the Housatonic

"And you, Miss Valiant, do you approve?"

The Honorable Peter's dinner partner was a tired-looking, pathetically eager blond girl, obviously awed by so opulent an atmosphere no less than the fact that she actually was seated beside the son of a viscount. Goodness! Just wait till Ellen Louise and Mason Brent heard about him!

"Why, Ah declare it's the *best* thing Ah evah did taste!" she tittered. "But Ah must confess Ah prefer a sweeter, yellow wine, like a — a —"

"Like a Graves, my dear?" suggested the hostess.

"Yes, of cou'se, Mis' Seymour, of cou'se. It's Graves Ah like," the Valiant girl directed a dimpled smile at her host. "Ah couldn't he'p wonderin', Captain, *wherevah* did you come by such perfectly go'geous wine in these po' times?"

Reynolds Seymour brushed a trace of sauce meunière from his lips, laughed easily. "I was fortunate enough to buy up a bankrupt cotton broker's cellar. Poor old Mr. Angier had been collecting choice vintages for years — used to travel personally to select his Pommards, Mersaults and Anjous." Louise noted that his French accent was good.

"Oh, yes. I remember!" It was Commander McBlair's plain but attractive sister, Verbena, who spoke. Sylvia had invited her at the last moment, largely because rumor had it that her brother, Charles, almost certainly would command the new ram.

"Wasn't Mr. Angier the poor man who killed himself when the news came that his third and last son had been killed in that river battle off Memphis?"

"He was a naval lieutenant in the *General Price*," said Charles McBlair, a dark-complexioned, black-haired and fierce-eyed individual who suggested Highland Scottish in every lineament.

Sam said, snapping a breadstick between powerful brown hands, "I wish I had even a little of your knack for finding good things to eat and drink, Rey. Louise and I rejoice if we come across a bit of brown flour. We get so blamed tired of cornpone!"

"Let me know whenever you want white flour," urged the host and his rounded silver epaulettes glittered when he reached for his wineglass.

"I *do* wish, dear Louise," Sylvia said smoothly, "that Sam hadn't insisted on your renting that miserable little house so near the shipyard. To have you nearby would have been simply wonderful. Our family's so dreadfully small these days, isn't it?"

Deceptively astute, Peter did not miss that sudden flicker of Louise Seymour's glance in her husband's direction. Um. And a band of color was creeping out along the blond Commander's strong cheekbones. Why? Only a few persons could have given him a reason. Even fewer knew the real reason: that, one wild evening up in Baltimore, Sylvia had conceived a son not by Irad, a husband unfortunately quite sterile, but by his handsome blond brother — the middle brother. So, in effect, Sylvia McGoffin had gone to bed with all three of the Seymour boys.

"Oh our house is a little horror, *bien sûr,* but it *is* convenient to Samuel's work," returned Louise equably. "Really, dear Sylvia, our home no longer is quite so ugly. We have contrived. Perhaps you and Reynolds will come to judge for yourself, no?"

"Mrs. Seymour has indeed accomplished miracles," Verbena McBlair assured them. "You have no idea how tastefully clever she is at making-do — a necessary virtue in a naval officer's lady. You can have no notion how little even a commander's pay will purchase nowadays. If and when he receives it," she added, bitterly.

"And how soon, sir, will your ship be ready for commissioning?" Peter inquired of Commander McBlair.

"She should be ready right now," came the acid reply. "If certain parts for our engines would arrive from abroad." McBlair glared about the dinner table. "Delays! Delays! Always delays. And most of the time no pay comes down from Richmond for my crew, so I keep losing hand-picked men. All the same," he growled, "the *Atlanta* will go to sea — and soon."

"Let us pray so," came Reynolds Seymour's enthusiastic comment. "Ladies and gentlemen, shall we raise our glasses to a successful cruise for the *Atlanta,* and a mass of prize money for her brave officers and men?"

"Will you be here for her commissioning?" Sam queried. "I'd like you to be on board."

"Why, as a matter of fact, I'm leaving town tomorrow. I've some business in Charleston. Army business," he amplified easily.

"Oh, darling, how long do you expect to be away?" demanded the hostess, a pearl necklace gleaming about the satin-smooth pillar of her neck. "I trust you will return in time for a reception I'm planning in Mr. Burgoyne's honor."

"I'll be back in ample time, dear, never fear," asserted Reynolds Seymour. "Possibly I'll fetch back some decent cognac, provided I can find some in Charleston."

"You will, all you want," predicted the Honorable Peter with a bleak smile.

CHAPTER III

C.S. Privateer *Rattlesnake*

DURING the second week of his stay at Beau Rivage, the Honorable Peter Burgoyne was aroused one night by an insistent rapping upon his bedroom door. The knocker proved to be Lieutenant Commander Sam Seymour. Hot, breathless, and reeking of horse sweat, he towered over his sister-in-law, who, clad in a voluminous negligee of pale blue voile, secured at its waist by a gay yellow ribbon, appeared anything but freshly roused from slumber. Sylvia's large and liquid dark eyes were fairly sparkling and her naturally bright color high.

Peter appeared swathed in a ruffled dressing gown of bottle-green silk. "I say. Anything gone wrong?"

"We've just learned at Naval Headquarters that, at dawn tomorrow, the privateer *Nashville,* I mean the *Rattlesnake* — that's her new name — is dropping down the Great Ogeechee to fight her way out to sea." He mopped powerful features. "Reckoned you might like to observe her in action against Yankee monitor that's patrolling Wassaw Sound."

The Englishman's bony features lit. "Of course. I'll be delighted to observe such an encounter and, I must say, it's damned decent of you to ride all this way to invite me. Can we get there in time?"

"We will. Fool pilot ran the privateer aground just above Fort McAllister. She can't hope to get off before high tide tomorrow morning."

"The *Rattlesnake* aground?" Sylvia cried sharply. "Heavens above! Reynolds has a big consignment of rice aboard." She caught Sam's sleeve and anxiously lifted her lovely face. He was so very tall. "What is going to happen?"

While Peter dashed back to dress, Sam accepted a biscuit and a cup of milk fetched by a heavy-eyed house slave. "Well now, I reckon for the first time I'm likely to see a monitor in action."

"A monitor!" Sylvia burst out. "I hadn't heard of any arriving in Savannah waters." She bit her lip. "Why didn't Reynolds or anybody else tell me about it?"

"That's surprising; we heard the monitor bombarded Fort McAllister the other day."

"What about this — privateer?" Sylvia inquired, peering up into Sam's ruddy features.

"As I told Burgoyne, originally she was the blockade-runner *Nashville* and has been refitted to become a commerce-raider, like the *Alabama*, the *Florida* and the rest."

Studiously, he avoided her eyes. It didn't help at all; the nearness of Sylvia's shiny, dark red lips stirred him profoundly. It just wasn't reasonable that Sylvia's overwhelming femininity could set his pulses to surging — not after the agonies of self-reproach he'd endured for the past two years.

Head tilted back, bright lips provocatively parted, Sylvia, in her filmy blue negligee, came closer. Her eyes seemed to shut, their long lashes lying like sable fringes upon the satin pallor of her cheek.

"Oh, Sam! Sam!" she cried huskily. "I'll never forgive you for this."

"What in God's name have I done wrong?"

"I was so sure it was *I* you came riding out to see." Her hands came to rest upon his wrists, gently drew him towards her. "I'm not mistaken — am I, dear?"

"Don't!" he choked and stepped back towards the staircase. "Don't say such things! Don't look at me like this. Oh, Sylvia, I can't bear it — this being so near you."

"Then your love for me is still alive?" Her voice was soft now and rich as a low note on a viola.

"I — no — yes. Sylvia, everything is different now." Desperately. "You see, I truly love my wife."

She stepped so close her hair brushed his cheek. "But *I* was your first love. How much we meant to each other, how much we shared. Poor little Jeff."

"Our child is dead." He groped backward with his foot, in retreat towards the staircase. "Now, everything is different. You have Reynolds. I have Louise."

"We can have them — and each other. Oh-h."

Still knotting a black silk cravat and looking unusually slim and long-

216

limbed in riding breeches and boots, the British naval officer reappeared in time to hear Sam saying, "Anyway, the report states that a Federal scout launch watched the *Nashville* — damn it, *Rattlesnake* — get piled onto a mudbank, then steam back towards Wassaw Sound at top speed. The Yankees, undoubtedly, must know she's in trouble."

"What was wrong with her pilot that he should run her aground?"

Sam shrugged. "It's sad to admit but, nowadays, we can't always be too sure of a pilot's loyalty."

Peter's straight red brows rose a trifle. "And why not?"

"Confederate shinplasters don't talk half as loud as Yankee green-backs." Sam gulped the last of his milk, then passed the empty silver cup to the waiting slave. "Her crew is trying to lighten her, but I doubt if they can accomplish much before the tide floods again."

Sylvia collected the negligee's skirt while treating her guests to a daz-zling smile. "Good night, Sam. I'll go pray that the *Nashville* — and Reynolds's rice — win safely past that nasty monitor." Graciously, she inclined her head in Peter's direction. "I trust that you, Peter, will be privileged to witness another Southern victory."

Returning to her bedroom, Sylvia smiled. How deeply the Honorable Peter Burgoyne had flushed when she had blown him that gay little kiss from the top of the staircase. Possibly, from his position, he had ob-tained just a glimpse of wondrously shapely ankles? Perhaps even more.

CHAPTER IV **Great Ogeechee**

FOR the first time Peter Burgoyne commenced truly to appre-ciate the varied and eerie charm of Georgia's tidewater country as this battered steam launch chuffed along densely wooded shores of the glassy, continually winding Great Ogeechee.

Of the grave and sleepy-eyed officers aboard — mostly artillerymen and engineers — Peter recognized but two: Sam, and that same alert North Carolinian he had met on the train coming down from Charles-ton.

How vast the world, seen by this deceptive half-light. Deer, surprised at feeding among the shallows, went crashing off under moss-hung branches. Raccoons scuttled away and, occasionally, a dog fox barked defiance at the hooting of an owl; successive flocks of invisible ducks kept taking wing, caused a soft, muffled roar.

"Too bad the 'gators are still hibernatin'," remarked a gaunt, black-bearded major of artillery. "To hear a big bull roaring is *something*."

"I should imagine so." Peter, shivering, gathered a boat cloak more tightly about him against the chill and lifeless atmosphere.

Inexplicably, the Englishman's thoughts reverted to Beau Rivage and a vision of his hostess throwing him — or was it her brother-in-law? — kisses from the top of the staircase. Most titivating had been his all too brief glimpse of white, superbly proportioned legs and knees.

How enchanting had been Sylvia's mature loveliness, set off by that flowing, filmy negligee. Jove! There was something maddening about the changing shape and expressions of her full and dark-red lips. Seldom had he encountered a female even half so appealing.

While the launch plowed on through tendrils of river mist his thoughts raced on until, gradually, a number of apparently unrelated incidents arising during the past fortnight commenced to form a pattern.

Sylvia Seymour was so intensely curious about all things English; about his family and their connections at Court; tactfully, of course. It seemed she could never hear enough concerning Oakleigh Towers and its surroundings — in detail.

She wanted to learn about his father's servants, their duties and what they were paid. "Mayn't always be able to keep slaves, you know."

Most insatiable had been Sylvia's interest in life at Court, and about London society.

Amid the darkness, Peter felt his cheeks warm on recalling her naïve eagerness when he gave her a heraldic description of the Burgoyne coat of arms — and a semihumorous description of the family coronet and Court regalia.

On that occasion, he recalled she'd sat so close examining the crest on his seal ring, that her hair had brushed his cheek and he'd come to appreciate a certain appeal stimulated by a French scent she wore.

On surged the launch. Her pilot with uncanny precision at the very last instant avoided half-seen sand bars and weed-draped snags.

"How long till dawn?" someone inquired over the boiler's sibilant hissing.

"Half an hour, mebbe."

"Just where is the *Nashville* grounded?" Everyone seemed inclined to call the privateer by her original name.

"She's hard stuck on a mudbank halfway around that big bend just above Fort McAllister. Hope to God they string her dumblock pilot by his balls," the speaker added savagely.

The launch's engineer circulated a can of steaming coffee heated on top of the boiler; it tasted surprisingly good.

"Where's McAllister?" a very short and stout engineer captain wanted to know. "Me, I don't know this terrain at-all."

"Stands on the south bank, 'bout five miles above where this river empties into Ossabaw Sound," Sam told him over a black stoker's shoveling noises.

When the Englishman lit a pipe, his strongly modeled features glowed gold-red.

"And how did this monitor fare in her fight against the fort?"

"The *Montauk?*" the bearded artillery major asked. "Well, suh, they fought to what one might rightly call a draw; the ironclad didn't hurt McAllister a mite and though the monitor was hit thirteen times, she steamed away when she was done, sassy as a catbird on a pump handle."

Sam asked, "Does the enemy have other monitors which may have come up during the night?"

"Near's we know, suh, there's only one hereabouts. But our spies reported three more at Port Royal, ten days back. They're named *Weehawken, Passaic* and *Nahant.*"

Below Harwick's Mill and Patterson's Island sinister, tangled trees receded from the river's edge giving place to rice fields shimmering wetly within earthen dikes. Here and there lay an islet, crowned by clumps of stately cypress or water oak supporting immensely long streamers of funereal-looking Spanish moss.

Peter shivered. How strangely depressing was this ghostly, yet desolately beautiful, landscape. Certainly, there could be nothing at all similar in England except, perhaps, among the Norfolk Broads or the fens of Lincolnshire.

Dawn by now had become something more than a presentiment

when, somewhere downstream, sounded the dull *boom-m-m* of a cannon's report. Another, then another . . . Men dozing in the launch started up, white-eyed and anxious.

"Damnation! We won't get there in time!"

"Sounded like a rifled gun to me."

"Can't have opened on the *Nashville* already! Yankee can't shoot by this light."

"Correct. Them shots was fired farther down-river."

"No. Those were McAllister's smoothbores firing."

"Hump yerselves, you lazy black bastards," the launch's engineer commanded. A pair of Negro stokers then made shovels fly, bathed the stern in a palpitating orange-red glare which drew brief flashes from hat ornaments. "We got to make tracks iffen we don't want to miss the whole show."

The distant smoothbores continued to play a diapason obbligato; but, presently, distinctive, flat-sounding and very loud reports became noticeable.

"Those will be Dahlgren rifles aboard the monitor," Sam Seymour announced. His broad jaw chewed hard on nothing.

"How can you tell?" demanded the Englishman.

"Heard plenty of such in action along the Mississippi River last year. Besides," he smiled wryly, "I'm supposed to be an authority on naval ordnance. I was installing the *Mississippi's* ordnance when New Orleans fell. Damned shame. Singlehanded, that ram could have chased Farragut right back to the Gulf."

"Why did New Orleans fall so readily?" Peter pursued peering past a reach of river screened by a row of long-leafed pines. "In England we read that the city had been defended by two strong fortresses, as well as a great flotilla of gunboats."

Queer that these now-familiar sounds of battle should set his pulses to leaping; Sam cocked his head towards that distant cannonading. "Because of divided command, Mr. Burgoyne. Believe me or not: we had not one, but *three,* flotillas in action on the river that day — each obeying a different authority."

The Briton looked starkly incredulous. "You must be jesting?"

"I wish I were," came the angry reply. "We had in action below New Orleans vessels of the regular Confederate Navy, of the

Louisiana State Navy, and of the River Defense Flotilla, which took orders from the Confederate Army!"

A low whistle escaped Peter. "God above! Why are you Southerners so fearful of acting in concert, so eager to defy your own central government?"

Lieutenant Dalton overheard and slewed around on his seat. "I've been wondering, Mr. Burgoyne, how long it would take you to recognize so obvious a paradox."

"Paradox?"

The North Carolinian nodded curtly. "Yes. Here in the South we fight for independence under the slogan of 'States' Rights.' However, we are carrying the notion to suicidal extremes. Governor Brown of this State won't lift a finger to supply Alabama, Carolina or Florida troops; the Governor of North Carolina imposes special taxes on certain goods of military importance exported from his state. What a God-damn', shortsighted policy! We'll pay dear for it."

CHAPTER V **U.S.S. *Montauk***

GRADUALLY, the Great Ogeechee widened until it was nearly half a mile across, then the launch steamed into sight of a great, fish-shaped sand bar, dotted with sickly-looking palmettoes and rising only a few inches above the highwater mark. Beyond it towered the black topmasts and funnel of a big steam sloop — those of the Confederate States privateer, *Rattlesnake*.

"Looks like she's stuck quartering across the channel," Sam commented. Through his binoculars Peter meanwhile identified two points of cardinal interest. The low outlines of a large, earthenwork fort showed gray-brown up on a low bluff beyond the bend and in a direct line with the stranded privateer.

At the moment, Fort McAllister was wreathed in billows of burnt powder smoke which was drifting out to draw gray streaks over the river's slate-colored and mirror-calm surface. The second object capturing the Honorable Peter's attention was a curious and barely visible silhouette.

At this distance it suggested a circular shed resting upon a raft. Those aboard the launch crowded forward, cursing in their excitement, to train field glasses and telescopes. Their weight depressed the bow and seriously slowed the boat's progress.

Certainly, U.S.S. *Montauk* created a less than imposing impression; she was so flat and seemingly insignificant-looking when one recalled lofty ships of the line and armored frigates.

Without orders, the engineer stopped his craft, allowed it to be borne along upon the current. No one offered objection; when nothing useful could be accomplished, it would be nonsense to steam into range of those distant guns.

Sam sucked his breath in sharply. Once more, fort and monitor commenced to duel. Even louder reports came slamming, banging over the water, scaring dense clouds of terrified birds into flight. A panic-stricken string of brown pelicans appeared, fleeing upriver and looking like relics from the Age of Saurians. Brief white waterspouts commenced to rise all around that ugly little Yankee vessel. Strangely, the gunners in the fort today could not seem to range a target so inadequate, although they had hit her often the day before.

Peter Burgoyne's breathing quickened on recognizing the unmistakable characteristics of a British-built merchantman. Next he perceived that water around the privateer was dotted with flotsam of all sorts. *Rattlesnake*'s crew must have labored all night to decrease her draft. Had they been able to lighten the privateer sufficiently to get her off? A good many cotton bales were adrift in the current, others already had stranded downstream. Were any of these Reynolds's property?

In a twisting column, smoke commenced to gush from *Rattlesnake*'s tall smokestack, building a sable, funnel-shaped cloud. Next came a furious threshing of the privateer's paddle wheels, churning the river into a froth with their efforts to get her off the mudbank.

In the distance, meanwhile, U.S.S. *Montauk* prepared to drop anchor, coolly ignoring salvos from the fort's heavy cannon, of which twelve could be brought to bear. Everyone in the launch saw a white V, caused by the monitor's wake, fade; watched her smoke commence to climb vertically like that of the cornered commerce-raider.

"Damned monitor's not paying McAllister's fire any heed at all," growled the artillery major, a muscle working in his leathery cheek. "See that shot glance off her turret just now?"

"Why don't the Yankee run past the fort and try boarding?" demanded a silver-haired officer wearing upon his sleeves a colonel's braid done in tarnished gold.

Lieutenant Dalton answered him. "Sir, do you see that row of ranging stakes across the river from the fort? Well, behind them is anchored a line of torpedoes. Somehow the damn' Yanks found out about their being there and won't try running by."

"And now what?" The expression in Peter's bright-blue eyes was intense. He was thinking back to a blustery day off the Crimean peninsula, of the bombardment of Kerch and of a very young red-headed midshipman desperately attempting to disguise his fears.

"Everything will depend on how well the raider's forward pivot gun is served," Sam predicted. "It's a 9-inch Brooke rifle. Saw it last week. If its gunners can score some quick hits the enemy may break off the action."

"What's the range now?" asked the engineer officer.

"Around twelve hundred yards," Dalton told him.

The speakers had to shout because Fort McAllister's gunners, evidently ranging on the stakes, kept up a continuous fire causing the whole river to resound and thunderous echoes to roll. For some reason the Confederate artillerymen must have become unduly excited; although many shots splashed close alongside the sinister black ellipse, hits were few and far between.

Apparently disdainful of the fort's cannonade, *Montauk* rounded comfortably to her anchor and prepared to deal with *Rattlesnake*.

Because the marsh which had caused this bend in the river was a low one the Union gunners clearly could discern the privateer's masts, funnel and even her pilothouse, but nothing at all of her hull.

Through his field glasses the Englishman, in ever-mounting interest, watched the ironclad's single turret revolve with majestic deliberation until its twin guns became trained upon the target. Then a great gush of fire and smoke burst from her scant seconds before a shell burst, like a deadly scarlet flower, some two hundred yards beyond the struggling *Rattlesnake*.

When the monitor's other gun spoke its projectile raised a cloud of mud and water on the far edge of that marsh interposed between the adversaries.

"God above!" groaned Sam. "They've got their bracket in salvo already!" Briefly, he conjectured as to whether some Annapolis classmate of his might be directing this fire; while awaiting exchange, after his capture by Federal cavalrymen, he'd met several wearing dark blue uniforms.

"Reckon we'll soon learn what's what. *Nashville*'s bow pivot gun is going into action." The artillery major's fingers commenced spasmodically to knead at the gunwale.

Heartfelt curses resounded when, far down-river, the Brooke's nine-inch shot raised a tremendous but quite harmless waterspout from the clay-colored current.

"Oh, God! If only I were aboard . . . !" Sweat appeared in high, bright beads across Dalton's forehead. "They've no excuse to miss so badly."

"Well," grunted Sam, "there's at least one consolation: it takes seven minutes to reload a monitor's battery."

"Seven minutes! How very interesting," came the Englishman's crisp voice. "Your ship should be able to fire twice as fast."

The privateer's secondary guns then opened up in rapid succession; one of them must have struck *Montauk*'s turret a glancing blow because a bright streak suddenly gleamed upon it. *Montauk* fired a second salvo and this time fuses had been cut to the precise instant for her shells burst squarely over *Rattlesnake*, sent huge, jagged splinters to flying in all directions and dropped her upper yards crashing onto the deck. Others dangled broken, and useless, from halyards and stays.

Miraculously the pivot gun's crew entirely escaped injury and could be seen, bravely enough, continuing to fight their piece. They fired again and yet again. So did a couple of *Rattlesnake*'s lesser guns.

"Good men," quietly commented Lieutenant the Honorable Peter Burgoyne.

Dense smoke in slowly shifting clouds soon enveloped both men-of-war, spread over the river. The fort continued its strangely futile firing. On their last encounter with *Montauk*, the gunners in McAllister had scored forty-six hits.

"Oh, *damn!* Here's another hit on the privateer," growled Dalton over the thundering uproar.

"Look! Look!" suddenly yelled the gray-haired colonel. "*Nashville's* afire! God help the poor devils aboard her."

It was so. Those aboard the drifting launch gulped, cursed and pounded the rail in fury when, with astounding speed, pale red-yellow flames soared from *Rattlesnake's* long, black hull, while calmly, as if at target practice, the Union ironclad maintained her devastating fire.

That, I fancy, about does for her, thought Peter, when, all at once, the privateer's riddled funnel, too many of its stays severed, began to reel drunkenly. Still exuding smoke, it crashed overside.

In silent misery, the observers watched *Rattlesnake's* men hurriedly lower small-boats; but many crew members, fearful of what would chance when those raging fires reached the magazine, dived over her side and struck out for shore.

Sam's jaws clenched themselves until they ached as, despite everything, tears of impotent rage gathered, commenced to course slowly down either side of his strong straight nose, when the privateer's bright new ensign was lowered, oddly streaming out straight under the impulse of gases generated by the flames.

When to the privateer's signal gaff appeared a white flag, *Montauk* ceased fire and, her mission completed, commenced to raise anchor.

Soon fire reached *Rattlesnake's* magazine and, with a mighty report, she blew up. Her masts tottered and crashed, but the privateer's shattered hull could not sink because of that mudbank which had proved her undoing.

CHAPTER VI **Catesby's Landing**

BY no stretch of the imagination could the aged gundelow, *Three Sisters*, be considered a thing of beauty. Even in her early days she'd suggested a bluff-bowed and broad-beamed Dutch housewife — which, of course, was just what her builder had intended. Before the firing upon Sumter, it had been the gundelow's occupation to navigate various small rivers and creeks entering the Sounds in search of the odd cotton bale or barrel of rice which could be bought from small or distressed planters at a low price. When no wind filled her loose and often-patched brown mainsail she could be propelled by four fifteen-foot sweeps at a snail-like pace along moss-hung waterways. Now she lay to an almost abandoned wharf which had served the Catesby estate before its "Big House" had burned to the ground.

The *Three Sisters* had no deck, only wide catwalks running parallel to her thwarts and ridged their whole length by blunt cleats designed to afford sweep swingers an additional foothold.

Joe Hasker shifted a seegar across his loose-lipped mouth while, with a jaundiced eye, he once again surveyed his cargo of cotton bales. Sprawled upon them dozed the lantern-jawed infantry sergeant charged with the cargo's protection. When he glimpsed Captain Seymour and another horseman dismounting at the wharf's end, he roused up, grinning and scratching himself. Cap'n Seymour sure was one of the boys. Sometimes he brought along a chaw of tobacco or a demijohn of popskull. But not today. The cap'n seemed in a hurry.

Reynolds Seymour said, after checking the cargo: "Here are your orders, Hasker. They tell you what route to follow. Sergeant, you and your men will defend this cargo with the utmost vigor, understand?" He sounded mighty authoritative for all his slight build and youthfulness. "It's worth above eighty thousand dollars."

He paused, stared straight into the sergeant's vitreous black eyes. "Of course, if you *should* blunder into some heavy-armed Yankee patrol boat, it wouldn't do any good to get you and your men killed for the sake of a few dozen bales of cotton, would it now, Morrison?"

The sergeant grinned, vaguely scratched a scarred jaw, blue with a three day's beard. "Naw, I reckon, Cap'n, we'll know when to show fight. Last time them Bluebellies was thicker'n turds round a school-house, so we just let the bastards grab your cotton."

"You had no difficulty in escaping?" was the soft query of Captain Seymour as he used his crop to dislodge a lump of mud from the side of his boot.

"No suh, Cap'n, not much," grinned Sergeant Morrison. "Cain't figger out why they kept such a mighty poor guard over us. Them Bluebellies kept only one man to watch us, so when he fell asleep, 'twas dead easy to mosey down to our boat and shove off. Never did try to catch us, I know of."

Reynolds Seymour stepped back onto the dock. Morrison followed without instruction. When they stood out of earshot of those aboard the *Three Sisters*, Reynolds said, "Here, Sergeant, are funds with which to purchase rations. Couldn't pry a requisition out of the regimental quartermaster."

The sergeant's chipmunk-narrow jaw briefly interrupted its eternal mastication. Heyo! This sure was a fat envelope the cap'n passed over; looked like it held money enough to feed a whole regiment and his guard detail didn't number over a dozen.

Briskly, Reynolds Seymour returned to the gundelow, lying low in the water under the overhanging branches of a great gum tree. "Understand, Hasker? You're to descend the Forrest until it meets the Little Ogeechee. Then head for Raccoon Island, but don't go down that far; stop when you arrive off Harvey's Creek. Understand?"

"Reckon I do, suh," grunted he in the coat of tattered homespun, exposing snaggle stumps of teeth. "Who gets the cotton this time?"

"Your consignee is the blockade-runner, *Tigress*. She'll be hiding somewhere. They'll send a small-boat out to guide you on."

"*Tigress*, eh? Blamed old hooker used to bum the Sounds 'twixt here and Charleston. But say, Cap'n, ain't she a mite old and slow to run the blockade?"

"The *Tigress*'s capabilities are no concern of yours," Reynolds coldly reminded him. "Your job, my friend, is to see my cotton safe aboard."

As expected, the slim young officer produced a plug of tobacco and, smilingly, passed it over. "One thing, and this is important. Navigate so as to arrive off Harvey's Creek at *exactly seven o'clock* tomorrow morning — no earlier, no later. Is that clearly understood?"

"I reckon, suh," drawled Hasker, pushing a frayed palmetto hat onto the back of his head. He winked elaborately. "We'll slow up, come seven; sure as death and taxes."

"Now mind you take care. This cotton's worth eighty thousand right now and a bit more overseas."

. . . A "bit" more? Christ a'mighty! This should fetch two hundred, mebbe two-fifty hundred thousand United States dollars over in Cuba or, more likely, up North. Plenty of cotton was finding its way up to the mills of New Bedford, Nashua, Fall River, New Haven and Providence.

"Now, Hasker, here's your expense money." From a navy-blue riding coat the figure in muddied boots produced a second bulky envelope. "If successful, you can count upon a bonus when you return."

The gundelow's skipper fawned, even touched the brim of his shapeless hat. "Thank you, suh, thank you most kindly! I'll get your cotton safe aboard that there *Tigress* — the way you want; so don't you fret none."

Reynolds Seymour shook hands, then climbed ashore and strode over to an orderly steadying a handsome half-bred bay stallion. No thoroughbreds for Reynolds Seymour, admittedly no accomplished horseman. Blooded mounts were apt to be far too unpredictable, too nervous.

In the saddle again, Reynolds lingered long enough to watch the guards wake up and go crawling forward over the cargo. Apathetically, they dragged after them long-barreled flintlocks, the only muskets left to the State Guards, nowadays. Wide-shouldered Negro bucks meanwhile poled the gundelow out into the oily and sluggish current. They then manned crude sweeps, braced themselves and pulled. Rich, sad voices lifted a chant:

> When I goes out to serenade, I dress so fine and gay,
> Heave, ho-ho!
> I'se 'bleeged to tek my dawg along jest to keep de
>   gals away,
> Heave, yo-ho!

CHAPTER VII The Fugitives

VERY slowly and cautiously the runaway slave, standing waist-deep in the river, parted a screen of reeds. His little, yellowish eyes, catlike in their unblinking intensity, surveyed the riverbank above Sibley's Island by the misty, early morning light. Then, yard by yard, he explored the opposite shore, much as his Ashanti warrior father might have reconnoitered a bend of the White Volta in hostile territory.

Except for a few snowy egrets and gray-brown bitterns wading in stately style along the shore and a line of shiny black cormorants sunning themselves upon limbs of a dead tree which, undermined years ago, had toppled into the Ashley, there seemed to be no sign of life.

228

Reassured, Limber Jim climbed, dripping, into a small pirogue and paddled out to lift his trotline. The baits he'd used proved to have been effective; soon the log canoe's bottom was agleam with briskly flapping fish.

To the runaway's ears came a faint sound as of hoofs drumming upon a road somewhere across the river. Instantly, he left off rebaiting and, with powerful strokes of hand-hewn paddle, drove the pirogue deep into the screening reeds and cattails.

While thrusting his canoe deeper into this green and fresh-smelling wilderness, the big Negro commenced to grin. This was a sure-enough elegant catch. Old man Josh and Missy would be right pleased; the night before the three of them had devoured the last shreds of a young doe he had snared. With care he beached his craft, then covered it with rushes after he'd strung his catch on a sapling branch.

Wisht Ah dast paddle over to the south shore, he reflected. Maybe Ah meet up with somebody's cow and milk her into mah bailin' gourd. De Lawd alone know' how much longer dat po' stranger gwine keep out of Shut-Eye Town. Don't seem, nohow, able to keep down even thin broth — must be too strong for he stomach.

Fo' God, somebody had treated the stranger powerful mean — mean as that head overseer on Ol' Cunnel Watson's plantation treated a rebellious or a runaway nigger. What a ornery buckra he was; when in liquor he'd claim he'd rather whup a nigger than eat. Well, Misto' Cruikshank wasn't whupping nobody no mo', not since a charge of buck-shot, fired from ambush and at close range, had taken his arm off at its elbow. Could have killed that overseer, easy as not, but reckoned 'twould be a greater punishment for him to wander round like a crippled cur-dog the rest of his days.

Jim had been head hunter and fisherman, and a damn' good one, too, supplying the Watson's "Big House." Everybody 'lowed so, 'cept Misto' Cruikshank. Since this war, there's been nothing for field hands to do. Can't give cotton away, rice, either — too much of it everywhere — nothing much to stop a fellow from taking to the woods if he'd the mind to. Most able-bodied buckras had gone traipsin' off to fight the Abolitionists, so mighty few slave patrollers remained to haunt the roads and game trails.

Silently as a wild turkey, the big, ugly and very black hunter, with his catch still squirming and flopping on the sapling branch, ferreted a

229

course through tangles of myrtle, Virginia creeper, persimmon and swamp gum covering the north end of Sibley's Island.

Abruptly, Limber Jim halted and sniffed, his broad nostrils flaring like those of a buck scenting danger. He spat angrily before starting on. Dat old man was being careless agin and usin' green wood on the fire. Smoke like that could be smelled half a mile off, and seen twice as far. His low forehead was furrowed in a scowl when, silently, he reconnoitered a tumbled-down, two-room slab shack, once utilized by those of the Sibley boys who liked to shoot ducks, gamble and drink to their hearts' content, safely removed from critical womenfolk.

When the runaways had discovered this cabin it had been pretty much of a wreck with glassless windows and door sagging from its hinges. Fortunately the roof had remained relatively intact, its stone fireplace still drew, and there were even moldy, mouse-infested mattresses on some of the bunks, therefore, it had been no great task to restore the place to a habitable condition — at least for folk so humble. Best of all, the shack occupied a little vale shaded by water oaks and loblolly pines and a clear spring bubbled through sand under a big cypress. So long as no one came to suspect that there was anybody living on Sibley's Island, Limber Jim reckoned they'd be safe and even comfortable here.

"Hey, you crazy Joshua! Pull 'at green log off de fire. You fixin' git us cotched?"

The angry lines faded from Jim's broad features when out into the early sunlight strode a young mulatto woman wearing only a red bandanna turban and a badly stained and faded calico gown. Her skin shone rich, copper-brown rather than chocolate-black, while her straight black hair, narrow head and slightly humped thin nose attested the presence of Seminole blood in her veins. Far gone in pregnancy, her belly strained hard at the calico, but her walk still was light and easy.

"My, I'm sho'ly sorry, honeyman. 'Tain't Joshua's fault; it's mine. Josh's gone to tend rabbit snares and pa'tridge traps. O, Cudjoe, I done missed you!" She always called him by his real name, the African one given him by his mother. Vital, almond-shaped eyes glistened as she sidled forward. "That's sho'ly a splendiferous mess of fish. You always the bestest woodsman round Walterboro."

Splendid muscles rippling, the half-naked hunter eased his catch onto

230

a split-log bench beside the spring, then took Melissa into his arms —
very gently for a change — she was so great with child.

"Oh, mah honey," he murmured finger curling under her chin,
"Missy, yo' *is* de beautifulest gal in all Ca'lina, but fo' Gawd's sake don't
ever put no mo' green wood on de fire."

A faint cough from the shack's interior caused their heads to swing
quickly about.

"How he?"

"A little stronger, mebbe." Dropping on her heels, Melissa commenced deftly to gut a still-quivering catfish. "Thought he sho' was
fixin' to head for Shut-eye Town last night; I heard a hoodoo owl
cryin' in the swamp. Seems more peart-like this mornin', though; his
fever ain't so bad and he's breathin' easier. You get that milk?"

"No, honey, didn't dast cross de wide water. Got bright real early
dis mawnin'."

"Well, you just *got* to get some soon, Cudjoe," the girl observed
gravely. "Directly he swallows broth, he spits it up. Same with pa'tridge
stew."

"How dat hole in he chest? Proud flesh sloughing?"

"I ain't looked. I don't aim to change the poultice today. His other
hurts is healing, exceptin' that burn in his belly's button. That's mean,
real mean festered."

When Jim thrust his head into the shack the unknown still lay
motionless on a locker bunk. He presented a ghastly sight, so deeply
sunken and dark were his eye sockets, and parchment-hued cheeks. A
fast-growing brown-black beard emphasized the taut, pale lavender
outline of his lips.

"India! India!" mumbled the sick man as his eyelids fluttered weakly.
"Where — you?"

There was that name again. Jim's bullet head inclined wisely. India?
That was Indian. This buckra must love some Seminole, or maybe
Yamacraw woman.

From a cracked chamberpot discovered among the vine-smothered
ruins of Sibley Manor, the big Negro removed a ragful of cool water
and wrung it out before clumsily arranging it across the stricken
figure's forehead.

Missy was right. The unknown's breathing did sound deeper, less
rapid, while his skin no longer felt quite so burning hot. Once again

the big hunter pondered. Who could this be? Mebbe an escaped Yankee prisoner — or some deserter from the Rebel Army? This seemed more likely because, when he raved, his voice was that of a Southerner, and a Carolinian at that.

Limber Jim had no idea how many days had passed since that night they had been terrified to hear a shot ring out among the plantation house's ruins. Scared half to death, the three of them had crouched in a canebrake until daylight.

Only after Limber Jim had heard the intruders' boat pulling away had they returned to the shack. Next morning was time enough to investigate. It was then that, among a jungle of weeds behind the Sibley stables, Jim and Josh had discovered this wreck of a human being sprawled in a bloody pool and narrowly watched by a line of buzzards settled upon the paddock's crumbling fence. Good thing they'd found him just then. For sure, them vultures would soon have begun picking and tearing.

The days lengthened, grew steadily more beneficent. Mud turtles and terrapins appeared, basked upon snags and sand bars. Along the sand beaches of Sibley's Island any number of migrating shore birds, sandpipers and snipe tipped up and ran about. Among the cedars and magnolias masses of varicolored and dainty little warblers and thrushes and other songbirds filled the air with liquid melodies. Then, one evening, Jim noted the sharp spoor of several large alligators upon a sand bar. While fishing or wading he'd have to take care, now. The scrub which had reclaimed most of the island glowed with blossoms; evergreens and palmettoes lost their sere, grayish look, and assumed vernal tints.

All this Alistair Bryson observed from his position upon a bed of palmetto fronds arranged on the shack's sunny side. How dismaying to discover that intelligence and strength could return so very slowly.

One particularly pellucid spring morning, his mind, still strangely dull and stagnant, occupied itself with considerations other than immediate problems such as pain, food and sleep. For instance, why should these fugitive slaves lavish so much undeserved care and tenderness upon him? He could understand concern on the part of gentle old Joshua; undoubtedly, he once had been a preacher. Every morning and at sundown he would kneel, with the gray-pink soles of his wrinkled feet showing, before a crudely contrived cross and supplicate God that his people, like the Children of Israel, might escape from bondage.

Joshua's voice had a simple, richly beautiful quality, and his eloquence touched the sick man as never had any sermonizing from a pulpit. Missy was respectful of the nearly bald old man and studied to anticipate his wants, but, naturally, her life was centered in Limber Jim, that sable Hercules whose skin shone like a bacon rind. One day, bashfully, he explained that he was descended from a line of Ashanti warrior-kings and, with pride, indicated those bluish gums in which his fine, strong teeth were set. His was a fierce and innate dignity. No wonder his owner had been sufficiently astute to make of him a hunter, not a field hand.

Gradually, as strength returned, the gates of Alistair's memory creaked open and Josh asked the only question ever put by these sable Samaritans.

"Please, friend; who dat India you loves so gre't? Ah'd admire to pray fo' her, suh. She come from the Injins down in Geo'gia?"

India! Missy would never quite forget the way the invalid's sunken eyes had rounded themselves.

"India? Have I spoken of her?"

"All de time, suh," gently assured the ancient.

"She is — or was — my wife."

Haltingly, he related a little of what had transpired before they had found his battered, bleeding body. Good God, what could have happened to her in all this time?

To his astonishment, among the few effects found on his person remained his sketchbook and the banknotes folded within it.

In anguish, the invalid begged Limber Jim to venture into Charleston and to seek out the Ramsay house. India must be given money, must be told that he still lived and loved her — despite everything.

Missy, however, would not heed his plea. "God knows Cudjoe willin' go, but he so much a man ever'body take notice where he go." Alistair couldn't argue that. The hunter did, indeed, present a figure noteworthy in any street. Therefore it was decided that Josh should venture across into town. A "darky" so small, humble and undistinguished might safely enter Charleston under pretext of purchasing worn-out clothing. Such was needed decently to clothe the patient's emaciated form.

Never had Alistair suffered more intensely than during Josh's absence.

"He be safe," Limber Joe assured him, but didn't look confident, for all that, during the night, he had landed the old deacon on an abandoned pier and had seen him go shuffling off, differing in no particular from those hungry and homeless slaves and freedmen with which the countryside was swarming.

"Please, Misto' Bryson, you jes' eat this one l'il rabbit's leg," urged Missy, smiling that wonderfully wide warm smile of hers. Firmly, she held the calabash of food under his nose. "How else you goin' git strong so's you can go lookin' fo' yo' lady?"

When, obediently, he choked down the meat, the mulatto woman used a mallard's lustrous wing to fan bluebottle flies from his ribby body, still hideously marked by dull red burns and scars. All his hurts were healing well, even the bullet hole in his side, save for that angry, suppurating burn where Cherokee had ground out the seegar upon his navel.

To pass the time during Josh's absence, Alistair called for his sketchbook and a charcoal twig and, to Limber Jim's childish delight, reproduced the mulatto woman's handsome Indianlike profile. He called Missy his "wife in de Good Lawd's sight." Someday, as soon as possible, they would "jump the broomstick" and be wedded.

When Josh failed to signal that night, he essayed to sleep, but did so only fitfully. Time and again he roused at the gibbering of an owl, at the *plop!* of fish jumping in the river, at the furtive crackling of underbrush caused by a passing deer, by a prowling opossum or perhaps by a foraging fox.

He must eventually have lapsed into an exhausted slumber, for when he roused it was to find the old man's wrinkled and lead-hued countenance bending over him.

"Joshua! She — she is all right?"

"Please, friend, peace!"

The wounded man's eyes caught the faint, silvery glimmer of the old man's hair. "Misto' Bryson, reckon it's best Ah remind you dat de ways of de Lawd often am deep and inscrutable."

Alistair's hand shot up, gripped the old man's ragged sleeve. "Joshua! Has anything happened to my wife?"

"Friend, Ah jest cain't 'zactly say. De house you done send me to am empty."

"Empty!"

"De do' am tight locked. Ah axed 'round de neighborhood, keerful-like, but nobody didn't know nawthin', 'cept Mistress Bryson suddenly done disappeared, complete, lak de hosts of Pharaoh in de Red Sea."

Then, indeed, did Alistair Bryson cover his face, turn to the wall, and groan out his despair.

Alistair next waked to read puzzlement written large on the faces of his benefactors. Off towards the east was sounding a sullen grumbling noise, as of distant thunder.

Limber Jim's brow furrowed itself deeper than usual. "Just cain't be thunder, hit keeps up too steady, and dey ain't no kind of stormy weather about."

"That's no thunder, that's a cannonade," the invalid said after a little. "It was like that at Manassas Junction. The Federal fleet must have steamed in to attack the forts."

"Now doan' you make a bad mouth 'bout it," Missy pleaded. "Settle back, please, Misto' Bryson." She had become deeply concerned by the patient's drawn expression and lethargic movements since Joshua's return.

"Befo' God," she muttered, "it's jus' like the poor soul was being tormented all over again."

Gradually, that diapason roar down-river swelled so loud and unbroken that Alistair concluded a major engagement must be under way. What could be going on? Were *Chicora, Palmetto State,* possibly reinforced by *Charleston,* again attempting to drive away the blockaders? No. A much more important action than their few guns could make provoked this noise. Dozens, if not hundreds, of cannon were being discharged — which argued that the harbor forts, too, must be engaged.

A shadow fell across Alistair and he glanced upwards.

"Heah yo' dinner," Missy announced in her soft voice. "Please eat somethin'. You looks like a haunt."

To the mulatto woman's surprise the haggard white man devoured every bit of catfish stew and asked for more.

"How can you eat so much, suh?" Josh demanded. "You really dat hongry?"

"No. But I aim to recover my strength. I must learn what's become of my wife; and," grimly, "I've some business to conclude with certain speculators."

CHAPTER VIII A Sunny Afternoon

NEVER had he found Charleston so unsubdued, so grimly determined, or looking so woefully down-at-heel, decided Captain Reynolds Seymour. The few troops he noticed idling about the streets were either cripples — and there were masses of them — spindly youths with fiery eyes, or gray-haired dotards. Some were wearing bits and pieces of uniform dating back beyond the Mexican War. Every able man, it seemed, had either been ordered North or to the city's outer defenses.

The citizenry went about their occupations wearing an air of defiant, if uneasy, expectancy.

Within an hour, the spruce young captain newly arrived from Savannah found out why. Two days earlier, the Army's always alert Coastal Signal System had semaphored that no less than *nine* Union ironclads and twice as many wooden men-of-war had cast anchor below Morris Island.

Inevitably, rumors increased the number of monitors to eleven, fifteen; some said eighteen had been sighted. The Union armada was reported to number nearly a hundred vessels of all types.

It remained inescapable, however, to the Confederate High Command, that the Union's entire mailed might had been placed under the command of Rear-Admiral S. F. Du Pont. The mission of this fleet, obviously enough, was to reduce Charleston — that ever-defiant hotbed of Secession. After the bloody disaster at Fredericksburg last fall, the North sorely needed a taste of victory.

All the same, Reynolds Seymour, sauntering back to his hotel, felt exceptionally pleased with life and the outcome of a discreet interview with Judge Riegler, Mr. Archer Wasson and his beetle-browed son, who had proved a bit more difficult to dicker with, yet the outcome of Reynolds's negotiations had exceeded his most sanguine expectations.

236

Talk about luck! He'd reached the city at *le moment juste.* Thanks to the threat posed by Admiral Du Pont's formidable collection of ironclads, Seymour's greenbacks — obtained never mind where — had secured for him, and at a ridiculously low figure, a substantial interest in the heretofore fabulously successful Excalibur Trading Company.

No sooner had the smoke of Du Pont's passing armada stained the sky off Morris Island than an unostentatious exodus began. Such stalwarts as Major St. George Lambkin, however, loudly refused to budge. That bellicose little man had proclaimed, in the Planters Hotel's bar, "My home may become a coffin for my loved ones, gentlemen, but I never shall desert it so long as the Stars and Bars fly above it."

Clad in the claret and gray uniform of the Cape Chatham Fencibles, Reynolds Seymour turned into Queen Street, revelling in this early April evening's mellow warmth. The only unpleasant consideration was that, tomorrow, he must board the train for Savannah. He must reach there in time to act upon intelligence that, in Upper Vernon Creek, a Yankee patrol boat had been successfully ambushed. Most likely it would have been captured by a detachment from the Cape Chatham Fencibles. Now wouldn't it be utterly astonishing if a generous supply of drugs weren't found hidden in her paint locker?

At this hour the silent, moss-hung streets were so deserted that the squabbling of sparrows upon the brick sidewalk attracted the stroller's attention.

At the entrance to a small park, Reynolds hesitated. It wasn't yet six o'clock, so why return so soon to his stuffy suite at the Charleston Hotel? It was so noisy and overcrowded. Reynolds pushed open a rusty, cast-iron gate to the park.

He was sauntering along, savoring a fine Havana seegar presented by Mr. Wasson, when he noticed a slim young female seated on a bench, apparently enjoying the warmth. She was wearing, of all things, a wide yellow skirt. What a cheery vision, illumined by golden sunlight! A lovely contrast to those somber and ever-present mourning garments darkening Charleston's streets.

His gaze lighted. By God, yonder *was* a lovely creature, finely formed and dainty, by the look of her. Especially, he was intrigued by the luscious curve of a tawny cheek just visible beneath this girl's dark green bonnet. Reynolds slowed his gait, halted, pretended an

237

interest in a row of scorched and blackened Ionic columns standing before the ruins of a dwelling half destroyed during the great fire.

Covertly, the young officer adjusted the plain black silk stock covering his throat, then checked his uniform's silvered buttons. Finally, he rubbed his cuff over a brightly gilded belt buckle adorned by CSA in silver letters.

From the corner of his eye, he felt convinced that, for all her downcast eyes, this demure young female probably had noted his presence. Why else should her fingers commence nervously to knead the jet-beaded reticule in her lap? Who or what might she be? Some young wife bored by a husband's long absence, a well-bred but penniless and desperate refugee? There were so many in every city from Richmond, south. Or could she be, as he was beginning to suspect, a clever harlot? Young and pretty enough to risk exposing her attractions by daylight? Reynolds, during the past years, had had pleasantly to do with all three categories.

Squaring shoulders in a military manner, he casually bore down, reconnoitered the bench, increasingly stimulated by glimpses of a delightfully retroussé nose and softly rounded chin.

As the grass-grown walk of chevron brick guided him closer his interest soared. Lord! How tiny were those slippers peering from beneath her skirt just a bit farther than should those of a thoroughly conservative young lady. Ha! Even as he drew near she shifted indolently on her seat and trim ankles became daringly exposed, even to the tops of prettily tasseled balmoral boots.

Reynolds was about to venture a cautious overture when this pretty young female's reticule slipped off her lap and landed upon the bricks almost at her feet. He pounced upon it with a celerity which instantly annoyed him. Gad! He would have done better to appear casual.

"Yours, I believe, ma'am?" Smilingly, he offered a graceful bow, became aware of heavily fringed blue eyes so dark that, at first glance, he mistook them for black.

"Why, why, thank you, sir." Vivid red lips glistened. "How very clumsy of me. I—I fear I have inconvenienced you."

Reynolds, suddenly a little breathless, stared in shameless admiration of the most distractingly beautiful face he had beheld in a long, long time.

238

"No trouble at all, ma'am," smiled Captain Seymour. "I see that you, also, appreciate the warmth of this magnificent afternoon. Surely, it ought to be enjoyed at leisure — and in peace."

Amazingly long black lashes fluttered downwards. Expertly or demurely?

"I quite agree, sir. Is it not especially enjoyable after such a long spell of wet and gloomy weather?" Never had he heard a voice sound quite so clear and melodious. What in the world had he here?

"Ma'am, will you permit me to present myself?"

"Oh, no, sir! That would be most unseemly."

"You are undoubtedly right." The supple young fellow's smile was curiously open and disarming. "Nevertheless, ma'am, I am Ralph Supplee, a humble and rather lonely captain in the Cape Chatham Fencibles — and very much at your service." His second bow would have won approval from the most critical of chaperones.

She in the yellow and black fluttered, tucked feet under her as if preparing to rise.

"Oh, sir, I — I really don't know what to say. What if some one should — notice?"

He extended a reassuring hand gloved in doeskin. "Please! Don't alarm yourself, ma'am. Really, I have not the least intention of forcing myself upon you. Say the word and I will depart on the instant."

The young woman hesitated a long instant, timorously undecided. "Oh, sir, I don't know what to say," she repeated.

"Then in Heaven's name take pity upon a poor, unlucky dog of an officer on detached service in an unfamiliar city." He flicked his hand to the brim of his kepi in a semimilitary salute. "I have heard it ventured, in polite circles, that the ladies of Charleston, because of this war, are at times hospitable to lonely strangers."

For once Reynolds found himself unable correctly to estimate the situation. Obviously, here was no common trollop. She dressed, talked and looked like a lady, yet there was no blinking the fact that she *had* permitted her bag to fall at his feet.

As further baffling and contradictory clues, only a trace of rouge was discernible upon her cheeks, yet her hair had been dressed into an intricate and alluring coiffure. Why? So elaborate a design could have been thus arranged but for a single purpose.

239

He seated himself beside her. "Am I correct that you, too, are a stranger in Charleston, Miss . . . ?"

She flushed becomingly and lowered her gaze. "I am Miss Iris Benson."

Across the park a pair of black-clad ladies in shawls and full bombazine skirts lifted chins and ostentatiously averted their gaze from the seated couple.

"Look there, Parthenia! Have you ever seen anything more brazen? From the first time I laid eyes on her I've thought India Bryson no better than a — a common trollop! Just look at her ogle that handsome young fellow. Do you recognize his regimentals?"

CHAPTER IX **Supper by Candlelight**

RELAXING her thin and weary body upon the divan's red plush cushions, India sighed. She was making a determined effort to retain complete control of her senses. When last had she been so comfortable — so, so warm, so well fed? When had she last tasted such a variety of delicate wines and been so amused by a man's conversation? Ages! Ages! Nonetheless, she decided to be wary about sharing a second bottle of champagne ordered up by this boldly fascinating and handsome young captain. But it would be difficult, so tenderly, so gratefully, did this clear and sparkling liquid warm her being.

Nombre de Dios! This Captain Supplee must be richer than that Lydian king called Croesus. Never once had he so much as inquired the price of this dish or that wine. In his shirt sleeves now, and sweating a little, he was working loose a cork. Heavenly days! What a prodigious amount of liquor this darkly handsome young fellow could tuck away! He broke off his efforts, to unknot his stock and open his shirt two buttons — without asking her permission, she noticed. Curly black hair kept falling over his dead-white forehead. Impatiently, he kept brushing it back into place.

Anxiously, India's gaze sought a dusty bottle of cognac — the headwaiter said it was really a brandy favored by Napoleon the First. She hoped her host wasn't going to try to press more on her. It was so terribly strong. Brandy *and* champagne? Recalling something Rafe once had told her, India arose, laughing lightly. Her bolero of black silk fluttered to the carpet, but she made no effort to retrieve it. The looseness of her blouse left not only her shoulders bared but exposed swelling curves trembling above the lace-trimmed top of a corset cover. She drifted over to the sideboard.

"You have been working too hard, and all alone, to make our evening a gay one — allow me, *amigo mío*, to pour this, our next drink."

"Why, that's damn' considerate." He wiped the sweating bottle with care. "I vow, Miss Iris, tonight I'm the luckiest soldier you'll find in all this lovely, and soon to be victorious, Southland."

Reynolds slipped an arm about her waist and kissed her on the mouth, while at the same time jerking loose strings supporting the yellow skirt. She swayed free and stepped out of the fallen garment before rolling her eyes ceilingwards, and in her best theatrical voice sighed, "Oh, Ralph! Ralph! Have pity. I am undone."

"Undone!" Reynolds yielded to a burst of deep-throated laughter. "That's quite the timeliest pun I've heard in years, my pretty. That lacework on your petticoat is really beautiful."

Teasingly, India pretended to resume her yellow skirt — the same she had danced in at Charleston Jail — but ended by draping it over a chair. Then, a trifle uncertain as to what might be the outcome, she commenced some spinning steps from an Andalusian dance which gradually elevated the hems of several petticoats above her knees.

Reynolds stepped eagerly forward, eyes alight. He restrained himself, however, in order better at a distance to survey this tawny-complexioned girl's impromptu dance about his suite's little dining room. Eventually, breathless and radiant, she halted beside the sideboard and splashed a generous measure of cognac into an empty glass — then, almost in the same motion, filled the goblet to its brim with champagne.

India raised her own half-filled glass, smiled a seductive little smile. "Well, here's to Ind —" She almost gave herself away. "Iris Benson and Ralph Supplee. Best company in all the world." After they had drunk deep India immediately cried, "Let's drink damnation to all Yankees."

Reynolds grinned a trifle owlishly. "Amen to that, and with all my heart. All the same, Iris, my love, I mus' say some Yankees have their uses." Perspiring still more heavily, he clasped his guest to him and showered her glowing neck and shoulders with moist caresses.

After kissing him lightly, India spun out of his grasp and hovered, poised and graceful, before embers glowing in the fireplace. "What did you mean by 'Some Yankees have their uses'?"

"Why, that we have Yankees to thank for all the pretty things I'm going to buy for you!" he murmured and swayed nearer, well-formed mouth red, shiny and slack while tossing off yet another jigger of cognac. "Just as it's the Yanks who furnished the wines, champagne and brandy we've had for supper."

"But, Ralph! I still don't comprehend —"

He winked over his glass. "You mightn't guess, thanks to this dear War, that a certain Captain of Militia Infantry is growing to be a rich man, Iris, a very rich man. Hope to God the fighting goes on forever."

She looked prettily puzzled, reached out to smooth his dark disordered hair. "But — but you're a soldier and soldiers are supposed to hate war — all I've ever met, have."

Reynolds flushed a dull red, slopped fresh champagne into their glasses and didn't seem to realize there was cognac in the bottom of the one India passed him. "Fighting is for fools, my pretty little bird. Stupid, unimaginative fools, so I leave the killing and getting killed to such fine patriotic clods as my brother, Sam Seymour."

"Seymour? I thought you said your name was Supplee?"

Laughing, he made a wide motion. "So I did, but think nothing of that. Generally use 'Supplee' as my *nom de boudoir*."

"Have you other brothers or sisters?" India fenced.

Momentarily, he sobered. "Had 'nother brother, older, named Irad; another sobersides dedicated to the cause. Poor devil's dead, God rest his soul."

Briefly, Reynolds recalled that unforgettable Christmas Eve when, in Richmond, he first had beheld Irad's wife, Sylvia. All at once he became aware that Sylvia and this Benson girl, in many ways, were similar, physically at least. Both were petite, but generously developed as to figure. They had the same kind of provocative, naturally vivid lips; wide and expressive eyes. Sylvia, he solemnly decided, might stand an inch or so taller; she'd be a few years older, too.

The girl in camisole and petticoats swayed lightly over to touch glasses. "Tell me, Ralph, do you have cousins by the name of Seymour?"

"Woods are full of 'em," Reynolds exhaled noisily as the last of his drink bubbled out of sight. "Why?"

"A while ago I met a Virginian called Dabney Seymour." She exerted a conscious effort to steady the red-and-gilt-painted walls' gentle swaying.

"Dabney? Dabney? Oh, yes. Think I have heard of a Dabney Seymour. Sure I have. Came from near Norfolk, but attended some Northern college — place called Dartmouth, I think. Why so curious?"

The pink tip of India's tongue appeared, described a saucy circle around her lips. "Don't be jealous, Ralph. I only thought him right attractive. Charm must run in your family. Tell me more about him."

Seating himself on the red-velvet-covered divan he pulled her onto his lap and kissed the damp nape of her neck. "Don't know much more. Somewhere, I heard he was studyin' somethin' or other in England, when this lovely, delightful war began — that's all." Unsteadily, he ripped his shirt the rest of the way open and pressed her head, sadly disheveled, against a thin coating of black hair covering his muscular and well-formed chest. "Forget about this Dabney fellow — only Seymour you're to be interested in is me — Reynolds. Understand? Me." Suddenly, he wound cruel fingers into the hair at the base of her head then jerked it back and, drooling a little, bruised her lips with a succession of kisses so ruttish that the room began to whirl about.

India took refuge in passivity. "Oh, Ralph, you're magnificent. Kiss me hard! Harder! You're so masterful — isn't it wonderful that we should have found one another?" Then, somehow, it became all too easy to act and sound convincing in her responses. Half-forgotten tides, deliciously warm and erotic, commenced to race through her breasts, her loins. What was so fascinating about this ardent young fellow with the insatiable lips and hot black eyes?

Reynolds's hand groped towards a kerosene lamp glowing under a beaded shade of rose-tinted glass and dimmed its flame almost to obscurity. "Iris," he whispered presently. "Oh, my darling, have you followed — this — er — calling very long?"

"Only recently," she whispered dizzily. "I'd no choice."

"Why?"

"My husband was killed last summer in a battle somewhere in Maryland. I think it was Sharpsburg. He wasn't rich — so I — I sold everything of value we owned. I tried to find work — but — but I guess I can't do anything useful very well."

243

She snuggled close against the sweat-marked cambric of his shirt, made no effort to hamper the questing of his fingers beneath her corset's top.

"Last week, honey, I — well, I guess I came to the end of my money. I haven't any friends here, so I starved a while and then — well, here I am." Lazily, her finger tips stroked first his fluffy black sideburns, then his chest. "You really like me, don't you, darling?"

"You're inexpert — and shy at the wrong moment sometimes, but that's exciting. Never did like a practiced whore."

"*Whore?*" India's lips flattened themselves against her teeth and she jumped up. "I am *not* a whore! I've never before earned money — like this!"

"Well, you're starting now." Rolling onto one thigh, he fumbled in his trousers' pocket and brought out a thick roll of banknotes. "Reckon it'll be fun breaking you in."

Blood-injected eyes veiling themselves, Reynolds belched softly. "Ever figured how much you're worth, for all night? Plenty. That's what you ought to charge. Plenty. I'll meet your price, you're so damn' lovely and warm."

India crossed on unsteady legs to the sideboard and swallowed a deeper draught of wine than she had intended. Fundamentally honest, she appreciated the soundness of his advice to charge a lot. Strange. Why did she no longer feel aghast at the step she was about to take? On the contrary, she was experiencing a voluptuous thrill over the prospect of, at long last, becoming what she had been so often called. How infinitely amusing it was to hark back on those days in the theater and recall how skillfully — and successfully — she had resisted all manner of advances.

Touseled head sunk on chest, Reynolds glassily was considering that delicate, yet well-rounded figure standing, half-dressed, before the sideboard and preparing yet another libation. For sure, this was a day to remember! He'd secured those Excalibur shares at the psychological moment, and now this exquisite creature, fresh as a spring dawn, but hot as noon in July, preparing to surrender herself — at once deliciously diffident, yet Lydian in every look and movement. Tomorrow, he resolved all at once, he'd look for some snug little place in which to install Iris; she was much too sweet, intelligent and refined to waste her charms on other men. After all, his new interests should bring him to Charleston more frequently now; certainly often enough to justify such an arrangement. God above, he was in luck, all right. The conviction brought with it a sudden increase in his intoxication — and his desires.

"Irish, pour me 'nother drink — not so much brandy thish time." How stimulating it was thus to be able to order, and not invite, her to obey.

She complied, wanton in her least movement.

"Well, darlin', wha's to be the price of your favors? As I said, don' be modes' about your firs' lapse from virtue. Funny, believe you're not lyin' 'bout it. You're lucky. I got money, plenty money — more where that comes from."

India drew a deep breath and, aware of a strange buzzing noise in her ears, she kissed with no lack of ardor. "You're right, Mr. — Seymour, so I shan't accept a penny under five thousand dollars for going to bed with you."

"*Five thousand dollars!*" Momentarily sobered, he heaved himself up on one elbow, blinked, incredulous. "Jesus God! Not even Ninon de l'Enclos or Pompadour dared name such a sum!"

"Possibly. But, after all, five thousand — Confederate — isn't an overwhelming sum."

"Oh, Confederate —" He grinned in sheepish confusion. "Thought you wanted greenbacks."

She watched his startled expression relax as his sensitive and tapering fingers closed over the stem of a continuously refilled glass. "All the same, tha's a lot of money."

"You don't really think so, do you, honey?" A slow, Cyprian curve shaped India's lips as, after shaking free the last pins restraining her hair, she jerked undone a gathering ribbon to stand revealed in a brief chemise.

"God, no! Come here!"

"First, we must drink to our — our new association, mustn't we? Please, dear, it's important. I want to."

While in a semidaze she, for an uncounted occasion, mixed champagne and brandy, he settled back on the divan, eyelids drooping. "Ralph? You don't mind presenting me with my fee — now?"

"For a beginner, you learn fast," Reynolds stifled a belch. "Here. 'S all yours — more 'n you've asked, I reckon."

"Thank you, darling. Aren't I the lucky one to have met with so generous a protector to start with? Because you've been so very sweet I'll dance for you."

245

"No! No!" he objected thickly. "C'mere. You — Want you. Here's money — come!"

"The appetite comes with the waiting," India mocked and, by the dim lamplight, executed an off-balance pirouette.

"You — you're maddening. C'm here." Unsteadily, Reynolds Seymour attempted to rise, but could only sink back on the divan; a shiny dribble of liquor escaped the corners of his mouth. India danced until perspiration commenced to spangle her body.

"Bravo! Brav —" his words degenerated into an indistinct mumble — " 'm 'ere."

"Oh, Reynolds, I mean Ralph, don't go to sleep — yet. It would be discourteous."

"Come 'ere," he repeated and lurched in her direction but only sagged limply onto the floor. His dark head lolled over sidewise and his breathing became stertorous.

CHAPTER X The Richmond Express

THERE was nothing unusual about the fact that, at twelve noon, the North Eastern Railroad's 10:30 express for Richmond remained motionless beside its platform in Pocotazlio Station. Its locomotive had suffered another breakdown so, resignedly, the passengers sought refreshment, alcoholic and otherwise, and stood about discussing the war.

It being a pleasant, balmy and windless day, only a few people remained in the decrepit old cars, but among them, sat a petite young woman wearing a commonplace gray poke bonnet and a black cape. She occupied the furthermost seat in the forward car, unfortunately close to a reeking privy, and sat facing backwards; by simply tilting her head a little she could obtain a view of the train's entire length.

India Bryson kept crumpling a copy of the *Richmond Dispatch* until, at last, she tossed it aside. Every time someone boarded one of the cars she gathered herself, prepared to escape, via the forward platform, and lose herself in the freightyard.

246

Had Captain Seymour gone to the police? Anxiously, India took to kneading that same reticule she had used to attract his attention.

I haven't stolen this money, she kept insisting to herself. Was it my fault if, after Ralph, no, Reynolds, made me that — that present he went sound asleep? I couldn't be expected to wait around till he woke up, now could I? And yet, the bargain was for all night, and I didn't stay all night. Why, oh, why, won't this wretched old train pull out?

Gradually, the car grew so stuffy and the privy's sour smell so strong she wished she dared alight and seek the refreshment counter; but she didn't. Somebody might recognize her and thus be enabled to report the direction of her flight.

What fate had befallen Alistair? To occupy her mind, she returned to that seemingly insoluble question. Surely, despite his anguish, a man so innately fine and honorable would not voluntarily abandon his wife forever without affording her opportunity for an explanation? Wouldn't this confounded train ever leave?

By an effort she controlled herself and her crisping nerves and, smoothing out the newspaper, reread an item which had attracted her attention. It stated that a Mr. Desmond Kilpatrick — she felt sure it must be the same actor she had played opposite to while a member of Mr. Edwin Booth's company — recently had formed a troupe of his own. At present, it was entertaining Richmond audiences with a popular comedy entitled *King Linkum the First*.

Next week, Mr. Kilpatrick's Thespians would offer *The Eton Boy* and *The Merchant of Venice*.

The Confederate capital, it appeared, was quite as avid for theatrical entertainment as New York, Philadelphia or Boston; just as eager to win momentary surcease from dreadful realities. A wonderful possibility occurred to her. Surely, Des Kilpatrick would at least let her try out for a part? Just a small one, to start with?

Aside from dancing, comedy always had been her forte. How exciting, how grand and glorious it would be once more to associate with witty and open-minded fellow artists. Among troupers she would no longer need to watch her every deed, word and look lest they be misinterpreted.

You poor, sweet ninny, she thought. You never should have quit the theater. From now on, matters are bound to improve.

Wonder what Richmond will be like?

She relaxed on the hard wooden seat and tried to visualize Desmond Kilpatrick. She succeeded in recalling a blond, boldly handsome and virile individual verging on middle age. She remembered him, too, as a consummate actor who gave his best performances when just a trifle under the influence of alcohol. The singular thing about him was that he kept on liking and helping her, even after she had repelled, in no uncertain terms, the raffish advances he invariably made to a young and pretty actress. He'd been thoroughly disgusted and had gotten whimsically drunk when he learned she was quitting the theater to marry a penniless Southern newspaperman.

A series of strident whistlings announced that, at long last, a locomotive was clanking up to claim the train of cars. Indescribable relief filled the girl in the gray poke bonnet when her fellow passengers filed noisily in to reoccupy their seats.

The engine's bell set up a clangor that sounded sweet as angel chimes in India Bryson's ears. The train shuddered and actually had commenced to move when a dull rumbling noise sounded in the distance. Startled, the passengers gazed at one another.

A sallow, sad-faced artillery captain who carried his arm in a black silk sling spoke up. "Reckon those damned monitors have come in to tackle the forts."

CHAPTER XI Battery Wagner

"WELL, seems like our friends out there are getting under way at last," calmly observed Captain A. Hunter Davidson, commanding the Naval Submarine Battery. He jotted down the time in a notebook.

A knot of sunburned officers, clad in a weird miscellany of uniform and civilian clothes, leveled binoculars, watched units of the Union fleet, one by one, quit their anchorage off North Edisto Creek. Soon the whole squadron began to steam on a northerly course, trailing long, lazy streamers of sooty smoke.

Artillery officers in Battery Wagner studied the enemy's approach with mixed emotions. So these insignificant-looking little ironclads out there

248

were the fabulous and dreaded monitors? Would they prove impervious to the fire of heavy coast artillery?

Certainly, those small, black men-of-war didn't offer a gun pointer much of a target, decided Major Huger, 1st South Carolina Artillery, and commander of the fort. Silently, he prayed that the Yankee ships might pass within reasonable range.

"Can anyone identify the various enemy vessels?" Captain Davidson inquired of the group surrounding him.

"The biggest ship out there, the one without any masts, is the *New Ironsides*," explained a very tall and painfully sunburned captain. "She's an armored frigate."

"Never heard of a frigate without masts."

"She must have had some. Reckon they've been sent down, though," a tall officer drawled.

The day was so still even the least noise was audible; no waves broke upon the beach immediately below Battery Wagner's sand-and-palmetto-log bastions; twitterings raised by a flock of silly little sandpipers sounded absurdly important.

In line ahead, the enemy paralleled the coast, brought death and destruction steadily nearer. Commented a sparsely bearded lieutenant, "It's past noon. Wonder why Du Pont didn't attack earlier?"

"On account of low water, I expect." Absently, Captain Davidson undid yet another button of a red-and-white-checkered shirt. The sunlight was growing hotter by the minute. "Besides, the Yankees have grown damn' scared of our torpedoes."

They had reason to be. All week long *Sumter*, a small coasting steamer attached to the Torpedo Service, had traveled about planting patterns of torpedoes and rows of rope entanglements at various strategic locations along the approaches to Charleston Harbor.

Lieutenant Dabney Seymour and a Mr. Cheves, an expert civilian electrician, had superintended these operations. It had been Cheves, a small, dark and tense individual, who'd insisted that the Submarine Battery's biggest torpedo — manufactured from a boiler from a rice mill, waterproofed and packed with half a ton of gunpowder — should be sunk in the main ship channel. Over it any vessel of considerable draft would have to pass; the Yankee flagship out there, for instance. *New Ironsides* must draw considerably more than any of her consorts.

The great mine, therefore, lurked squarely in the center of this channel. Mr. Cheves himself supervised the connecting of its electrical detonating wires to wet batteries protected by a small shed beyond Battery Wagner's southernmost gun emplacement. Not a man in Battery Wagner but was joyfully aware of the boiler-torpedo's existence, and its approximate location. By Grabs! It should be quite something to watch an ironclad get blown sky-high.

Those assigned to the Submarine Battery expected either Mr. Cheves or Lieutenant Seymour to be in charge of the detonating knife-switch, but it appeared that Captain Davidson, as Commanding Officer, intended to set off that monstrous charge.

Tensely, gun crews, half-clad and turning salmon-pink with sunburn, waited beside a long-barreled, thirty-two-pound rifled gun; a twenty-four-pound rifle and a brace of thirty-two-pound smoothbores. Most of these bronzed fellows wore dirty, broad-brimmed palmetto hats and had stripped to the waist. They kept shading their eyes and, in their anxiety, chewed spasmodically on lumpy cuds of tobacco.

Dabney Seymour squatted upon a bombproof, the better to observe the approach of this, the greatest ironclad fleet yet to appear upon the high seas, and steadied field glasses upon his knees.

Muscles hardened in the big Virginian's scarred cheeks as he studied a number of small yellow flags drooping above buoys set to identify various ranges for the gunners.

Far off to the left, between Cummings' Point and Fort Sumter, could be recognized the squat outlines of *Palmetto State* and *Chicora,* ready and eager to close action should the great guns in Forts Bee, Beauregard, Sumter and other batteries fail to check the Federal assault.

Out yonder, Donald Bryson must be gnawing his lip, along with cheerful young Duncan Mullinix and the rest of the regular Navy men. Lord! How long had these fellows serving in the rams been looking down their noses at the Torpedo and Submarine Services!

"It's a damned shame," remarked Captain Davidson, "that we've ready not even one torpedo boat! A *David* would come in right handy about now."

Commented Lieutenant Steedman, very tall and thin, "Thought they'd only seven, but I count eight monitors out there."

Fellow officers pushed up hat brims and, refocusing, agreed that yonder indeed cruised seven single-turreted monitors, followed by a curious, double-turreted vessel which somewhat resembled them in size and silhouette.

"Say, that's a queer-looking craft."

"She's called the *Keokuk*, and was designed not by Ericsson but by a fellow called Whitney," Seymour explained. "She differs from the Ericssons in that her turrets don't revolve. Her guns can be aimed only by pointing the entire ship, which, to my mind, is a damned stupid notion."

Steedman, the tall lieutenant, blinked in the strong sunlight. "Wherever did you learn all that, Mr. Seymour?"

Deliberately, Dabney eyed the fellow. "Apparently, sir, you are unaware that, for some time, General Beauregard has enjoyed the services of an excellent espionage agency and a semaphore system which transmits intelligence of such a nature the length of his department."

The inane mewing laughter of sea gulls and terns sounded shrill over the rhythmic throb of propellers and laboring of engines; inexorably, the Union fleet churned near, nearer, under a canopy of smoke Stygian against the softly blue heavens. When almost abreast of Battery Wagner, the leading monitor suddenly slowed and veered out of line, spewing clouds of silvery steam from her exhaust pipes.

"That there will be one of our obstructions going to work, sir," a freckled young sergeant of the Torpedo Service grinned at Dabney. "Reckon her propeller's got fouled."

"Hope you're right, son."

Meanwhile, Captain Davidson nervously fingered a slender brown goatee, attention centered upon the progress of the enemy flagship — she was the fifth in column. He thought, "This *New Ironsides,* however deadly, is no thing of beauty; dismasted like that, she's ugly — looks like a coal hulk."

Suddenly, he snatched up his binoculars. Yes. The great, armored frigate *had* begun to yaw along her course! She, too, must be experiencing steering trouble right among that treacherous maze of shoals and sand bars which rendered the approaches to Charleston Harbor so difficult.

Everyone who had glasses of any description focused them on *New Ironsides,* reportedly the most powerful man-of-war in the world, her side armor being no less than four-and-a-half inches thick! Her battery, the informed knew, consisted of two one-hundred-and-fifty pound rifles and fourteen eleven-inch guns — truly monster cannon.

An Intelligence officer then rapidly identified the enemy ironclads by means of the varicolored stripes painted upon each vessel's pilothouse. *Passaic* was second in line, then steamed *Montauk*, then *Patapsco*, followed by *New Ironsides*. After the flagship came *Catskill*, *Nantucket* and *Nahant*. Last in line labored *Keokuk*, she of the fixed twin turrets.

In momentary expectation of a salvo from the enemy, officers watching in Battery Wagner followed Major Huger's example and sought shelter behind parapets of sand and palmetto logs. Thus they were forced to content themselves by squinting through the embrasures. Around them gun crews handled their training tackles, rammers and spongers, and fidgeted. Gun captains profanely begged for permission to open fire.

Sad-faced Lieutenant Webb's expression lit. "My God, Captain! Looks like the Yankees are about to pass right over that boiler-torpedo!"

An atmosphere of almost unbearable suspense invaded the electrician's shed, froze the men grouped about the detonating switch into strained immobility. Just as the line of monitors neared a tiny black buoy indicating the great torpedo's position, *Nahant*, now heading the enemy column, lost headway, just like *Weehawken*. As in her case, steam escaped from her exhaust and a crowd of men swarmed out of her turret and ran forward. Apparently something must have gone wrong with the monitor's antitorpedo rake — another invention of the imaginative Dahlgren.

To avoid their temporarily incapacitated consort, the next monitors veered out to sea; *away* from the torpedo. "Damn!" growled Mr. Cheves, acid-stained fingers curling and uncurling themselves. "The whole damn' Yankee fleet's going around my mine!"

He was in error, though.

"Why the hell don't they shoot at us?" growled a gray-bearded gun captain.

"Reckon them Bluebellies is saving their fire for Sumter and Moultrie — which is all right with Mrs. Beasley's boy!"

Dabney, his sunburned features drawn and tense, nodded agreement. How fast the enemy vessels seemed to be advancing towards their doom — yet, actually, they were barely crawling along at quarter-speed. He turned to a sergeant in a striped cotton jersey and baggy gray pants supported by a gallus of bright red flannel. "Mullins, the enemy aren't going to fire, it seems, so I reckon this is about as good a time as any to send over that load of shells they want in Emplacement Number Four."

"But, suh, suppose them Bluebellies gets minded to start shootin' after all? Ah don't aim to git mah mules hurt."

"They don't intend to open fire or they'd have started long ago," Seymour said crisply. "Now get going. Better go along the beach, sand's hard there."

"It had better be hard," grunted the sergeant. "Them shells make a danged heavy load and my wheels dig in something fierce." He saluted and sought his long-eared team.

A murmur of surprise circulated the artillerymen in broad-brimmed hats when, to the staccato cracking of a whip lash, the ordnance wagon rolled out onto the beach sand with its four mules leaning hard into their collars and holding low their heads. Derisive jeers arose.

"Come awn, Pop! Keep them Missouri nightingales movin'! Leave them Yankee jackasses admire their kin."

Derisively, the driver squirted an arc of tobacco juice at the distant men-of-war and used his whip. He had to. The mules were straining, struggling to turn wheels digging deep, deep into the damp gray sand.

"Who ordered that wagon sent along the beach?" shouted Major Huger. "It'll get stuck for sure and, my God, suppose a shell hits it?"

"I reckon, Major, it must have been somebody down at the torpedo station," drawled Steedman.

The ammunition wagon, however, did not stop while paralleling Battery Wagner's entire length and, to a triumphant cracking of the sergeant's whip, it disappeared behind Emplacement Number Five.

"It's really getting hot!" Dabney Seymour commented and blew beads of perspiration from his eyebrows before once more scanning that grim, black line of ironclads drawing silvery streaks over the glassy sea.

Nahant's work party quickly enough disencumbered the torpedo rake, so now she was smoking furiously in her effort to catch up with her consorts. But *New Ironsides,* for some reason, still seemed unwilling to obey her helm. The Federal flagship continued zigzagging ponderously along the main ship channel towards the boiler-torpedo.

"Praise God and all His angels!" yelled Captain Davidson. "He couldn't steer straighter for that torpedo. The switch ready, Mr. Seymour?"

"Aye, aye, sir," Dabney told him. "The wire ends are secure in the terminal posts." A series of icy ripples descended his spine while, inexorably, that ugly great vessel steamed on towards her doom.

"Oh God! God! She has less than a hundred yards to travel!" Features working strongly, Captain Davidson bent over the switch; at the same time he kept his gaze riveted on that little black buoy.

Louder swelled an excited babble in the emplacements. Glory hallelujah! Out yonder the giant armored frigate had almost reached the fatal spot.

"Oh, my God! Look! Look!" yelled Lieutenant Webb. "She's going to anchor right over the boiler!"

Seymour licked sun-cracked lips, and, from a corner of his eye, watched Captain Davidson bend forward, squinting through a telescope long since mounted and aligned upon the torpedo's position. When the enemy flagship's bow moved up to the buoy, then passed it, he experienced an overwhelming urge to yell.

Those others in the command shack watched Captain Davidson's thumb and forefinger close over the switch's blade handle.

"God pity the poor devils out there," breathed Lieutenant Webb. "They've not the least chance for their lives."

The forward progress of New Ironsides ended and she let go an anchor. Among those emplacements fronting the ocean sounded a fierce shout of anticipation, but in the shack such penetrating silence prevailed that everyone heard a little *click!* caused by the switch blade on being jammed down.

As in a nightmare, Dabney Seymour felt himself grow twelve feet tall. Lieutenant Webb raised the Rebel yell but, quickly, it died away. No explosion took place out on the bright blue water; nothing at all happened, except that the Union flagship gradually rounded to her anchor to swing *directly* above the boiler-torpedo!

"Christ above!" snarled Mr. Cheves, his features gone a sickly gray. "Throw that switch again, Cap'n. Throw it hard!"

"I have, Mr. Cheves," rasped Davidson, "so it does no good to blaspheme our Savior."

"What the devil's wrong then?" Dabney choked, wiping away a sheen of sweat from rigid features.

"Possibly the connecting wires are loose, sir?" Webb suggested.

"They're not loose!" snarled the civilian. "See?" Savagely his fingers drove at brass set-screws securing the detonating wires' ends to the terminal posts.

"Maybe the battery's dead."

"It's not. Look!" Seymour jerked loose the wire ends, and caused a bright blue spark to leap between the battery's posts.

Mr. Cheves commenced to rave. "What in God's name's gone wrong? Look at that damn ship out there. Somebody tell me what's gone wrong!"

"Maybe the switch is defective," Dabney said. "I'll connect up a new one."

While *New Ironsides* lay motionless offshore with smoke from her single funnel spiralling lazily into a cloudless sky, exasperation and frustration reigned within the torpedo shack. Nothing, nothing, could be found wrong. Mr. Cheves, cursing like a madman, again and again closed the detonating switch, but no geyser of destruction erupted from the mirror-smooth ocean; nothing happened.

At last the tide flooded sufficiently to permit Rear Admiral Du Pont's flagship to proceed, so *New Ironsides* steamed off to join the eight monitors awaiting her in Swash Channel. She had lain over the mine, calculated Dabney Seymour, exactly one hour.

CHAPTER XII **Fort Sumter, April 7, 1863**

IN an expanse of clay-colored water separating Fort Sumter from the Battery Gregg on Cummings' Point, C.S.S. *Chicora* and C.S.S. *Palmetto State* waited with steam up and guns run out. To the captains, their orders had proved to be disappointing, to say the least. Both rams, so General Beauregard had ordained, were to close with the enemy *only* if enemy ironclads managed to batter their way past Forts Sumter and Moultrie and into the harbor proper.

So Medical Lieutenant Bryson, with most of his fellow officers, glumly ascended a wooden ladder temporarily placed against *Palmetto State*'s carapace to give access to the casemate's top.

Already quite a number of men had collected on that point of vantage and sat on the hot, rusty iron trailing legs over the edge. Everyone, it appeared, wanted to see for himself what those dreaded monitors could accomplish against land forts. So many rumors had been circulated as to their invincibility.

Before squatting on a folding campstool he had thought to bring along, the physician cleaned his spectacles, then looked back at the city. How beautiful the old town looked at this distance! None of the damage, none of the unpainted shabbiness showed in the luminous April sunlight; only the graceful spires of St. Philip's, St. Michael's and the other churches.

He wondered if Serena's people had been affected by a near panic which started when a report spread that the Union's entire ironclad fleet was off the bar. All he knew, surely, was that even before the rams had quitted their berths, all manner of wagons, carts and carriages had been loaded hastily and could be seen departing inland. But, by and large, residents who thus far had endured the siege merely climbed to rooftops and other points of vantage to witness this battle which well might end with Admiral Du Pont's ironclads lying off White Point, ready, willing and able to blast Charleston from the face of the earth.

"Well, there they come!" called Lieutenant Porcher, recently recalled to duty aboard *Palmetto State* after laboring over the *Davids* — those torpedo boats so slowly reaching completion in Stoney's boatyard.

It seemed uncanny that, thus far, neither the ironclads nor the forts should have fired a shot; but now, with the enemy bearing down in an irregularly spaced line-ahead formation, Moultrie's gunners fired a salute of thirteen guns — Oh, shades of the chivalrous past!

Disdaining to acknowledge this courtesy and trailing dense clouds of smoke, the ugly little monitors, one after the other, boldly entered the main channel and, with a disconcerting certainty, avoided a line of torpedoes anchored there!

Atop the Rebel rams, men cursed, looked angrily at each other. How could those damned Yankee pilots tell so surely which buoys marked the position of dummies and which indicated those of real torpedoes? Already a number of blockade-runners, blundering off course, had been blown sky-high.

Aware of an odd, plucking sensation in his bowels, Donald Bryson

256

watched the leading monitor display a big Union flag at her stern and commence to lose speed when some fourteen hundred yards short of Fort Sumter's long, gray outline. Suddenly breathless, they all saw the enemy's turret deliberately revolve until her twin guns became trained upon that very edifice over which this conflict had begun.

Sumter still showed many a scar sustained during that historic first bombardment.

At exactly five minutes after three, *Weehawken* let fly with her eleven-inch Dahlgren rifle gun; she scored a solid hit on Sumter's northwest face. The fort replied with a thundering salvo that ruffled the still waters below its gunports.

A dense smoke cloud burst into being, smothered Sumter. Moultrie, across the channel also, spouted smoke and fire. Then the other monitors, which also had hoisted huge national colors, opened fire and the battle commenced to rage in tumultuous, ear-torturing fury.

All eight monitors now had attained predetermined stations, and from them commenced a concentrated and devastating bombardment of Sumter. Moultrie and the other outer defenses, although firing with increasing effectiveness, remained ignored by the Federals.

The effect of the monitors' ponderous projectiles was obvious. Large sections of the fort's brick glacis and parapets could be seen sliding into the harbor amid billows of mortar dust.

Confederate gunnery, too, was proving amazingly accurate; thanks to stakes driven into the mud, men in the fort knew the exact range.

The cannonade raged louder and louder until the very sky reverberated to a breath-taking tumult. When powder smoke, clinging now to the windless water, at last drifted aside, those aboard the rams and watching from Cummings' Point, could see the iron ships being hit. Shells kept bursting close aboard and punctured their smokestacks. Solid shot gouged and dented their turrets. The water in their vicinity fairly frothed under the lash of flying iron splinters.

Round-eyed, Duncan Mullinix watched a big chunk of iron fly crazily from *Weehawken's* funnel, already riddled by bursting shells. As in a dream, he saw roundshot glance off *Keokuk* and *Nahant's* turrets, then go skip-skipping on over the glassy water like flat stones hurled by small boys. Every now and then some gun would blow a perfect smoke ring to waver, halolike, in the sky.

Soon it became apparent that the great draft of *New Ironsides* was preventing her from advancing into effective range of Sumter. The flagship therefore vented her spleen by rounding to a sheet anchor and hurling a broadside into Moultrie.

Equally ineffective in the engagement were the Union's wooden ships. They dared not venture into range of the forts, so contented themselves watching the contest from beyond the bar. Whitely, their topsails gleamed in the bright sunlight as they cruised about the harbor's outer approaches.

At length the Whitney monitor, *Keokuk,* in her efforts to avoid collision with *Nahant,* was forced to steam within five hundred yards of the fort and instantly became smothered by shellfire. Because of engine trouble this unhappy ironclad was forced to endure a fiery torment for thirty minutes before she managed to limp away, oozing steam through a dozen gaping wounds. Her superstructure was so riddled as to resemble a colander.

Lieutenant Glassell danced an ecstatic jig on *Chicora's* casemate. "Will you look at our boys shoot! Those monitors are being so hard hit they're firing slower."

He was not in error. Because of solid hits which had twisted turret tracks on the Ericsson monitors, *Wissahickson, Montauk,* and *Patapsco,* their commanders, in order to reload, were forced to turn the whole ship away from the enemy. After that, the guns had to be re-layed so the whole operation required many minutes, during which the Rebel fire slackened not at all.

Now Sumter's sweating artillerymen, dodging flying debris, deafened and black-faced, concentrated their fire upon *Passaic,* somehow isolated and dangerously close in under the guns.

Observers upon the rams watched the little monitor reel under the impact of heavy shot, heard her armor *clang* like a tolled bell when struck by shell splinters. Bright smears streaked her turret and her funnel was half amputated, but still her people kept on shooting. Finally, oozing smoke and steam, she turned and, pursued by Rebel projectiles, limped painfully away.

The monitors' fifteen- and eleven-inch solid shot, however, had struck smoke-smothered Sumter with such punishing effect that a whole casemate collapsed amid clouds of dust and wood smoke, and huge holes were punched into various curtain walls.

At the end of an hour's furious bombardment, strings of bright little signal flags could be discerned fluttering up to *New Ironsides'* signal yard. Only when the recall signal flew did the battered little men-of-war back away, wreathed in smoke and drenched by waterspouts raised by near-misses. Several monitors leaked steam through their riven armor. All had had enough.

Although Captain Tucker raised binoculars and hopefully watched the fort's signal mast, only a tattered Stars and Bars showed out there; no orders to attack the retreating ironclads.

"God's love!" he raged. *"Now is the moment* to pursue. They're so crippled even we could catch them! Damn those idiot Army officers in the fort. Look, Glassell, Clarke! Two of those monitors are hardly able to move."

"True enough, sir," gloomily agreed Lieutenant Glassell. "But you'll notice, sir, the *New Ironsides* is moving to cover the enemy's retreat, and she's reported to mount a number of eleven-inch Dahlgrens. Solid shot from them could penetrate our armor as easily as a sword goes through a sheet of paper."

"I presume that's why we are being restrained," sighed Tucker, and returned his glasses to their scuffed leather case. "All the same it's damned small and jealous of the Army not to let us fire a single shot."

CHAPTER XIII **Hosanna! Hosanna!**

THERE was jubilee in Charleston and broad grins of relief on the faces of those manning the harbor's inner defenses. Hosanna! The dreaded Yankee monitors had come in and done their worst. And they'd been beaten, badly punished and driven off, running with their tails between their legs. Right now, Admiral Du Pont was calling in his wooden ships to take punch-drunk *Weehawken* and dying *Keokuk* in tow. Hosanna!

Church bells began joyously, wildly to sound, and victory salutes were fired by batteries immediately defending Charleston.

The instant *Palmetto State* was secured to the dock her crew, saving for unhappy guard detail, swarmed ashore, whooping and shouting like schoolboys let out from school.

"We whipped the monitors! Ain't so much, after all."

"Fired slower'n cold molasses."

"We'll sink the lot."

Standing on the wharf, Donald Bryson hesitated. Should he take advantage of this moment to risk a call on Serena? Possibly, by this time, the Major might have recovered from his outrage over poor Alistair's accusations; he might well have, especially since Virginius Roadheaver had printed the most abject of retractions.

Donald got to thinking of India, alone and forlorn in this happy hour. She'd have no one with whom to celebrate. His Presbyterian conscience pricked him because he hadn't been near his sister-in-law since that awful day when Alistair had disappeared.

Conscience prevailing, he set off along East Bay Street and even bought a bright armful of camellia branches. Had he been entirely fair in her regard? the physician wondered. Possibly not. Soon the Ramsay gate loomed ahead, partially obscured by the trailing, yellow-green branches of a weeping willow tree.

Possibly India had received word from Alistair? He fervently hoped so. All their lives he and his brother had been so very devoted. These past weeks he'd felt like a man trying to walk on one leg.

He found a pair of shirt-clad Negro children tussling in the driveway and called out a cheery greeting but, at the ring of his boot heels, they fled like scared young rabbits.

Donald's wide smile faded when he noticed a blanket of dead leaves sprinkling grass long uncut, and an accumulation of dirt and twigs on the stoop of white marble.

He pulled the silvered glass bell knob. No one appeared; not even when he used the knocker.

Circling around to the rear, he peered inside the kitchen but noted no fire in the stove and saw its big table quite bare.

Footsteps sounded and, turning, he watched an aged, clubfooted Negro shuffling up, his shapeless hat respectfully held with both hands.

"Yassuh! Kin Ah do sumpin' fo' you, suh?"

"I'm calling on Mrs. Bryson, but she seems to be out."

"She ain't out, suh, she done gone away."

"Gone?"

"Yesterday Miz' Bryson call me — Ah belongs Mr. Brownell yonder." His grizzled head inclined towards an ochre-fronted house across the street. "Misto' Brownell, he look out fo' Cunnel Ramsay's propity —"

"Do you mean Mrs. Bryson has moved away?"

"Reckon so, suh, but not till she done tidy ever'thing up slicker den a eel's back."

A sour taste welled into Donald's mouth. "Did Mrs. Bryson say where she was going?"

"No-suh. Never a word."

"Did she leave in company with anyone?"

"No-suh. De po' lady done been livin' all a-lone." The caretaker batted dim, thick-lidded eyes. "Didn't nobody come see her a long time. Reckon she got mighty hongry."

"Hungry? However would you know that?"

"Why — why, Miz' India wuz so good and kind, Ah, well, Ah reckon mebbe Ah toted some eatments fo' her. She didn't have no money buy some."

Donald groped for his wallet. "Look, Uncle, here's ten dollars. Tell me where Mrs. Bryson's gone and it's yours."

The cripple's eyes bulged. "Ten dolluhs! Fo' God, suh, Ah sure tell you iffen Ah knew, but Miz' India she jest pass me de key and say, 'Ah'm leaving Charleston, Ben, fo' good and all.' Dat's all she say, suh. All."

"If she comes back, you hurry right down to my ship, the *Palmetto State* — and you'll get this ten dollars."

Contrite and miserably ill at ease, Donald sought the Lambkin mansion and was fortunate enough to encounter Serena and her sister returning from the kindling of a victory bonfire. How wonderfully gentle and poised and lovely Serena looked after all this time. What unspoken thoughts might be troubling her mind? After all, her Papa had broken off the engagement, and she was a most dutiful daughter.

"Ah, Doctor Bryson!" exclaimed Cordelia, blue eyes shining. She looked fresh as a crocus blossom. "What a wonderful, what a memorable day! We are so very glad our rams came through without a scratch. You — you didn't notice whether Mr. Bears — Harry Bears that is — took any noteworthy part?"

Unhappily, Donald blinked behind his glasses. "I'm afraid not, Miss

Livesey. None of us Navy men were afforded the opportunity of distinguishing ourselves. Neither ram went into action at all."

Serena's smile was radiant as, suddenly, she extended mitted hands in greeting. "Oh, Donald, I'm so very happy none of you got hurt. But why so solemn? Haven't the Yankees just been soundly whipped?"

The girl lingered, warmly lovely, in the twilight.

"To be sure," he admitted. "The monitors won't come this way again for a long while. What I really came here for was to learn whether you might have heard anything — anything at all — concerning the whereabouts of my brother's wife. First, Alistair, and now India, have disappeared, and I'm worried — deeply anxious."

Cordelia's pink mouth pinched itself into an ugly ellipse. "It is only natural, Doctor, that you should feel concerned over your brother, but as to that — that — hussy he married — Well!"

Donald blinked through the twilight, brows merged into a single line.

"What do you mean, Miss Cordelia?"

The girl's little rounded chin went up and she sniffed. "I must presume that you have not heard of her latest escapade?"

"Please, 'Delia," Serena implored piteously. "Don't say anything more on the subject."

"Say what?"

"That you need not worry further over that scandalous sister-in-law of yours. It's all over town that she spent last night in the Charleston Hotel with a speculator from Savannah. He is an associate of Major Lambkin's so I know this to be a fact."

CHAPTER XIV **Stoney's Boatyard**

FOLLOWING the gallant, and almost bloodless, repulse of Mr. Lincoln's vaunted monitors, a rebirth of confidence so pervaded Charleston that, for several days, recruiting offices were crammed with would-be volunteers. Eagerly, citizens read General Beauregard's statement that the Union ironclads had been terribly smashed up. For example,

Keokuk, after having been hit ninety-one times, had finally filled, rolled over and gone to the bottom off Morris Island, while under tow.

Deserters reported that Admiral Du Pont had been utterly shaken on learning that his *Weehawken* had suffered fifty-three hits, *Nantucket* fifty-one, *Patapsco* forty-seven, and the other monitors almost as many. Months would be required to refit them for usefulness. True, the fast and powerfully armed *New Ironsides* still patrolled off the bar, but she could be reinforced or relieved only by wooden men-of-war.

Investigation finally had revealed the cause for the boiler-torpedo's failure. Somehow, the electrical wires connecting it with the battery switch had become severed near the water's edge; but not even shrewd Intelligence officers could decide just how this misfortune had been brought about.

How to destroy the lone remaining Union's ironclad became the first consideration of almost every senior naval officer on duty in the Southeastern Military District. *How?* How? Seemingly, the most occupied of all with this problem was dapper little General P. G. T. Beauregard. Enduring far into the night were his consultations with General Ripley, second in command; Flag Officer Ingraham, Captain Davidson and a Captain Francis D. Lee of the Army Engineers.

Lee was a native-born Charlestonian, and of an inventive turn of mind. For some time now, he had devoted all his energies towards perfecting a new type of offensive weapon — the spar torpedo. This invention consisted of a copper cylinder head that could be charged with from fifty to one hundred pounds of gunpowder and contained a hand-operated fulminate of mercury cap detonator — no electrical nonsense here. This slim but deadly warhead, when affixed to the end of a pole some fifteen or twenty feet in length, could be mounted above the surface upon a swivel on a torpedo boat's prow. At the right moment this spar could, by means of hand, be depressed well under water and so grope under an enemy's bilges. On being detonated, the cylinder charge could blow a huge hole in an enemy's bottom, a fact successfully demonstrated by Captain Lee upon a number of tired old hulks.

Probably no one, other than its inventor, knew more concerning the spar torpedo's use and capabilities than Lieutenant Dabney Seymour, he being charged with adapting these new weapons for employment aboard the *Davids.*

263

In increasing numbers, officers in the Navy Department made the weary trip down from Richmond to inspect Stoney's boatyard where, at almost any hour, they might find George A. Trenholm, that patriot merchant, scanning blueprints of designs prepared by another inventive and distinguished Charlestonian, Dr. St. Julien Ravenel.

At Stoney's, nowadays, hammers rang, saws whined and armorers sweated over their forges from dawn to dusk. Around the stocks a mere handful of experienced shipwrights fumed and, unsuccessfully, struggled to conceal their disgust over the clumsy carpentry of house builders attempting to build boats. Nevertheless *David Number One*'s hull was completed at last and, at Lieutenant Glassell's suggestion, painted a hard-to-see blue-gray. Thirty-five feet in length and with a beam of six feet, this boat would be some fifteen feet shorter than *David Number Two*, and three feet smaller in width.

Ingeniously, Dr. Ravenel had designed both torpedo boats to attack all-but submerged, thus offering enemy gunners a target almost impossible to hit when conical ballast tanks fitted over stern and stem became filled; only a scant ten inches of coaming showed above the surface — a fact which unfortunately precluded use of these torpedo boats in heavy weather — as Flag Officer Ingraham sourly pointed out. Lord! How unrelentingly that dour individual hated all torpedoes, torpedo boats — any form of underwater warfare.

To render his invention even more invisible, Dr. Ravenel had designed a telescopelike smokestack which could be attached to the ordinary steam launch's engine furnishing a *David*'s motive power. Optimists at Submarine and Torpedo Service Headquarters calculated that the new boats should cruise at about seven knots; might even do better. Everyone prayed that they would.

Among those answering a call for volunteers to navigate these new warcraft were Lieutenants W. T. Glassell, Henry Bears and, of course, Dabney Seymour. The tall Virginian, as a British-trained naval engineer, was immediately accepted.

Eagerly, earnestly, and without respite, these officers collaborated with Francis Lee — recently promoted to Major — and one Sam Easterly, a civilian in charge of completion.

By April's end two of the scheduled eight *Davids* had been plated with boiler-iron and otherwise lay almost ready for service, while the keels of four more slightly larger torpedo boats had been laid amid considerable fanfare, fond hopes and soaring oratory.

Meanwhile, at the Naval Depot, various types of torpedo were tested upon worn-out ships with results so generally promising that Duncan Ingraham at last agreed that his rams, as well as the great new *Charleston*, should be fitted with spar torpedoes. Soon even lesser vessels of the Palmetto Squadron such as *Ettiwan*, *Stono* and *Chesterfield* could be seen steaming about the harbor with torpedo spars rigged to their bows.

As spring advanced and the weather grew warmer, it became the fashionable thing for ladies and their escorts to drive out to Stoney's to view these wicked-looking little men-of-war and admire the new boats of which so much was coming to be expected.

For Cordelia Livesey, now prettily and properly affianced to Lieutenant Henry Bears, the chip- and sawdust-strewn boatyard long since had lost the attraction of novelty. All the same, life was so dull and there was so little to do except attend funerals, sew and roll bandages, it was a relief to drive out along dusty, oak-shaded Bay Street, now that people had quit gaping and putting their heads together on sighting the sister of that giddy young lady who had eloped with Rascal Rafe.

More often than not, Serena Lambkin accompanied her, since it afforded the possibility of encountering Medical Lieutenant Donald Bryson. He often visited Stoney's to attend some injured artisan.

On this drowsily warm spring evening a stillness had settled over Stoney's now that the day's work was done and the workmen had gone home. One could not only hear the liquid warbling of mockingbirds and wrens but the *plop!* of fish jumping in the river. Grotesquely suggestive of gargoyles decorating some Gothic cathedral, pelicans dozed upon a row of rotting, lime-whitened pilings. The sweet odors of pitch and of fresh-sawed pine was strong in the air.

From an armorer's forge a slender blue spiral escaped its moribund fire and traced lazy designs through the still air. Out on the smoothly flowing river, Negroes were fishing, motionless as statues in their pirogues and patiently awaiting a bite.

Cordelia, gay and bright-eyed as a catbird, lolled against her cabriolet's cushions conversing with Dabney Seymour and twirling a ridiculously small parasol while awaiting her fiancé to make an appearance.

The scarred Virginian's gaze wandered thoughtfully to *David Number One* and, with satisfaction, considered the four-bladed bronze propeller which he had himself installed. Um-m. Tomorrow, if all went well, her boiler could be lowered into place. The twin iron posts to which the torpedo spar soon would become hinged rose from the torpedo boat's smooth, iron skin like fingers raised above a balled fist.

Dabney slapped a persistent mosquito, inquired, "Have you decided when you and Harry will be getting married?"

"I fear that remains impossible to answer," Cordelia sighed, then pouted a little. "So much depends on whether Mr. Mallory will approve Harry's promotion. He insists we can't possibly make out on a lieutenant's pay. But *I* claim he should be guided by the motto of our Navy."

Dabney's big blond head swung upwards. "Do you know?" he grinned. "I'm ashamed that I've never even heard it."

"*Aide-toi et Dieu t'aidera.* Ah! There's Harry!" She closed the parasol and stood up to wave so suddenly the pony between the cabriolet's shafts started and snorted.

It was wonderful to watch the weary young officer's face light up. You could see he burned to kiss her, but Dabney and a little black groom were present. Manners dictated that he could only bend over her hand and put his lips to it.

"Granted the opportunity," drawled Henry Bears, "I'll surely sink a Yankee warship. Then the Navy Department will *have* to promote me." Over his shoulder he considered *David Number One*. "Dabney, in your opinion, are Dr. Ravenel's calculations correct? Are the ballast tanks large enough to sink the hull even with the surface?"

The Virginian drew a deep whiff from the pipe he'd just lit; he stared hard at that sleek, gray shape poised on the ways. "Hard to say. Personally, I'd venture that the ballast tanks should be larger."

Cordelia rounded lovely eyes and tried hard to appear interested. "Please tell us why, Mr. Seymour."

"If our *Davids* aren't to be sunk, they must remain undetected until the very moment of attack."

"Then — then you must attack at night?"

Bears patted Cordelia's hand. "Of course, my sweet. Even submerged, Yankee lookouts would detect us by daylight." He frowned, stared at the chip-littered ground. "To be successful our attempt must be made on a still and very black night."

"Which is a major problem," the marine engineer pointed out. "A black night without wind doesn't occur too frequently."

"Why must there be no wind?" the girl asked.

"With a freeboard of only ten inches, a *David* would quickly swamp, the boiler would blow up and her crew with it."

The pony inched forward to reach a tuft of grass.

"By the bye," Dabney remarked, "as I was leaving my boardinghouse this morning, I *thought* I saw the *Grey Ghost* in the harbor."

Cordelia lost her radiant expression. "That wasn't Rascal Rafe's boat, I can assure you; only a runner very like her. Serena says she's named the *Banshee*."

Fiercely, she added. "I only wish she were the *Grey Ghost!* So does my brother. Poor, silly Sister Julia!"

"Come now, honey, don't fret your pretty self. What proof is there that Julia isn't properly married?"

"If they'd got married Julia surely would have written, and half a dozen runners have come in from Nassau since she — she disgraced us all."

"Now, honey, please don't take on," Bears pleaded. "I'm certain-sure Julia and Captain Bryson were married long ago. Don't you think so, Dabney?"

The Virginian only nodded because he couldn't inject sufficient conviction into his voice. He hurried on to say, "I've had a letter from Peter Burgoyne, the English naval officer."

"Oh, where is he? He was so perfectly charming, so distinguished and so well dressed."

"He's in Savannah, watching the *Atlanta* being finished."

"What did he say about her? Everyone around headquarters claims she'll perform miracles."

"Burgoyne didn't say much," Dabney told him. "You know how reticent the English are. Funny thing, though. He says he's lodging at present with a family of the same name as mine."

Henry Bears looked his surprise. "Didn't know there were any Seymours around Savannah, and I used to hunt and visit there a lot."

"The name, I think, is Reynolds Seymour," Dabney amplified.

"Any kin of yours?" Cordelia queried as, smoothing wide skirts, she gracefully resettled herself on the cabriolet's seat, then nodded for her groom to secure the pony's checkrein.

"I've never heard of any Seymours living south of Virginia."

"These mosquitoes are getting pretty bold," smiled Cordelia. "What do you say, gentlemen? Shall we drive into town?"

CHAPTER XV Boom Port

DAZZLING tropical sunlight, reflected from whitewashed houses across the street, caused Alistair Bryson to blink and shift his chair about on the second floor balcony of this rather dilapidated boardinghouse. It was no mean feat to have come across living quarters of any description in Nassau, what with the continual stream of ships arriving from Europe and the United States, and so many runners clearing for such ports of the Confederacy as remained at least partially accessible.

From where he sat fingering the short and curling brown-black chin whiskers he wore nowadays, Alistair could see a small forest of masts and yards rising above a lower tier of smokestacks. Every wharf in Nassau's small harbor was so occupied; sometimes as many as three vessels lay secured, side by side.

Today the sun seemed particularly merciless and the air dreadfully humid and lifeless. Under normal conditions nobody would have been abroad at this hour but sensibly enjoying a siesta under a mosquito bar. As it was, sea captains, mariners, merchants, factors and a sprinkling of scarlet-jacketed soldiers from the garrison mopped streaming faces as they trudged dispiritedly along, hugging every bit of shadow.

Using a hooked forefinger, Alistair scraped an accumulation of perspiration from his brow and so caused a few drops to spatter the sheet of foolscap before him.

In the distance sounded the doleful strains of a military band playing a dirge; although the worst of this most recent outbreak of yellow fever was past, there still were many deaths every day.

The newspaperman unbuttoned his shirt over a chest which, during the past month, had filled out considerably and become healthily tanned. It was God's own mercy, he ruminated, that he'd not taken the yellowjack; certainly, he'd offered a prime target for any disease the day he'd shakily descended the blockade-runner *Hattie*'s gangplank.

He'd been lucky, too, that the run over from Charleston had been accomplished without the *Hattie*'s sighting so much as a streak of smoke on the horizon. Yes, lucky. Only thanks to the epidemic had he found immediate employment. Jim Caldwell, Nassau correspondent of the *Richmond Despatch,* when looked up, had betrayed symptoms of the fever and had been pathetically eager to welcome him.

No wonder. Jim had sunk into a final stupor and had died less than forty-eight hours after their reunion.

It had proved a simple enough matter to take over Caldwell's responsibilities, and get himself hired as a replacement under the name of Bryant — a necessary precaution in view of his real reasons for being in Nassau.

He tilted back in his chair and, catching up a palm-leaf fan, attempted to create cooling currents of air while watching the lazy evolutions of a buzzard planing about the brazen sky.

A good thing that, at least thus far, the editors in Richmond had appeared content with his efforts — in fact, had commented favorably upon his selection and interpretation of foreign news forwarded.

Purple blossoms on a bougainvillaea vine shading the balcony began to move, stirred by a hot breeze commencing to beat in from the turquoise-and-sapphire-hued ocean. How truly beautiful and replete with color were these islands! Especially during the early morning, and at dusk; then, black fishermen came sailing home from their toil.

After darkness fell, the light of little cooking fires, flaring upon sandboxes on each fishing boat's deck, tinted patched and faded brown sails a rich and glowing crimson. Always, it seemed, there was music or singing of some sort in the distance. Otherwise, Nassau was proving a journalist's paradise; there were so many ships coming and going, so many distinguished personages passing through, and so many plots afoot to circumvent the Federal Navy's vigilance.

Rumors, of course, flew like bats at sundown. One could hear any kind of news one wanted. For instance: Abe Lincoln had gone insane; Jefferson Davis was soon to be assassinated; the Northern armies in the West were in headlong retreat; the blockade had been abandoned off Galveston; the French Emperor was about to sell four seagoing steam rams, ostensibly to the Khedive of Egypt, but really to the Rebel government.

Into the street below Alistair's balcony turned a two-wheeled oxcart, the ungreased axles of which screeched like fiends dipped in holy water. Nonetheless, Alistair dried sweaty fingers and resumed writing his dispatch.

Once the sun really lowered, the torrid air commenced almost magically to cool; shutters banged open, and slatternly women vendors appeared, singing their wares while balancing baskets and trays on brilliantly colored turbans.

A sigh escaped Alistair when he put aside his pen and folded his work into an envelope which should be delivered aboard the *Nighthawk* in good time. He glanced across over the housetops and was reassured to discern the runner still at her dock with smoke climbing only lazily from her funnel.

He started. A new arrival lay berthed beyond her: a small, iron ship strangely resembling the *Grey Ghost!* Heart hammering, he ran for a pair of field glasses; they proved the stranger not to be the *Grey Ghost*, but, evidently, a sister ship built in the same Liverpool yard and named *Banshee*.

It hadn't taken long after his arrival in this heat-drenched port to discover that Rascal Rafe, after having twice run the blockade into Wilmington, North Carolina, had sailed away to pick up cargoes in England.

Patient and very discreet inquiry also revealed that a lovely young woman describing herself as "Mrs. Raphael Bryson" at present was occupying a villa on Hog Island, a pretty palm-dotted sandbank across the harbor from Nassau.

It was as well, the journalist reflected, that he had not found Rafe. During hot, insect-tormented and humid nights, he pondered endlessly over what he might say and do when he came up with his cousin; probably something he'd later regret, for certain it was that Rafe must be held responsible for India's disgrace and the shattering of his married happiness.

In misery, the lonely man often wondered why he had refused India even so much as a sentence in explanation? That Rafe might have forced her was entirely in character. Also, India invariably had repelled all manner of advances. How well he recalled the evening she'd so resoundingly slapped the face of a lascivious cavalry major who'd attempted to steal an embrace following a performance before officers convalescing at Drayton Hall.

Whither might she have fled? Home? No. There was none to seek. God only knew where Captain Villepigue, her seafaring father, might be — were he still alive. Her mother, that gravely gay Spanish lady, long ago had perished of that same dread plague which recently had filled so many Bahamian graves.

From the very beginning in composing dispatches to Richmond he had taken care to include a certain number of Scottish words and phrases about which India had often gently teased.

For instance, he would write, "Such crews as can be enrolled in Nassau are not worth a penny wheep." Or "The daffling indecision of our foreign policy is woesome." Finally, he always signed his work "Dorlach," a cognomen he'd employed when a very green dramatic critic on the *New York Herald*. In the fulsome enthusiasm of youth he had selected "Dorlach" because such a Gaelic dagger was reputedly both keen and penetrating.

Perhaps, wherever she might be, India might recognize his *nom de plume*? During certain tender and intimate moments she often had called him thus.

A trace of a smile curved Alistair's lightly bearded lips. Odd to recall that, to the day of his death, Grampa, when excited, employed certain curious Highland oaths which, fortunately, none of the Bryson ladies ever had understood, and that his own father had always referred to his sire as "Feyther."

Some kitchen down the street began to give off tendrils of smoke tinged with the inevitable odors of frying sea food, of baking plantains, of curry and of saffron.

Alistair was sealing this week's dispatch when a knock sounded on the latticed door to his bedroom and presently there shuffled in a small, bullet-headed Negro with a regular piano's keyboard of a smile.

"Mister Bryant, sir? Here you are, sir." It always gave the journalist a start when a black Bahamian used English inflections. He passed over an envelope marred with oily fingerprints. "I am required sir, to await a reply."

Alistair's bronzed features broke into a broad smile. This ragged scarecrow of a messenger really should have been wearing livery, he stood so straight and was so formal of manner.

The note was addressed in a flowing feminine hand. Without waiting to read the message he glanced at its signature. "Your old acquaintance, JULIA BRYSON."

Julia *Bryson!* Happiness flooded Alistair's being. So, at long last, Rafe had righted the old wrong; had scotched the serpent of scandal.

> DEAR MR. BRYSON:
>
> Can you perhaps take supper with me this evening? This is unpardonably short notice but please allow me to assure you that I do not act upon impulse. Ever since recognizing you on the waterfront last week I have been summoning sufficient courage to address you.
>
> The reason for my seeming lack of courtesy is that it seems necessary to dispatch certain letters by a packet clearing for England tomorrow morning. Therefore, if it is possible for you to join me this evening — as I pray you will be able — I will have a rowboat awaiting your orders at seven o'clock at the foot of Queen Street.

Alistair drew a deep, quivering breath. Perhaps Julia had received news from Charleston? Possibly she might have learned something concerning India's whereabouts?

Hurriedly, he delved into his pocket and produced a shilling bearing Queen Victoria's likeness as a young girl. "Tell your Mistress that I will be pleased to accept her kind invitation."

"Thank you, sir. Mistress will be overjoyed." The messenger bowed solemnly, then his bare feet pattered away down the corridor.

Raphael Bryson's dwelling, set amid a grove of lacy coconut palms, proved to be neither elaborate nor extensive. At the same time it looked comfortable and proved to be attractively furnished, in the West Indian fashion. Softly creaking punkahs stirred the air without creating a draft. Unaccountably, the caller's heart commenced to pound while his heels crunched along a walk bordered by pink-lipped conch shells.

Julia greeted him in the small hallway which, bisecting the house, permitted breezes to pass uninterrupted through the house. At first glance he guessed that Julia must be pregnant, although the folds of her carefully arranged Paisley shawl all but concealed the fact.

"Ah, Alistair! Alistair! How wonderful it is to see someone from home!" She tilted her dark head a little to one side. "My, that tan certainly becomes you; but haven't you put on just a bit of weight?"

He almost said, "Haven't you, too?"

"How very kind of you to appear on such shamefully short notice!" Full white skirts asway, she led him to a sitting room floored in gleaming mahogany and equipped with cool, rattan furniture. She indicated a chair beside which a silver pitcher stood sweating gently on its tray. Certainly, Cousin Rafe was not being stingy with his bride! Ice in these latitudes, he knew, was akin to pearls and fine gold in value.

Her smile was wide, yet somehow wary, as she indicated the pitcher and goblets. "Have you yet become acquainted with this form of punch? The natives here call it a rum swizzle and Rafe swears it is well suited to this climate. Alas, we have no whisky."

"Not yet, but I am sure I'll enjoy it. It looks delicious."

A little later he said, carefully, "I'm sorry Rafe's away. I had hoped to meet my cousin."

Her long eyelashes fluttered downwards. "Unfortunately Raphael left, very unexpectedly, on a voyage to England; six weeks ago. I hope for his return any day."

Something in her tone caused him to survey this tall and stately young woman with a trained reporter's unostentatious attention. "And what do you hear from Charleston these days?"

Color darkened the lustrous pallor of her face and neck. "Nothing," she replied in a low voice. "In fact I was hoping that you might bring me some news."

"But, surely, *some* letters must have come through?"

"No letters are being written to me." Julia stared out at the starlit ocean, past silhouetted palm fronds. "Perhaps because I have written none."

Alistair looked his bewilderment. "But why not?"

"Because . . . I must tell you something I trust you, as a gentleman, will not repeat." Julia drew a halting breath that lifted her bosom into lovely, full-blown contours. "Although I am known here as

273

Mrs. Bryson," she turned her head aside and her expression crumpled, "I — I remain Julia Livesey in the eyes of God, and the law."

He could only stare across the lamplit room in shocked surprise. "You have my word I'll keep this confidence. I'd never have believed it if I didn't know — all too well — how completely wicked he can be," Alistair said, and his original sense of outrage came flooding back in doubled intensity.

Julia got out of her chair, went to stand before a screened door leading out onto a verandah. "Please don't judge him too harshly. He's such an irresponsible creature of impulse."

"Not judge him harshly?" Alistair burst out. "Not judge him after what he's done to you, and to my wife and to me? Just let me find him within gunshot! I'll judge him all right."

"He wronged India?" Julia Livesey asked.

"He did." And in brief, bitter sentences he related the miserable story.

"No wonder you hate Rafe." She turned to face him, eyes luminous. "Nevertheless, please hear me out. Once we reached Nassau Rafe confessed to having married some woman in England, years ago — a foolish, transitory affair." Julia's gaze sought a flaming poinsettia standing in a jar of terra cotta. "He said he was returning to England to obtain a divorce."

"You really believe this — after all he's done to you?"

"I *must* believe him, Alistair. I don't dare not to." Her chin quivered and, to hide it, she lifted a handkerchief to her mouth. "Besides, I'm certain Rafe will return — because of this." Her fingers came to rest upon her rounded abdomen.

"I hope that you are right and that I'm wrong. We'll see."

"You won't try to kill him?"

"If I try, I won't miss. I can promise you that," he evaded grimly.

Later, while the sea broke over coral barrier reefs and land crabs created dry, rustling noises among fallen palm fronds, the bearded journalist described his life since being kidnaped; Sibley's Island and the great goodness of Missy, Joshua and Limber Jim.

"And so . . ." He got up and took a turn across the room. "Here I am, under an assumed name." A faint smile curved the corners of his mouth. "We would seem to be in the same boat in that respect — How did you know where to find me?"

274

"I had Eustace follow you home. But why have you changed your name?"

He started to explain his purpose in Nassau and the stark necessity of finding evidence to support his accusations, but remained silent. St. George Lambkin was her uncle.

He became aware of her intense regard, of an anxious curiosity. "Tell me, Alistair Bryson, why did you publish those calumnies concerning Serena's father?"

"They were not calumnies," said he quietly, and got to his feet. "I have trespassed long enough on your hospitality."

"But — but — why couldn't you prove your charges?"

He told her. "That's what happened, believe me or no. And that was what the speculators of the Excalibur Company have had done to me. Only I've not told you the half of it." He shrugged. "I've learned to be careful when crusading against men quite so rich and reputable."

She crossed hurriedly to his side, placed a hand on his arm. "Please don't go. I — I, God help me, I believe what you say, Alistair Bryson. How else could Major Lambkin and the others stay so rich when everyone else seems to be losing everything they own?"

"Thank you. I need a vote of confidence these days — you've no notion how badly."

"Can I help you in any way? This trade in luxuries is truly despicable."

"Are you acquainted with any factors? Any shipping agents?"

Julia brushed away a stray mosquito, deliberated, then nodded.

"I know a Mr. Lafitte who is the agent here for Fraser, Trenholm & Company. You will find him a true Southerner with sufficient vision to interpret events in their real value and perspective. And then there is Major Huse, also a devoted patriot, who represents our Government here. He would be Consul if only the British would recognize our independent status."

Julia's full, dark red lips compressed themselves. "Why, oh why, won't the British Crown grant us recognition? Are we not a nation in being? Are we not governed by a legally elected Congress and President?"

He looked long into the delicate oval formed by her features.

"The answer, I think, lies in the matter of slavery."

"I fail to grasp your meaning. Very few of our slaves are badly treated."

"But they are *slaves*," Alistair pointed out gently. "And, whether we like it or not, the great mass of the British public abominate the institution. The French as well. They can afford to be smug because they freed *their* slaves, and at a very considerable cost, many years ago."

"But how can you say that? You have only to read the English papers to realize how bitterly the British hate Mr. Lincoln and the North! Just walk along the waterfront and listen. Everywhere, you will hear the most violent denunciation of the Federal Government."

What good would it do to explain that this animosity stemmed largely from the arbitrary manner in which United States Navy officers were enforcing the blockade? Their treatment of captured British seamen often was contemptuous, severe beyond reason. Few people hereabouts would recall that, at the start of the War, Bahamians had favored the Northern cause, but, after the highhanded way the U.S.S. *San Jacinto* had, on the high seas, seized and searched the British-owned *Trent,* all that had become altered.

Alistair sipped his swizzle, could not resist slapping away the most persistent of the gnats and midges which continued to whine and circle about his head while, briefly, they spoke of old times in Charleston.

"I do hope Major Livesey has relented concerning Serena's engagement," Julia said in her rich, slightly husky voice. "She's truly in love with your brother, you know."

"I don't know, although it's utterly unfair that Donald ever should have been blamed, even a little bit, for what I chose to publish."

A bugle over in the barracks at Fort William — the same Esek Hopkins's squadron had taken during the Revolution — commenced to sound "Last Post" and its notes came winging mellowly across a phosphorescent expanse of jet water separating it from Hog Island.

Alistair arose. "I presume you have no notion of exactly when Rafe may return?"

"Oh, I'm sure, positive, the *Grey Ghost* will appear any day, now." For a long instant Julia's sensitive features retained a radiant expression, then suddenly she placed hands before her face and burst into dull and heart-rending sobs. "Oh, Alistair, if only I *could* be sure he returned to England only for a divorce. You can have no conception of how shameful it is to have to masquerade in — in my condition."

"Surely, you are not destitute of friends here?" he queried. When he placed an arm lightly about her shoulders she turned, clung to him like a frightened child.

"Some English officers' wives have been kind; really very sweet beneath their prim reserve." She dried her eyes and attempted a smile. "There are, of course, a few South Carolina and Georgia women; scarcely of the sort I knew at home but, all the same, eager to assist me in my — my condition."

Alistair caught up a broad-brimmed, low-crowned straw hat. "If I can serve you in any way, Julia, please let me know. You'll understand there's not much that a man in my peculiar position can accomplish." He patted her hand reassuringly. "Once more. You need never worry that I'll betray anything about the matter of you and Rafe."

CHAPTER XVI **Mr. Lafitte**

MR. J. B. LAFITTE, Bahamian agent for the wealthy and long-established firm of Fraser, Trenholm & Company, sat in the shade with a sallow-looking young woman gloomily viewing a cricket match between officers from Fort Montague and those ashore from H.M.S. *Racer*. When the *Richmond Despatch*'s correspondent drew near and lifted his broad-brimmed hat he glanced up, a morose expression clouding a squarish, sun-darkened countenance.

"Mr. Lafitte? May I have a few words with you?"

"Good day, Mr. Bryant, and what do you want now? We have no inward cargoes due at present. What amusement our British cousins find in so dull a game —"

"What I have to speak about concerns no mercantile matter."

"Eh? What then?"

"I must speak to you in private, if I may, Mr. Lafitte," he jerked a little bow in the wan girl's direction. "Hot day, eh, ma'am?"

She smiled faintly for, certainly, this wiry, dark-bearded stranger with the glowing dark eyes and strongly modeled features was not unattractive.

"Your pardon, Polly," the shipping agent murmured. "I'll be gone for only an instant, but for Heaven's sake hold that parasol so the sun don't strike your head. Don't want you coming down with heat stroke again."

"Well, what can I do for you?" Lafitte demanded once he and his companion had seated themselves on an artillery limber abandoned for some reason at the cricket pitch's far end.

Briefly the correspondent reviewed his connection with the *Richmond Despatch*, then said, "I have just received word that my editors are most anxious to obtain news, at the very first instant, of the arrival here of a great shipment of munitions."

Alistair glanced about and lowered his voice. "Mr. Lafitte, General Lee is preparing his army for a mighty thrust at the heart of Yankeedom."

"That's scarcely news." Mr. Lafitte's eyes were gray, red-rimmed, and their whites were yellowish from malaria.

"Have any of these munitions arrived?" came the tense query.

"I wish I could report the arrival of thousands of stands of small arms; hundreds of fieldpieces; tents, shoes, uniform material and such," the agent snapped. "But I can't, Mr. Bryant. Damn it! I can't, because none have appeared, despite all Mr. Trenholm's and Major Huse's efforts."

"But sir, what of those three ships which made port today? There were two from England and one from France? Weren't they reported to be importing blockade goods?"

"Oh, right enough, right enough! But between them they brought in not a thousand muskets, not a hundred thousand rounds of small arms!"

"Their cargoes were not consigned to Fraser, Trenholm?"

"No. These cargoes are for such firms as Mordecai & Company, Clingend & Company and such low-class riffraff." A harsh laugh escaped the shipping agent. "You'll never find *them* bothering with heavy weapons or sheets of boiler iron, let alone machine tools; the profit isn't sufficiently attractive."

Alistair spoke cautiously. "I take it, then, that your firm disapproves of speculation in liquors, perfumes, silks and laces?"

"Disapproves!" Lafitte's jawline hardened. "There's a fine piece of understatement. None are more devoted and resourceful patriots than

278

Mr. Trenholm and the vast majority of the merchants in Charleston, Wilmington and Savannah. We both know of notorious exceptions," he growled. "I'd give considerable to find out how the Columbian Importing Company, for instance, manages to clog so many precious holds with illegal freight."

"The Columbian Company, did you say?" the journalist demanded slowly.

"Yes. They do business in Richmond and are utterly brazen about flouting Government regulations concerning the importation of unwarlike freight. Oh, it's a crime! A damnable crime!"

Angrily, Lafitte beat one hand against the other. "Here's an example. For over six months, we've had launch engines on order in Liverpool. They're intended for some torpedo boats now under construction in Charleston. Well, those engines still are at dockside in England. No space available in any hold."

A military band commenced to play while, solemnly, the cricket sides exchanged positions and white-jacketed stewards circulated, offering tea. A low cheer broke out when the music began to play that hauntingly mournful tune, "Lorena." Why this air should have become a sort of unofficial anthem for the Confederacy was hard to say. In later years Rebel veterans would claim that this lugubrious song had done more to dispirit soldiers in the field than all of Grant's victories put together.

"About this Columbian Company, Mr. Lafitte. Who are its principal stockholders?"

"Nobody seems to know. The same goes for the Excalibur Company, a similar rotten concern operating from Charleston."

"But, surely, Mr. Lafitte, someone *must* know the identity of these speculators?"

"Perhaps Mr. Baylor, the agent here for many reputable British shippers, might have some knowledge. Then, again, some of Collie & Sabel's supercargoes might find a certain amount of proof."

"Would you mind if I write a story to my paper on this traffic in illegal freight?"

The saturnine shipping agent's dark eyes gleamed. "Mind? Hell, no! Nor would any other decent Southerner around this plague-ridden hellhole of a port."

"Then you'll present me to Mr. Baylor? You see, Mr. Lafitte, I am

279

most anxious" — he didn't explain how anxious — "to identify and expose speculators in luxuries."

"Good ! Baylor and I will help you all we can. God above. I've one brother dead at Shiloh, two others with the Army of Northern Virginia and God knows how many cousins fighting as best they can, short of weapons and equipment."

He looked Alistair squarely in the eye. "Now suppose you tell me your real name? You're not by any chance that fellow who turned Charleston upside down a while back?"

"Yes. I'm Alistair Bryson — but I won't be, long, if it gets to be known, hereabouts."

The other's hand clamped down like a vise as, in a voice hoarse with emotion, Lafitte said, "This is a great moment for me, Mr. Bryson. I wondered what sort of man would dare defy the speculators, in, and out of, uniform." He got up from the limber and mechanically dusted his trousers' seat. "Meet me at Fraser, Trenholm's office at eight. By the bye, did I hear somewhere that you had been murdered?"

"You probably did. It was no fault of certain parties that I'm not dead. You understand why I've taken the name of Bryant?"

CHAPTER XVII Intruder by Moonlight

THE evening being well advanced, the Gothic tangle formed by spars and rigging lining the waterfront showed, boldly etched, against a sky of purple-black when Mr. Lafitte and his guest strolled amidst a jungle of high-piled freight. Even at this hour stevedores toiled by lantern light to trundle ragged cotton bales from the decks and holds of the *Owl* and the increasingly famous *Robert E. Lee.*

Further on, they lingered among pungent shadows watching freight being manhandled aboard the runner *Banshee.* Too many cases were very easy to lift.

"Who are her agents?" Alistair queried softly.

"Messrs. Isaac Campbell & Company, of London. They specialize in the luxury trade."

"Are you acquainted with anyone in their employ? Here in Nassau, I mean." Alistair's gaze lingered on one of the few triple-storied warehouses looming above an avalanche of white houses descending the hill above the harbor.

"Yes. A young Englishman in their employ named Wolfe — Geoffrey Wolfe. His mother is Southern — a relation of President Davis's, I think. He's so disgusted with Campbell & Company he just might find the evidence you want."

That Nassau was enjoying an unprecedented prosperity was inescapable; exhorbitant prices were demanded for even the most commonplace of necessities and local Negroes went about better dressed than any of their race Alistair had ever beheld even in the North.

"I expect you know it's not safe to wander about the docks at night," Lafitte said. "Let's take dinner, then I'll go talk with Geoffrey Wolfe." He hesitated, cast a swift, sidewise look. "As near as you know, has anybody recognized you as Bryson?'

"Only one person. The wife of a cousin of mine."

"Cousin?" Lafitte stopped so suddenly that a passing cart grazed his shoulder. "You can't mean Rascal Rafe!"

"Yes. I took supper with Mrs. Bryson last night."

"And how do you feel towards your dashing cousin?"

"For very personal reasons I'd rather not answer that, Mr. Lafitte. You don't happen to know when the *Grey Ghost* is due here?"

"We've had advices that she'll make port almost any hour now."

"How do you know this?"

"Fraser, Trenholm are Captain Bryson's agents. Perhaps marriage has changed him. This time he is importing more munitions than luxuries."

Rafe's *marriage*? What an evil jest! Julia alone, pregnant, unmarried, and callously abandoned, it would seem.

The Bower Anchor Inn proved to be a not unattractive eating place boasting a wide patio on the eastern edge of town; but, like all other restaurants, packed to capacity. The air was thick, hot, redolent of a hundred kitchen odors. Everywhere could be seen perspiring men discussing cotton prices, the tobacco market or the parlous state of Confederate finance.

Observed a merchant in a sodden cotton shirt and grimy duck

trousers: "Why Jeff Davis embargoes cotton so long I'll never make out. Through export the damned fool could have got credit enough to stabilize his currency. He could have got foreigners to snap up those Government bonds Erlanger was offering, at top prices."

"If that's so, why haven't Rebel bonds lost more value than they have?" inquired his red-faced companion, obviously a British merchant marine officer.

"Guess it's because Southern armies won so damned many victories last year and the North's howling over the butcher's bill. Besides, you've heard about the Copperhead movement up North?"

"What might that be?"

"A separatist movement on the part of the Northwestern States. It's led by a fellow called Vallandigham."

Alistair's companion consumed a leisurely dinner of a delicious kedgeree of fish, shrimps and spiny lobster. As the evening wore on and spirits became more rapidly consumed voices grew proportionately louder, and the air grew grayer still with smoke from pipes and Jamaica seegars.

"Suppose we take coffee and liqueurs on the terrace?" Lafitte suggested. "Smells like a nigger whorehouse in here."

The newspaperman started to rise but shrank back and shielded his features so abruptly that Mr. Lafitte gaped. "You sick?"

"No. Know that man by the entrance?"

The journalist had gone so white under his tan that Lafitte put a steadying hand on his shoulder. "Only the ugly one. He comes from Charleston, I think. Sometimes he sails as supercargo for Isaac Campbell. Why?"

"That man was one of several hired to murder me last winter. He's called Doggett." He shivered. "Should he recognize me, my life won't be worth a shinplaster."

"How long has he been here?"

"Don't know. I just noticed him," Alistair replied peering through his fingers. He felt sick, sick as he had back there on Sibley's Island.

A soft sound from across the bedroom caused Mr. Charles Doggett slowly to open his eyes. Moonlight, streaming through a glassless French door, cast the shadow of a man's head and shoulders upon mold-specked plaster beside him.

282

The sleeper pretended to sigh, then started to grope beneath the pillow for a derringer.

"Stop that!" a low harsh voice directed. "Reach any further and I'll gladly kill you for a murdering swine. Sit up!" The intruder stepped squarely into the shaft of moonlight, revolver dully gleaming. "Recognize me, Mr. Doggett?"

A whistling gasp escaped him upon the sweat-sodden sheets. "Christ A'mighty! But I saw you lyin' dead!"

"Almost, but not quite. Get up! Go and stand against yonder wall."

"All right, Mr. Bryson, just as you say." Hairy legs scrambled to the floor. In his nightshirt Doggett presented a sight at once ludicrous and repellent. "For God's sake don't shoot me down. I'm worth plenty. I — I'll give you five thousand, gold."

"No doubt, Mr. Doggett; but that won't do."

"I can get more," came the quavering voice. "This trip, I've brought out ten thousand Excalibur gold. I'll get it in the morning."

"You miss my point. Do you think ten thousand would be enough to leave you alive and free to murder me at the first opportunity?"

The fellow's little black eyes shone, white-ringed, with a mortal terror. "Please don't shoot! I'll give you the money, then go right aboard the *Owl*. She's sailing first thing tomorrow morning."

"No, Mr. Doggett, I'll not trust you or anyone who participated in that business on Sibley's Island."

Doggett clasped hands in entreaty and dropped to his knees so suddenly that Alistair almost fired.

"For the love of God!" quavered the kneeling wretch. "Don't kill me like this. I've too much on my conscience."

"I don't doubt that. Now stay as you are."

Revolver leveled, Alistair with his left hand groped under the pillow until he found the derringer.

"I'm a colossal idiot, Doggett, not to shoot you dead this instant," Alistair remarked. "Right now, my stomach still hurts because of that seegar burn you gave me. However..." He crossed to a table in the center of the room and placed Doggett's pistol upon it. "Now listen carefully, you mangy coward: you're to pick up your derringer, raise it over your head and then cock it, understand? I'm keeping you covered, so best try no nonsense."

Panting like a hard-hunted fox, the other shook his head. "Please,

Mr. Bryson, don't do this! I've been drinking. I — I couldn't noways hold a gun."

"Yes, you will! After you've raised that derringer over your head and cocked it," Alistair grated, "I will also raise my pistol. I will then count three."

"I won't do it! I'm going to yell!"

"Go ahead. Then I'll not take this absurd risk. Go ahead, you yellow bastard. Pick up that pistol!"

Dark hair streaming in wild disorder over his moon-silvered forehead, Doggett grabbed at his weapon and cocked it with almost incredible speed. Still, he was not fast enough. A slender shaft of yellow-red flame raked the table's surface, momentarily illuminated the high-ceilinged bedroom before a report, deafening in that confined space, numbed the eardrums.

Charles Doggett's white nightshirt lurched far over the table, then his hands scrabbled in an attempt to straighten up. The effort failed because his fingers went lax. Inch by inch, his body sank back upon its haunches, trailed a dark rivulet across the table's top.

CHAPTER XVIII **The Summerhouse**

EVERYONE was aware that, up in Virginia, Robert E. Lee was gathering his magnificent, battle-tested armies and preparing to launch a great campaign which, once and for all, must determine the outcome of this struggle.

For weeks now, replacements and new units, recruited from all over Georgia, had departed from Savannah, rattling northwards over railways which, every day, exposed more inescapably than ever a pitiful lack of equipment, maintenance, shops and replacements.

As spring waned, citizens assumed a new, and hopeful, interest in commerce. Shippers looked to their wharves and repaired warehouses, merchants commenced to seek out clerks, discharged long since, and shipowners made tentative preparations to restore their vessels to running condition.

Everywhere, from spacious drawing rooms to the rowdiest taverns fronting the river, conversation centered on how soon the Union blockade might end and the port thrive as in the good old days.

The *Savannah Republican* had taken to publishing, each day, a special report on the progress of finishing touches to the ram recently, and proudly, christened *Atlanta*.

Every day, people from all over the countryside packed basket lunches and made excursions to the Tift Brothers' shipyard, there to gape at the great, two-hundred-and-four-foot ironclad lying so low and menacing beside her arming dock. This, they assured each other, was not another *Rattlesnake,* not another wooden merchantman hastily converted into a man-of-war.

The new ram's armor was reported capable of deflecting the heaviest shot a Union ironclad could hurl. After all, four inches of railroad iron, bolted tightly together, had been superimposed upon three inches of oak and fifteen inches of pine!

Atlanta's battery, although consisting of but six guns, was the very best procurable in all the Southland: two seven-inch Brooke rifles, mounted fore and aft, and in such a fashion that they could also be fired in broadside; her four other guns were modern six-inch rifles of the same manufacture.

All day, curious citizens were permitted to wander about this fearsome craft which smelled so sweetly of freshly sawed timber. Observant visitors noted than an iron ram-bow had been added to *Fingal*'s hull and that a torpedo spar protruded thirty feet ahead of her. It was said to carry a charge sufficient to blow up any enemy known to exist.

During the early spring, Commander William A. Webb had been hand-picking his men down to the last stoker and oiler; gun crews, under the exacting direction of Samuel Seymour and Lieutenant Alexander, had toiled for days on end to familiarize themselves with the least details of loading, sighting and firing.

On several occasions during the past few days the citizenry had been startled to hear the dull, reverberating boom of *Atlanta*'s battery at target practice downstream.

Yes, expectations ran high in Savannah while the long days grew hotter, more humid, and rice grew tall and softly green in the flooded fields. These days, any man wearing naval uniform was showered with all the hospitality his constitution could stand.

Out at Beau Rivage, serene and beautiful above its terraced lawns, several dinners were given in honor of *Atlanta*'s officers, repasts so lavish that guests again fell to wondering about the source of this splendor. Reynolds Seymour, however, remained politely, and effectively, noncommittal about his affluence. He seriously offended public opinion, though, when he purchased a steam launch and dressed its crew in quasi-naval uniforms — to the pained disgust of Sam Seymour and his fellow officers.

No one devoted closer attention to the great ram's reconstruction and armament that did Lieutenant the Honorable Peter Burgoyne. Indeed, not a few of the occasional suggestions he made later became adopted by the brothers Tift. Indeed, as Sylvia Seymour once was heard to remark, one might have imagined that the ironclad was being built for service in the Royal Navy.

It became the Englishman's conviction that, being far better designed and somewhat speedier than either *Palmetto State* or *Chicora*, *Atlanta* should find small difficulty in defeating *Weehawken* and *Nahant*. These two Ericssons had hurts suffered before Fort Sumter hurriedly remedied at Port Royal; then had been dispatched to maintain the blockade of Savannah.

June 16, 1863, proved to be an especially calm and peaceful day, but Savannah seethed with excitement. Somehow the word had got about that, with tomorrow's dawn, *Atlanta*, Georgia's pride and joy, would enter Wassaw Sound to engage the blockading monitors!

Peter Burgoyne was enjoying this trip up the Savannah with Reynolds Seymour — a major in the Fencibles now. Many wondered how he, who smilingly admitted never having smelled a grain of gunpowder burned in anger, could have won promotion, when many who had been campaigning so long were passed over.

Not that Major Seymour was alone in this: all too many well-fed and handsomely uniformed officers were riding about town. Never had this lazy, always fascinating river appeared more beautiful, decided Peter Burgoyne, than with the sunset gilding trailing beards of Spanish moss and glistening amid reed beds. No wonder Georgians loved their country so deeply.

He glanced at Reynolds, who, wearing his gray uniform turned up in claret and silver, was absorbed in conversation with a pair of corpulent bankers. These gentlemen, also, seemed not to have suffered unduly from the rigors of war.

The current continued to whisper past the launch's smooth sides until, somewhat to his surprise, Peter found himself eagerly awaiting his first glimpse of Beau Rivage. Would his hostess be waiting in her little summerhouse overlooking the river? Inexplicably, his heartbeat quickened. Sylvia Seymour, without doubt, was the loveliest woman he'd encountered this side of the Atlantic. She was so gay, so witty yet tactful, and always charmingly gowned and coiffeured.

All at once, he found himself puzzling over her husband's seeming indifference towards her, especially during the past few weeks. Certainly, Reynolds paid little attention, and made few excuses for his frequent absences. Not that she asked many questions. It had come about, therefore, that often at a mealtime he, rather than Reynolds Seymour, occupied the armchair opposite Beau Rivage's beauteous mistress.

Yes. He must admit he was coming to anticipate a return to Sylvia's home. Often, during visits to *Atlanta* and a curious floating battery named *Georgia,* he found himself recalling some remark of hers, or a lovely expression on her warm and shiny, dark red lips. Peter was honest enough to admit that to her he was becoming the object of considerably more than passing admiration, and an interest in his title and family connections.

A flock of snowy egrets took off from the limbs of a tree overhanging the water, went flapping languidly upstream ahead of the launch.

Ah! Beau Rivage was opening up beyond the next bend and, sure enough, on the terrace nearest the water seemed to drift a generously crinolined yellow gown.

When the launch churned up to the plantation's sturdy little dock, Sylvia blew her husband a dutiful kiss, then called, "Welcome back, Peter!" and waved gaily.

Reynolds stirred on the stern seat, looked preoccupied as he announced: "I'll set you ashore, Peter, then take Mr. Ainsley on to his plantation. We've not had time to conclude certain business affairs, so, probably, I'll not be back until late, Sylvia. You needn't wait up."

The Englishman arose, mechanically fanned away clouds of mosquitoes emerging from nearby reed beds. He raised a quizzical red brow. "I say, do you still intend to watch your ram in action? Or shall I ride into town and go aboard a tender? Must observe this bicker. Duty, you know."

"My launch will take us downstream in plenty of time," the master of Beau Rivage assured him. "Lord knows I hate early rising, but I want to see the *Atlanta* sink or capture those confounded monitors."

The banker called Ainsley laughed a little too heartily. "If half Webb's claims prove justified it won't take her long and we'll be back in time for breakfast at the Club."

Once again, Sylvia and the Honorable Peter Burgoyne dined alone. It proved to be a relatively silent meal. Sylvia appeared puzzled, and even put out, by her husband's casual defection, and did not become animated until sherry was served.

"Suppose we take our coffee in the summerhouse?" she suggested, looking steadily over the gleaming width of mahogany between them. Her warm beauty seldom had been better accentuated than by this gown of yellow marquisette ornamented by large, white silk blossoms. Her golden-brown hair was swept back, in lustrous smoothness, into a large chignon above the white sheen of her neck. "We should have nearly an hour in the coolness before those pesky mosquitoes drive us indoors."

They sat in high-backed wicker chairs facing the peacefully flowing Savannah and watched twilight shadows deepen from blue to violet. A faint fragrance of late spring flowers lingered in the air, overcoming the sour reek of rice fields upstream. Thought Peter, Sylvia has never appeared lovelier.

Indolence personified, Sylvia manipulated a silk and tortoise-shell fan to drive away the first insects that came to whine about the summerhouse. In the distance could be heard the voices of the house servants and the lively twanging of a guitar over in the Quarters.

"And what do you make of us Southerners, Peter? Now that you have been among us this long."

He smiled faintly. "Why, that is difficult to explain, there are so many contradictions amongst you. I can understand, nonetheless, why so many of my countrymen come over to live in this beautiful land."

"But, surely, England is just as beautiful?"

288

He leaned towards her, elbows resting on knees; his ruddy wavy hair glowed copper by the fading sunset. "Many parts of it; but there are also ugly regions, parts of the Midlands, of Wales, and there are many bleak and forbidding sections of Scotland."

"Would you like to settle, to live in Georgia?"

"If I could own a place like Beau Rivage, I fancy I wouldn't hesitate long." He shrugged and settled back in his chair, gaze fixed on a rice barge drifting downstream. "You see, my dear, as my father's second son, the best I can hope for is a small property in Norfolk.

"Of course"— his uneven, but very white, teeth glistened in a wry smile — "I may succeed to the title. Poor Hubert has been sickly since birth. His lungs, you know. Lives in Switzerland now."

The wide arcs of her brows climbed a trifle. "Then there's a chance that you will become Viscount Oakleigh?"

"I fear so; but, of course, there is no certainty."

"Please, Peter, tell me more about the galas and balls in London." Her voice thrilled, rich and melodious amid the semidarkness. "Ever since I was little, I have yearned to be presented at Court, and have wanted to travel about Europe; to live, perhaps, in France; perhaps in England. Over there, so much is to be enjoyed, learned and accomplished. Here in Georgia, and in most of the Tidewater for that matter, life is so wretchedly dull, so arrogantly insular." Her laughter sounded flat, mirthless. "Especially here in Savannah, people are so narrow-minded, so mean-spirited and envious. Of course, if we win this war it will all be very different."

" 'If'? You seem to doubt that your people will win eventually."

"Any clear-witted person doubts."

Peter looked his astonishment.

"We have neither the population, nor the energy, nor the industrial capacity, to match the Northerners. This may sound disloyal, but I don't think it would be a good thing if we did win. Rey thinks so, too." She put out her hand, let it come to rest lightly on his. "Perhaps you understand, now, why we aren't always popular hereabouts?"

"Then why not move abroad? After all, your husband is a very clever man."

Her expression became masked. "Oh, Reynolds is clever, all right, but he lacks depth of character. I fear he lacks the capacity for true greatness. Besides," her long lashes flickered upwards and her shining, sherry-colored eyes widened, "Rey'd get entangled with the first shrewd woman who approached him."

"Really," murmured the Englishman, "aren't you — well, under-rating your husband?"

"I'm not! Not one little bit. Reynolds was unfaithful within a month of our marriage." Abruptly she closed her fan. "Just because I don't choose to berate him, or rail like a fishwife over his crude in-fidelities, doesn't mean that I haven't been stung. Oh, I know all about that Creole he keeps here in town, and the common creatures he consorts with in Richmond, Charleston and half a dozen other towns." Anger faded from her tone and became supplanted by crisp, calm accents. "You see, dear Peter, I know considerably more about Rey-nolds's various undertakings than he, or anyone else, suspects. He really would be shocked, perhaps frightened, if he found out."

The Englishman produced a pigskin case of seegars. "You don't mind? Discourages the mosquitoes."

"Not at all," Sylvia said pleasantly. "As I was saying, I've made it a point for quite some time to keep myself informed concerning my handsome husband's business, as well as his social activities. No. I've lost the few illusions I had when I married him. He's utterly un-scrupulous. There is nothing Rey won't do to turn a dollar, honest or dishonest. I venture he'd cheerfully knife his best friend in the back to win an advantage in some commercial enterprise."

She arose, and went over to face the river, wide skirts swaying to the sharpness of her movements. "A wife can do without true love; many of us have to; but while one can at least respect one's mate, life together can remain tolerable."

She spun about, eyes intent. "May I confess to you, dear Peter, that I'm truly wretched here? I must, and I will, be rid of Reynolds and escape this crumbling, demagogue-ruined Confederacy! How very tragic it is that so many hundreds of thousands of fine men are throw-ing their lives away for the sake of greedy cowards like Reynolds!"

"Of course, the way your husband pretends to play the patriotic sol-dier is wrong — it's outrageous." The young Englishman's voice thick-ened. "Least of all can I condone his neglect of so lovely, so gracious and tender a lady as yourself."

She sped to him, heart-shaped face uplifted, lips parted. "Then you *do* understand? I must escape this existence. But I must leave with security in sight."

He peered into her half-seen features. "There are an infinite number of things we could enjoy doing together. How wonderful it would be to tour the Continent, to show you the Towers and other country homes. How your beauty would shine out there!" He smiled whimsically. "Of course we do have beauties in England, but all too many of our wellborn ladies resemble horses; nice horses," he added, loyally. He drew a slow breath. "I'm talking out, am I not? You're married. Wouldn't do at all for you to come abroad under less than honorable circumstances. You could not do that, any more than I could —"

"Could what, Peter?"

"Violate the trust and hospitality of a gentleman who has taken me into his home, who has done everything in his power to make my stay in Savannah as agreeable as possible."

"Peter! I — I — Oh, dear!" A quick, involuntary gesture sent the fan flying. When he straightened from recovering it Sylvia Seymour was within his arms, lips parted and eager for the kiss.

For many instants they clung together, trembling, mouths avid.

"You *will* take me away, won't you?" she begged. "I — I shan't mind your waiting for the title. I won't mind a bit — and I'll make you happy. You've no idea how happy."

Gently, he disengaged, but held her at arm's length and struggled to speak evenly. "But we can't do such a thing, dearest. It wouldn't do. After all, I am still a commissioned officer in the Royal Navy. Were I to run off with the wife of an officer in the service of his country I would be immediately cashiered, and rightly so."

"But Peter, can't you understand? I need you. I crave you. I — all these weeks I've been eating my heart out for you!" She stepped closer into his embrace. "Do you remember that night Sam rode out from town to tell you about the *Nashville?*"

"I'll never forget it."

"Well, darling, that night I was on my way to — I wanted you so much I actually was on my way to you when I heard his horse on the driveway."

In the firefly-lit gloom he felt blood pouring hot into his face, his neck, his loins. "Let's not make our situation more difficult. I'll confess, my dearest girl, that I was enchanted when first we met." He let her

291

go, stepped back. "Dear God in Heaven! Why must we be inflicted with that incubus called 'honor'?"

Sylvia's smile became inscrutable. "Why, then, Peter darling, since we cannot have each other dishonorably, we must behave honorably, mustn't we?"

"What do you mean by that?"

"Have patience, my beloved," she breathed, her hair softly fragrant about his nostrils, "and you will soon find out."

CHAPTER XIX **The Pride of Georgia**

THE Confederate States ram, *Atlanta,* lay to her anchor below Coulson's Bluff, trim under a new coat of gray paint. By starlight, the pride of Georgia appeared even longer, larger and more sinister than she did by day.

Upstream, the lights of Savannah winked and glowed, in unprecedented numbers for such an early hour: half after three. Everyone in town above the age of five knew that a crucial trial of strength for their beloved ram impended, so were up and about.

Carts, carriages and saddle horses kept clattering down to landings at which a trio of old excursion steamers waited with steam up and lanterns lit. Swarms of citizens, it appeared, were anxious to witness this struggle upon which their lives and fortunes depended. Many had been the toasts offered the night before to victory, to the port, and to deep confusion for those monitors lurking in Wassaw Sound.

Nowadays, people weren't so fearful of those cheeseboxes-on-rafts, since their futile assault on Sumter. They'd learned how terribly the Ericssons had been hurt. Amateur tacticians were given to pointing out that a monitor's rate of fire was much too slow to be effective.

Out on the river, a pencil-thin column of smoke climbed from the ram's single, squat funnel and starlight glanced dully off her iron carapace. Lights winked through *Atlanta*'s gunports and shone in her wheelhouse.

292

From upstream appeared the running lights of several steam launches; more were putting out from docks below the bluff.

"Wouldn't miss this for a farm."

"You got the lunch bag?"

"Bet you she sinks both them Linkum gunboats 'side ten minutes."

"Ought to. She mounts six cannons to their four. Hurry up, Billy. There goes the warning whistle."

"Oh, Mamma, will the cannons sound awful loud?"

"Damn it, Jennie, I believe you forgot to bring my corn squeezings."

One of the excursion boats commenced importantly to toot her whistle and, after a small stampede of stragglers, smoke poured from her funnel and she began to back out into the stream, paddles threshing loudly amid an almost unearthly stillness over the earth. The quiet was so perfect that the sleepy crowing of cocks and the clamor of distant dogs were easily to be distinguished.

Deep in the remodeled blockade-runner's vitals, stokers, already black as minstrels from coal dust, streamed sweat, joked and laughed tautly. On the iron deckplates over their heads rang the hurrying of gunners' feet. A supreme confidence pervaded the whole man-of-war from Commander Webb to raw infantrymen selected to round out the gun crews for, thanks to unforeseen delays in readying the ship and failure of a paymaster to appear, many well-trained men had slipped away not to return.

Although pierced for eight guns, *Atlanta* mounted only six pieces — this was because the other two guns would have increased her already frightening draught of sixteen feet to a perilous depth. However, the ram's present battery consisted of powerful modern pieces which, fired at close range, should shatter a monitor's armor or dislocate and so immobilize her turret.

Sam Seymour's broad, always lean face appeared unusually gaunt and strained by the battle lanterns' dim light when, accompanied by Lieutenant Dalton, he checked and rechecked the position of every item of equipment essential to efficient service of the guns.

While clumping along, his thoughts ran back to unlucky *Mississippi*, over which he had toiled so hard and in vain. He still could visualize her, minus engines, spouting smoke and flame and drifting down towards New Orleans and David Farragut's triumphant squadron.

Well, in a short while, he should attain his life's ambition: he'd go into action aboard a proper ironclad. How different, in every respect, was this iron monster from the dainty little *Sumter,* aboard which gallant commerce-destroyer he first had sniffed the smoke of battle.

Louise, he reckoned, probably was standing right now on the porch of their home and trying not to cry, for, sternly, he had forbidden her to go aboard an excursion steamer or to accept a place in his brother's sleek steam launch.

He hadn't seen much of Reynolds since he'd bought that launch and dressed her crew as naval seamen. Besides, it made him wince to see Rey riding about Savannah so prosperous-looking and dressed in that preposterous uniform.

That the ram's other commissioned officers, without exception, also had come out of the Old Navy, was reassuring. They brought with them traditions of technical excellence and steadiness in combat. The conviction grew that, this time, a Confederate man-of-war was about to win, not an indecisive draw, like that duel of *Virginia* — née *Merrimac* — nor a partial success, such as had been won by *Palmetto State* and *Chicora,* but a crashing victory that the whole world would hear about.

A fierce impatience pervaded him. He, personally, was to fight *Atlanta's* big bow rifle, whilst Ham Dalton would command Number Two gun on the ram's starboard broadside.

Lord, it was getting hot in this casemate. What would it be like when the sun came up? Wiping sweat from his brow, he fumbled for a cumbersome, nickel-plated watch.

"It's nearly four," he told his red-bearded gun pointer. "We'll be getting under way any minute now."

The sour reek of sweating bodies and mingled fumes of coal gas and oil momentarily grew stronger. The stokers must have been ordered to get up steam, for the ringing scrape of scoops began to reverberate within *Atlanta's* six-foot casemate.

Curious, in what directions a man's thoughts ran at such a moment. Graduation Day at Annapolis; that night in Baltimore when Sylvia had prevailed; Irad lying, with his neck broken, on a muddy street in Richmond beside the body of an infant he'd believed to be his son. Recollections of smotheringly hot days on a ways where *Mississippi* was under construction; Raphael Semmes, watching yet another Yankee merchantman sink in flames; Louise's horror-stricken face peering from the balcony of her looted home; Louise's lovely features framed in long, black hair as she dreamed beside him.

Aide-toi et Dieu t'aidera! Well, he reckoned, every man aboard was out to help himself; surely, this time God must favor their cause.

When, imperiously, a bell clanged in the ram's engine room, an electric tension pervaded the entire ship. Pilot Jim Fleetwood had judged the tide to be at flood, which was necessary if *Atlanta,* needing nearly sixteen feet of water, were to avoid stranding on one of the innumerable mudbanks above Wassaw Sound.

The hull shuddered, steam hissed like a pitful of snakes; *Atlanta* started downstream.

Aboard Reynolds Seymour's launch the guests crowded impatiently, noisily, about a Negro steward engaged in lacing strong black coffee with even stronger whisky.

"Hurry, Mose, my glow's fading!"

"When's the sandwiches comin'?"

"Any champagne?"

Lieutenant the Honorable Peter Burgoyne spoke to his nearest neighbor — he did that more readily, now. "Fancy the ram's commander will have to attempt to engage on wide water. Isn't much room for maneuver in the river."

The other, a morose-looking artillery colonel, emitted a grunting noise, then squirted tobacco juice over the rail. "Like hell he will! He'll be better off if he can engage at close quarters. Those monitors, Mister, mount eleven-inch and fifteen-inch Dahlgrens; a damned-sight weightier than Webb's seven-inch and six-point-four rifles."

"You seem to have had naval experience?"

"Used to be an officer of the Old Navy."

"Why are you Army?"

"No ships to serve in, that's why. Besides, our Navy Department is being starved to death. Old Jeff Davis can't tell a tug from a ship of the line — and doesn't want to. He's all Army."

Reynolds offered a cup of coffee. "What odds were being quoted at the Club when you left, MacGregor?"

"The monitors get whipped to hell and back; five to three. Ten thousand was offered."

"Wish I'd been there. I'd have taken a piece of that," laughed Sylvia's husband.

Colonel MacGregor stared. "You don't seem extra confident over the *Atlanta*'s success."

Reynolds swallowed a deep gulp from a mug of shandygaff, then winked a little drunkenly. "I'm not, really. Besides, the fewer blockade-runners in operation, the greater the profits for those in the business."

Peter blinked. "Do I understand correctly," he inquired, "that you would just as soon *not* see the blockade broken below Savannah?"

The other's slight shoulders lifted under the Cape Chatham Fencibles' silver epaulets. "I own heavy interests in certain concerns operating from Charleston. Why should I welcome competition down here?"

Then, indeed, was Peter Burgoyne forced to suppress a contempt that bordered on loathing. He found it especially disgusting that Reynolds must know that his own brother was aboard yonder ram and stood an excellent chance of being killed in a little while.

"Look, boys! The ram's getting going at last!" A fat little man, showing an enormous expanse of waistcoat, raised a pocket flask. "Here's luck to the old girl."

Off to starboard, an excursion boat, gay with lanterns, puffed steadily along. She had a band aboard. It was pumping out "The Beauregard Quickstep," a tune recently grown popular. Other sightseeing craft were steaming downstream, too, but were hugging the north bank.

The light now strengthened sufficiently to reveal the great ram in stark silhouette relieved only by the twinkle of sparks shooting from her smokestack. Men could be seen busying themselves about a torpedo boom rigged upon her flat and pointed prow.

"There's a plenty cold chicken in the hampers, boys," Reynolds called out. "Help yourselves and drink up. Let's all enjoy this cockfight."

In *Atlanta*'s pilothouse, a low, wooden affair protected by steel railroad rails and roofed with the same material, stood Lieutenant-Commander William A. Webb, his handsome, aquiline features glistening with perspiration. By his side waited the best procurable pilot, James Fleetwood, wearing a rusty-black frock coat and flat leather cap of the same color.

In a taut voice, the latter continually called instructions to a brawny quartermaster handling the ironclad's wheel. Dawn remained little more than a presentiment, so Fleetwood had to look hard to find his landmarks.

Webb, ever religious, prayed silently that God grant to his ship a clean-cut victory. Nothing, at this time, was more necessary to the new nation's fortunes. The Confederacy's six million inhabitants needed something to be proud of afloat, something to prove that their Navy, no less than their magnificent armies, could defeat the Northerners.

Valiantly, Webb attempted to discount Commodore Tattnall's misgivings concerning the probable invulnerability of *Weehawken's* and *Nahant's* ten-inch armor. What most concerned him was his ironclad's fifteen feet and nine inches of draft.

Soon the river widened and the lead-hue width of Wassaw Sound opened up beyond a final bend. At eight knots an hour, *Atlanta* steamed on, pursued by frivolous music aboard the excursion boats and flanked by sight-seeing launches. Some people aboard these waved bottles, shouted inane encouragements.

"Well, there they be!" suddenly remarked the pilot. "And firing up in a hurry."

'Way down toward Wassaw Island's eastern tip, at that point where the river's waters emptied into Wassaw Sound, arose two tiny smudges of coal smoke.

The enemy captains, Commander Webb soon decided — and Lieutenant Dalton agreed — would make no effort to close the range, but would remain on the Sound's broad waters.

While stars paled and the east assumed the colors of sunrise, the pride of Georgia, the Confederacy's mightiest man-of-war, steamed onwards. As on the day which had witnessed *Rattlesnake's* destruction there was scarcely a breath of wind; only the ram's forward movement stirred a bright new ensign dangling from *Atlanta's* after flagstaff.

The water parted evenly under *Atlanta's* bow and rose in little white jets about the shaft of that spar torpedo which, it was hoped, might soon be exploded under a Yankee.

Now, there was very little movement among the hot and hairy crew — they only chewed tobacco and cracked feeble jokes to relieve a tension growing all but intolerable.

Peering past the muzzle of his big English rifled gun, Sam sighted a monitor. Judging by the clouds of smoke she was emitting, she was closing in, under forced draft. Then he glimpsed her consort, for some reason astern by a good three quarters of a mile.

How long and sandy was the shore hereabouts; just pale dunes indented by patches of marsh and topped here and there with wind-twisted, flat-topped pines.

He directed a sidewise glance at his Right Shot Man, a lean artillery sergeant from the mountains of Georgia. What could he be thinking about?

"Peters, I want you to —" He got no further for, sick at heart, he recognized the cause of a soft, jarring impact which swiftly impeded *Atlanta*'s progress. Followed a furious jangling on the engine-room bell; the ram lurched onwards a short distance, then came to a dead stop.

"What in hell's wrong with that dunderhead pilot?"

"Oh, Christ! We've been run aground."

"Jesus God! What'll we do now?"

Down from the pilothouse raced Lieutenant Dalton, face white and furious. "Run aft, everybody! Must try to lift our bow."

Through hot semidarkness in which a few battle lanterns still swayed, the gun crews pounded aft and, upon order, commenced to leap up and down in concert once the ironclad's ten-foot screw had begun to labor in reverse.

Men, crowded against the after gun, cursed loudly as, with arms around each other, they jumped. Foam gushed from beneath *Atlanta*'s fantail, spread far out over the glistening water. Sam Seymour's mouth went sour. This simply must not happen.

Loud cheers arose when everyone felt the hull slide smoothly off the sandbank. Creating furious, coffee-colored eddies, the ram backed into deep water.

"Shoal must have built up during the spring storms," opined Jim Fleetwood. "Ain't no ship this size come this way since last year."

Gradually gathering speed, *Atlanta* circled southwards towards the onrushing Ericssons; confidence reigned supreme along her gun deck. "Thank God! We're free to fight them Yankee bastards the way we aim to."

The sightseers, meantime, had taken alarm and, turning tail, were threshing upriver as fast as their paddles could drive them.

Lieutenant Barbot, face aflame with excitement, descended to the gun deck. "Mr. Seymour!" he shouted. "Captain's compliments. Please fire a ranging shot at the *Weehawken;* she's the leading monitor."

Sam would, and gladly, being quite unaware that his shot might slay Captain John Rodgers, a former classmate.

"What's the other one called?" It was necessary, for efficient fire control, to give specific names.

"*Nahant,*" Barbot said, and returned to the pilothouse.

Sam squinted through the gunport, drew a deep breath. "Range nineteen hundred yards!" The Brooke's training gear was set into operation; he, himself, supervised and adjusted the elevation.

"Fire!" The bow gun's captain jerked the lanyard; a deafening explosion resulted and the great rifle recoiled smoothly, to the hurters at the end of its carriage tracks; a small whirlwind of heated, rotten-smelling smoke beat into the casemate, set the gun crew to coughing.

Sam vented a staccato oath when his seven-inch solid shot raised a lazy waterspout about halfway between *Weehawken* and *Nahant.*

"Range fifteen hundred yards!" he barked. The gun was reloaded with speed, but not before *Atlanta* had blundered onto another shoal so hard that many gunners were thrown flat and the ram slewed ponderously around to starboard so far as to ruin the bow gun's aim and render it all but impossible to train the ram's starboard broadside.

Exasperated profanity sounded in all directions when once more the engine room's bell clanged in a frenzy of urgency.

Despite her crew's frantic efforts *Atlanta,* this time, remained hard and fast aground, a fact immediately noted by the enemy.

The only thing to do, Sam realized, was to fire as best he might. A lucky shot just might cripple one of those ugly little juggernauts.

Hamilton Dalton's piece fired also, but, because of *Atlanta's* position, it could not be properly trained, and its shot missed by a disgustingly wide margin. Hope soared when the after broadside gun went off and its projectile raised water less than a hundred yards off *Weehawken's* starboard bow. Surprisingly, she was maintaining a course calculated to bring her under fire from the ram's broadside.

In frantic haste, Sam had his piece traversed until its sights seemed aligned on *Weehawken's* turret but just then she veered to port, an evolution which abruptly eclipsed the Stars and Stripes flying over her stern.

Seymour himself sighted the gun, but was sickened to see the enemy run so far to port that the Brooke soon became masked by the after edge of its gunport.

It came as a measure of consolation that, thus far, neither Federal ironclad had fired.

Atlanta's bow gun was discharged for a second time and missed by only a few feet — but missed, all the same. The fury of undeserved impotence clouded Sam's vision. Why? *Why* did such mischances seem, inevitably, to dog Confederate men-of-war?

Sullenly, he ordered the bow gun reloaded, aware that, unless a miracle occurred, it could not possibly be trained on either enemy.

Now, surely, the Ericssons must open fire and, when Sam recalled that devastating marksmanship which had shattered *Rattlesnake* in such short order, his stomach went cold and his intestines writhed.

What would it be like to receive shot fired by eleven- and fifteen-inch Dahlgrens? Would *Atlanta's* armor really withstand the impact of such projectiles? Sam bent over the Brooke's rear sight but could see no monitor through it. The big rifle simply could not be traversed far enough because the gunport was far too narrow.

Four hundred yards; three hundred and fifty yards. Smoothly, *Weehawken* came bearing down the glassy Sound with horizontal rays from the newly risen sun brightening her turret's gray-brown armor.

"Lie down!" he heard Dalton shout. "Down — everybody! *Weehawken's* about to fire."

There was barely time to obey the North Carolinian's command before a hellish thing happened. A fifteen-inch solid shot struck *Atlanta* squarely on the beam of her casemate. While the projectile failed actually to penetrate the carapace, it nonetheless hurled inwards a murderous cloud of iron and wooden splinters and its concussion stunned or flung flat to deck all hands manning the ram's forward division.

Shrieks, howls and bubbling screams bespoke men terribly wounded. Blood gushed from Samuel Seymour's nose and stained his shirt as, half-stunned, he reeled about the bow gun's breech and stumbled over the prostrate bodies of his men. In a semicoma, he heard *Atlanta's* Number Three gun fire — hurl its shot not at *Weehawken,* but at

300

Nahant. The acrid fumes of burned powder eddied through the casemate, yet failed to disguise the sickish-sweet smell of freshly spilled blood.

Somehow, Sam raised himself onto hands and knees, but was forced to remain in that position, shaking his head to clear it. His Number Two gun pointer began screaming horribly when a handspikeman tried to pull out a jagged oak sliver driven deep into his shoulder.

When *Weehawken* fired her eleven-inch gun she scored a clean hit on *Atlanta*'s pilothouse, knocking out the quartermaster and Pilot Fleetwood.

Commander Webb was hurled down the ladder leading to the gun deck, but Lieutenant Barbot remained rigid at his peephole, frozen into immobility by the awful impact of that shot which had caved in the pilothouse sides and roof while bending its protective steel rails as easily as if they had been pieces of macaroni.

Commander Webb rolled over and over on the gun deck, then swayed to his knees, eyes staring and face ashen.

"Keep firing!" he choked. "For God's sake, keep on firing!" But, strive as they would, the Rebel gunners could not bring their cannon to bear.

Seven minutes of agonized waiting ensued before there came another shattering impact followed by wild screams and the thump and thud of flying debris. Sam had no idea where his Brooke pointed, but jerked the lanyard all the same.

One by one, various gun crews struggled to their feet and, by instinct alone, attempted to serve their pieces.

Weehawken's fourth shot dislocated an iron gunport cover from its hinges and started joints in the armor so wide that daylight came streaming in through splintered wood and riven iron. Again and yet again, *Weehawken* fired point-blank into the helpless, steam- and smoke-oozing ram. Even so, *Atlanta*'s crew managed to fire an eighth shot which did no damage at all, only caused the excursion boats to flee faster still.

"Captain, reckon we'd better call quits," Lieutenant Barbot could be heard crying. "The other Yankee is coming up."

Through cupped hands, Commander Webb called down to the gun deck, "Mr. Dalton! Have there been any clean punctures of our armor?"

"No, sir, not yet; but if the enemy closes the range any further we'll surely get riddled."

As if to attest Dalton's opinion, *Weehawken's* next shot tore a great section of armor from the casemate's top, permitted light to come flooding down to reveal, in pitiless detail, the destruction and confusion prevailing along the gun deck. Bloodied, insensible men sprawled everywhere between the guns dazedly holding hands over their ears, or attempted to bind up dripping wounds.

Samuel Seymour would never experience a more bitter moment than when he staggered over to the wheelhouse ladder and called up into the wreckage above. "We must strike, sir! Their next shot will go clean through us and this place will become a slaughterhouse."

So it came about that a white cloth was poked through the pilot-house's roof just in time to prevent *Nahant's* opening fire.

Tears streamed down Commander Webb's cheeks when he lowered himself to the gun deck, to stand swaying like a man far gone in drink. Said he:

"My brave fellows, I have surrendered our vessel because circumstances, over which I had no control, have compelled me to do so. I know that you started upon this expedition with high hopes and you have been disappointed. I most earnestly wish that it had happened otherwise, but Providence, for some good reason, has interfered with our plans and we have failed of success.

"You all know that if we had not run aground the result would have been different. Now that a regard for your lives has influenced me for this surrender, I would advise you to submit quietly to the fate which has overtaken us. I hope that we may all soon return to our homes and meet again in a common brotherhood."

The shaken figure drew breath to continue but, suddenly, Webb's legs buckled and he collapsed, inert, across a gunner's half-naked body.

Later on, a Union steam tender appeared; took off *Atlanta's* crew while surgeons toiled to save the wounded. At sundown a pair of tugs appeared and pulled *Atlanta* off the mudbank, then started towing the prize to Port Royal.

CHAPTER XX

Supper in a Boudoir

SOMETHING, decided Sylvia Seymour, must have gone very wrong. Reynolds never rides like that except when he's been drinking too much. So blown and lathered was his mount he must have galloped all the way out from town. He roared for a groom, dropped his bridle reins and strode angrily out of sight under the portico.

When Rey gets excited, he's easy to talk to. She went over to preen herself before a tall pier glass and was pleased with her reflection. Seldom, recently, had she appeared so delectable, so desirable, for beneath her gown of pale green she was wearing nothing whatever.

Lord's mercy! How long since she had invited Reynolds to sup in her boudoir? Many months. In the early days of their marriage they usually had dined up here, because a titivating minimum of clothing could be worn. Mirrors, arranged at advantageous positions about the boudoir, had multiplied the flames of a single candelabrum and had reflected the diners from unusual angles.

Sylvia loved this room with its pink-and-green satin draperies, its voluptuous Louis XV furniture and, most especially, a soft-cushioned chaise longue.

Using a rabbit's foot, Sylvia expertly applied rouge, then wetted her finger tips to smooth winglike brows. Quite unruffled, she listened to the front door bang open; to Reynolds, cursing the inattentiveness of his servants; to the noise his riding boots made crossing parquet flooring towards the staircase.

"Sylvia! Sylvia! Damn it, Sylvia, where are you?" She heard him shouting as he clattered upstairs. She remained quite calm before her *poudreuse*. Her door was locked because, in warm weather, she invariably enjoyed a siesta in the nude. When it got very hot she would allow Hecuba, a slim mulatto woman bought in Richmond, to cool her with a huge ostrich fan Reynolds had brought from some blockade-runner's captain.

"God damn it, why is there no ice water in my room?" She heard her husband's voice demanding.

"We wasn't expectin' you, suh."

"Damn it! Always expect me!"

Before the mirror Sylvia straightened lazily and flattened her shoulders until the points of her breasts stood out under the pale green gauze. The nipples were visible, all right, she decided, but not sufficiently, so, for the occasion, so she dipped a finger tip into her pot of lip rouge and, smiling, brightened both budlike nipples and the neat, concentric aureoles surrounding them. She again dusted powder over her bosom and paid no attention at all when a furious hammering began at her door.

"Open up! How dare you lock me out?"

"You'll have to wait, Rey. I'm dressing."

"Let me in!"

"I'm sorry, dear," she called softly. "But I want you to wait — it's for your own sake, Rey." Deliberately, she secured her gleaming hair with pale green ribbons.

"My sake? What in hell do you mean? Come on, open this door."

"Be patient, lover, and you won't be sorry. Why don't you go change your clothes? It must have been miserably hot in town."

"Hotter than hinges of hell!" came the petulant assurance. "All right, I'll be back in twenty minutes and you'd better have that door unlocked."

"Dear, dear, Reynolds! How impetuous you are. Is Miss Enriquez indisposed?"

"Ah-h. You're too damn clever for your own good." He broke into a peal of that wild laughter which sometimes left her frightened, and tramped off down the hall shouting for his valet.

The Reynolds Seymours' supper had been perfectly planned: a bisque of shrimp, sweetbreads with truffles under glass, an endive salad with delicate French dressing and a slice of iced melon for dessert.

Inviting but not heavy, the wines selected by Sylvia were a delight. Seldom, she reflected, had Reynolds looked more dissipated than tonight, but by candlelight, his overfine features lost something of their bloated look. In a dressing gown of mulberry-hued silk turned up in turquoise blue, he remained one of the handsomest men she had ever beheld.

"And what, my sweet, has prompted this intimate little soirée?"

Reynolds drawled, oscillating a brandy snifter while reclining on her chaise longue.

"I don't really know," she smiled. "Perhaps it's been so long since we have had an evening to ourselves. Besides, I suspect you are at last growing tired of Miss Enriquez."

He stiffened momentarily, then relaxed. "*Touché!* You're a penetrating creature." He raised a brow. "Or could it be, Wife of My Bosom, that you are becoming bored with your English aristocrat?"

"What gives you that idea?"

"Didn't dear Peter move out, bag and baggage, the day after the *Atlanta's* miserable showing?"

Sylvia peered into a glass of Graves beaded with condensation. "That might also be the case, though I'll not admit it."

"Well, we're well rid of that supercilious swine," drawled Reynolds, dangling a heelless slipper from his big toe; hairs on his legs showed surprisingly black to the movement of his thigh muscles. "He was getting too envious to be tolerated."

"Yes," sighed the girl in the green gauze negligee. "Seems as if the number of envious persons increases every day."

"Let them be envious," he smiled. "Haven't I the loveliest home? The prettiest wife?"

"And the swiftest growing fortune in all Georgia?" She bent forward, allowing the outlines of her breasts to become more pronounced. "Tell me, were you angry this evening about something besides your quarrel with that Creole girl?"

"Why do you think that?"

She laughed an ascending scale. "You understand me so little, Reynolds."

He lifted the snifter, inhaled daintily, but did not drink. "Why, as to that, Sylvia my darling, you may very well be right. I had an unpleasant interview with Sam's wife."

"Oh! So Louise went to your place of business?"

"She did." He sat up frowning. "Imagine it! She had the nerve to march into my office towing Sam's brat by the hand."

"Did she really? I would never have imagined she possessed such courage or imagination. And what did she want?"

Across the shadowy boudoir Reynolds laughed unpleasantly. "She demanded that I drop everything and travel straight up to Richmond

— demanded, mind you — to see Secretary Mallory of the Navy Department. She wants me to *demand*, no less, that he arrange for Sam's exchange. When I said that I would see what I could do when opportunity offered, she fairly withered me. She spoke right out, said that the least I could do for our country, since I was growing so rich out of this war, was to secure Sam's release."

Ineffably graceful, Sylvia picked up a peacock feather fan, commenced to cool herself. "And what else did dear Louise say?"

"She was unpleasant enough to accuse me of shirking my duty, of only masquerading in uniform, of fattening on the blood of worthier Southerners." Reynolds made a sharp motion with his brandy glass, then bent his handsome head and drank deeply. "Her voice wasn't loud, but it carried. I could hear clerks in my outer office fall silent."

Steadily, the young woman in green considered her husband. He was worried all right, hadn't given a sign when she passed between him and the candelabrum, her every opulent curve fully visible; it disconcerted her no little.

"That was most unfair after all we've done for her and Sam. Was there anything more?"

"Yes. She even mentioned certain connections I have in Charleston: the Excalibur Company. Wonder where she heard about that?"

Here, Sylvia perceived readily enough, was what really had aroused his concern.

"Oh, don't you fret, darling. It's really nothing to get upset over." She placed cool fingers on his wrist. "We'll be wealthy and secure when Louise is taking in laundry." She kissed him lightly on the lips, then sank onto the floor beside the chaise longue.

When he slung bare legs over the edge of the seat and sat up, she rubbed her cheek against his knee, ever prettily posed.

"Things were never better! Oh, Sylvia, you can't believe how hard put I was to restrain my satisfaction when the monitors won. Now the Excalibur people needn't fear competition out of Savannah; not for a long, long time at least." Almost absent-mindedly, he reached down to fondle her firmly yielding bosoms.

"Rey, I must be stupid, but I don't understand. Surely, if this port were reopened, you could operate your own runners out of here?"

"I could, but it would mean a greater division of the profits. Whew. It's hot in here, and all that cologne makes me dizzy."

306

"I suppose so, but I daren't open the windows with the malaria season so near at hand. There now — let's both be comfortable." She let the negligee slip from marble-smooth shoulders into her lap while Reynolds settled back, wrenched open his dressing gown and exposed a mat of gleaming black curls.

"You see," he continued, "Louise isn't the only one who has been giving me a hard time. Often when I ride downtown these days, a good many friends — I've done a lot of them big favors, too! — look aside, or through me when I draw near. It isn't pleasant. Silly fools, if they only knew how much I'm about to realize on just one little transaction!"

"Oh, Rey!" she stroked his thigh, murmured, "I reckon I've not given your cleverness half the credit it deserves. This . . ." she hesitated ". . . is another blockade-running venture?"

"In a way, I suppose. Damn it, Sylvia" — he chuckled and patted her bare shoulder — "I've got the Midas touch these days. Everything turns into gold."

Having long since observed that silence is a most effective questioner, Sylvia rearranged the skirt of her negligee.

"This is merely the climax of a scheme I've kept in operation for months, and don't let anybody fool you into thinking there aren't just as many Yankees ready to grab at a quick dollar as there are — others."

"But you said it wasn't exactly blockade-running?" Her long-lashed eyes rolled up at him.

"It isn't. It's a wonderful dodge Sam learned about. It's been done along the Mississippi ever since the start of this war."

"Sam?"

"Of course he wasn't in on it; he just described the technique that's being followed."

" 'Technique'? What can you mean, Rey?"

"Why, it's simply this. We have certain commodities the Yankees badly want, just as there are certain things the Yankees have which we want even more badly. What could be simpler than to ship what the Yankees want — cotton, tobacco, rice, for example — to where it surely will be captured? One of the captors, then, er — indemnifies the shipper — ah — *very* handsomely, let me assure you. Do you understand, my pet?"

"I'm beginning to, but continue on."

"Then, as per agreement, the captor becomes shipper and sends what we need near enough our lines to have it captured by certain of our troops. Most of them, bless their stupid, poor-white souls, have no real notion of what's taking place."

Ice, melting in a bucket, tinkled softly and Sylvia smiled, as if only half interested in talk. "A little champagne would be cooling, don't you think?"

She arose from the swirl of fallen draperies and, quite nude, crossed to fill their glasses, her exquisitely formed limbs gleaming rosy-white by the candlelight.

To her sharp annoyance he continued to stare unseeingly at his own reflection in a bull's-eye mirror on the wall opposite. "Imagine it: within two days I stand to clear a hundred thousand dollars on a single transaction."

"In greenbacks, I presume?" Sylvia turned, the bottle poised.

"Better than that. I'll be paid in English gold. *That's* the stuff to salt away."

"But, dear, isn't it difficult, even dangerous, to carry about such a fortune? Especially between the lines?"

"No. Two nights from now, I will meet a Captain Higgins near Tod Hardwick's old rice-pounding mill — the one that got burned at the start of the war. Higgins has only to ascend Great Ogeechee Creek and go ashore. I meet him. He gives me the gold. It's as simple as that."

CHAPTER XXI **Settlements**

NIGHT birds still twittered drowsily among trees beyond rice fields lining Great Ogeechee Creek's banks. The *plop!* caused by fish jumping and the sad, thin complaint of screech owls lent an air of surpassing peace and repose. A listener equiped with sharp ears, therefore, might have recognized subtle sounds from around a wooded bend in the stream as those of muffled oarlocks. He would have heard also the soft *clip-clop* of hoofs following a sandy road towards the ruins of Tod Hardwick's rice-pounding mill.

But a listener would have had to possess even sharper perceptions to detect scrabbling noises in underbrush hemming in the factory's vine-draped ruins. Its tall brick smokestack seemed to rise as a monument to commemorate the victory of Decay.

Major Lucius Kershaw, 2d Georgia Infantry, emitted a low, birdlike whistle. "Look alive, you men. There's a boat somewhere out there."

"Yes, sir." Captain Charles Knowles, on detached duty from the Provost Marshal's office, peered through the shadows and presently was able to discern several of the figures lurking in his vicinity. Furtively, these men crushed a few of the mosquitoes which had made a real torment of the past two hours. Itching little lumps were standing out all over Knowles's face, hands and neck.

A thin mist began to arise, and the sour, wet smell of rice fields grew stronger, and then the dew-drenched watchers stiffened on distinguishing an indistinct and somber outline. The crew of a four-oared gig was pulling it easily along on a rising tide which, according to calculation, soon must turn and bear it as swiftly back towards Ossabaw Sound.

By now it had become possible to tell that the gig's occupants were clad in blue, but how many men were aboard couldn't yet be determined.

Perhaps two hundred yards inland from the landing, a pair of gangling privates — the elder might have been sixteen — nervously handled their muskets behind trees beside a sandy road.

"Some fellers acomin' up fast. His hoss canterin'."

"I don't hear nothin'."

"Then you must be deef as a adder. I heered him ten minutes ago. Where I come from a feller don't git no deer iffen he don't hear him a long ways off."

The youths started because, at that moment, a pair of deer did rouse up, alarmed by the approach of what now sounded like not one, but a pair of horsemen. White flags asway, the deer bounded off into the silent woods.

Pretty soon the riders appeared. A slight figure rode in front followed by a bigger, long-legged man a couple of lengths behind.

"Don't you dast shoot, no matter how purty a target they offer," hissed the older soldier. "Remember Major's words. Don't shoot lest they try to go back."

They stiffened, froze like rabbits at the approach of danger. The younger boy sighted the road, then hooked a finger over the trigger. Cripes! These riders were mighty careless: didn't notice nothin'. They'd pass not ten feet away. Must have come a far piece, though; they rode heavily and the horses were white with sweat.

"So far so good, McCurdy," they heard the smaller man saying, "you ride ahead and I'll wait behind the old tool shed."

The other nodded and rode on, shoulders rising and falling rhythmically. By this dim light he looked simply gigantic.

Captain Knowles was struggling to even his breathing, when out onto the landing trotted a single horseman. He reined in and sat looking about. Major Kershaw eased a foreign-made hand gun free of its holster. He was mighty proud of the weapon, a Volcanic patent pistol: by a simple pulling of its trigger, four barrels could be made to rise and fire in succession. Fellow officers had ridiculed its short barrels, had claimed Kershaw couldn't hit a barn at thirty paces. But he knew better.

At the same moment, to the commanding officer's ears, came a dull *thud* of wood bumping wood. "Easy all! Back, you numskulls!"

The horseman, far from taking alarm, rode deliberately back to the clearing's edge, and whistled.

Unintelligible conversation followed below the dock, then onto its weed-tufted surface clambered a stalwart figure. He was in Federal uniform and wearing a black campaign hat pulled low over his eyes. Then another man appeared lugging what appeared to be an extra-heavy valise. Both the Federals stood silent, peering in all directions. Then one of them gave a very poor imitation of a whippoorwill's cry.

The rider, meanwhile, was leading his heavily breathing mount over to a crumbled pile of brickwork that once had been the boiler house. Here he was joined by another horseman who called out in a low voice: "It's all clear, sir. They are here."

The twenty-odd infantrymen concealed about the mill watched a second rider — he wore civilian clothes — advance towards the men waiting on the dock.

Politely, Captain Reynolds Seymour of the Cape Chatham Fencibles lifted his hat to the Union officer, Captain Higgins, Second Rhode Island Artillery. The latter acknowledged this courtesy with a careless half-salute.

"You're right on the nose, Captain," greeted the Federal, a stocky, clean-shaven individual. "Don't nobody tell me you Rebs got no sense of time. Got a list of wants for our next trip?"

Reynolds reached into the front of a dark frock coat. "Yes. Here's what I reckon will bring the best prices. Not bulky, either."

The black slouch hat inclined.

"Look at that slimy little bastard!" the man from the Provost Marshal's office was whispering. "No wonder he can live like a king."

"He'll hang — damn him!" promised Major Kershaw. "For the scabby traitor he is."

"That's good," the Yankee was saying. "Say, Captain, that was extra fine long-staple cotton we found in our last 'capture.' Should fetch top prices in Nassau."

"I try to deliver only superior merchandise, Captain Higgins." He failed to restrain a certain eagerness in his tone when he noted that big valise by the sergeant's side. "You've brought my — er — compensation?"

"Every sovereign of it, in English gold. Here. How are you going to carry this? It's heavier than lead."

"My man and I have brought saddlebags," Reynolds explained; then, watched by his companions, he bent over the valise.

With bated breath the ambushers heard the supple figure emit a half-stifled cry as he allowed a succession of richly clinking coins to drip through his fingers.

"Very well, Captain," they heard the traitor say. "In that envelope I gave you you'll find explicit directions about the place and hour for your next 'capture.'"

Captain Higgins offered a cigar. "Fair enough. God, what a soft touch this is! Best thing is, I can't see why we can't keep right on. Come another month I'll send North and buy me the handsomest spinning mill in Pawtucket." He uttered a snorting laugh. "Know what this business has brought me? Thirty thousand dollars, gold. Now listen —"

The Federal got no further because Major Kershaw jumped up and raised a piercing yell. Along the perimeter of a semicircle facing the stream underbrush threshed, twigs cracked and snapped.

The Federal hesitated not an instant but spun about and leaped into his gig, shouting: "Shove off! For Christ's sake, pull!"

For a long instant, Reynolds Seymour and his lanky companion remained gripped by the paralysis of horrified surprise; helpless, they watched broad-hatted infantrymen running, converging upon them.

"Surrender! Come back here, you Yankee bastards," yelled infantrymen at the downstream end of the cordon and opened fire on the boat which, with oars scrambling wildly, nonetheless was getting away. Some bullets must have scored because howls of pain sounded out there. The whole river reverberated to musketry.

"Damn your black soul, Seymour! Do you surrender?" rasped Captain Knowles.

"Don't shoot! For God's sake, don't shoot me!" screeched Reynolds. "I'm unarmed! I — I'll make it worth your while." He raised hands above his head but, as Major Kershaw was racing onto the dock, the sergeant who had appeared with Reynolds jerked out a derringer.

"So *this* is what you was up to! Oh, you God-damned Judas!" The lanky soldier fired point-blank; his weapon's ball blew a ragged hole in Reynolds Seymour's chest and sent him spinning crazily over the weed-grown planks until he fell heavily and ceased to move.

"Damn you!" roared the Provost Marshal's officer. "Why'd you have to shoot him? He was surrendering. Now, you blasted idiot, we'll never learn who was in cahoots with him."

The sergeant's long and hungry-looking features contorted themselves in a vicious grin.

"Well, now, suh. Mebbe I'm wrong, but seems to me first man gits the chance to kill a traitor has got a duty to do so." Deliberately, he spat into the dead man's bloodied features. "Me, I got no use for a Judas, even if he's from my own regiment."

"What regiment?"

"Cape Chatham Fencibles, that's what," came the sullen reply.

" 'Regiment'?" jeered a voice from the background. "Who in hell called that bunch of yellow-bellied home-huggers a 'regiment'?"

CHAPTER XXII **At the Jockey Club**

LIEUTENANT the Honorable Peter Burgoyne, RN, wrote the final paragraph of a report, critical and analytical, concerning an encounter between two American ironclads, entitled, "Observations on a Monitor in Action: U.S.S. *Weehawken* vs. C.S.S. *Atlanta.*" He summarized his findings in succinct, official terms approved by the Admiralty. Using his own crest, he sealed the envelope in red wax and addressed it to His Majesty's Consul at Charleston.

This done, the red-haired Britisher arose and went over to stare down into sun-drenched McDonough Street. Passers-by merely shambled along; they had hoped for so much from the great ram.

He recalled the sum of his observations:

> Strive as they will, let them bravely devote lives and fortunes to their Cause, yet the Southerners cannot build ships capable of defeating the Union on the surface. Their real hope lies not only in submarine defense, but in submarine offense.
>
> I plan, my lords, to quit Savannah tomorrow, and return to Charleston. There, I intend to survey certain torpedo boats reported to be near completion. These, for some reason yet unknown to me, are designated by the Rebel authorities as 'Davids.' Such craft are not designed wholly to submerge, but to attack very nearly on a level with the surface. Their sole armament consists of a torpedo which, I understand, is very deadly in effect; quite capable of sinking the most powerful ironclad in existence.

He sighed. How smotheringly hot it was this afternoon. From the public rooms of the Jockey Club — he had lodged here since quitting Beau Rivage — sounded voices wearily ordering juleps and other cooling drinks.

Aware of perspiration trickling under his shirt and soaking waistcoat, Peter postponed packing the balance of his effects until the evening should cool off and was sponging his face when someone knocked and one of the club's servants appeared. He presented a slim, square envelope, bowed and silently withdrew.

Curiously, Peter fingered the missive, noted that its envelope was of fine quality French paper, light gray, ruled by very pale blue stripes. He sniffed it and detected only a hint of perfume. The scent was not strong enough to admit identification. Um-m. The writer must be well off for one thing. Stationery of all sorts was at a premium in the

South these days, and here was certainly no common stock. Using his penknife, he slit the envelope and read:

PETER DEAR:
Please come to me without delay. I am in dreadful distress. Reynolds is reported suddenly dead, killed under mysterious circumstances.

I implore you, therefore, to seek Beau Rivage with all speed. I am sending a saddle horse for your use to your club at half after seven tonight. Please, dear Peter, *do not fail me!* I am utterly distraught and I do not know what to do without your advice and comfort.

Distractedly,
SYLVIA

The Englishman drew a deep and quivering breath. So Reynolds Seymour had been "suddenly killed"? Probably, Peter'd failed to hear of the tragedy because he had spent the day at Willink's shipyard where certain indefatigable Georgians already were laying the keel of a new and more powerful ironclad. Certainly these Southerners were not easily to be discouraged.

Peter Burgoyne's face, already peeling and scarlet from sunburn, reddened still further when he recalled his last encounter with Reynolds. It had required quite an effort to play the gentleman, because, say what one might, Sylvia Seymour was undoubtedly one of the loveliest, most alluring and fascinating ladies Peter had ever beheld in a not too limited experience. There was a certain warmth of disposition and an essential, powerful femininity about her. And those glorious, sherry-colored eyes! Always alert and observant, their expression at times became definitely languorous, if not sensuous.

So Sylvia needed him? Now, come to think of it, no barrier of honor was there to prevent it. Then he realized that her messenger had not waited for a reply. Obviously, she had not entertained the possibility of refusal, a fact which brought home a stimulating sense of satisfaction that she should, so instinctively, turn to him amid her tribulations.

In the club's lounge Peter noticed an unusually big percentage of civilians seated about. Day by day, the number of convalescent officers, or those on leave, had decreased, probably because Lee's Army of North-

314

ern Virginia, and Pemberton's forces defending Vicksburg, were girding for the supreme effort.

This evening the only military members present were a handsome young captain, an amputee with a leg gone below its knee, and Colonel Beresford, a severe-appearing old officer with long and silvery hair. They sat to one side, sipping drinks and listening, in manifest disgust, to the perfervid opinions of a group of merchants.

The Colonel, whom Peter recognized as the Provost Marshal for the Savannah District, waved him over and, smiling grimly, said, "Pray sit down, Mr. Burgoyne. Young Wilkins, here, and I grow bored with this silly civilian chatter. If those fat windbags would go and fight half as earnestly as they breathe fire, we'd have this war won in jig time."

Young Captain Wilkins's classically fine head inclined. "Damn hard lines having to stay home and listen to such tripe while my battery is probably rolling across the Potomac right now."

Burgoyne ordered his julep made with cognac; he'd found such much more palatable than the more usual drink prepared with whisky of local distillation.

"Sorry to hear you are leaving us, Mr. Burgoyne," the cripple said presently. "Any chance of your going up North?"

The Englishman shrugged. "No telling, I expect I'll find orders in Charleston."

"A great shame our losing the *Atlanta* the way we did. If you can do something towards getting Sam Seymour exchanged —" he broke off lamely. "But of course you can't. You're British."

At the mention of Sam Seymour, Colonel Beresford's parchmentlike brow momentarily furrowed itself, but then he sighed and settled back in his wicker chair to light a thin black seegar. "Hasn't today been a real scorcher! Of course, I'd *have* to have one of my busiest days in months."

"Why? What's happened?" the wounded officer asked carelessly. "Hang some deserters?"

"A most singular thing," explained the Provost Marshal: "Very early yesterday morning, my orderly brought to my quarters a note, an anonymous note, informing me that a certain gentleman of local prominence was about to enter into treasonable negotiations with the enemy."

Captain Wilkins's bored expression vanished. "Treasonable negotiations! You don't say! You've no inkling who the informer was?"

"None. At any rate, the note gave the exact hour and place of this treacherous rendezvous and the information, gentlemen, *was absolutely correct!*"

The clatter of iron-shod wheels rolling past the Jockey Club's open windows caused a lull in the conversation. Now that the sun was low, traffic was commencing to appear upon Savannah's broad, live-oak and moss-shaded streets.

"What happened?" Wilkins demanded over the rim of his glass.

"While I don't generally pay much heed to anonymous warnings, there was something about this particular tip-off which prompted me to dispatch an officer of mine, and a number of troops, to the spot indicated." The white-haired officer's expression grew grimmer still. "Believe it or not, the traitor was caught while in conference with a Union officer. Unfortunately for us, he was shot dead."

"Who was he?" Peter inquired casually, though his heart seemed to be shrinking in his chest.

"I'm not at liberty to disclose that. The fellow, it appears, was an officer in our Army, so his reputation is entitled to a Court of Inquiry," came Colonel Beresford's courteous explanation. "There must — *might* be extenuating circumstances which would spare a family, well-known hereabouts, from scandal. You understand, don't you?"

"Of course, of course." Peter put down his julep cup, bent forward on his chair. "I am wondering what sort of person would dare betray a man of prominence; a servant do you suppose, or some underling bearing a real or fancied grudge?"

Colonel Beresford fumbled in the side pocket of a faded, long-skirted uniform coat, worn unbuttoned because of the heat. "Since the note is not signed, sir, I will allow you to examine it and draw your own conclusions; provided, of course, that you keep them to yourself."

Suppressing a small gasp of pain, Captain Wilkins also bent forward to inspect an undated, unheaded sheet of notepaper. When he took the note Peter Burgoyne's bright blue eyes became white-ringed and his face redder than ever. Despite the temperature, trickles of ice water seemed to flow the length of his back.

"Very interesting," he managed to mutter. "Seems to have been penned by a lady of quality. The paper seems of excellent texture, therefore very expensive. Like to look at it?"

He offered the message to Wilkins, who, in seizing it, lost his balance and snatched at the sheet. Sounded a brief snarl as a corner of the note came away, remained between Peter's fingers.

"Sorry, sir," Wilkins, red-faced, apologized to the Provost Marshal. "Seems I still can't get used to being shy a flipper."

"It's quite all right," the old officer reassured him. "The message hasn't really been damaged, for which I'm thankful. I will need to produce it before the Court of Inquiry."

CHAPTER XXIII **A Stillness in the Library**

STRETCHES of starlit water glimmered to either side of the River Road. The windless air reverberated with the diapason croaking of countless bullfrogs and the cries of nocturnal waterfowl. Numbers of bats, feasting upon dense swarms of mosquitoes, kept darting about the heads of two riders trotting briskly in the direction of the plantation named Beau Rivage.

The horses kept shying when bats circled too close about their heads, and snorted. For Peter Burgoyne it had proved an easy matter to talk with the Negro groom who had led the promised saddle horse, a gaunt mulatto named Petronius whom Peter recalled having seen working about the estate's stables. Mechanically, he soothed his horse when a young raccoon suddenly scuttled across the road.

"Yassuh. It were a terrible thing, Captain Seymour gittin' kilt like that."

"How did it happen?" Peter asked, rising to his thoroughbred's trot.

"No one seem rightly to know, suh, but 'pears like the captain got caught in rookus between some Yankees and our folks. There was a turrible lot shootin'," he added with relish.

"Then your master was slain in a skirmish?"

"No, suh, not 'zactly; 'twere more like a ambush, so they says." Petronius rode closer alongside, slanting eyes narrowed meaningly. "Well, suh, one of the captain's men who was there got drunk and 'lowed as how 'twas one of Captain Seymour's *own Company* shot him down after he done surrendered."

317

"That's very strange. Who was it?"

"That big-mouth, no-good Sergeant McCurdy. I ax you, Mr. Burgoyne, why he shoot after the captain done hold up his hands?"

"I am sure I don't know." Peter slapped away a halo of whining insects and ducked under low-sweeping festoons of Spanish moss. "What do you make of it?"

"I tried real hard, but I just cain't figure it out, suh, specially on account of the cap'n was extra good to Sergeant McCurdy, and the Mistress, too. She been mighty kind to Sergeant McCurdy, all along.

"Why, only two days back, when it was so extra hot, didn't she send out to the stables and ax him to come cool hisself in the Big House? Jonas he done tole me Mistress ordered up cool wine, treated him like he was a gentleman."

A buzzing infinitely louder than that caused by the insects commenced to sound in Peter's small, close-set ears. "He stayed quite a while, then?"

"Oh, yassuh, McCurdy he in that great, big cool house a hour or mo'e, then sergeant come out grinnin' like a hoss collar and lookin' almighty pleased with hisself. Why, suh, he felt so good he went round and paid off borrowin's from the house folks. Reckon he must have been chancy in some crap game."

"That, of course, is entirely possible," Peter admitted. "Let's pick up a canter, Petronius, these beastly mosquitoes are eating the horses alive."

When Lieutenant the Honorable Peter Burgoyne, streaming with sweat and wearing his red hair tumbled over his forehead, strode through a gleaming mahogany door into the library of Beau Rivage, Sylvia Seymour was awaiting him. She stood poised in the center of the room wearing a black velvet ribbon in her hair and clad in flowing garments of light gray.

A long instant she remained motionless, looking searchingly at him with a pathetic droop to her mouth, then she sped forward, sobbing, "Oh, Peter! Peter! Thank God you're here! I — I've been so shocked! So utterly wretched!" She flung cool arms about his neck, raised her lips and pressed herself so fiercely against him that, perforce, his arms closed about her. For several moments she clung, weeping softly.

He explained presently, "I came as soon as I could, so you must forgive my shocking appearance. It's really a hot night, you know."

She stepped back blinking wet eyes and dabbing at them with a tiny

318

square of cambric. "What a thoughtless creature I am! You must be perishing of thirst." She crossed to an octagonal brass and mahogany wine cooler and produced a glass and a beaded bottle of white wine the cork of which already had been drawn.

"I am sorry," he went over to stand, damp and disheveled, before the empty fireplace. You could see his mount's sweat had stained his neat, white riding breeches. "I am sorry for what I've learned."

She seated herself amid a swirl of light garments and, momentarily, concealed her face behind her palms. "Wasn't it dreadful? Poor Rey!" She looked slowly up at him. "What is being said in town? What *are* they saying?"

Moving stiffly, Peter crossed to the wine cooler, hair coppery in the lamplight and, quite deliberately, poured himself a glass of wine which he swallowed at a single gulp. The he turned to consider the girl's distraught figure.

"Why, nothing much, except that Reynolds's death will be a great loss to the community and that it seems damned unfortunate your husband should have lost his life in so petty a skirmish."

"Oh!" Sylvia looked relieved. "So he was slain in battle? Did you hear how it happened?"

While mopping his neck, the Englishman asserted that Captain Seymour had been reported killed in a brush between Union and Secessionist outposts.

"You heard nothing else? No rumors?" Her amber-hued eyes, pink-rimmed now, bored into his.

"Why? Should I have?"

"Oh, no! No!" Presently she said, sipping a glass of Chablis, "Is it true there's to be an — an inquiry?"

"Yes. I believe so."

"I hope they'll hurry it so that Rey's body can be brought home. Our family has a pretty little graveyard down by the river, you know."

"Yes, I've visited it frequently, if you'll recall." How many times had he and Sylvia not strolled among its darkly green cedars, myrtles and willows weeping, so gracefully, over ornate tombstones?

Said he abruptly: "I wish I could remain for the funeral, Sylvia, but I fear that will be impossible."

She started as though stung by a scorpion. *"You are not leaving Savannah?"*

"I fear I must leave at once and report to Her Majesty's Consulate in Charleston."

"Oh, but you can't!" she wailed. "You mustn't leave. I don't know how — how I am going to manage."

"I am afraid I must go," said he in clipped accents. "But I have every intention of returning to you, dear Sylvia, because —"

"Because why?"

"Because by that time," he explained with a stiff smile, "there should be no reason for my not marrying you — after a decent interval, of course."

"Oh, Peter, how very wonderful!" Again she flung herself into his embrace. "You'll take me away to England? Oh, darling, make it soon. I don't want to live here any more. I've grown to hate Savannah, its poverty, envy and malicious gossip."

Over the top of her head Peter's eyes roved the library, scanned rows of tomes expensively bound in rich reds, blues and greens. "Yes. We'll go abroad the moment we're married," he promised, and lightly stroked her golden-brown ringlets. "It's cursed bad luck, having to leave just when I should be here to lend you strength for your ordeal, my dear." He kissed her lightly on the forehead.

"Don't ever kiss me like that!" she blazed. "I want it like this!"

A long instant they swayed in the center of the library; then she stepped back, tear-swollen face lifted. "I wonder if you will ever understand how terribly, how deeply, I love you?"

"How 'terribly,' yes," he smiled. "And now, if you will find me a bit of notepaper, I'll write down the address of my lodgings in Charleston."

Her wide and filmy gray skirts swayed over to an escritoire. She pulled open a drawer. "You can write it on this."

Peter Burgoyne appeared inordinately tall as he strode over an elaborate West Indian grass rug to seat himself before the desk. "Be a good girl, and refill my glass, will you?"

While she recrossed the room he pulled out first her note summoning him to Beau Rivage, next that corner torn from the anonymous letter received by Colonel Beresford. Hands trembling gently, Peter placed his specimens to either side of the sheet she had just given him.

"What are you doing?" she inquired over a pleasant gurgling from the wine bottle.

"Making comparisons. Fancy you might be interested to hear certain conclusions I have just arrived at." He arose and stood before the desk, rigid as though on parade; his forefinger indicated her note to him. "You recognize this?"

She smiled uncertainly. "Why, certainly, Peter. Of course — I wrote it. Isn't that why you are here?"

"The paper you wrote on came from this desk?"

"Of course. Where else?" Eyes grown round with uneasiness flickered upwards. "What in the world are you getting at?"

He held up the torn shred, and his voice sounded like the rasp made by a steel blade being drawn over a whetstone. "Pray examine this closely, madam. It was torn from an anonymous letter received by the Provost Marshal; a message which accomplished your husband's death. But it was his companion, a Sergeant McCurdy to be exact — mark you that, McCurdy of his own Company and a favorite of yours, I understand — who shot Reynolds *after* he had surrendered to the provost's men!"

Every vestige of color ebbed from the girl's piquant features.

Inexorably he continued: "I direct your attention, madam, to these three sheets of paper. Do you not find them uniform?"

"Oh, no, Peter! You leap at conclusions!"

"I fear I do not. I examined the note received by Colonel Beresford." Casting her a look of anguish and loathing commingled, he started over the gleaming floor for the door.

"Don't desert me!" she wailed running after him. "Oh, Peter! Peter! Can't you realize what I did I did for you? For both of us! Did I do so wrong in exposing Reynolds's treason towards his country, his shameless self-seeking?"

A harsh laugh escaped the tall figure in dusty riding boots. "Somehow, my dear Sylvia, I find that last comment inordinately funny."

"But I can't live here any longer," she wailed. "Not after the Court of Inquiry's findings are made public. For God's sake, take me with you, Peter."

Again she flung herself upon him and clung, panting entreaties.

"If you leave me what *will* become of me?"

His face rigid, Peter pushed her aside; said in a weary, dead tone of voice: "My dear, I really don't care a damn. Good night."

BOOK THREE
Aide-toi et Dieu T'Aidera

PLAN

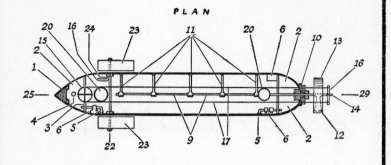

ELEVATION

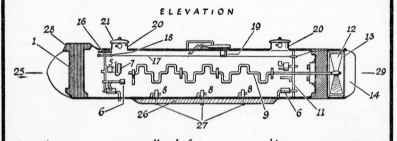

1 casting	9 propeller shaft	18 rod braces	26 cast iron
2 water ballast tanks	10 stern bearing and gland	19 air box	keel ballast
3 tank bulkheads	11 shaft braces	20 hatches	27 bolts
4 compass	12 propeller	21 hatch covers	28 butt end
5 seacocks	13 propeller guard	22 shaft of	of torpedo
6 pumps	14 rudder	side fins	boom
7 mercury gauge	15 steering wheel	23 side fins	29 stern
8 keel ballast	16 steering lever	24 shaft lever	
stuffing box	17 steering rods	25 bow	

C.S.S. H. L. HUNLEY
(The "American Diver" or "Fish Boat")
BUILT, MOBILE, ALABAMA · 1862

S·H·B

CHAPTER I *King Linkum the First*

WHEN Miss India Villepigue sped lightly off stage, wild applause was marking reception of Mr. Heriott's popular satire, *King Linkum the First.* The hand-clapping reverberated even to a crammed little dressing room India shared with another actress. Fortunately, Miss Huntington had no part in this presentation, so India had the place to herself. Humming happily, she pushed aside a row of voluminous costumes hanging on a series of rusty hooks and turned up the kerosene lamp on her dressing table.

After making certain that her make-up remained undamaged, that her coiffure was as it should be, India unhooked her costume's stays. She sighed in relief. They were really a little too tight; the costume hadn't been made for her, but for another ingenue in *The Unknown Dead.* All the same, she must have gained weight, despite Richmond's summer heat and almost continuous performances.

Not being due on stage until the middle of Act Two, she yielded to a devilish impulse, reached into her make-up box and brought out a tiny Cuban seegar of the type it was growing fashionable for ladies of the theater to smoke in private.

After lighting the weed over the lamp chimney, India coughed, then settled in a lumpy armchair and started to run through her lines in the next act; soon her mind wandered to recollections of supper last night, when, at Mr. Desmond Kilpatrick's insistence, they had shared a private dining room in the American Hotel. There could be no denying that Desmond *had* been patient, accepting good-natured rebuffs with far better grace than one might expect from so fiery a temperament. What was it he'd said? India closed her eyes, deliberately relaxed her body — as a trained actress learns to do between scenes — and visualized the actor-manager.

He exuded virility and was undeniably handsome in a dark, aquiline way despite slight pouches beneath his eyes and subtly dissipated lines about his mouth.

"Damn it, my gel!" he murmured. "Why won't you heed my suit? I could do so much to further your career. One little word from me, my lovely, and Mr. Taylor will alternate you with Miss Cassidy as his leading lady."

"If you really admire me," she'd pouted, skillfully enough, "you'll see that I play the lead in *Les Vivandières*."

Intense, fine eyes aglow, he'd seized and fondled her hand. "Perchance that yet may happen. O thou cruel jade! Why dost ever repel me? Thou art a widow and I shall soon win my divorce."

" 'Soon win' isn't the same as 'have,' O my friend, guide and philosopher! Therefore pray grant me a stay ere I decide whether to enter into this — this relationship."

"Then — then you'll actually consider?" He'd leaned so far over the table as to upset the coffeepot. "Ah, India, priceless pearl among women, can you not grasp the power of your witchery? I have a devil of a time when we are on stage and I kiss you — damn it all, I, Desmond Kilpatrick, almost forget my lines!"

It was then she'd taken refuge in attacking an extra tough piece of chicken. "I am attracted to you, dear friend," she'd murmured. "Tremendously so. 'Tis far from easy for a female of my humor to dwell in celibacy."

"Then, in the name of Thespis, why not accept my ardor? In the theater anyone not a Caliban, or a Gorgon, has his moments."

"Not everyone," India had corrected mildly. "You see, I love my husband very much."

"Say 'loved' rather. You believe him dead, do you not? Look, look at me. I am alive and you are alive. We need one another as the sea needs a shore. I need your love so desperately, India, darling. You are so very exquisite, so incredibly passionate beneath that schooled exterior."

"Grant me but another fortnight, then we shall see," she'd fenced. "You *have* been very gentle, generous, and so patient."

To her astonishment the actor had glowered at her. "That won't do! I can't, I won't wait. Now attend what I say. The day after tomorrow

Mr. Taylor and I will cast *Les Vivandières*. You must play the star role, otherwise I can imagine no suitable part."

"And, I foresee," she'd observed in a small, frightened voice, "that you might experience difficulty in finding suitable parts for me in the future?"

"Oh, don't talk rubbish!" All the same Desmond had flushed and she'd known he didn't mean what he said.

The thumping noises made by stagehands moving scenery impinged dully upon India's consciousness.

Oh, dear! To be forced into so critical a decision after having adhered steadfastly to the pitiless dictates of her conscience — and Alistair's memory. No. It hadn't been easy at all to pass up so many attractive roles, and now that the war was going so badly, theaters were not being too well patronized. By consequence, one troupe after another had disbanded, so the Variety's stage door daily was being besieged by veteran Thespians seeking even the most insignificant of parts.

Not that she, herself, was living at an address on Easy Street. Out of her never munificent salary she was adding to, and keeping in repair, her wardrobe, an expensive matter in wartime Richmond. Even needles and thread had become almost impossible to come by. Little remained after paying the broken-down actress who ran a theatrical boardinghouse.

India had grown sufficiently practical to perceive the stark alternatives of her situation. Why not become Desmond's mistress? Time and again, he'd sworn he'd espouse her the instant he became divorced. And Desmond really seemed to mean it, she assured herself — at least for the present.

Oh, to enjoy a measure of security once more! What a delight to go home with someone to share the problems of life. What could have happened to Alistair? To her father? Poor Papa. It wasn't at all unlikely that that genial *bon vivant*, Captain Villepigue, might be at present languishing in some Northern prison — with so many other blockade-running captains.

Of course, she was far from alone in her uncertainties. The Southland was in ever-increasing turmoil; family links everywhere were snapping; sometimes for good and all. What with the postal service having become an evil jest and the telegraphic service nearly as bad, few could be sure how, or where, their loved ones might be.

To see so much black being worn, to look into so many tragic, memory-haunted faces was infinitely depressing. Since the disasters at Gettysburg and Vicksburg, the whole tempo of life in Richmond seemed to have slowed. All the same, a sublime determination to continue the war remained strong as ever, despite the manipulations of speculators, profiteers and grafters. Never before had these creatures dared to be so brazen, so crass about flaunting their success. Never had so many balls, so many lavish dinners been given in the semistarved and distracted capital.

Luxuriously, India extended her legs and so noticed a tear in her costume's brown taffeta. With her skirts pulled up onto her lap she was mending it when someone knocked. Hurriedly she bit off the thread, stood up. Desmond Kilpatrick or possibly young Paul Thebaud, that aspiring juvenile who kept showering her with examples of puerile poetry . . .

To her surprise, in the doorway stood a straight, humorous-looking young fellow in naval uniform. She recognized him instantly. "Why, Henry Bears!" she burst out. "What in the world . . . ?"

"I've been in the audience." He colored, revolved a salt-stained kepi. "When I saw you I couldn't help wondering whether Miss Villepigue and Mrs. Bryson weren't one and the same. After all, your given name isn't exactly common. May I enter?"

"Oh, do! Please come in!" To India it proved astonishing that she could be delighted to meet anyone from Charleston; yet, certainly, other Charlestonians must have sat in this theater. Covertly, she tucked her quarter-smoked seegar beneath a varicolored make-up towel and summoned an engaging, encarmined smile as she indicated a cane-bottomed chair. Lieutenant Bears's uniform, she noted when he seated himself and crossed his legs, looked badly worn and frequently had been mended.

"I — I trust you will forgive this intrusion, Mrs. Bry — er — Miss Villepigue; but — but, well, unlike some others, I've never forgotten how awfully generous you were about singing and dancing for our wounded. I especially respected you for including those poor devils in Charleston jail among your entertainments. Must be pure hell to be a prisoner of war."

"You really don't hate me for dancing before the Yankees?"

"Of course not. Your entertainment must have created the only bright moment those poor devils ever had." He heard the music strike up, lifted a quizzical brow. "How much time before you go on stage?"

"Fifteen minutes." Prettily, she lowered false eyelashes before his avid gaze. "I — I wish it were possible to offer you refreshment, Mr. Bears. But, alas — you know how it is here in Richmond?"

"Yes, I know." When he laughed fluffy yellow sideburns glinted. "May I state that I've greatly admired your performance? You lack affectation."

She arose, exposed an ankle in executing a mock curtsy. "Why, sir, may I thank you from the bottom of my heart? Tell me, have you and Miss Cordelia Livesey set a date?"

His powerful, wind-burned countenance lit. "Yes. We are to marry in the late spring."

"Mercy! Must you wait so long?"

He shrugged.

"And how is Serena? She's a dear girl."

"Well, and occupied with good works. She and Dr. Bryson again are officially affianced," he said, staring shyly at her make-up. "They, too, plan to wed in the spring."

A sudden constriction closed India's throat. "For Heaven's sake tell me, Mr. Bears, is there any news of —"

"Of your husband?" he finished swiftly. "Nothing, I am sorry to say, but I've heard all sorts of rumors: that his body was found in the Ashley River and secretly buried; that he's been recognized in Mobile, or seen in Bermuda. I am dreadfully sorry, but I doubt if there's reliance to be placed on any of them."

"Thank you for your honesty." She straightened and faced her mirror to tighten little yellow bows in her hair. "Did you attend this performance just to see me?"

From his coat tail pocket the weather-beaten young man produced a copy of the *Richmond Despatch*. "A dinner I was supposed to attend tonight was canceled because Major Pendleton suddenly died of wounds. When I noticed the name 'India' in this paper I decided to satisfy my curiosity. Hope you aren't annoyed. I return to Charleston tomorrow."

"I see. Tell me, has the new ram *Charleston* been finished?"

"No. But she's complete save for her engines." He beat one fist into the palm of its mate. "Oh, dear Lord! If only we could import some good French or English machinery!"

"I'm sorry about that. I know how much completion of the *Charleston* means to you all. What of the 'Davids'?"

His manner brightened. "Oh! There you've touched on a happy subject. We have two in operation, another will be in —" He broke off, flushing down to a none-too-clean paper collar. "Sorry I can't say more. God knows, there's been so much loose talk the enemy seem able to circumvent or anticipate our every move."

"You really believe these 'Davids' can break the blockade?"

Seriously, he nodded. "It is entirely possible. The torpedo boats have had several trial runs, and I, myself, have blown up a couple of old hulks higher than kites. I wish you could see —"

Bears felt silent because a callboy knocked. "Five minutes, Miss Villepigue."

Henry Bears heaved himself to six feet of stature, hesitated. "I must go. You've been most gracious. Could I bear a message to anyone in Charleston?"

"No one," India said briskly, and, patting on fresh rouge, added: "Except possibly Dorcas Mullinix. Should you see her, tell her I'm well — and succeeding, in a modest fashion."

Once Henry Bears had taken an absurdly ceremonious departure, India lingered in a state of unhappy turmoil. Why, of all times, had this link with Charleston had to appear?

Recollection of the slights, snubs and slurs, so patiently endured for the sake of Alistair's career, rushed back in a bitter tide. And to what end? Alistair was lost, almost certainly dead, physically as well as emotionally.

India opened her door, listened to on-stage voices, sniffed the odors of cold cream and grease paint and fumes from badly trimmed kerosene footlights. She commenced to smile again.

"And so, O most noble Senator, I do pronounce you wise . . ." It was Desmond's speech and she knew the callboy had been previous. She had three more minutes to wait.

When she reclosed the dressing room's door she saw the newspaper Bears had brought: the *Richmond Despatch*. Why had she never read any newspaper but the *Examiner*? Probably because the latter journal

330

printed more startling headlines and fulsome rhetoric than its competitors. And how bitterly its editions opposed Mr. Davis; almost persecuted him.

To the pleasant rustling of four petticoats, the actress reseated herself, then narrowed her eyes because the print was so very small and the lamplight hardly adequate. She skimmed usual reports of this day's doings in the Capitol and skipped entirely a speech made by Secretary Judah P. Benjamin.

News from abroad appeared on the reverse of this quarter-sheet. The dateline was "Nassau," she read — "ARRIVAL OF ENGLISH-BUILT BLOCKADE-RUNNER" — then followed the name of her builder, her tonnage, cargo capacity, and so on. Dull reading, indeed. She was about to seek the advertisement for *King Linkum* when she happened to notice the Nassau correspondent's signature. *Dorlach!*

As certainly as if Alistair had spoken from the doorway she knew he was alive! None but he could have written that dispatch, for, here and there, appeared some of those quaint Highland words or phrases with which he had amused her during the early days of their marriage.

"It *is* Alistair! It is!" she cried aloud. "There's a theatrical quotation for me." He had written: "The visit of the *Lynx* to this Port, was, as Hamlet has it, 'Brief, my lord . . . As a woman's love.'" She groped to steady herself while, with fast-hammering heart, she reread that inconsequential report on shipping movements. So many implications, questions, possibilities, flooded her that her head reeled and she stared when the callboy came rushing back.

"On in a half-minute, Miss Villepigue. Hurry!"

CHAPTER 11 Dorlach

THE *Richmond Despatch*'s foreign editor, during these difficult times, was also in charge of advertisements. He peered over old-fashioned, square-lensed glasses at this handsome young woman waiting so tensely before his desk, then mopped a red and juicy nose on a bandanna handkerchief.

"I regret, ma'am, that it is against our policy to disclose the names of correspondents who choose to sign their work with a pseudonym. Generally, they have some reason for wishing to keep their identity concealed."

"But, sir," India drew on her histrionic abilities and set her lovely dark-blue eyes to brimming, "I assure you I believe myself to be 'Dorlach' 's wife. Enemies separated us violently and against our wills last winter."

The old fellow's faded gray eyes swung upwards under a green celluloid eyeshade. "Were you now? Well, that's quite possible; since this war began we've heard of many similar cases." He offered a sheet of manuscript. "Would you recognize this handwriting?"

"Oh, God, I thank Thee! That *is* Alistair's writing!"

"Are you positive, ma'am?"

"Of course. Look! Look at this." She fumbled in her purse for the first note he had ever addressed to her. "Do you see, sir? The writing is indeed identical."

For an exasperating interval the editor cleaned his glasses, then deliberately compared the two specimens. "Well, it seems that they were written by the same hand, but really, ma'am, I really must obtain Mr. Bryant's —"

"Bryant!"

He snapped fingers which might have been cleaner. "There now! Haven't I gone and spilled the beans!" He smiled thinly. "I trust you will not inform the publishers of my slip?"

Swiftly India circled the table and pressed a kiss on the old man's leathery cheek, left a red semicircle upon it. "Oh, bless you!"

"Then you really are Mrs. Bryant?"

It was on the tip of India's tongue to correct the name, but, barely in time, she restrained herself, nodded evenly. "Yes, I am Mrs. Bryant. I am an actress in Mr. Taylor's troupe of Thespians."

"Reckon you must be that winsome Miss Villepigue I hear young bucks talking about in the bars? You are, are you not?"

"Yes. When I returned to the theater I resumed my maiden name," she explained, but her imagination raced onwards. Immediately, she sensed the reason for his use of a pseudonym, but since Alistair was using an alias, what now would be his Christian name?

Very little guile was required to produce a letter signed "Andrew

Bryant." So intolerable was her sense of relief she found it difficult not to start whirling about in a madly joyous dance. Alistair was alive! *Alive! ALIVE!* Yes, alive and attempting to get in touch with her.

She felt happier than at any time since the war had begun. She said, "Please, sir, when next you communicate with Mr. —" she almost said "Bryson" — "Bryant, will you inform him that you have seen Miss Villepigue and that she lives only to be reunited with him?"

"I'll do so, ma'am, but the Lord alone knows when we'll get mail through to Nassau. That damned blockade grows tighter every day. No less than three runners were run down and captured off Wilmington last week, and two off Charleston."

"May I scribble a note to be enclosed?"

Something about this big-eyed and fresh-faced young woman appealed to even a cynical old newspaperman's sympathy. "Go ahead but I won't guarantee it'll get through, any more than my letter."

To condense such torrents of emotion into a single page was not easy. She would join him whenever he wished, India declared, and would await instructions through the *Despatch*. Surely, he must have learned the truth about what Dorcas Mullinix had seen? Of course, otherwise he'd not have adopted a pen name only she would recognize.

"You have been wonderfully helpful and kind. How can I thank you?"

The wrinkled old fellow chuckled. "Reckon I've still got one cheek that hasn't been kissed."

In a happy daze, India wandered down Broad Street noting with radiant, but unseeing, eyes the antics of small boys noisily chasing each other about in the bright October sunshine. She took delight, too, in the play of newly fallen leaves over the uneven brick sidewalk.

Alas, for Desmond Kilpatrick's aspirations! A sobering realization occurred. How would she fare were the actor-manager to make good his scarce-veiled threat? If *only* she hadn't just purchased a certain plum-colored merino cloak with a lovely, warm astrakhan collar. But she had. By the end of the week her purse would contain barely enough to satisfy the landlady. Of course she *might* linger at Mrs. Brown's another week on credit; then, undoubtedly, news of her fall from grace with the Taylor troupe would reach the boardinghouse.

She was in no hurry to return to her lodgings, and how she dreaded the prospect of tonight's performance and the subsequent meeting with Desmond!

The crowds were thick along Main Street. An afternoon so beautiful had brought out all manner of invalid soldiers who hobbled along on crutches and canes, or just sat on stoops soaking up the last warmth of Indian summer.

Few private carriages rattled along the streets these days; the bulk of the traffic was composed of forage wagons, horsemen and a few oxcarts.

Opposite the American Hotel a hand came lightly, but strongly, to rest upon her shoulder. Angrily, she whirled about and found herself staring up into the willful, bronzed features of Raphael Bryson.

She slapped him so resoundingly his cap fell off; then, in tones sibilant as a cat's angry hissing, cried, "I have nothing to say to you! Now, or ever!"

She pushed by him and hurried off. Rafe paused only long enough to retrieve his cap, then swiftly fell into step beside her.

"Reckon I richly deserved that, India, and more besides."

"You do! Leave me alone."

"No, my dear. It's been much too long since I've refreshed my vision with your beauty."

She strode on in stony silence, wondering what she should do.

"Will it do any good if I swear to you that I've never regretted a misdeed a fraction as much as the one I committed against you?"

"No. Please leave me alone!" she repeated coldly. "Your presence is odious."

"No doubt," he admitted, but continued to walk at her side. "I'll admit I'm everything you deem me; but please, India, allow me to talk to you. You see, I know where Alistair is living."

"I already know, and no thanks to you!"

"Then I'll immediately relieve you of my company." Gravely, he touched his cap's brim.

"No. Wait. Have you yourself seen him?"

"No, but Julia has written in detail. Look. We can't talk like this on the sidewalk. Let's drop in at yonder café."

Although wondering that she could even converse with Rafe, she nonetheless accompanied him into the dim confines of Mr. Duke's

334

Coffee Shop. It being mid-morning, patrons were few, confined to legislators and a handful of Army contractors.

Once coffee was set before them, Rafe settled back while his finger tips ruefully tested marks left by her fingers. "For a person of your size you're surprisingly strong."

"Dancers become so." Firmly, she concealed neat Congress gaiters beneath the hem of a brown barege skirt. "Now, Captain Bryson, either you will talk to me about Alistair — no other subject — or I shall depart immediately."

He shrugged, made a wry face over the taste of a liquid made of burned acorns and chicory and served in place of coffee. He repeated Julia's description of Alistair's call.

"At present he dwells in a rather scruffy boardinghouse on Queen Street." He went on to say that Alistair had taken to dropping in for supper on occasion, patently hopeful of news concerning his wife.

She forgot to be angry. "Then Alistair still loves me?"

Rafe hunched over a patched and badly spotted tablecloth. "Julia writes that he thinks of nothing else, except finding proof of those charges he leveled at certain patriotic speculators.

"So you see, despite my ill-advised attempt at gallantry, Alistair hasn't lost faith."

For the first time, she looked full into Rafe's lively dark eyes and became aware of lines in his face which had not previously been there. She was surprised to hear her voice inquire: "Answer this truthfully, Raphael — do you *really* love Julia?"

He spoke quietly. "Believe me, yes. I now appreciate the true beauty of Julia's nature and the depths of her love for me. You've heard that we've a son?"

"No! Oh, Rafe, how very wonderful!" She never realized that she'd again employed the contraction of his name. "You must both be so proud and happy."

The passage down Main Street of a band playing a funeral march before a hearse drawn by a single, bony old horse, momentarily stilled the coffeeroom.

"Please, dear India," he inquired once the doleful music had faded away, "is there anything I can do to make amends — however in-adequate?"

335

"Yes," she told him without hesitation. "You can help me rejoin Alistair. Will you take me to Nassau?"

"Gladly. If you dare trust yourself aboard my vessel."

"I dare. I must find Alistair."

Her impatience was rather pathetic, he thought.

"Is the *Grey Ghost* in Charleston?"

"No. In Wilmington." He tugged at sideburns grown considerably longer than in the past. "Unfortunately, my dear, I cannot, as you assume, take you direct to Nassau. However —"

She stiffened, reached for her bag. " 'However,' nothing! I was a fool even to ask."

"A moment, please. Don't jump to conclusions." Smiling, Rafe extended a restraining hand. "I was going to say that I'm on my way to England, but I can drop you off in the Bermuda Islands."

"So you're for England again?" she jeered. "Buying more frills and furbelows for speculators?"

"This time I intend to import munitions," said he sharply, shaking his head. "Enough to satisfy even Cousin Alistair Bryson. I'd no conception of the desperate need of our Armies."

"Dare I believe you? You and Truth have been such casual acquaintances."

"I deserve that, India; but on my honor, whatever that's worth, I intend to charge the *Grey Ghost* deep as I dare with medicines and the materials of war." He raised a straight, dark brow. "Well, my dear, will you sail as far as Hamilton with me?"

"Yes!" she burst out. "Oh, yes! Yes!"

He arose and bowed formally. "Very well. Now listen with care, my dear. You will find me in the second passenger coach from the end of the train which departs for Wilmington at nine o'clock tonight."

"Oh, thank you! Thank you! Only death can prevent my being there." She jumped up, to press an impulsive kiss upon the dull red marks left by her fingers, and ran back out into the brilliant sunshine of Main Street.

CHAPTER III A Matter of Hours

AMONG the first passengers to descend from the steamer
St. George, out of the Bermudas, was a vivacious, dark-haired young
lady followed by a seaman, obviously her devoted slave.

"Quick! Quickly!" she cried. "Please, find me a carriage at once. Oh,
I'm in such a hurry."

"Aye, aye, ma'am." The sailor presently returned, riding a two-
wheeled shay driven by a sinister-appearing mulatto.

"One hundred and seven Queen Street, driver. It's not far, I hope?"

"No, maum. Isn't five minutes drive at the most."

She tossed a half-crown to the seaman, but he shook his head and
passed back the coin. " 'Twas a pleasure. All of us hands have been well
paid, mum, by your being so pretty and sweet and kind."

"Thank you. You've all been wonderful."

To the driver India said, "I'll double the fare if you'll gallop the
whole way."

"Aye, maum!" No sooner had her valise been tossed aboard than the
whip snapped loud as Chinese fireworks and the shay went careening
along the waterfront. It being still early, there was little traffic; so
the bony old nag, stung by this unaccustomed whipping, clattered
loosely, recklessly down one narrow street after another.

Alistair! *Alistair! ALISTAIR!* . . . The beloved name resounded in
her ears as India held on for dear life with one hand and clung to her
hat with the other. To think that, within minutes, she'd be kissing those
cherished features, feeling the ecstatic firmness of his arms about her.

Alistair! Mongrel dogs and improbable, half-naked gamecocks scattered
in belated terror until the shay came to a jolting halt.

"You are here, maum!"

The numerals 107 in faded blue shone on the mildewed walls of the
galleried two-storied house.

"Wait, I'll pay you well!" India sprang from the shay, pelted into a
dark, musty-smelling hallway shrilling, "Alistair! Alistair, darling! Where

337

are you?" A Negro crone thrust her startled face from behind the door. "Maum?"

"Where is Mr. Bryson?"

"Bryson? Nobody named Bryson boards here."

An agonizing pang squeezed India's heart, then, in delicious relief, she remembered. "Mr. Bryant, I mean."

"Oh. He boards on the second floor, maum. First door to your right."

India flew aloft, all the while calling his name. It was disconcerting, therefore, that Alistair did not appear, because the door of the second room to the right was standing slightly ajar.

"Heavens! He's already left for work." India's elation faded with an agonizing swiftness. Trembling, big straw hat in hand, she pushed the door open wide. At least she'd have the comfort of seeing his possessions, his clothes.

She stood rooted. The room was in perfect order: plain wooden bed, battered chest of drawers, and table desk and washstand. Not a single garment hung on wall pegs, no shoes were under the bed, no paper or ink on the desk.

That stupid darky must have told me wrong, she thought and whirled.

"What ails you, Miss, hollering fit to wake the dead?" A huge white woman, pendulous breasts sagging beneath a discolored housecoat, filled the doorway. "This is a respectable establishment and don't you forget it."

"My husband, Mr. Bryant, where is he?" India gasped, lips aquiver. "I must see him at once."

The slattern's hairy features softened. "Why, I reckon, Mistress Bryant, you must be almighty unlucky."

"*Unlucky!* He hasn't been hurt?"

"Why, no, but you've missed him by just a matter of hours. He packed and sailed this very morning; he was in a terrible hurry." The woman's voice sounded as if it came from a far distance.

India swayed, put out a hand to steady herself against the door's jamb. "Sailed? To where?"

"Didn't say, except he was taking ship, unexpected-like," the landlady vouchsafed while picking her teeth with a long fingernail. "He paid me in full. Mr. Bryant always was a perfect gent — neat, quiet and no trouble, ever."

CHAPTER IV **Man Overboard**

THE steam brig, *Trident*, out of Nassau for Havana and sundry Central American ports, bored sturdily through the Gulf Stream's warm and darkly blue billows. Since this half-gale was blowing from astern, the Scotch skipper ordered steam cut off and canvas spread; no point in wasting expensive coal.

In a microscopic cabin, Alistair Bryson lay upon his bunk with feet braced against the violent plunging and listened to the protests of the ship's fabric. Occasionally, he extended his hand to prevent a loaded derringer, lying on the bunk beside him, from falling to the deck.

By now he was growing somewhat less aware of a shallow nick in the top of his right ear caused by a bullet which had buzzed out of an alley the night before. That shot had been just what was required to make him decide that his none too effective disguise and alias had been pierced.

There could be no doubt concerning that shot which had come so near to spilling his brains across the turd-splashed cobbles of Wellington Street. Yes. He'd been almost fatally unalert not to catch on when a sailor, simulating drunkenness, had tried to knife him. Still, such fracases were commonplace. Then a stew which seemed a trifle "high" hadn't been spoiled at all; it had only contained so much poison he'd vomited, and thereby saved his life.

"Reckon I've shaken them off," he ruminated while staring up at drops of seawater seeping through his cabin's ceiling. "Probably my speculator friends figured I'd board the next runner headed for Wilmington or Charleston."

To further the illusion, he'd actually booked passage in the *Banshee,* due very shortly to depart for North Carolina, and prayed that he'd been unobserved while boarding this brig during the dead of night. He hoped he was right, for, protected by waterproof case of oiled silk and sewn securely into his jacket's lining, was a selection of manifests, invoices and correspondence which should prove, beyond any

339

room for doubt, the highly illegal composition of most cargoes imported by the Excalibur and Columbian concerns.

The *Trident* gave a particularly vicious heave. She was an old vessel, so old her owners must have been very greedy, or ill-advised, to have ordered engines put into her at this late date. Far too slow for blockade-running, she had been diverted to the safer business of transporting blockade goods to Bermuda and the Bahamas for transshipment.

He heaved a sigh, thankful that the sea appeared to be moderating. What a pity he hadn't had opportunity to bid Julia farewell. Poor girl! Her cheery personality had sobered considerably since her baby — a lusty little boy — had been born, and day after day passed without bringing even a line from Raphael. What an arrogant and supremely selfish scoundrel the fellow was, for all his charm.

Nor did it help matters, Alistair mused, that he had to quit Nassau without hearing from India Villepigue. How overjoyed he'd been on recognizing her stage name in the same journal for which "Dorlach" had written for so many weeks. He'd written to her immediately, care of the Taylor troupe, but had heard nothing.

He tried to encourage hope by reminding himself that the runner bearing his letter might well have been captured or sunk — so many were. To think of India Villepigue's being in the theater once more he found far from reassuring; especially when one recalled the dissolute and quite Bohemian characters she would be forced to associate with. It was especially tormenting to think that she might deem him dead, and herself at liberty to remarry, or to indulge in whatever intrigues her fancy dictated.

A little stab of pain shot through his wounded ear so he tested the bandage, found it secure.

To his satisfaction the derringer no longer kept sliding about so violently; after a bit, he'd go on deck and breathe fresh air — the *Trident* being more than commonly replete with the stenches of unclean bilges, malodorous past cargoes, and the sour, musty smell of an old ship.

Lying there on the bunk with shimmering tropic sunlight dancing on the cabin's top, his mind returned to India. How could she be faring? Probably well. She had been a most promising ingénue. A hunger seized him for sight of that gay and unaffected smile, for that sparkle in her eyes, and for the unstudied grace which characterized his wife's every movement. Oh, to experience again the pressure of that supple young body, those sudden, fierce clutchings, those panted, sometimes tenderly salacious, endearments.

He arose, wiry figure yielding to the brig's motion, and went over to a cracked and far from perfect mirror. He found looking back at him deep-set, passionate, almost fierce-looking eyes. Gone from the mouth's corners were those certain, humorous lines; the cheekbones now were so pronounced he must, to a considerable degree, resemble that ancestor who, wisely, had emigrated to the Carolinas after Culloden.

Suddenly, he grinned. Only a great ninny would stand there, analyzing his own features.

Good. Seas no longer were pounding against the porthole, but it was growing dark and cockroaches two inches long were beginning to sally out of the woodwork. A good thing the passage from Nassau to Havana should last but two days, barring really foul weather.

He began speculating on the possibility of discovering a runner destined for Mobile or one of several minor ports along the Gulf; ports so shallow that only very small runners could enter. The Federal cordon was reported to be looser drawn off such places.

Thanks to a concentration of intelligence peculiar to Nassau, Alistair knew that, during the past weeks, Mr. Lincoln's blockade was being ever more efficiently enforced. So much so that only two out of five runners could clear for the Confederacy with any real hope of reaching their destination unharmed. Too many fast new cruisers were steaming down from the North, ready, able and willing to match speed with the swiftest products of England's shipyards. Possibly it was a disguised blessing that he was being forced to try re-entering the Confederacy from the Gulf?

A gong clashed and a Cockney steward yelled that the evening meal would soon be served. After dressing, Alistair tested the position of that oiled-silk packet, more precious than jewels and fine gold, beneath his left armpit, then slipped his derringer into a waistcoat pocket. Although double-barreled, the little pistol caused only a minor protrusion in the fabric.

Only three other passengers appeared at table: a pinch-faced young Frenchman, restless and observant as a cat; a muscular bravo who, through thin, cruel lips, declared himself a shipmaster on his way to assume command of a runner in Havana; and a sallow, cadaverous individual with coffee-colored eyebrows. He spoke in monosyllables and gobbled his food like a starving wolf.

"You won't have no trouble findin' passage to some port along the Gulf," predicted the merchant captain; the name he gave was Bellows. "There, you won't come across nothing as big or fast like you saw in Nassau, but you won't pay so fancy for your passage, neither. Where you headed, Mr. Bryson?"

"Haven't yet made up my mind." Alistair was learning to appreciate the use of caution. "I'll ask about, once we reach Havana."

"Oh, you'll like the place. That there's the liveliest town east o' Marseilles. Liquor's cheap and a dollar, Mex, will buy you a pair of the youngest and prettiest whores you ever saw."

" 'Ow young?" the Frenchman wanted to know.

"Eleven, mebbe twelve. They ripen early, and love it."

After eating, Alistair lit a seegar and went on deck to find the weather completely cleared. Though there was no moon, the stars shone bright enough to create shadows from rigging and bulwarks.

Trying to forget a persistent throbbing in his injured ear, Alistair lingered near the main shrouds listening to a mournful hum caused by the Trade Wind in the rigging, and the hoarse rushing of waves along the side. A member of the watch, off duty, was playing a concertina, but Alistair couldn't see the man because of deck cargo; it had been stowed so closely that only a narrow aisle had been left traversing the ship's beam forward of the quarter-deck; up yonder, a quartermaster and officer of the watch must be conning the brig towards El Morro. Here and there a light blinked on the horizon. A brief flood of radiance brightened the deck beyond the main companion before Captain Bellows appeared. He nodded in friendly fashion.

"How do? Know what I was just thinkin'? Many's the maidenhead'll get popped under stars like those."

"It's a fine night, Captain, and that's a fact."

"Ain't I seen you round Nassau?" Bellows queried, looking out over the ocean.

"I have been there a short while, but I don't recall seeing you."

"Oh, reckon I'm out o' Nassau more'n I'm there. Used to run into Wilmington, you know."

They stood by the rail watching starlit billows endlessly rush away towards the horizon. They talked for a time about the war, agreed that, because the Army of Northern Virginia had been defeated at Gettysburg, foreign recognition, barring a miracle, seemed unlikely.

"All the same, we'll whip the bastards," Bellows grunted, "once the *Stonewall Jackson* and our other ironclads reach this side."

He produced sulphur matches but, in striking a light, dropped the box. He stooped to retrieve them. What gave Alistair warning he had no notion, but when Bellows gripped his leg and gave a mighty heave which should have sent him spinning over the rail, he grabbed a shroud and lashed out with his free leg. The heel of his boot impacted with such sickening force upon the other's chin that he collapsed without making a sound.

Coldly furious and infinitely alarmed, Alistair glanced up at the quarter-deck, but could see no one in sight. The foretop lookout was concealed by the main topsail.

There was no help for it. Allow this fellow to go on living and there'd be no certainty of ever regaining the Confederacy alive.

Locking his teeth, Alistair stood swaying, waiting until the *Trident* should start her next roll to starboard. Only then did he heave his would-be murderer over the rail.

Panting gently, he forced himself to count twenty before cupping hands and raising a shout of, "Man overboard!"

CHAPTER V *David Number Two*

THERE was practically no wind blowing the night of October 4, 1863, and a haze hung thick and eerie, low over Charleston Harbor. Collected upon the Naval Station's rigging dock stood a little group of men. Only half-revealed by lantern light and looking down at the fifty-foot outline of *David Number Two* were most of the leading military and civilian figures in the Southeastern Military District.

Present was Mr. George A. Trenholm, that patriot whose open purse largely had made possible the construction of this, and other, *Davids;* Theodore Stoney, contractor and shipbuilder; Dr. St. Julien Ravenel and Commodore Tucker. The last recently had enjoyed

343

promotion and appointment as Naval Commander of the Southeastern District. Flag Officer Duncan Ingraham's duties now were merely those of Officer Commanding the Charleston Naval Station. Ingraham was not in attendance; that gentleman still clung to his oft-mentioned credo that underwater warfare at best was ignoble, if not downright cowardly.

Standing around in silence, too, were Lieutenant Webb, Captain Gray, Dabney Seymour and General J. J. Raines. Henry Bears, looking on, suddenly felt as if he had attempted to hold his breath over an impossible length of time. Why couldn't he have drawn command of *Number Two,* instead of *Number Five,* still on the stocks and awaiting an engine?

He offered his hand to Lieutenant Glassell. "The best of luck to you, Bill; hope you blow that damned *New Ironsides* clear back to New York."

Glassell, a lively, imaginative young fellow, was wearing only a jumper beneath a dark loose-fitting civilian coat which would be easy to shed if it became necessary to start swimming.

"Thanks, Harry. We'll do our best." He shook hands, saluted his superiors, then clumped down a set of slippery wooden steps to a float beside which the *David* lay, a long, seegar-shaped outline only a little blacker than the motionless water.

Looking downwards, Bears glimpsed a glow of light from the engine's firebox. The boiler, for some reason, had been seated forward of a small transom, while the engine itself was aft. Between them was located that little cuddy in which the torpedo boat's crew of four must be crammed. Moisture had collected on *David's* skin of boiler iron, lent it a polished effect.

"Good luck to you, Toombs. Hope that scrapheap hangs together," Dabney called down. He'd known *Number Two's* engineer while serving in *Chicora* and had grown to like him. He knew the other two members of the little crew equally well: lantern-jawed, roisterous James Sullivan, a fireman off *Chicora,* and Jim Cannon, who, until recently, had been *Palmetto State's* assistant pilot. On the pilot's short black beard drops of moisture had formed and glistened in the lantern light.

On the bow the torpedo spar had been raised to the horizontal, secured and balanced upon a pair of stanchions rising midway along her forward deck, just forward of *David Number Two*'s collapsible funnel.

A lantern, swung near the surface, revealed the conical shape of a copper torpedohead containing a mechanical fuse and approximately sixty pounds of high-grade gunpowder; quite sufficient to blow a big hole in the *New Ironsides*'s bottom.

Curious, mused Bears, how very little emotion was to be read on any face, for all that everyone privately had been convinced *Number Two*'s chances of coming through unscathed were slim indeed. Equally, the men on the float understood the deadly seriousness of this new and significant attempt to break the blockade. If the most powerful vessel in the Union's Navy could be sunk by a *David*, then, surely, monitors would fall a relatively easy prey.

Captain M. M. Gray, of the Submarine Battery Service, bent over the cockpit's low coaming and warned, "Remember, Billy, you must depress the boom all the way, and shove your torpedo *as far under* the enemy's side as possible."

"Aye. I'll do that, sir. Please get under way, Mr. Toombs."

A pair of seamen cast off the mooring lines; then, while Fireman Sullivan shoveled coal, Toombs eased open his throttle. A soft, hissing sound ensued, the engine uttered an oily, clanking noise then a piston, motivating the propelling gear, commenced to move.

Sh-h! Hiss! Sh-h, hiss. A low cry of encouragement swelled from the onlookers as, almost imperceptibly, *Number Two* commenced to move off.

Lieutenant Glassell, watching Cannon handle the wheel, experienced an exalted, lifting sensation now that his command's two-bladed propeller had commenced evenly to revolve and that at the far end of yonder boom lurked death for several hundred men — and himself, perhaps?

"Once we pass Sumter, we will commence to fill the ballast tanks; but not until then," he informed Toombs. *Number Two* passed under the stern of *Stono*, lying to the next wharf, then headed boldly out on the Cooper with smoke and a few sparks trailing after her.

Once the engine's beat quickened and set the torpedo boat vibrating; Glassell glanced at Pilot Cannon, whose always prominent cheekbones were jutting like those of an Indian brave as he peered through the haze. When *David* passed *Chicora* her crew collected on the ram's stern

345

and raised a deep-throated yell. Somewhere, a steamer's whistle screamed; another and another.

"Blast them to hell!" growled Glassell in impotent rage. "Why don't those idiots send up rockets to warn the enemy we're coming?"

Six o'clock of the evening; Billy Glassell had selected this departure hour with care. Should his command become disabled, as well she might with this feeble old engine, a flooding tide would carry her back towards safety rather than out to sea and Yankee guns.

Only wavelets lapped against *Number Two*'s iron skin when she steamed stealthily past Sumter at her top speed of seven knots. The light of myriad stars was surprisingly effective and, out on the harbor, the haze had thinned to vagrant wisps.

Billy Glassell thought, Must remember to keep cool and push that damn' torpedo 'way under the frigate's side. Why'd I forget to pay Joe Pringle for that box of percussion caps? Had the money right on me, too. Poor Esther — she'll be having a bad time right now. Wonder whether the baby will be a boy? I really wish I knew — want our name kept alive. I suppose they'll call him Billy, too. Yes, I certainly wish I could know about that. Maybe I will. Poor Harry Bears, he tried so damn' hard not to look envious! Maybe he'll get his chance later. Won't the effect be terrific if we really should sink the frigate? We'll all be famous, I reckon.

He joined Cannon in peering into the translucent darkness for a first glimpse of the blockade ship's lights. Ought to raise them any minute. Funny, how very alone a fellow could feel at a time like this, for all that three other men were within easy reach. It wasn't at all pleasant, he discovered, to realize that he was about to drown or cause an indeterminate number of human beings to be blown into bloody shreds.

Glassell swallowed nothing several times. What might happen to *Number Two* when her torpedo exploded? Stoney was certain that, lying so low to the water and being shaped as she was, the torpedo boat would suffer no damage whatsoever; that the explosion's force would be directed vertically, not laterally.

Charley Toombs lifted a dark lantern to inspect a pressure gauge, then settled onto his seat saying, in undertone: "All right, Sullivan. This is your last chance to stoke, so pile on plenty; can't risk glare from your fire being sighted."

346

"Aye, aye, sor. I'll soon have a full head o' steam, and our smoke thinned out like a gnat's breath."

Toombs settled back against the coaming's damp wood, listened to the rustle of water alongside. A barb of anxiety came to further his uneasiness. The engine's throb became uneven.

Please God, he silently prayed, Don't let that damn' piston guide jam again when it heats up. I'm sure the crazy one to get off the *Chicora* and go volunteering for a job like this. Wonder if I'll live to finish that compensating gear I've got into models.

To keep his eyesight unconfused, he averted his gaze when Sullivan jerked open the fire box. Jim was almost attractively ugly; had the map of Ireland written over that long-lipped, flat face of his.

What will the newspapers say about us? Too bad Mr. Bryson isn't still around. Wonder whatever happened to him? Some say the Wassons had him put away for keeps for writing about them like he did. *Argus* sure has gone to hell since he disappeared. If we bring this off handsomely I'll maybe get promoted.

Toombs felt surprised at finding himself tugging at his mustache. Can't be nervous. I haven't any nerves. Everybody says so. Wonder what Glassell's thinking about? There's a cool one.

Pilot Cannon felt the tide slacken so altered his course two points to starboard. Pretty soon the current should start setting in towards Morris Island.

What the hell are you doing out here with sixty pounds of gunpowder about to go off not ten yards away? And you not even a military man. Just a big-mouthed commercial pilot who got a little drunk at the wrong time and bragged he was the best damn' harbor pilot south of Mason and Dixon's line.

His lips formed a wry grin. Yep, you're shore smart as a mud turtle, Jim Cannon. Out here in a floating coffin — you, who cain't swim worth sour apples.

His attention became focused upon a double row of lights, tiny as pinpoints, and low to the surface. There, by damn, would be the Yankee. That blasted armored frigate which, all alone, was maintaining the inner cordon.

She lay, Cannon reckoned, about a mile away.

"My God, Charley, does that old engine have to make so much noise? Cain't you run her quieter? They'll sure hear us comin'."

"Sorry. Always makes a hell of a racket when she gets heated up. How's your fire, Sullivan?"

"Well, sor, 'tis good English coal we're usin'. Note the little smoke it gives off? Warn me just before the skipper wants the chimbley cranked down."

"Why?"

"Me draft will be almost cut off entire. We'll loose speed faster than Ould Satan grabs a sinner."

"Don't worry about that."

Jim Sullivan didn't. He had other cause for worry; a talk he'd had with pretty Katie O'Boyle last night, for instance. Ye'd better come back, Jim Sullivan, she'd wept. I'm in the family way for sure, ye big Odmahaun, what promised to take care.

Well, he wouldn't mind marrying Katie. She was a fine, strapping wench with plenty of bottom to keep her off the ground — and strong! Och! The O'Boyle girl was stronger than many a man. No, he'd not mind marrying Kate. Was her father not a master cabinetmaker? But if he did, there'd be the devil to pay, and no pitch hot, over to the Hennesseys. Their Mary would be expecting him to do right by her; then there was saucy Maureen Maguire, whose apronstrings weren't being tied so tight any more . . .

James, me boy, if you don't come back from this foray, ye'll save yourself a donkey's load o' grief.

CHAPTER VI **A Pillar of Fire**

LIEUTENANT GLASSELL's watch indicated the hour as nine when, some three hundred yards distant, the armored frigate loomed as a long and sinister blur.

Softly, he ordered the telescopic smokestack cranked down. This accomplished, *Number Two*'s crew flattened in the cockpit until just the tops of their heads showed over the coaming. They blinked because little particles of spray kept driving into their eyes.

Billy Glassell's heart commenced to thump like the tom-toms of runaway slaves hidden in Great Dismal Swamp.

The propeller's every revolution brought nearer the "Moment of Truth." How soon would some Union lookout hail? Glassell pressed his cheek hard against the coaming's unpainted wood, scented its raw, pine odor in ridiculous sharpness.

Certainly, *Number Two* did not offer much to be seen; only her funnel's fuming stump and the coaming lifting barely twelve inches above the surface. The things most visible were the torpedo boom and the stanchions upon which it was hinged.

Ready to hand lay twin lines designed to pull Captain Lee's deadly invention below the surface.

Back in Charleston, he reckoned, a lot of people must be perched on rooftops, training night glasses from church spires, and praying to sight a pillar of fire which would indicate that *Number Two*'s torpedo had been successfully exploded.

Black and ungainly loomed the target, now only two hundred yards distant. How ungraceful she looked deprived of masts; her smokestack was giving off a funereal smoke spiral. Magically, *New Ironsides*'s silhouette grew larger and larger; her gunports became visible. Obviously, she had been anchored from both ends.

Still no challenge.

The tips of Billy Glassell's fingers commenced to tingle unbearably. At his side Engineer Toombs began to yawn silently, uncontrollably. Now the hiss of steam and the clanking of the piston sounded incredibly loud.

Another twenty yards towards deathless fame and victory! Surely, a very slack watch must be kept aboard the iron frigate.

Then, faint as if let in by a pinpoint on the horizon, a voice bawled, "Ahoy! What vessel is that?"

Shivering in their excitement, the torpedo boat's crew crouched flatter; Glassell's hand crept out towards a double-barreled shotgun charged with buckshot. He had brought the weapon along in order to disconcert sharpshooters.

"*What vessel is that?*" The voice sounded alarmed, and much louder.

If only *Number Two* could close in quicker! Now that *New Ironsides* loomed, big as a ridge, scarcely one hundred yards distant, many voices began shouting in alarm.

"What vessel is that? Answer, or we fire!" Quite distinctly, could be heard the clatter of feet running. The great man-of-war's sides seemed to rise cliff-high, her lights on a level with the stars.

"Steady! Steady!" Glassell warned himself. "Only fifty yards more and we're there!"

Pencils of flame sparkled along the enemy's deck, musket balls began to whistle over the little craft and Cannon's sphincter contracted at the vicious *thwack!* made by a bullet splintering the rail at his right. Ringing, metallic noises were created by musket balls piercing the smokestack.

"Reduce speed!" Glassell was surprised that any sound at all issued from his throat. Toombs throttled down, Billy caught up his shotgun and aimed at a black figure standing on the frigate's bulwarks. He fired once, twice, evoked a scream the agony of which he would never forget, then dropped the smoking shotgun to grip the depressing lines and pulled with all his strength.

Jerkily, the torpedo boom disappeared beneath the sea's Stygian surface to grope under the armored side. Rows of rivets, securing plates, now were distinguishable.

The spar stuck. Helped by Cannon, he heaved at the stubborn lines, but the torpedo boom only inched downwards. Damn! Why wouldn't that spar respond? *Number Two* lay barely her own length from the frigate's beam.

Right overhead loomed the muzzle of a big rifled gun; any instant it might spout flame. The concussion alone would serve to kill the attackers.

Glassell felt a scraping sensation caused by his torpedo in sliding over *New Ironsides*'s plates. "Down! Down!" he screamed and jerked the warhead's lanyard.

It seemed as if the whole world were disintegrating in a cataclysmic spout of fire, an outrageous detonation and a terrific concussion which blew the torpedo boat's crew flat and left them only semiconscious.

So effective was the explosion that the huge Union ship was rolled far over onto her starboard beam. A gigantic waterspout soared high over both crafts, then came cascading down in a smothering blanket.

Bleeding from nose and ears, Billy Glassell clung to the cockpit, felt his body savagely whirled about by waves that eddied furiously about him. The sky spun crazily around and around, then tilted over sidewise.

A roar of steam escaping *Number Two*'s boiler warned that the engine fire had been swamped. Water was surging about his hips. Where? What? Glassell swayed, groped blindly amid white-hot vapor clouds.

"Reverse!" he managed to gasp. "For God's sake, Toombs, reverse!"

"Can't — piston's jammed!" Toombs's voice sounded as if it were rising from the bottom of the ocean.

Impossible to guess what had happened to the enemy — swirling clouds of steam and smoke were impenetrable.

Water now lapped at the coaming. "All hands abandon ship! Quick, boys, or we'll be dragged under."

It proved an easy matter for the torpedo boat's men to ease over the side into cold water, lapping hungrily.

The sum of Billy Glassell's strength was required merely to keep afloat while the flood tide commenced to carry him away from the tumult aboard the stricken ironclad.

Of *New Ironsides* Glassell could see nothing; no more of *Number Two,* either.

Well, we've done it. We've torpedoed the enemy. Lazily, he turned onto his back; drifted helpless and semiparalyzed off into the dark.

The chill of the water was so numbing as to make him feel sleepy; the drag of his clothing slowed his efforts to keep afloat. Then, as if his head were swathed in a thick blanket, he heard a rattling of oarlocks, voices. A small-boat. Meant capture, of course; there'd be no friendly boats out here. He struggled to draw breath enough to raise a croaking outcry. Oars and a hull loomed above him.

"All right, friend, you're safe now." Hands gripped the collar of his blouse; a lantern's beams splashed into his face. "Friend? Hell, it's a God-damn' Reb'! One o' them cowardly bastards what blew up our flagship without warnin'!"

CHAPTER VII **The Survivors**

WHEN that blinding shaft of fire leaped towards the stars it seemed to Fireman Sullivan that he'd been conked on the head by a shillelagh. From amid a cloud of fiery sparks he heard Pilot Cannon yelling hysterically, "Oh, God! We're sinking, and I can't swim!"

If *Number Two*'s headed for Jones, came Sullivan's subconscious thought, I mustn't get meself sucked under. Spitting blood, he squirmed over the coaming and numbly commenced to dogpaddle through the smoke, steam and turbulent water.

Helpless as a drifting log, he felt himself bumping along the armored frigate's wet and slimy plates. Why wouldn't his arms and legs respond better to orders issued by his brain?

He realized he was being carried past the stricken man-of-war's bow, so, when his shoulder impacted against something hard, he grabbed links of an anchor chain and held on for dear life.

How long Jim Sullivan remained in the chill water before his head cleared, he had no idea; but, eventually, a sickening realization penetrated his consciousness. *New Ironsides,* although obviously badly hurt, was betraying no indication of sinking!

Presently, he recognized the *whir-r* of a boat's falls and heard the *smack!* made by her bottom on striking the surface. Not much later, a gig's crew found the fireman clinging to the flagship's anchor chain. He was hauled aboard, promptly to be thrown, *incommunicado,* into the brig.

As for Engineer Toombs, that worthy had delayed not an instant upon Glassell's command to abandon ship, and struck out at top speed away from the water-logged *David* and that bitter reek of burned powder. Ever a strong swimmer, Charley Toombs headed in the general direction of Morris Island, or where he thought it to lie — for it was hard to be sure, what with darkness and the tide running so strongly.

At the end of half an hour he descried some black object floating low in the water. What? It looked like — he shook his head to rid his eyes of water — looked again. It was *David Number Two,* drifting almost awash — and there was a man aboard her: Pilot Jim Cannon.

"Thank God, you, too, have been spared, Mr. Toombs," the pilot called.

"What about the others?" gasped the engineer and hoisted himself inboard.

"Don't know. Probably they've been picked up. Sea's fairly crawling with Yankee small-boats." The pilot must have been bailing hard, for water sloshed only knee-deep in the torpedo boat's cockpit.

Towards dawn, the sea began to roughen and waves to lap hungrily at the cockpit's coaming but the two hollow-eyed men had reduced the water in *Number Two* to a level well 'way below her firebox.

"Think that's enough?" panted the pilot.

"Reckon so," Toombs said and fell to cleaning out the firebox. From a waterproof locker Cannon pulled slabs of pitch pine.

"Think we sank the *New Ironsides?*"

Cannon shook his head. "I hate to say it, but I didn't hear no noise like her boilers was blowing up; would have, if she'd gone down. All the same I reckon we hurt her pretty bad. Must have blowed a big hole in her bilges."

"Next time, we'll have to use a bigger torpedo — that's all," Toombs said. He felt utterly exhausted and more than a little sick from all the salt water he'd swallowed.

Daylight found *Number Two* drifting through a light haze and, seemingly, as alone as if she floated in mid-Atlantic.

Employing double handfuls of waste saturated with coal oil, the engineer had succeeded in rekindling the boiler's fire from a dark lantern that still burned. Blue smoke commenced to curl reassuringly from the bullet-riddled smokestack. Toombs then went aft carrying a peen hammer and a wrench. In a short while he'd got the mechanism oiled and otherwise in order.

It must have been around six o'clock when the boiler's loud hissing suggested that there was sufficient head of steam to turn over the propeller.

"Hope to God that junk heap works," sighed the pilot. "My Missus'll be runnin' out of prayers by now. Think they sighted the flash in Charleston?"

"Couldn't help but see it," Toombs reassured him. Breathing a silent

353

prayer, gingerly he opened the throttle; *Number Two* shuddered, then, while her reduced crew exchanged delighted grins, the screw commenced to revolve.

CHAPTER VIII *The American Diver*

MR. C. O. FORSYTHE, editor in chief of the *Mobile Register*, blew a pellucid bead of sweat from the end of a slightly bulbous nose and, wearily employing a palmetto fan, made his way over to a red clay *olla* sweating gently in a far corner of his office.

He yawned, wished he had returned home to nap. After all, there would be nothing much to do until his copy boy turned up with whatever dispatches he'd found at the magnetic telegraph office.

Mr. Forsythe drank the cool water slowly while regarding, with a jaundiced eye, the expanse of Mobile Bay, all a-shimmer with heat. The usual gunboats lay at anchor out there, together with a scattering of blockade-runners awaiting a break in the weather. Um-m. A runner must have made port during the night and now was being towed over to Belden's dock.

The harbor looked vaster, emptier than ever, it being much too hot for local craft to put out. In the dusty, sun-drenched street reposed an oxcart the span of which had lain down in the shade of a tree to chew their cud. The driver lay, loosely sprawled and snoring, under the vehicle itself.

Sighing, Mr. Forsythe picked up this day's edition and grimaced over the dreadful quality of paper upon which he had been forced to print. God willing, a supply of real newsprint might show up on some runner before the end of the month; failing this, he would just have to suspend operations. There wasn't even a roll of wallpaper left in the vicinity of Mobile.

The editor reached for a plug of tobacco and bit off a chew, then went back to his seat and stared on a series of time-yellowed auction posters; one advertised ice for sale. He really ought to order it taken down. What wouldn't he give for a pitcher of ice water! Especially on a day like this.

354

While awaiting the copyboy he riffled through the *Register's* recent back numbers and extracted the one in which appeared a brief account concerning the loss of Horace L. Hunley's extraordinary submarine boat. Many termed it the *American Diver,* but its inventor invariably referred to this innovation as a "fish-boat."

Sweat formed on Mr. Forsythe's brow but he just let it trickle into the collarless and unbuttoned neckband of an already sodden shirt.

How well he could recall that first visit to Park & Lyon's yard to inspect the queer craft designed by Messrs. Hunley, McClintock and Watson. Quickly, he'd ascertained that the fish-boat was, almost entirely, the product of Horace L. Hunley's imagination.

Poor Hunley! At the outset of hostilities he'd been an enormously wealthy cotton broker in New Orleans, but his fortune had reached rock-bottom, and he'd moved to Mobile. Apparently, the former broker's whole remaining interest in life was centered upon his submarine boat; granted the least excuse, he would advance the most extravagant of claims.

"My fish-boat will be able to sink the biggest ironclad afloat," he'd boasted. "Give me a dozen fish-boats — they're cheap and easy to operate, gentlemen — and I'll guarantee to clear the Gulf of Yankee ships within a month! They'll blockade New Orleans, starve the enemy garrison into capitulation, re-open the Mississippi, and so restore communication with the Southwest."

In appearance, Mr. Hunley was as far removed from the usual concept of a New Orleans Cotton King as could be imagined.

He had intense eyes, a craggy countenance and a long gray beard which bore an unfortunate resemblance to the late John Brown of Ossawatomie and evil memory. In the ex-broker's steel-gray eyes burned a Messianic light and he seemed without fatigue or capacity for discouragement. Like John Brown, he also possessed an ability to arouse devoted enthusiasm among his associates.

Columbus Forsythe's memory ran back to that day when most of Mobile had crowded the waterfront to watch the so-called *American Diver* attempt her first run, fully submerged. Smoothly, she had sunk from sight, had traveled better than half a mile and had surfaced triumphantly at her destination, amid wild huzzahs and thundering salutes.

Mobile would be long in forgetting the celebrations that night.

355

Those eight brave fellows who, sitting four on a side, had cranked and supplied the motive power to turn the fish-boat's propeller were fêted as heroes; they deserved to be. The mayor gave an impromptu banquet in honor of the fish-boat's only officer, and the men who had designed and built her.

Two further successful dives were performed and then . . . Mr. Forsythe's sweating fingers tightened over a black-ruled copy of the *Register*. His eyes focused upon an announcement centered on Page One:

> We regret to inform our readers that the *American Diver*, a privately owned submersible, was lost with all hands yesterday in the harbor during exercises. We take this opportunity of extending the deepest of sympathy to friends and families of the nine heroes who perished in this tragic mischance.

A week later divers who succeeded in raising the fish-boat reported finding her nose plunged deep into adhesive mud on the harbor's bottom. No water was in her, but the crew was discovered in the hideous attitudes and wearing the contorted expressions of men who have perished through suffocation.

Poor Mr. Hunley had locked himself in his room for a week and had refused to see anyone. Later, on examining the salvaged craft, he discovered that, somehow, her pectoral fins had become locked in such a fashion that they could not guide her back to the surface,

None knew better than Columbus Forsythe how pitifully, and persistently, the inventor had pled for another crew and further test dives; the military authorities had only scoffed and refused. No more lives would be hazarded, they declared, in so dangerous and impractical a contrivance.

The fish-boat, therefore, had lain on the shore, rusting and derided by all save her inventor and an incorrigible enthusiast, Lieutenant George E. Dixon of Captain Cothran's Company, 21st Alabama Volunteers.

Finally, a great day dawned for Horace L. Hunley. A telegram from General Beauregard in Charleston had been received, requesting information about the *American Diver*. Possibly she might be put to use in the Southeastern District? Delirious with excitement, the inventor

356

had offered, at his own expense, to take his fish-boat East and demonstrate its potentialities. Following an exasperating delay, a second telegram was received:

PLEASE EXPEDITE TRANSPORTATION OF WHITNEY'S SUBMARINE BOAT FROM MOBILE HERE. IT IS MUCH NEEDED.

Signed: P. G. T. BEAUREGARD
General Commanding S. E. District

Mr. Forsythe slapped a fly which had discovered sufficient energy to settle upon his nose. Now where in blazes had Beauregard got hold of the name "Whitney"? Had he confused Hunley with Eli Whitney, that Yankee inventor who had effected such monumental changes in Southern economy and had made Cotton King?

Um-m. Not one, but two, sets of feet were ascending his office's stairs. Were these shipping agents reporting the arrival of newsprint aboard that freshly arrived runner? No. The age of miracles was past.

One of his printers, a poor young devil whose twisted left leg had precluded service in the armed forces, knocked and entered. "There's a gentleman outside to see you, sir."

Forsythe spat accurately into a cuspidor at his side. "If he's a bill collector, take him away."

"No, sir. Says he's a friend of yours; used to know you in New York."

"New York! I've no time for any damned Yankee. Tell him to —" Mr. Forsythe got no further, for the caller strode in, hand extended. "Clip Bryson, by God! What in hell are you doing in this stewpot of a port?"

"By God, Columbus, you haven't changed a bit." Clip! He had not been called by his cub reporter's nickname in years. He liked the sound of it.

"You're brown as a Seminole and you've lost weight, haven't you?"

"I've run through some rough patches lately."

"Who hasn't? Well, well, sit down, Clip, have a chew, maybe? Bixby, just you trot 'round to Glancey's and fetch a bottle of brandy — French brandy — none of that Cuban hogwash."

The two lingered late mulling over high old times on the *New York Tribune*. "Remember 'Jasper' Salter? I hear he's the *Times's* principal correspondent at the Seat of War, as the Yankees put it. And whatever happened to 'Spareribs' Roberts?"

357

"He was editing the *Vicksburg Whig* until he got his head blown off by a Yankee cannon ball."

"Too bad. Always liked the way old 'Spareribs' played poker. Never learned not to try to fill an inside straight." Forsythe took a deep gulp from his glass, sighed and leveled a searching look at his caller. "Hope you are not, by any chance, hoping for a job; I'm publishing with a skeleton staff. No business these days, no advertisements, and my circulation's down to ten men and a dog."

"I wasn't, Columbus," said the brown-faced visitor. "Truth is, I want to get back to Charleston in a hurry, but —"

"What's to stop you?"

With a wry smile Alistair turned out his trousers' pockets. "Broke. Like any good journalist."

Forsythe grinned, fingered a day-old beard. "Let me see, as the blind man said. Um-m. It's damn' difficult getting anywhere on the railroads nowadays — even if you've got the cash."

Suddenly, he snapped his fingers. "Tell me, Clip, are you in such a hurry to reach Charleston you don't care how you travel?"

"Don't give a hoot, just so I get there, and," his expression grew grim, "tend to some unfinished business. You see I —"

Forsythe cut him short with a gesture. "Ever heard tell of a craft called a 'fish-boat'?"

"What do you mean? A commercial fishing vessel?"

"No." In concise sentences, Forsythe reviewed the story of Horace Hunley and his *American Diver*.

"All very fascinating," Alistair nodded, "but what has this to do with me?"

"Well, they've cut poor Hunley's floating coffin in two, preparatory to loading her onto platform cars. In a day or so they're expected to depart for Charleston; ought to get there in jig time, too." He described General Beauregard's second telegram.

"Interesting. Makes a wonderful story," agreed the younger journalist. "I still don't understand how all this affects my problem."

"Why don't you travel East on that special?"

Alistair's bronzed features kindled, made him look years younger. "You really think I could get aboard that train?"

The other reached out and splashed fresh liquor into their tumblers. "Yes, provided you're a military man. Are you willing to enlist? No!

358

By God, that won't be necessary! Clip, I believe I can land you a commission in our Home Guard; colonel's a brother-in-law of mine."

The other looked his bewilderment. "Commission?"

"Of course it won't be a regular Confederate States of America commission, nor even one in the Alabama Volunteers; still, it's a valid commission, and makes a military man of you."

Columbus Forsythe threw back his head and burst into roars of laughter. "My God! To think of Clip Bryson, booted and accoutered in the panoply of Ares!"

"I can't be commissioned under my own name. Here's why." He told Forsythe the whole story.

CHAPTER IX The Caboose

DESPITE General Beauregard's telegram requesting that Mr. Whitney's submarine boat be dispatched to Charleston with all speed, a special, bearing the fish-boat's two sections, clanked north, then east, at a speed, calculated by Lieutenant Dixon and Mr. Hunley, averaging five miles an hour.

The Fish-boat Special, as the train came to be called, consisted of two platform cars, an ancient daycoach in which camped a squad of infantry from the Mobile Home Guards, and a caboose occupied by Lieutenant Andrew Bryant, Mr. Hunley and Lieutenant George Dixon.

Day after bakingly hot day, the Special panted and clattered across Alabama towards Georgia until fewer trees lining the right-of-way were draped in Spanish moss; clumps of mistletoe grew denser and dog-run cabins, inhabited by poor whites, became more numerous.

The trainmen often had trouble at various woodyards along the Mobile & Ohio's route, in finding hands to replenish the fuel supply, so thoroughly had recruiting officers and the Provost's men combed the countryside for cannon fodder. Labor, too, was required frequently to hoist the fish-boat from one flatcar to another — the gauge of many a railroad failed to match that of its associates.

Tempers grew shorter as beards grew longer; days dragged by amid humid weather until, in a fit of furious impatience, Mr. Hunley and Lieutenant Dixon boarded a military express and rode on ahead to see what could be accomplished towards expediting the fish-boat's snail-like progress.

Lieutenant Bryant, with a sad-faced and tubercular sergeant named Nast, became entrusted with the product of Horace Hunley's imagination.

It grew so unbearably hot that Alistair at last was forced to shed his uniform coat, an old, red-collared militia tunic purchased in Mobile. He hated to have to take it off, for, sewn into its lining, was that limber, oiled-silk packet. Regretfully, he hung it in the caboose's clothes locker, which wouldn't lock.

It seemed almost too good to be true, when, at the end of ten days, the *American Diver* was, by dint of sweat and profanity, transferred for the last time — on this occasion onto platforms belonging to the Railroad of Central Georgia.

"Yes, suh," drawled Mr. Huse, the Special's newest conductor. "Come any luck, we'll roll into Atlanta tomorrow."

"When?"

"Oh, sometime."

"With any luck," of course, meant that the locomotive would not break down, that dry fuel might lie ready in the woodyards, and that the line's single track did not become clogged by troop trains rumbling northwards to re-enforce troops facing the blue Armies of Grant and Thomas. These, slowly, but steadily, were biting ever deeper into Tennessee.

What would he find in Charleston? A hope flared, then flickered out, that he might find India returned from Richmond and waiting. Not to possess the least inkling of her present whereabouts was proving sheer agony. Still, it was to be expected; even in times of peace, theatrical people seldom could predict where the passage of even a few weeks might find them.

At Roberts Junction, below Macon, the Special again was shunted onto a siding to permit the passage of trains bearing the rawest kind of recruits and recovered invalids towards Atlanta.

Eighteen hours the Special idled; twice was sent back from the main line by the trains appearing all unannounced.

In midafternoon Conductor Huse, who much resembled an old turkey gobbler, swung up the caboose steps and drawled, "Mebbe it's just as well we've been held up. Brakeman declares that's a cracked axle on Number Two platform car; says 'twon't last down to Charleston. I'm fixin' to get a substitute."

It came about, therefore, that the flatcars, together with the guard's daycoach, rolled into Roberts Junction's freightyard; there, a crane might be utilized to shift the fish-boat's after-section. The caboose remained forsaken on the siding because the spur on which the transfer must take place was too short to accommodate the entire Special.

Mindful of his responsibility towards the *American Diver*, Alistair set out for the repair yard and left Sergeant Nast snoring in the caboose. He was lifting down his tunic when a blast of suffocatingly hot air deterred him from taking it; anyhow, this time-honored tunic was too greasy and threadbare to tempt a thief.

The switching engine's bell clanged, and, presently, the Special was backed onto the siding to recover its caboose.

A little air fanned Alistair's forehead; it would be sheer luxury to wash up, providing Sergeant Nast had remembered to refill the water tank.

Once the Special had chuffed around a clump of jack pines a deep sigh of relief escaped Alistair on glimpsing the caboose, waiting and tinted dull red by the sunset. For quite a space he'd been reproaching himself for leaving behind his tunic and the documents it concealed.

Then Conductor Huse said, abruptly: "Why'd them dim-wits shift my caboose to Number One siding?"

"Don't know," Alistair remarked amiably. "But it'll sure be nice to wash. Maybe, I'll even shave." He tested a black, week-old beard grown so long it was beginning to curl.

Slowly, the Fish-boat Special bumped onto a siding. "Say, Lootenant, know what?" Huse said. "That *ain't* my caboose. We're Number 78, and that there's Number 64. God-damn! I left a near-fresh plug of eatin' tobacco aboard."

Sergeant Nast, oysterlike eyes contrite, came shambling down the right-of-way. "Well, what do you know?" he called with a conciliatory grin. "Me, I wuz drawing water, when some danged supply train backed in and hitched onto our caboose. Reckon mebbe they mistook it for that one, yonder."

Alistair could only gape miserably at the strange caboose a long instant. Then he galvanized into action.

"Huse! Where was the train routed?"

" 'Deed, I don't know, suh," confessed the conductor. "Maybe we could find out over to the freight shed."

But the dispatcher claimed he had only recently come on duty. All he knew was that three trains had cleared; one heading west, one going northwest and one east.

"My uniform coat's in that caboose," Alistair kept yelling. "My — my orders are in it. I've *got* to get it back! Come on, you lunkhead, get busy on that key and find out which of those idiot engineers picked up Caboose Number 78."

Grudgingly, the operator seated himself at the key and commenced to tap out messages; but with little success. The northwest-bound train had just rolled by the station called by him, and he could arouse no operators at check-points for the other two so caboose Number 78 continued to roll on towards a destination unknown.

On Siding Number 2, the Special's engineer commenced to sound strident summons.

"We gotta go, else we'll lose the right-of-way, and we're 'way late already. Now don't you worry none, Lootenant, I'll shorely get your coat back," promised Huse. "Yessir, I'll raise such holy hell in Charleston you'll get it back in a hurry."

From amid the black miasma of despair, Alistair watched the lights of Roberts Junction recede around a bend.

The ex-journalist lay upon a sour-smelling bunk and stared, sleepless, into the dark now that each turn of the wheels was bringing him back to Charleston. Back, unarmed, into the ken of Judge Riegler, Major Lambkin and the Wassons . . . Dared he risk being seen in, or about, Charleston?

Obviously, his only course now was to slip aboard a blockade-runner and trust that luck would permit a return to Nassau. There, he'd claim a file entrusted to Julia Livesey and containing supplementary evidence. While its contents was not as damning as those documents which, in all likelihood, were lost beyond hope of recovery, they might serve.

"I'll have to risk it," he decided and stirred, irritably. Even at night, it remained so hot in the caboose that perspiration trickled into his eye sockets and the hollows above his collarbones.

Um-m. Well, in another couple of days his beard would certainly grow long enough again to serve as a passable disguise, while a razor, skillfully employed, should alter not only his hairline, but the shape and direction of his brows. Were he to add to that a pair of weak, or unground spectacles, he might pass through a crowd without anyone's recognizing the *Argus*'s former managing editor.

On the other hand, little could be done about his profile; that strong, straight Bryson nose and his prominent cheekbones were not to be disguised.

Bump-bump! Bump-bump! There must have been a flat place on one of this caboose's wheels. When he reached Charleston, Alistair decided, he'd have to occupy himself with whatever job he could find on the city's outskirts. Most certainly, he must keep away from the center of town.

When he remembered what had been done to him on Sibley's Island, he shivered.

CHAPTER X **Staff Meeting**

NAVAL HEADQUARTERS for the Southeastern District were situated on the second floor of the old United States Customs House; to it climbed a majority of the officers charged with the defense of Charleston, South Carolina.

To tall, good-humored Lieutenant Commander Dabney Seymour, attempting to adjust his lanky frame upon a small and uncomfortable wooden chair, the faces of most of these gentlemen were intimately familiar.

Yonder was Major General Beauregard, looking less like a romantic cavalier today — only hot, weary, and frustrated. To his right sat Brigadier General J. J. Raines, and, beyond him, slouched dour Flag Officer Duncan Ingraham. Deep wrinkles scoring his craggy Scotch face seemed more pronounced than ever, now that he no longer commanded the Palmetto Squadron — only the Naval Depot.

Handsome Commodore John Tucker, sitting directly across the table from Beauregard, now commanded the Confederacy's vessels of war. Praise the Lord, his flagship, the brand-new *Charleston,* had been adequately armored and her armament was superb, if only her engines . . . those weary, tugboat's engines! True, they could propel her, when they chose to work, but at a speed even less than that of *Chicora* and *Palmetto State.*

Until adequate engines turned up, the city's pride could not hope to close with the nimbler Yankees, except on their own terms. To subscribers it was frustrating in the extreme to witness their new ram reduced to little more than a floating battery. Because of this unhappy fact the Naval Arm perforce directed its hopes, attention and energies towards submarine offense and defense. Hence this unprecedented staff meeting.

General Beauregard arose, bowed with courtly grace to the assembled officers. "In a few moments," he announced, "I shall have the honor, gentlemen, of presenting to you a Mr. Horace Hunley, of New Orleans and Mobile, and his most able assistant, Lieutenant Dixon of the 21st Alabama Volunteers." He paused.

Dabney watched Duncan Ingraham scowling at a pencil gripped in both hands. Obviously, the Flag Officer was in an evil humor, merely wanted an excuse to explode. Everyone present, of course, was aware of his Old Navy hatred of innovations, especially underwater ones.

"I have taken it upon myself, as General Commanding this District," General Beauregard continued, liquid black eyes ceaselessly roving about the council table, "to invite Mr. Hunley to demonstrate the use and capabilities of what I have come to consider to be a very powerful threat to our enemies' supremacy on the sea.

"His invention, I might add, is unique in conception and design, but I shall count on your imagination as much as upon your clear recognition of the problem confronting us: How can we sink, or drive away, a formidable enemy fleet by other than conventional means?"

Duncan Ingraham's scowl deepened but Commodore Tucker straightened, smiling, in his chair. "We shall be honored, General, to entertain any suggestion you care to make. Is it not our common determination — and duty — to rid our shores of the enemy by any possible means?"

General Beauregard nodded his appreciation, then instructed an aide to fetch in the inventor.

364

"Gentlemen," Beauregard said in a rich, melodious voice, "I have the honor of introducing Mr. Horace L. Hunley of New Orleans, my native city. His generosity and unselfish devotion to our beloved country has been equaled by few and excelled by none. I trust that you will make him most welcome here in Charleston." The General's narrow black goatee quivered. "Gentlemen, I must be fair to all of us and warn you that Mr. Hunley's invention has not been without its disappointments."

A loud, "Harumph!" escaped Duncan Ingraham.

"He will explain to you the nature of this *American Diver* or 'fish-boat,' as I believe Mr. Hunley prefers to term this submarine boat. Incidentally, the vessel remains his private property until, as I hope, it is purchased by the Navy Department."

Captain Gray arose. "May I salute so gifted an inventor who, perhaps, is about to present a solution of our problems."

About the table the officers pushed back their chairs trying to forget a hot wind beating through windows.

In a metallic, almost inflectionless tone, Mr. Hunley put forward his conviction that the naval war against the Federal Government could not be won upon the surface, the shipbuilding resources of the Confederacy being so hopelessly inadequate.

"You need not go into that, sir," came Ingraham's harsh accents. "We are painfully aware of the handicaps under which we labor."

"My apologies, gentlemen, for commenting upon the obvious," the former cotton broker said, then told about building his first fish-boat, and how the untimely capture of New Orleans had necessitated the scuttling of his uncompleted invention in the Mississippi. Next, and in mounting enthusiasm, he described in detail those successful dives in Mobile Bay.

"Is it true that your fish-boat sank?" Captain Gray wanted to know.

"Yes. On her last practice dive the mechanism of my craft's pectoral fins — they direct her course vertically — somehow became jammed and caused her to bury her nose in mud on the bottom." Hunley's heavy brown brows merged. "She was unable to free herself, so her crew perished of suffocation."

The rustling of paper from those taking notes became absurdly audible.

"I will not attempt to deny that my original design for the pectorals

365

was inefficient, but that error has been rectified, and" — his voice soared — "I can solemnly assure you, gentlemen, that, on her next dive, there will be no repetition of such a disaster."

Captain Gray peered over gold-rimmed spectacles, steel-gray eyes narrowed. "And just what changes have you made?"

"Why, sir, I have lengthened the fins and moved their axis farther aft; this also tends to increase my fish-boat's stability when under way."

Lieutenant Commander Dabney Seymour glanced up from his notebook. "And just how, sir, does your craft propose to attack an enemy? With a spar torpedo, in the fashion of a *David?*"

The big-bearded figure standing at General Beauregard's right shook his head. "No. Although she can do so, if the notion seems practicable. No. My invention is designed to swim beneath an enemy trailing a torpedo at the end of a length of cable. This torpedo will navigate at a higher level than the fish-boat. Once my submarine boat has passed under the enemy, the torpedo it tows will detonate under the target at her most vulnerable point — there is no armor below the waterline. This mode of attack is entirely feasible, I assure you."

Low cries of approbation, even enthusiasm, arose.

"Further, gentlemen, my craft cannot possibly be harmed by enemy gunfire when she approaches, concealed beneath the surface —"

"— and blows unsuspecting Christians denied the least opportunity of defending themselves into Eternity, unprepared to meet their Maker," rasped Duncan Ingraham.

"Now, now!" General Beauregard spoke sharply. "The use of submarine weapons has become accepted and is a legitimate form of waging war, Mr. Ingraham. The Federals use torpedoes as well as ourselves."

Ensued a question and answer period: General Beauregard's secretary and Dabney Seymour for the Naval Forces were pressed to record the conversation completely.

At the end of half an hour it became inescapable that, although Commodore Tucker and the other naval men favored purchasing the fish-boat and commissioning her as the C.S.S. *H. L. Hunley*, Duncan Ingraham, speaking as the senior naval officer present, remained unalterably opposed.

"Let this deathtrap prove her worth," he rasped and snatched up his cap. "Let her demonstrate that she can perform even half as well as our learned friend from Mobile claims; then, and only then, I might agree to her purchase."

"Come, come, Duncan." Mild exasperation marred General Beauregard's usual urbane manner. "Upon my own responsibility I have had this craft brought halfway across our nation. I *invite* —" he lingered on the word — "at least a measure of co-operation on your part."

"What do you mean by co-operation, sir?"

"I mean that you should detail suitable officers to learn the use and operation of Mr. Hunley's invention. Far better that they be so employed than wasting their time in endless drills aboard those sluggish rams of ours."

Had not Beauregard been commanding the Southeastern District and had he not thus been, by several grades, senior in rank, Duncan Ingraham, looking much like a minor prophet from the Old Testament, would certainly have made a hot retort. As it was he jerked a stiff bow, put on his cap and strode from the room.

General Raines shrugged. "I regret, Mr. Hunley, that we seem unable at present to persuade Flag Officer Ingraham towards purchasing your vessel for the Confederate Navy."

"But I will gladly *give* you my fish-boat," Hunley stated.

"Our thanks, sir, but it would do no good if Mr. Ingraham refuses to accept your invention and commission her in the Regular Navy. However, please rest assured, we of the Army will not rest until she becomes commissioned. We have the fullest confidence in her capabilities."

Commodore Tucker said, "I shall be pleased to detail any of my officers from the Submarine and Torpedo Service, sir, to study the *Hunley*." He smiled faintly. "There, you hear? We intend to have the fish-boat and call her by the name of a great patriot."

"I am overwhelmed, sir." The brown-bearded man beamed. "The honor is too great. Why not call her *Bushnell* after the man who devised torpedoes during the Revolution?"

Commodore Tucker shook a blond, leonine head. "No, sir. May I particularly recommend Captain Gray here, and Commander Seymour?"

"Thank you, gentlemen. Thank you very much indeed. This is far better treatment than I had been led to expect." His voice swelled, until the whole hot room resounded. "In return, I can promise you that my invention can sink not just one, but so many of the enemy that our ports soon will reopen to the use of all nations. Gentlemen, I bid you good day."

CHAPTER XI "Nigger in the Woodpile"

ONCE General Beauregard, elegant and colorful as usual, and his staff officers had ridden away from the Customs House, the naval conferees commenced to collect their notes and were starting to leave when Commodore Tucker, suddenly grave of mien, signaled them to stay.

"Before we disperse, gentlemen," said he, his eyes suddenly bayonet-sharp, "I fear I must broach a most unpleasant subject. Mr. Bears, go make certain that no one lingers in the hall outside. The rest of you, pray seat yourselves."

There now was in Tucker's manner something ominous enough to spread a chill over the room, even on this hot afternoon.

"What's up?" Captain Gray queried of Major Francis Lee, new commander of the harbor's submarine defenses.

The other drew a deep breath. "We believe that someone on duty with this naval establishment is furnishing the enemy with information; there's 'a nigger in the woodpile' somewhere."

"What! Are you certain?"

"Yes, it has become fairly obvious."

The Commodore, hands locked behind back, commenced an uneasy parade across an end of the room affording a view, depressing in the extreme, of ship after ship rotting away at docks and wharves growing green with weeds and disuse. Recently, precious few blockade-runners had come in. The Federals were just too alert.

"Gentlemen, it has become inescapable that someone among us is an enemy agent of the most dangerous sort — because he's a patriotic spy," Tucker amplified — "a man who considers espionage as a dangerous duty to be performed, not as a source of personal gain."

An undertone of incredulity circulated the humid atmosphere.

"Surely, sir," Lieutenant Porcher burst out, "this must be pure imagination!" His gaze flickered from one taut and sweaty face to the next. "Who among us could be so lost to truth and honor? Surely, Captain Gray, the traitor must be among the civilian employees?"

Nervously, Gray fingered his short, dark beard. "I wish I could agree with you, Mr. Porcher. However, I have maintained a record of certain occurrences and incidents in which carefully made and well-guarded plans have been accurately foreseen and thwarted by the enemy." He then enumerated several occasions on which the rams had thought, under cover of fog, to approach and surprise the few Federal craft vulnerable to attack by such slow-moving ironclads.

Placing steel-rimmed spectacles upon his beak of a nose, Captain Gray ticked off a number of dates upon which Confederate patrol vessels, on special missions, had been ambushed and captured; upon which certain Union scout vessels had been able, and without suffering the least damage, to penetrate that intricate pattern of torpedo lines protecting the forts and harbor. He spoke also of how the enemy seemed to guess just when certain blockade-runners might attempt to run in — especially those carrying munitions.

"I'd call that mighty conclusive evidence," grunted Lieutenant Webb, recently attached to Charleston Naval Headquarters by the Secretary of the Navy himself.

It was far from pleasant, thought Henry Bears, to observe the covert and uneasy manner in which his fellow officers now looked about. Each seemed to be asking himself what instance he could recall, no matter how trivial, which would tend to implicate someone.

A sea gull planed past the open windows of the old Customs House and uttered its plaintive cry as Captain Gray also arose. "From now on, we must be especially on our guard, because, as we all know, a new and terrible weapon soon will be placed at our disposal, the *Hunley*."

Captain Lee nodded to himself, he having directed that telegram to B. A. Whitney, Mr. Hunley's agent in Mobile.

"The Almighty in His wisdom," continued the Commodore, "has seen fit to place in our hands a weapon which can well determine the outcome of this struggle on the sea. Oh, by the bye, I hear that Mr. George Trenholm feels such confidence in the capabilities of this fish-boat that he has offered one hundred thousand dollars, prize money, to any crew sinking either the *New Ironsides* or the *Wabash*."

Men's eyes lit and they stopped drumming their fingers.

369

"This hundred thousand dollars will be matched by subscriptions from the Patriots' Committee of Merchants. I have received Mr. Wagner's written promise on that score.

"Further, a hundred thousand dollars is being offered by the same people for the sinking of any monitor."

Dabney Seymour called out, "How may one volunteer for service in the *Hunley?*"

Henry Bears jumped to his feet. "Please, sir, may I head the list? Any reward, should I win one, I wish paid to the Navy Benefit Fund."

One after another various officers volunteered, among them Lieutenants Webb and Payne. A sobering look appeared on Commodore Tucker's fine features. "Thank you, gentlemen, but perhaps you will wish to reconsider when I remind you that this same fish-boat sank in Mobile Harbor and suffocated her entire crew?"

He plunged hands in the pocket of his long-skirted frockcoat. "I should be less than fair were I not to warn that, however sanguine we may be concerning her eventual success, this submarine torpedo boat remains an unpredictable experiment, and that anyone electing to serve aboard her does so in danger of his life."

Lieutenant Dixon, the slow-spoken, terrier-small Alabaman, jumped to his feet. "What the Commodore says, gentlemen, is true; I would be the last to disguise the fact that service aboa'd the *American Dive* — er, the *Hunley* — can be hazardous in the extreme. However, I hasten to tell you-all that I've made several successful dives and that changes have been made in the fish-boat's design which will render her operation considerably less dangerous."

His voice, surprisingly large for so small a man, rang out: "We, who will serve aboard the *Hunley*, will be initiatin' a new fo'm of naval warfare; one which may well determine not only the outcome of this war, but of wars to be fought by our descendants. Gentlemen, I'm feelin' mighty proud and privileged to serve amongst you-all, but I'm sure mortified that Charleston, rather than Mobile, has found the courage to use the *Hunley*."

CHAPTER XII

Twilight Garden

THE late afternoon sun was reddening warehouse roofs along East Bay Street and a hush descended upon the city. It was almost time, everybody realized, for the Swamp Angel, that pestiferous great cannon the Federals had emplaced on Morris Island, to resume its daily bombardment. Of course, the big rifled gun could, and did, at any hour, lob shells into Charleston, but sundown, invariably, marked a period of firing.

The Swamp Angel, indeed, had come to supplant nearly all other interests although most of its projectiles missed entirely. All in all, the bombardment thus far had caused surprisingly little property damage, and had resulted in very few casualties. Nevertheless, a fear remained in most minds that, someday, a shell would explode with ghastly results.

Only one shell from the Swamp Angel thus far had fallen near the Lambkin mansion; a projectile which had landed squarely on Mr. Hunter's house and knocked its two top stories into brickbats. Fortunately for the family they had been in the garden seeking relief from the heat. Since the Hunters lived but three dwellings removed, the Lambkin household for quite a time remained quietly apprehensive.

Serena, lovely as a print in *Godey's Lady's Book,* watched Cousin Cordelia's willowy figure emerge from the side entrance and drift idly along a brick walk leading to that bower in which she and Cordelia had taken to greeting their lovers. By tacit agreement, if Henry Bears appeared first, Serena, after a polite interval, would betake herself to a bench in a pergola nearer the house. If Dr. Donald put in an earlier appearance, then Cordelia would disappear.

Because Cordelia's wedding day now was but a short while distant, Serena, ever tactful, quite often surrendered her advantage; she and Donald weren't going to marry until he received a promotion and increased pay. She was finding it difficult quite to forgive Father over this enforced delay. What with his continued prosperity, surely, he

371

could have given her a wedding present sufficient to permit their moving into one of many houses deserted since the Swamp Angel's bombardment had begun.

Mockingbirds were raising liquid notes amid an unaccustomed stillness when Serena, lovely in a gown of lemon-yellow batiste, went down to join her cousin.

How very little our poor diet and the bombardment is affecting Delia. She's still lovely as an angel. Wish I'd candy-colored hair that could be drawn into such a shining knot. My, her color's bright. Heavens, could she be using *rouge*? Now aren't you downright ashamed of yourself, Serena Lambkin, for even suspecting such a thing?

"Mercy!" Cordelia settled upon an Italian marble bench, began to fan herself with a handkerchief and wriggled a little. "I do declare this cool stone feels mighty good — you know where — and me wearing a single petticoat."

Serena giggled. "How times are changing! Imagine either of us admitting we own, er — er — posteriors, let alone how it felt?"

Cordelia laughed, looked reproachfully up at her cousin. "You've had another letter from Julia. Why does she write to you, rather than to me, her own sister?"

"Please don't be hurt, darling," Serena begged, "for I really don't know. Somehow, we've always understood one another."

"And what does she say? Anythin' interestin'?"

Serena's handkerchief flicked an insect from her wrist. "A most extraordinary thing. Honey, do you remember India Bryson?"

"Who doesn't! That — that hussy!"

"Julia says she's turned up in Nassau. It also appears her husband's been there, too."

Cordelia's clear blue eyes grew hard and incredulous. "Alistair Bryson! But Hugh Wasson told me he was dead. Your father said so, too."

"Well, evidently they are wrong. Julia writes that Alistair left Nassau very suddenly a while back." Serena's smile faded. "Seems that poor India reached the Bahamas only a few hours after her husband went away."

"And where has he gone?" sharply queried Cordelia.

"To Cuba, she thinks."

"Won't Uncle St. George be interested to hear that?" She rearranged her wide skirt. "Do you know, honey, I've always wondered why your Papa took those absurd accusations the *Argus* made so very seriously."

She fell silent. In the distance had sounded a dull report followed by a moaning noise which swelled into a scream. Both girls sat rigid and round-eyed, then laughed nervously. They had learned that when the scream of the shell was prolonged like this, the projectile would not land nearby. "There goes that old Swamp Angel. I wish it would blow up and all those damn' Yankees with it."

Both girls ignored the fact that another shell might, at any instant, start arching over from Morris Island. Sometimes one would trail smoke and sketch a graceful white arc across the sky. A clattering of horse's hoofs ceased as a rider drew rein before the Lambkin residence.

Like the wistaria vines trained along its balconies of cast-iron filigree, the Lambkin house looked faded and tired, thought Lieutenant Bears. The summer's long heat seemed to have drawn all the freshness from it. Eagerly, he swung through the driveway's gates of wrought iron because, on such a warm evening, Cordelia would be waiting in the garden.

By an effort he steadied himself, as with a long, swinging stride he bore down upon the summerhouse. "Honey!" he called. " 'Delia, honey! You in there?"

The lemon-yellow batiste dress, one of the few new ones in town, glimmered in the summerhouse's entrance.

"Oh, Harry! What can have happened? You sound so jubilant." She danced towards him, pale arms outstretched.

"I've wonderful news, honey!" he cried as he caught her close, kissed her eyes and lips while Serena turned aside, pretended to pinch off a rose-apple.

"Tell me!" pleaded Cordelia. "Don't you dare be an old tease-cat."

"Please, come over, Serena. This should interest you, also. You've both heard about the submarine torpedo boat that was brought from Mobile?"

"Why, of course." There had been a description of it in both the newspapers — the *Argus* long since had given up, adumbrated by Mr. Roadheaver's alcoholic breath.

Young Bears's countenance described his delight more eloquently than words. "Why, 'Delia dear, you're about to marry the luckiest officer in the Confederate States Navy — or one of them."

373

"I should hope so!" Serena's quiet laughter rippled. " 'Delia couldn't very well marry more than one. But tell us what's happened, Harry."

"Four officers have been picked to be trained to navigate Mr. Hunley's wonderful invention. She used to be called the *American Diver,* but now it's been named after him. Well, ladies, soon we will be strewing the ocean floor with Yankee men-of-war!"

Cordelia's radiant expression fled as she peered at his bronzed features with that strained look so characteristic of Southern women these days — of Northern women, as well. "Stop talking like an orator. What are you saying?"

"Why, Johnny Payne, Dab Seymour and a tough little Alabaman officer by the name of Dixon and I are going to start practice-diving within a week's time."

Serena's crinolines swayed forward. "But, Harry, you said this affects me — how is that?"

"Why, Don is to prepare a study of the physical effects of being submerged. He's also to care for the volunteers. I expect it'll be up to him to figure out how many of us can live on the air contained in the hull, and for how long. What's wrong, honey? Why aren't you happy?"

"I'm not!" Cordelia wailed. "When I think of you going down in that nasty old boat, out of the light and air! Oh, please!" she squeezed his arm. "If you truly love me, Harry, you won't accept this appointment."

He looked utterly crestfallen. "But, darling 'Delia! Don't you understand? I will be one of the first men ever to cruise beneath the surface of the water. Why, I might even come to command the *Hunley* after we sink the first enemy. Then you'll be married to a famous man!"

A brief stillness reigned in the garden where a few early fireflies had commenced to wink among the magnolias.

"— Or a widow before my time, more likely. Harry Bears, what do you know about this — this crazy contraption?"

"Nothing yet," came the cheerful reply. "But I soon will — tomorrow, the armorers will commence to reassemble her. You must come see her."

"I don't want to see her!" choked Cordelia. "Tomorrow, or ever."

"Why don't you two seek the summerhouse? I think I hear Donald arriving."

He appeared presently, flushed with enthusiasm. "Yes, Harry's right," he told Serena after a quick kiss. "I'm ordered on special duty at Railroad Wharf tomorrow."

"Was this submarine boat really brought all the way from Mobile?"

"Yes, darling, she was. Cut in two pieces and under guard."

By the half-light Serena's eyes seemed enormous as, with studied casualness, she inquired, "Did you happen to see any of the escort?"

"Only Mr. Hunley and Lieutenant Dixon. Why?"

"Where are the fish-boat's guards encamped?"

"Right near to Railroad Wharf. Why all this interest, darling?"

"Please come over here," she begged, and led the way to a marble bench darkly overhung by mimosa. "The most extraordinary thing happened this afternoon. Someone, I am not at liberty to state just who it was, offered the most incredible piece of information."

"And that is?"

"Among these Alabamans was an officer, a lieutenant in the Home Guard, who bears a striking resemblance to your brother!"

"To Alistair! But you told me he was last heard of in Nassau."

Serena's lovely blond head inclined. "My informant couldn't be quite positive, because the man he saw is bearded, wears glasses and keeps his hat pulled low over his forehead, but he did notice this Alabaman's profile, and when he heard him talk a little he felt strongly reminded of Alistair." Her hand came to rest on his sleeve. "Tell me, Donald, do you think it *could* be he?"

"I don't know what to say, because if he were daft enough to come back here, which I doubt, he'd undoubtedly return on some runner."

The sounds of more men dismounting in Legaré Street caused them to rise and step apart.

"There's Papa," Serena announced a little breathlessly. "I expect that will be Judge Riegler, too."

"They see a lot of each other, don't they?" Donald asked very casually.

"Yes, and there's young Mr. Wasson."

In an undertone Donald said, "Thank you, love. I'll be at the railroad yard the first thing tomorrow; if it is Alistair, he'd better get away in a hurry. His life won't be worth a pinch of ashes in a gale of wind if he stays."

Major Lambkin and the Judge appeared, mopping heated faces, just as the other couple hastily emerged from the summerhouse.

" 'Evening, Doctor. 'Evening Harry. Ladies, my service." Immediately, he demanded, "Harry, what's this nonsense I hear about your serving aboard that crazy fish-boat of General Beauregard's?"

375

"Make him stop, Uncle," begged Cordelia. "That iron fish sounds like the maddest notion, ever. How can it float?"

Judge Riegler nodded, caressed a noble white beard and gravely considered Serena's pale beauty. "I suppose you've heard, Mr. Bears, about this invention's fatal dive in Mobile Bay?"

"Yes, Judge, both Dr. Bryson and I have heard of it."

Mr. Wasson shrugged. "Well, I only hope Hunley's invention works. Something must be done to drive off those blockaders. Just yesterday two more runners were driven ashore and set afire."

"I know," Bears said. "The *Petrel's* loss hurt especially."

"Why?" Cordelia wanted to know. "Were — there some new styles aboard?"

"No. She was loaded deep with engines for some *Davids,* and other supplies they're aching for at the naval depot."

"You know, St. George, it's a mighty strange thing," commented Judge Riegler, fanning away a mosquito. "Somehow, the enemy nowadays seems to know where to lie in wait for runners bringing in materials of war. Last week it was the *Emilie St. Pierre* and *Night Hawk;* a week earlier the *Penguin* was driven onto Drunken Dick Shoal and shelled to pieces."

"But how can this be explained?" Cordelia demanded. "It sounds so mysterious!"

"A spy at work. Someone who must be very well informed," snapped Major Lambkin. "There's only one thing to be done, I say. This damnable traitor must be caught, tried and hanged — in public!"

CHAPTER XIII *H. L. Hunley*

THE sun had barely risen amid a welter of bright red clouds forecasting yet another torrid day to be suffered during this already unusually hot season, when Medical Lieutenant Donald Bryson stepped ashore from the gig which had pulled him and Lieutenants Payne and Bears, over from the naval depot.

The hour was so early and relatively cool that the birds yet were singing, and dew glistened on the rusty iron skin of the fish-boat's two sections.

From Railroad Wharf's construction shack briskly appeared Horace L. Hunley showing traces of lather about a clean-shaven upper lip.

"My thanks for being so prompt, gentlemen. I had particularly desired you to witness the reassembling of my invention."

When he led the way to the platform cars, their cradled burdens and the crowd of curious workmen waiting to start, Donald found opportunity, unobtrusively, to drift away. He sought a group of soldiers — evidently the guards from Alabama, consuming breakfast around a smoky little cook fire. His anxiety became relieved: certainly none of those roughly dressed, unshaven and, for the most part, aged individuals could possible be his brother.

He announced his profession and duties and ended by circulating among the group and lancing a boil on a gap-toothed corporal's neck.

It was only when he was wiping pus from his scalpel that he noticed a dark-bearded individual seated some distance away, busy over a sketch pad.

Barely in time, Donald stifled a groan. It *was* Alistair yonder, squatting on a pile of timbers and drawing, as of yore! The physician, however, took a measure of courage: to anyone else, the ex-journalist would have been difficult to recognize, what with those unfamiliar steel spectacles, short bristly beard and close-cropped hair. He had done something to his eyebrows, too; they looked slimmer and straighter than before. Further, Alistair had become tanned to a deep bronze.

"Nice morning for drawing," Donald commented as his shadow fell across the sketch. "Must be soothing for the nerves. Ought to be, anyhow."

"Why, thank you, sir. I like to sketch before it grows so hot that my sweat stains the paper." Casually, Alistair glanced upwards, quite as if he had never before beheld this man in the worn gray uniform. "I presume, sir, you have come in connection with the fish-boat the boys and I have fetched from Mobile?"

"Why, yes, Lieutenant." Donald raised his voice for the benefit of a passing mechanic; he was lugging a wooden box containing the tools of his trade. "I'm the physician designated to care for the health of those who are to work, guard and serve aboard the *Hunley*."

The physician adjusted his spectacles and bent over. "That's an interesting cross-section you have drawn of the bow half. May I look at it?"

Alistair passed up not only the pad but his pencil.

"Very interesting, indeed. I see provision for a water ballast tank, but is there no reserve for air?" While talking Donald wrote: *Meet me at once in the boat shed beyond the derricks.*

"A beautiful piece of work, Mr. . . . ?"

"I am Lieutenant Andrew Bryant, of the Mobile Home Guard and at your service, sir."

Fascinated, volunteers clustered about a drawing board to which had been tacked the plan of the fish-boat in cross-section, side elevation, and as viewed from above and below.

"She certainly is uncomplicated," commented Lieutenant John A. Payne, until today *Chicora's* gunnery officer.

"And what, Mr. Hunley," Henry Bears inquired, "is the craft's maximum diameter?"

"Five feet," came the prompt reply. "Her over-all length is thirty-five feet."

"Can nine men actually be accommodated in so confined a space?" Dabney Seymour sounded dubious.

The inventor frowned, then spoke briskly. "It will be cramped in there, sure enough, yet plenty of room remains in which to revolve the propeller shaft." Employing a bow pen, he indicated that piece of mechanism. "As you see, crank handles have been offset from the main shaft and will be turned by eight of the crew, seated four to a side, and facing one another. Here are braces to lend their feet extra purchase.

"This is the forward hatch, which I like to call a conning tower, because, when my boat is not submerged, the captain or helmsman can put his head out and see where he's going."

"Mr. Hunley, how does one see to steer when the craft is under water?" Lieutenant Payne asked, intently.

"There is a heavy glass disk — a bull's-eye — set into each of the hatch covers; this will admit a certain amount of light when the boat is not too deeply submerged. Two more are set into the manholes."

"Manholes?"

"The same as conning towers or hatches. Below thirty feet, it is generally too dark to see anything."

"Surely there is a lantern provided?"

"Yes, but a very small one because a large flame would consume too much air." The inventor sighed. "I wish there were some means of compressing air for use as a reserve under water; alas, we in the South have not yet sufficient technical knowledge to make this possible. . . . But such will come in time," he added quickly.

"How long can your boat remain beneath the surface?" Johnny Payne wanted to know.

Again the inventor looked uncomfortable and took refuge in fast talking. "Why, young sir, everyone should be safe for from between one to two hours — at least, so my calculations indicate."

"Um-m. Two hours would allow ample time to proceed, submerged, to and from even a fairly distant target," Dabney muttered to himself. "How fast do you estimate the fish-boat can travel under water?"

"If her crew is well drilled, from three to five knots."

Lieutenant Dixon, the Alabaman, spoke for a first time. "I have been thinking, sir, and have become convinced, that were the *Hunley's* outer surfaces to be highly polished, her speed could be considerably improved."

Stripped to shirts and trousers, now that the shed was heating rapidly, the volunteers bent, intent, above the drawing board. With rapt attention they noted the position of ballast tanks at either end of the little vessel, and hand pumps designed to empty them when she wished to surface.

"Somehow," said Dabney, squinting and tugging at light brown sideburns, "I still find it hard to believe, sir, that even eight *very* strong men could propel the fish-boat at five knots, submerged."

"You are as much entitled to your opinion, sir," came Mr. Hunley's courteous observation, "as I am to mine."

"Tell me, sir," Bears put in, "have you ever considered placing an additional pair of pectoral fins near the stern?"

"What are pectoral fins?" Donald Bryson inquired from the background.

"Why, sir, they are the blades which direct the fish-boat upward or downward; just as the rudder directs her in lateral directions."

"Suppose, gentlemen, we repair to the vessel? It should be easier to explain her parts and operation, especially since at present she lies in two sections."

Eagerly, the volunteers inspected the tubular hull's exterior, then crowded inside the forward segment and discovered that none save the steersman could possibly stand erect.

"For what use are these eye-brackets designed?" Bears inquired.

Smiling happily, Horace Hunley indicated a long slab of cast iron, roughly rounded on one side, and lying beside the platform cars. It looked to be about ten feet long and inordinately heavy.

"That is what I term a 'ballast keel.' " Mounting enthusiasm characterized the former cotton broker's manner. "Normally, this keel is secured to the bottom by pins and eyes. In the event of distress those pins are pulled free and my vessel is immediately relieved of the keel's great weight and so can rise more readily. I consider it, gentlemen, a safety device of enormous importance."

The tails of a soiled and badly wrinkled linen coat flapping about his legs, Mr. Hunley entered the forward section. "Please observe these projections. They brace the propeller's driving shaft; these are sea cocks which admit water to the ballast tanks to induce quick submerging."

He backed into the sunlight again with rust smears showing on knees and shoulders. "This is the forward tank bulkhead, and here is a mercury gauge which serves to indicate how deeply the fish-boat is navigating."

Peering towards the bow, Henry Bears recognized the bracket to which a compass would be attached and noted a small, brass steering wheel mounted horizontally, rather than vertically.

He simply couldn't get over the small size of this engine of destruction. The crew must certainly be forced to work jammed well together in that dank, dark hull.

Mr. Hunley now moved around to a metal cone forming the extreme bow tip. "This," he explained, "is fashioned of cast iron — as is the stern end. All the bearings and the gland through which passes the propeller shaft are brass-lined. Here we have a waterproof valve through which goes the line that will tow the torpedo. It can be fed out, or reeled in, on this little windlass; also the line can be released altogether at the moment of contact."

Watched all the while by sunburned armorers and workmen prepared to bolt the fish-boat's two halves together, the little knot of officers circled the invention. One and all, they were wearing serious, if not anxious, expressions.

Lieutenant Dixon, meanwhile, entered the hull, raised the hatch cover and popped out like a jack-in-the-box.

"See?" he encouraged. "There's plenty of room in case one has to get out in a hurry; there are two hatches, you'll observe."

Mr. Hunley looked proud as he explained, "I designed the escape hatches perhaps a trifle large for just that purpose. Please note the heavy glass ports I mentioned, let into each side of the conning towers."

"I'm all impatience to see this contraption in operation, aren't you, Dab?" Johnny Payne said. "Shall we toss up to see who first takes her out? Say, Mr. Hunley, how soon do you figure she will be ready to dive?"

"In about three days, I should think. It all depends on whether your rivets match the holes we cut in Mobile."

It was growing breathlessly hot in that boat shed in which Donald was concluding his account of Julia's correspondence.

For the first time in months, Alistair was smiling broadly. "So India came to me as fast as she could when she recognized that signature in my dispatches?"

"Yes. It's a damned pity you had to miss each other by so narrow a margin!"

The ex-journalist's happy look faded. Said he, grimly: "If I hadn't been gone, she'd have found a very dead husband. Tell me, Don, how soon do you reckon India can get here? I 'most can't wait."

Violently, the younger man shook his head. "You *can't* wait. Not here, at least. It's too terribly dangerous. The very fact the speculators keep on attempting to kill you proves their guilt and desperation. If only your coat hadn't got lost! You have heard nothing from the railroad, I suppose?"

"Nothing. Nobody's going to bother much over an old uniform jacket."

Blinking nervously behind his spectacles, Donald got to his feet and brushed sawdust from the seat of his pants. "Then you refuse to wait in Beaufort, or some other place nearby?"

"Absolutely. I'm going to be in Charleston when India appears; besides, Don, I intend to justify the commission I have been given. Don't worry, I won't go downtown or wander about, and I'll keep well in the background. Every day my beard gets thicker and blacker."

"Don't be a fool! All Charleston will come swarming out to look at the fish-boat. Somebody's bound to recognize you."

CHAPTER XIV **Trial Run**

WITH recollections of *David Number Two*'s semisuccessful attempt on the Union flagship fresh in mind, the inhabitants of Charleston awaited an initial glimpse of Mr. Hunley's famous fish-boat with a breathless impatience. Had not the gigantic *New Ironsides* suffered such severe damage that she had had to be detached and sent North for extensive repairs? Thus, an appreciable gap had been left among the blockaders and many runners got in by consequence.

Speculation as to *Hunley*'s lethal possibilities were rife. Although, up in Richmond, the Navy Department remained callously indifferent, many naval officers, somehow, obtained permission to come from Wilmington and Savannah in order to witness the fish-boat's first trial run.

Today, considerable crowds had collected, because, as usual, news of the supposedly secret test had been widely circulated. They congregated in swarms along the Cooper River's shore and crowded as near to Railroad Wharf as a heavy cordon of guards would allow.

The only civilians permitted within their line were members of the Submarine Committee, and immediate relatives of the volunteer crew. Of course, General Beauregard, Commodore Tucker and their staffs were in attendance.

Serena spied Mrs. Mullinix, wearing a taut expression and standing quietly to one side, so beckoned her near. Drummond stood in a single rank composed of four commissioned officers and thirty-two men; four complete crews for *Hunley*.

Decision as to who would take the submarine torpedo boat down for the first time rested with Commodore Tucker and Horace Hunley.

Serena, glancing sidewise, watched Cordelia's slim hands repeatedly open and close by her sides. Every now and then her cousin would shut her eyes and seem to pray. The widow stared with unseeing eyes upon a slim, gray outline riding easily in the clay-colored river.

382

"Of course, I don't know anything about it," Serena ventured, "but I'd imagine the weather is about perfect. The harbor resembles a mirror."

Somewhere in the background, a band began to play "Dixie's Land," gaily colored parasols bobbed and swayed, and a low cheer arose when the Mayor of Charleston's carriage rolled up.

The volunteers mostly were clad in old civilian clothing and, because of the late August heat, only a few wore coats. Even the officers wore checked or striped shirts above their uniform trousers.

The band music died away as, accompanied by Mr. Hunley, looking solemn as an undertaker in his tall, stovepipe hat and rust-streaked frock coat, Commodore Tucker approached the volunteers.

Cordelia's lovely eyes widened and filled when she saw her fiance's curly, yellow-gold hair flash in the early afternoon sunlight. He was standing third in that short row of officers.

The selectors passed Dabney Seymour. When they hesitated before Henry Bears, Cordelia felt invisible hands compress her throat. Oh, dear God, I thank you, she whispered. The naval commander had moved on and was beckoning Lieutenant Payne who took two steps forward and, flushed with pleasure, stood to rigid attention.

Serena's hand crept out to close over the Widow Mullinix's. One, two, three enlisted men had been selected before the party drew near to Drummond. The widow's breath made a soft, choking sound, but the selectors moved on and the youth stood where he'd been, looking mightily disappointed.

Loudly cursing their misfortune, the unselected men broke ranks while Medical Lieutenant Bryson treated each of the selected men to a cursory inspection — and found nothing wrong.

Of all tunes to be played at this moment, the bandmaster chose that dismal and depressing air, "Lorena."

Major Lambkin and his associates, as usual, had obtained an excellent point of vantage from which to watch *Hunley*'s crew board their vessel. Ringing noises, caused by shoes crossing the submarine torpedo boat's iron sheathing, were distinctly audible.

Lieutenant Payne, his head and shoulders protruding from the forward hatch, saluted, then waved gaily to the crowd. A terrific clamor arose. Not a soul present but hoped that in the river floated a weapon which might defeat the implacable Northerners.

Well apart from the crowd, a wiry figure sat sketching upon the gull-whitened forecastle of an abandoned hulk. What surpassing courage, what sublime patriotism, he was musing, must burn in a man to enter that cranky little craft which already had served as a drowning cage for nine brave men.

Oh, the inspired writing this scene should justify! If only the *Argus* were still in existence, and that which had taken place had not happened.

As if to emphasize the city's peril, a shell from the Swamp Angel burst far down-river, somewhere in the vicinity of White Point Gardens.

The band still was blaring when lines were cast off and the fish-boat moved smoothly out over the Cooper's turgid current. Gradually, the grotesque little craft settled in the water until only her cylindrical escape hatches showed above the surface; ripples began to break at the base of the forward conning tower.

When *Hunley* had cruised some two hundred yards offshore, Johnny Payne disappeared and the iron hatch covers were swung shut. The submarine boat must be preparing to dive.

Horace Hunley drew a shuddering breath and prayed. The last time those hatches had closed in this fashion it had been spring in Mobile.

"Citizens!" cried the Mayor. "Look, and remember that we witness a great event."

"Look! Look!" yelled the volunteers, left behind on Railroad Wharf. "She's going down!" "No, she's not!" "Yes, she is! You blind? You cain't see her bow no more!"

Effortlessly, the *H. L. Hunley* disappeared under a line of pelicans flapping by, faithfully mirrored on the river's unruffled surface. For a little while a streak of bubbles followed. From some point up the Cooper appeared a stubby supply boat, bound for the harbor forts. Her crew came crowding to the rail to wave their caps. Tooting her whistle in honor of the occasion, the supply boat drew near at a fast clip, her paddles churning.

"How brave they must be to toil there in the dark!" Serena whispered. Cordelia nodded, and her heart was light at seeing Henry Bears near the end of the wharf.

Some five hundred yards out from shore, the mirror-smooth water became marred, a ripple showed, then the conning tower's round top

384

appeared above the surface, then the afterhatch; then *Hunley's* full length, bright with moisture.

A mighty cheer went up. The fish-boat had gone under and re-appeared! The crew of the supply boat joined in the tumult.

Both hatch covers crashed back and Johnny Payne's dark head poked out like that of a turtle from its shell.

"No! No!" suddenly screamed Horace Hunley. "Close those hatches! Quick! Quick!"

In frozen horror the onlookers foresaw the tragedy. Whitely curling billows, raised by the wake of that speeding supply boat, were rolling at and over the surfacing fish-boat's open hatches.

Shrieks, screams, groans and howls of profanity made the shore resound. Icy shivers coursed down Serena's back and into her legs. Cordelia, wailing, covered her face. Successive waves were cascading into the open hatches. Lieutenant Payne's arms could be seen flailing wildly a moment, then a residual wave must have filled the already swamped hull and sent Mr. Hunley's invention sliding to the bottom amid boilings of frothy water.

A black dot, the head of a lone swimmer, could be seen marking the spot of the *Hunley's* disappearance. Nobody could guess who he might be.

CHAPTER XV **Salvage**

FROM the parapet of a battery, poorly placed and therefore abandoned, Lieutenant Commander Dabney Seymour sat with a telescope braced upon his knees. Through it he studied a tug and a barge-crane anchored over that spot where *Hunley* had foundered. He was able to discern a suit diver's attendants preparing him for another descent; the air pump's half-naked crew leaning over the rail and spitting into the water.

Other workmen were busy adjusting a loop of heavy chain to a huge block-and-fall, a mate to that which already had been passed under the submarine boat's stern. In a few minutes now, the diver would endeavor to pass yonder loop under the sunken vessel's bow. What Dabney wanted to learn was whether it would prove powerful enough to heave the fish-boat and her cargo of dead men to the surface. This, he knew, must be accomplished before the tide should change.

How dreadful the fate of those eight men — only Johnny Payne had managed to swim free of the vortex caused by *Hunley*'s death throes. Yet, perhaps, they had not suffered so agonizing a death as that of the fish-boat's first crew. To suffocate must mean a long-drawn agony; imagine gasping, feeling life slowly ebb. A man dying thus, in fetid darkness, probably would be granted all too much time to recall those things he'd done which he ought not to have done — those loved ones he must leave behind.

Other people, Dabney realized, were watching the salvage efforts, but not very many because attempts to recover the fish-boat now had gone on for five days.

He readjusted his telescope's focus, for now the suit diver was being eased over the barge's side waiting for his helpers to turn a set of butterfly nuts securing in place his helmet of gleaming copper.

"Think they'll get her up?" Dabney Seymour started, so silently had the speaker approached. Glancing over his shoulder, he saw Mr. Elisha Peake's saturnine countenance looming against a slate-gray sky.

"We'll soon learn," Dabney replied and replaced his eye at the telescope.

"For one reason, I hope they'll succeed out there; for another, I hope the fish-boat stays where she lies."

"Why so?"

"If the *Hunley*'s raised, she may drown more people. Seventeen already have lost their lives because of her."

The Vice-Consul clicked his tongue. "You've trained to serve aboard her, I believe. Don't blame you for being, well, apprehensive."

"I'm not," Dabney said slowly. "Still, I've a premonition that submarine boat will — Oh, I'm talking nonsense. Forgive me."

"Then, surely, you don't want to see her raised?"

"Of course," Dabney Seymour rose, dusted the seat of his trousers and offered his telescope. "Like to take a look?"

"Don't mind if I do." Mr. Peake tilted a stovepipe hat onto the back of his head, adjusted the lense. "Now this is what I call a

386

right smart spyglass! You can nigh count the hairs on that feller's mustaches. I expect you can see pretty well across the harbor?"

"Why, yes. I've even been able to watch the Yankees building earthworks on Morris Island and some shacks on the beach of Long Island."

"Now can you really? Now that's right smart. I presume you can make out some of the blockaders?"

"If I climb a steeple I can sometimes sight ships in the outer cordon chasing a runner," Dabney admitted.

"Well, if you want to watch another chase," drawled the Vice-Consul, "you'd better get up your steeple early tomorrow." Mr. Peake returned the telescope, pulled out an apple and commenced calmly to gnaw at it. "Heard tell there's a pair of runners, *Intrepid* and *Grey Ghost*, going to make a run for it, either tomorrow or, mebbe, the day after."

"You don't say," Seymour drawled. "Well, I'm not much for early rising and I've seen enough runners chased. Besides, I'll have plenty to do if they do bring up the *Hunley*."

The Vice-Consul's narrow jaws worked regularly. "Mr. Seymour, your wits must have been addled when you volunteered for service in such a nonsensical deathtrap."

A mirthless laugh escaped Dabney. "I'm an engineer, you know, so I'm bound to be interested in original mechanical ideas — especially any that can cause hurt to the Federals."

One of the nearby onlookers called to his companion: "Look, Jenny! The diver's comin' up."

It was so. Dabney watched a cumbersome, rubber-clad figure being assisted aboard the lighter, saw the helmet unscrewed and noticed the diver's head move in a series of nods.

An hour later, while the floating crane's donkey engine chuffed and strained, a crowd collected in time to see the fish-boat's stern and propeller guard slowly appear. Gradually, the slings were adjusted until she swung on an even keel beside the tender.

"Well," said Mr. Peake, "looks like you'll likely get your chance to risk your neck after all."

"That's just what I want," said Dabney Seymour gravely.

The Swamp Angel, for some inexplicable reason, this day lobbed no shells into the beleaguered city, which was just as well, because a blacker mood had never settled over its inhabitants than when the fish-boat was towed, still awash, back to Railroad Wharf.

It was commonly conceded, however, that the *Hunley's* foundering was not attributable either to faults in her design or to the performance of her crew. She had successfully submerged and had regained the surface after traveling all of five hundred yards under water. Lieutenant Payne, before a Court of Inquiry, had reported the air supply adequate and the functioning of all mechanisms perfect. The only cause for the disaster had been swamping through water pouring down hatches left opened at an unfortunate moment.

Powerful pumps soon sucked water from the submarine boat's hull and a detail of sober-faced workmen prepared to descend into her dripping interior. Onlookers watched an Army *fourgon* drive out upon the dock. From it eight rough coffins were unloaded and readied to receive the dead, but so grotesquely contorted and so inflexible were they, that they were pulled out of the submersible with no little difficulty.

In their present condition the bodies were so bent and twisted they could not possibly be fitted into the coffins. So, one after another, the corpses were concealed beneath a tarpaulin.

From beneath the brim of a palmetto fiber hat he had taken to wearing and seldom removed, Alistair Bryson watched his brother identify the victims and fill out their death certificates.

Poor Mr. Hunley stood silent to one side, ashen-faced and quivering like a colt scenting a bear. No doubt he must be recalling a similar scene in Mobile.

Already they're talking about more test dives, mused Alistair. Is Johnny Payne crazy? Why does he insist on navigating the fish-boat? George Dixon, Harry Bears and Dab Seymour are kicking like steers over being denied their turn in command; it's wonderful, but they've had no trouble finding replacements for the drowned men.

Wish I dared volunteer. Somehow, that submarine boat is getting to fascinate me — more and more. Maybe that's because I helped guard it coming East? Come to think of it, except for the inventor and George Dixon, I've been more intimately associated with the *Hunley* than anyone. But I mustn't risk being recognized. Hope Donald will show up in the boatshed tonight. Maybe he won't. He looks too upset.

"By God, Bunk, I don't know how such news gets about, but I've heard some shipments of arms are due within two days."

"Arms?" came Alistair's bitter query. "What's happened? Have the fat-cat speculators suddenly got religion?"

"Don't know. Anyhow, two runners are expected. But here's what'll really interest you." His eyes bored into Alistair's. "One of them is reported to be the *Grey Ghost.*"

"The *Grey Ghost?* Good God! Then Rafe will be fetching in Julia and India. Oh, Don, just to think of India near again . . ." Later he said, "D'you suppose Julia will bring the duplicate evidence?" Angrily, he flung away a chip he had been fingering. "Every time I see Major Lambkin riding around in style and the Wassons spending money like drunken sailors, I want to throw up."

"They make a lot of other people sick," the physician agreed. "Need they be so damned vulgar about it?"

India! The prospect of soon again clasping her fragrant, softly firm body, of listening to the rich music of her voice, of hearing the quick light sounds made by her feet!

"Let's hope some really bad weather's on the way," he said. "The calcium searchlights the Yankees have begun to use make ordinary darkness no real help."

Donald nodded. This was no less than the truth. Of late the block-aders had been equipped with lights capable of flooding the harbor's entrance with a radiance which could pick up even rowboats and skiffs.

Whatever gods direct the winds for once favored the Confederacy by sending a stiff gale out of the southeast which forced the inner cordon to claw offshore. Eerily, the wind moaned among chimneys and eaves, and bent trees with the savagery of a hurricane.

Successive blasts shook the spire of St. Philip's Church so violently that Captains Gray and Davidson heard its timbers groan and felt it sway. Fortunately, the atmosphere remained clear, enabling them to view not only the guardian forts but the sandy white outline of Long Island.

"Don't expect we'll see what we're looking for till it gets dark," Gray predicted.

"If we see anything at all," Davidson shouted over the tumult. "All the same, I'm convinced that if anyone intends to warn the enemy, he'll have to attempt it tonight. Weather like this is the answer to a blockade-runner's prayer."

Patiently, their glasses scanned the tip of that peninsula upon which Charleston had risen; then Davidson briefly viewed the giant new flagship *Columbia*.

She looked very imposing lying there at her berth, yet was really quite useless because of engine-room troubles. Two piers away, showed *Chicora's* squat funnel; *Palmetto State* was doing guard duty behind Fort Sumter.

Gray sighed and blew his nose, so much dust was flying about. "What we need is a light to appear where it shouldn't."

Presently, Davidson inquired, "Have your suspicions narrowed on anyone during the past few days?"

"Yes. I'm almost certain I know who the spy is," came the grim reply. "But I'm not saying anything until I obtain positive proof."

An hour passed. Only a few lights gleamed in the streets below St. Philip's, so almost uninhabited had become the lower end of Charleston since the Swamp Angel's advent. Bright lights, however, glowed out in Castle Pinckney, Fort Moultrie and in that stubborn bastion called Sumter.

Gray's hands began to ache from supporting the heavy night glasses and his eyelids grew hot and weary. He was about to traverse his glasses away from Moultrie and Battery Marshall when, suddenly, out there a rocket lanced into the sky. It burst, scattering a number of blazing red sparks far and wide.

"See that?" snapped Gray. "Look! Look! There's another."

"Yes, but they're being fired by our people in Moultrie."

"No, they're not. Look at these bearings on my map." He held up a lantern and his eyes seemed prenaturally large. "See where the signals were sent up? It's about halfway between Moultrie and Marshall."

"Come on." Stuffing glasses into their case, he caught up his map and, a moment later, he and Hunter Davidson were scrambling down a series of ladders. They startled orderlies holding their horses by the suddenness of their appearance, then mounted and clattered off to the Provost Marshal's office.

CHAPTER XVI **Battery Marshall**

BECAUSE there were no repairs of consequence to be made on the *Hunley,* she having suffered no appreciable damage as the result of the fatal dive, her maintenance crew found themselves with little to do. It was not therefore difficult for Lieutenant Andrew Bryant, on detached duty from the Mobile Home Guard, to obtain leave and go aboard *Juno,* that supply boat which transported food, ammunition and replacements to defenses and batteries studding the harbor's northern shore.

To him it came as a shock that he could, unchallenged, stroll all over Fort Moultrie. Nor did anybody say him nay when he quitted that defense to start over a series of sand dunes separating it from Battery Beauregard, next up the coast from Moultrie. Never a soul was exposing himself to the sting of hard-driven sand and spindrift that came roaring in from the sea. He kept on, shielding his face from storm-driven particles. It was still dark and dawn would not break for some time. Come what might, he intended to watch the *Grey Ghost* run in, bringing India and a precious cargo of munitions.

A wild night. Fervently, he prayed that the Yankees might be keeping equally bad watch.

While toiling along in the lee of a particularly tall dune, Alistair noticed the outline of a curious contrivance near its crest and paused long enough to examine a long wooden trough tilted on end and supported by two legs. At their earthward end the boards looked charred.

What . . . ? Then he remembered. Just such a contrivance, in the good old days, was employed to launch rockets on Christmas, New Year's and the Fourth of July.

Dully, he decided that this was, indeed, an odd place to mount a rocket launcher; then trudged on through clumps of wildly whipping dune grass.

For a time he lost direction and wandered perilously about a

391

labyrinth of runlets and creeks; long since, he should have entered Battery Beauregard. As it was, when it became light enough to see anything certainly, he found himself well inland of his objective, but quite near to Battery Marshall.

This expedition probably would be in vain, he decided, for the gale had grown too violent for any blockade-runner's captain to risk being driven among the maze of sands and shoals lurking offshore.

Alistair again was wiping away wind tears when, on the lowering horizon, showed a brief flash. Shielding his eyes against flying sand particles, the ex-journalist peered into the turbulent gloom. Ha! Another flash. That meant some Union gunboat had opened fire.

Great God! Suppose India was on those raging waters and being shelled? She mustn't be! . . . More flashes . . . Five, six, seven of them . . . The blockade ships must be in hot pursuit. All at once the sky brightened sufficiently to reveal three vessels plunging wildly, perhaps a mile distant. More spurts of fire sprang from two of the ships: the enemy. The nearest steamer, of course, must be their quarry.

Bitterly, Alistair began to curse his failure to foresee the need for field glasses. To stand there, unable to tell whether or not it was the *Grey Ghost* under fire out yonder, was agonizing. Gradually, the conviction grew that the fleeing runner was Rafe Bryson's, or — a wild hope burgeoned — perhaps it was the *Banshee*, which so greatly resembled the *Grey Ghost*.

"It must be! It's got to be!" The wind snatched the words from his mouth.

How quickly all three vessels showed shape and detail! They were tearing along towards a line of shoals spouting menacingly off Long Island, urged on both by their engines and by the force of the storm.

A sickening certainty suddenly seized him that it *was* the *Grey Ghost* out there, and running for her life.

Alistair's mouth went dry as he stood on the summit of a dune. "She'll have to turn soon and offer her broadside as a target," he told himself over the wind's howls.

The pursuers looked like screw sloops; one of them, the ex-journalist felt sure, must be the new and powerful U.S.S. *Housatonic*.

Closer raced the fleeing blockade-runner. Now she seemed to be plunging right among the boiling sands. For her to turn and attempt to claw offshore would have been a suicidal maneuver. Her only chance lay in running parallel to the shore, and try to gain the entrance to Sullivan's Island Channel. From there she could steam into Maffitt's Channel, and so come under the protection of Forts Beauregard and Moultrie.

The *Grey Ghost* turned to port and her low silhouette became presented; beyond question or doubt it was Rafe Bryson's ship; no other vessel had so exaggerated a rake to her funnels and masts.

Farther out on the raging water, *Housatonic* also turned broadside to the beach; a series of smoke puffs burst from her. The Blue gunners must have been expert or very lucky because, just as the *Grey Ghost* had Battery Marshall abeam, they hit her twice.

Icy spikes seemed to pierce Alistair's brain when a great cloud of steam and splinters burst from the runner amidships, then one of her funnels tottered and plunged overboard, trailing smoke as it fell.

There was no need for that sleek, black-painted cruiser to reopen fire. Already the *Grey Ghost* had fallen into the trough of the seas; huge combers were pounding her and vaulting high over her superstructure. Sickened to the depths of his being, the lonely watcher on the dune's top watched the runner's bow gradually disappear until, not a quarter of a mile distant, she struck a shoal and broke her back amid a furious welter of white water.

Louder than the howling of the wind, harpy voices screamed in Alistair's ears. His stomach writhed and griped to see all manner of débris commence to break away. In his mind's eye he saw precious rifles, fieldpieces and medicines spilled onto the bottom. And India was out there. Rafe, too, and probably Julia. Rafe, who had done them both such incalculable harm.

The ship's company began trying to launch a boat and a dark, antlike horde of figures swarmed about it. It capsized before it got well clear of the wreck. Black dots showed, then most of them disappeared.

Already, the iron ship had begun to break up — her never too substantial fabric yielding under the titanic pounding of billows racing in from the Atlantic. He saw survivors succeed in reaching and clinging to the overturned small-boat, now being hurled towards a throng of troops racing along the beach from Battery Marshall.

Alistair began running in great, bounding leaps down the dune. Once he reached the wet sand's hard-packed surface he looked towards the wreck and was astonished to realize how little of her now remained visible. This, of course, was due to her iron construction; her hull had no bouyancy, such as would belong to a wooden vessel.

None of the wildly excited artillerymen even noticed his approach. Many of them were wading out towards the overturned lifeboat, stretching out and trying to clutch half-drowned swimmers.

Alistair was up to his armpits in the icy seas before he realized it, and hauled a dark young fellow to safety. There were no more survivors in the water, so he staggered over to a place where the dead were being placed. Wildly, he stared upon limp, sand-smeared figures placed in a tragic rank, but found no female among them.

Survivors were being swathed in blankets fetched hurriedly down from the fort, and a medical officer forced liquor between purple-blue lips. Of those who had sailed in the *Grey Ghost,* only eight remained alive.

Somehow, Alistair Bryson was not surprised to find his cousin among the living, but semiconscious and bleeding from a long wound across his forehead. Like jagged teeth, splinters of bone protruded from the fabric covering his right leg.

Captain Raphael Bryson lost the tenuous hold he had retained upon consciousness through the pain of being carried up to Battery Marshall's rough-and-ready dispensary.

He lay with particles of sand speckling his dark, wavy hair and sideburns, and breathed heavily through retracted lips.

"Can't you bring him to?" Alistair demanded through chattering teeth. "I fear my wife was aboard."

"No. He'll not likely regain consciousness for hours," the Army doctor told him. "And with a fancy compound fracture like that I don't envy him when he does."

Chilled to the bone, Alistair repaired to a casemate in which rescued men crouched over steaming bowls of soup. They were all suffering, in varying degrees, from shock. For the most part, they only stared at an interrogator from dull and uncomprehending eyes. One, a bandy-legged little English sailor, however, could and did answer questions once he had consumed nearly half a pint of straight bourbon.

"Ladies? Aye, there were ladies aboard — don't know how many, sir. Me, I'm a stoker. I only watched 'em come aboard."

"Do you know any of their names? Please, for God's sake, try to remember," quavered the distraught figure wearing a blanket, Indian fashion.

"No, sir."

"Did you notice any of them once the chase began?"

"No, sir. It were dark and I was firing the boilers."

A seaman, whose badly broken arm the doctor was dressing, roused up. "Weren't no petticuts ever on deck, Cap'n. Me, I reckon that shell burst right in the passengers' quarters." He shivered. "Doc, ain't you got no laudanum? This here arm's like to kill me."

"It won't hurt you much longer, son," grunted the medical officer. "It'll have to come off." The wounded man screeched.

"Christ no! Let it hurt. I *won't* be no cripple."

"A terrible thing, the way that shell burst, sir," the stoker gasped. "Whole ruddy ship rang like a gong."

No amount of questioning could elicit anything further than the fact that a few women, nobody knew exactly how many, had boarded the blockade-runner in Nassau. No steward or any other individual who might have observed the females at close range had survived.

Alistair, therefore, returned to the wind-swept beach and assisted in hauling a further succession of corpses out of the surf's reach. When a pair of artillerymen began dragging on shore an unmistakably female figure his throat contracted. The body they lugged, with drenched skirts flapping heavily, was slight and approximately of India's stature.

"Oh, no! *No!*" Alistair ran heavily over to the dead woman. A whistling gasp escaped him when he perceived that it was not India who lay there so stiffly on the sand.

Until midafternoon, when no more bodies came tumbling in, Alistair ranged the beach, his haunted expression so apparent that soldiers commented, or awkwardly commiserated.

Around five in the afternoon, the *Grey Ghost*'s master's eyes finally fluttered open, probably because of the pain caused by an orderly in cutting cloth from the shattered leg. Alistair from the doorway heard his cousin choke, "You — save it?"

"I am afraid not. You see, Captain, these punctures are very ragged and both the fibula and tibia are badly fractured."

"No wonder. Damned shellburst blew me clear off — bridge. Give

395

me — drink, Doctor." He gritted his teeth. "When — you expect you'll amputate?"

"Not until tomorrow, sir, when you should have regained strength. You must be made of steel and rawhide to survive the battering you took. Is the bandage on your head too tight?"

The doctor had adjusted gold-rimmed spectacles and squinted at the head showing up so white against a folded Army blanket.

"Got any morphine or laudanum?" Rafe wheezed. "My leg hurts like hell."

"Sorry, Captain, we haven't had any for weeks; you runners should bring in more medicines —"

"Instead of French corsets and brandy, eh?" Rafe manufactured the ghost of a laugh. "Well, there's irony for you. This time I was running cargo almost entirely of munitions — medical supplies."

He must have seen Alistair's figure outlined in the door for, painfully, he turned his bandage-crowned head. "We seem to have a visitor," he croaked. "Pray make him welcome."

"You *are* a tough specimen. Are they going to pull you through?" There could be no analyzing his emotions when, at long last, he and his cousin thus confronted each other. He could only marvel that his chief reaction was pity.

"He'll pull through, all right," the doctor said. "Who are you?"

"Cursed if it isn't Cousin Alistair!" Rafe whispered. "What in hell you doing round Charleston? Thought — town too hot for you."

"Rafe, for God's sake tell me. Was India aboard your ship?"

"Neither Julia nor India. Too hazardous risk 'em — a cargo of munitions." When he fell silent the gale's diminished moaning invaded the dispensary.

The doctor said shortly, "I'm going to change some dressings on one of your crew who's going to lose an arm. So, Captain, if misery really loves company you'll have it."

Alistair dropped onto a camp stool beside the stricken man and, for a long while, they conversed in low voices. Every once in a while Rafe weakly would ask for coffee laced with brandy while describing how he had chanced upon India in Richmond. He related how, having won forgiveness, he had carried her to Bermuda when he was en route to England. From thence she had sailed for Nassau where Julia had taken her in and had grown to respect and to love her.

Gradually, Rafe's voice grew less distinct and his eyelids kept sagging.

"When will India be coming to Charleston?"

"Not until — the *Tam o' Shanter* — very fast new runner, comes from England. Damn' Yankees — growing altogether too 'cute 'bout intercepting —"

"Hate to keep after you like this, Rafe, but did Julia mention any documents I left in her care?"

"Yes. She spoke about the patient way you collected evidence; but didn't you take — most telling documents along? Haven't you already exposed our patriotic friends Riegler, Lambkin and company?"

Hurriedly, Alistair described the loss of his tunic and his furtive existence in Charleston. "And so the best of my proof is lost; people still think me an overzealous journalist who'd stop at nothing to boost circulation."

Rafe grimaced, stifled a moan. "Don't worry. Done a lot of thinking recently — running arms proves it. If I pull through my visit to — butcher's shop . . . I'll tell anybody — who's behind — Excalibur and Columbian . . . how much — profit is — and . . ." He actually winked. "And how much those heroes have salted away in English banks. Julia'll bring documents you left, and others I found — bear out your accusations. So, Alistair — will you forgive . . . dreadful thing I did — to you . . . India?"

CHAPTER XVII **Rope Obstruction**

FOR over a week after the surgeons took off his leg, Raphael Bryson lingered more dead than alive; only the blockade-runner's magnificent physique weighted the scales in his favor.

It was patent, however, that not for many a week would Rafe be capable of making a detailed deposition. He did, however, manage to dictate a letter to be sent to Nassau aboard the *Ella and Annie*, captained by the capable — and lucky — Frank Bonneau.

In Charleston, public attention once more became centered upon Mr. Hunley's fish-boat. A crew, new except for Lieutenant Payne,

397

took her out and conducted a series of eminently successful dives until, one evening, she submerged then suddenly struggled back to the surface. The two conning tower lids crashed back just before Hunley filled and sank in five fathoms. Again, Johnny Payne was spared, along with three others.

Lieutenant Payne reported to his superiors: "We had just submerged when, very suddenly, men cranking the propeller were thrown about in all directions. Despite their best efforts the shaft refused to revolve and the fish-boat commenced to sound. Barely enough headway remained to permit my ship to regain the surface, but when the hatches were open we were not sufficiently clear of the surface and water poured in.

"Only four of us, those right under the towers, were able to escape." He shook his head. "I — well, gentlemen, I just don't know what went wrong."

The explanation was found when, two days later, a steam crane and divers again raised the ugly little craft. Wound about her propeller and its protective housing of sheet iron was a section of rope netting which must have formed a part of those obstructions strung about the harbor to discourage sudden incursions. Obviously, the netting had broken loose from its moorings long ago, it was so green and slimy.

Again bands wailed the funeral march and five more graves were dug beside the original eight; upon them a little grass already had sprouted.

"A deathtrap, an iron coffin for brave men" was how the newspapers now described the *Hunley*. Only the indisputable fact that extraneous and unforeseeable forces had caused the disasters brought about no lessening of confidence on the part of the submarine detail. General Beauregard, therefore, sanctioned further practice dives. Lieutenant Payne, however, quietly requested a return to duty aboard the *Chicora*. Possibly he saw himself cast in the role of Jonah; if so, he said nothing about it.

CHAPTER XVIII Many Happy Returns!

ONLY because so few of the old families still clung to their homes, in defiance of the Swamp Angel's never predictable shelling, had so many ancient social barriers tottered and fallen. Before the war, the Lambkin girls would never had dreamed of setting foot in the late Major Mullinix's modest residence. True, Tom Mullinix had been born among the elect, but the fact remained that his widow once had been a governess in Mr. Bull's employ.

Serena, Aurora and her cousin gladly accepted an invitation to a celebration in honor of Passed Midshipman Drummond's nineteenth birthday along with various Pringles, Rutledges and representatives of other equally aristocratic families.

Fortunately, the evening proved to be as beautiful as only June or late September can be, so it was possible to utilize a lovely little garden which had always been Dorcas Mullinix's especial pride. True, the variety of her flowers was limited, and yellow rust showed upon iron palings enclosing a space beneath a weeping willow in which the Major and the Major's mother lay taking their long rest.

Refreshments, necessarily, were of the plainest, but the birthday cake had been decorated with cut up tapers and sugar icing. Duncan's initials even had been sketched in pink by the Pringle's pastry cook.

A banjo tinkled, and a string of faded Chinese lanterns glowed very prettily in the twilight — so thought Cordelia and Henry Bears as they stood at the garden's far end.

"The next celebration, I hope," she smiled wistfully, "will be in our honor."

"February nineteenth's a long way off, but it's at least something to have set a date," said he. "Surely, by that time, I'll have won a lieutenant commander's commission."

Cordelia cast a sidewise glance, drew him behind a pendant of Spanish moss, ardently pressed her supple body against him as they kissed. "Oh, darling, I do so wish we didn't have to wait this long,"

399

she whispered tenderly. "If only Cousin George hadn't got himself killed at Corinth. If only Mamma hadn't insisted on our mourning a whole year!"

Her expressive dark blue eyes sparkled with impatience. "Every day, people are marrying even though they've lost close relatives only a few weeks earlier."

"Then why don't we just slip quietly off and get married?"

"Oh, I can't! I can't!" sighed Cordelia. "I have promised Mother we would wait. She wants us to have a lovely church wedding."

A banjo struck up and soon a Scottish reel set the tall young fellows in uniform and their bright-eyed partners to skipping, bowing and whirling. Foremost among them stepped Drummond, gallantly handing about Aurora Lambkin. Serena's sister had matured during the past year into a pretty dark young thing, with a shining mass of curls and ready dimples. She'd have been really striking had she not been wearing a badly remodeled gown of Serena's.

When, at length, the number had been danced, Mr. Midshipman Mullinix was perspiring freely while Aurora only "glowed," as a lady should. Impulsively, she took his hand. "Oh, Drummie, is it true that you're about to be promoted?"

"I expect so, Miss Aurora." He flushed happily, made faint blond sideburns perceptible all at once. "I sure hope my lieutenancy comes through. You see, I aim to command a new submarine boat we intend building."

She clapped hands in lively enthusiasm. "Will you? Will you, really?"

"I sure will. I'm built right for submarine duty. Being short, I can move about easily in that damned — er — confounded cramped hull —"

"You were put in for promotion?"

"I expect it was Captain Gray, along with Lieutenant Commander Seymour. I went out yesterday with Dab. He's a wonderful fellow and as cool as they come. You'd have thought the fish-boat had never — er — met with bad luck, the way he took her up and down. Twice, we passed under our receiving ship, slick as an eel."

"Receiving ship? Which is she?"

"Sure — the *Indian Chief*. Right now we are berthed almost along-side of her. Next time, we'll actually tow a dummy torpedo."

Drummond's face lit when he beheld Dabney Seymour and Captain Rutledge entering the garden. They were easily the two tallest men

400

present, and the most distinguished, in contrasting ways. The Charlestonian was dark, the scarred Virginian essentially blond. Gallantly, the new arrivals bowed over the widow's callused hand, and murmured praise of her son.

Cordelia, back among the shadows, felt Henry's arm tighten about her waist. "Isn't Drummond handsome? But such a child!" She herself was exactly eighteen.

Bears said quietly, "I venture someday he'll command a great ironclad. Drummond's a hard worker and not afraid of man, God or devil. And levelheaded. You ought to have seen him one time our propeller shaft jammed." He felt her shudder. "Why, what's the matter, honey? Cold?"

"No, but I shiver every time I think of you going down in that dreadful little fish-boat. Papa says it's about the same as committing suicide."

"Now, now," he patted her cheek. "Haven't we been all over that?" He reached out, removed a couple of punch glasses from a tray being passed by Lieutenant Payne — there being no servants to perform that pleasurable task.

"I presume you've heard about Rascal Rafe's ship being chased ashore and wrecked?"

"Yes, but they said he was saved, badly hurt," the girl said. "How is he progressing?"

"Not very well," Bears said. "They had to take a leg off at the knee. He's suffering from internal injuries, as well."

Cordelia sniffed. "All *I* say is — it serves him right, after the way he treated Cousin Julia."

Harry Bears looked uncomfortable. "But hasn't he married her?"

"Oh, I suppose so, but I've yet to hear of anybody who's had much to do with Rascal Rafe and come out the better for it. Look! I believe Drummond is about to cut his cake."

Gaily, the guests congregated about a card table covered with a bed sheet for want of a proper cloth; even that had been patched in several places. A pair of candles, protected by storm glasses, attracted haloes of moths, bravely illuminated the cake and its various-sized candles.

The widow — intense, dark eyes alight — stood opposite her son. "You had better cut it, Drummond. I see hungry faces about us."

"Many happy returns, Mr. Midshipman!" called Captain Rutledge, magnificent brown beard asparkle as he raised his glass. "Here is to your lieutenant's commission in a hurry!"

"Before we proceed," Drummond said in his clear young voice, "may I invite you all to lift your glasses to the most devoted, unselfish mother in Charleston — to my knowledge, of course," he added smilingly.

Gravely, he raised his glass, looked his mother squarely in the face, called out, "God bless you, darling! I hope I shall always make you proud of me."

Serena's eyes filled, blurred the candlelit scene. So proud, yet so tender was the look Mr. Bull's former governess bestowed upon her son.

CHAPTER XIX **A Call from Mr. Peake**

FROM his back room window, Lieutenant Commander Dabney Seymour looked out upon Charleston Harbor and noted that pelicans were flying low over the water in the usual ragged formations.

Um. There were but two runners in port. He had no trouble in distinguishing them; no longer did yards, rigging and funnels create small forests along the waterfront.

For some weeks now, a curious lethargy seemed to have settled upon besiegers and besieged alike, and one uneventful day became deplorably like the rest. People moved in a somnolent routine; so little good news now was posted on the bulletin boards of the *Courier* and the *Mercury*.

The Virginian sighed on recalling a time-honored definition of warfare as 95 per cent boredom and 5 per cent being frightened to death.

He glanced down into the street, noted that the one-armed veteran was at his usual post, rather hopelessly attempting to vend smoking tobacco. Why doesn't he go elsewhere? He's been there a week now and with so few people passing, his sales can't have amounted to anything. Why doesn't he move nearer the taverns and hotels, or the railway stations? Probably, he'd meet with too much competition? Military cripples and beggars swarm about such places.

Dabney's elongated shadow followed him across the spotlessly neat bedroom to another window from which he could see the wharf at which the fish-boat now lay. How very tiny she seemed, especially by comparison with the *Indian Chief*, anchored a short distance out in the river. His interest quickened. Activity was visible on the float. Then he recalled that Mr. Hunley, himself, intended to conduct a practice dive; probably in order to banish any suspicion that faults in his design, not chance, had rendered so tragic his vessel's record. He turned, glanced at his desk, noted a fat envelope, well sealed, addressed to Mrs. Robert Ashton Seymour.

How curious that another Seymour should have served in the ill-fated *Atlanta*. Briefly, his mind delved into family history. How long had the Ashton and Seymour genealogy reflected association with America's naval power? As Dabney recalled, the saga had commenced with one Robert Ashton who, in 1776, had taken the privateer brig, *Grand Turk II*, to sea, glory and riches.

His interest sharpened still further when he recognized an angular figure turning into the street below and, a moment later, a half-grown mulatto slattern knocked: "Dey is a Misto' Peake heah, see you, suh."

A moment later, Elisha Peake strode in. His craggy features were expressionless, but profound excitement shone in his deep-set eyes.

"I was just going by, Commander," he explained in a voice loud enough to be heard downstairs. "Thought I'd pass the time of day."

"Glad you did, Mr. Peake. Perhaps you'll join me in a glass of sherry?"

"Don't mind if I do. How are things going aboard the fish-boat?"

"Well enough, I believe. Mr. Hunley's going to take her out for a test in a little while."

"You going aboard?"

"No, isn't my turn; damn the luck."

The two men sipped in silence.

"Notice you've got an admirer down on the corner."

"Oh, you mean that old soldier selling tobacco?"

"Yes, doesn't budge from that place all day long, does he?"

"No."

"What can he be finding so interesting in this neighborhood? He can't sell much."

"Funny. I was just speculating on the subject."

Mr. Peake was aware that the housemaid had not descended the staircase so offered his host a black Jamaican seegar. "Sure is duller than ditchwater 'round here. Practically no ships entering or clearing."

"It certainly is."

Mr. Peake looked up suddenly, brightly, like a bird. "Now if I were you, I wouldn't waste much more time 'round Charleston. Me, I'd head for the Navy Department in Richmond. Things keep happening up there. Yessir. Heard tell you people are building a fine new steam ram down in Mobile. I'd clear out of here in a hurry."

"Now would you really, Mr. Peake?" Dabney settled his big body upon the edge of his bed and bent forward, elbows on knees; the scar across his cheek gradually became noticeable.

"Yessir. I'd waste no time. Do I presume correctly that you've been figgering such a move?"

Dabney drew a deep breath. "Reckon so. I expect everybody does, once they get bored with inaction."

"How soon could you leave?"

"If it were necessary I would pack up in an hour's time."

"You couldn't manage it any sooner?"

While the Virginian deliberated, a board creaked in the hall outside. Dabney nodded.

"Yessir. Should think you'd like to get away for a while. Heard tell they're going to call in certain officers for a conference at Naval Headquarters — in fact, their messengers are on the way.

"Well, Commander, thank you for the drink." When he arose and extended a bony hand, his eyes met the scarred Virginian's. "Good-by, Commander. Maybe sometime we'll meet again."

"I hope so," came the level reply. "Wish you continued good luck in Her Majesty's service."

As the Vice-Consul's footsteps died away Dabney went over to the brassbound sea chest he'd brought out in the *Grey Ghost* — ages ago, it seemed — and extracted from it a long envelope which he set afire and, while the flames reduced it to wrinkled black shreds, hummed softly an old English air. Then he lifted from their pegs his third-best uniform coat and a round civilian hat he had taken to wearing aboard the fish-boat; next he stuffed the letter to his mother into his pocket and descended the back stairs even as someone began tugging imperatively at the front door's bellpull.

Once in the alley he turned sharp left, and headed for the waterfront.

Announced Medical Lieutenant Bryson: "You, Musgrove, must not serve in this test. You've a fearsome cold and I won't have you sneezing and coughing in that damned confined hull."

"But, sir," the sailor protested, "cold or no cold, I can turn the crank better than most. I've learned the knack, sir."

Decisively, Donald shook his head. "Nevertheless, I'll not certify you for this test. Won't have you infecting the rest of the crew. Best go home and to bed."

He glanced at reserve volunteers drawn up on the float under command of Passed Midshipman Mullinix.

"Mr. Hunley, you must select a replacement."

The entire reserve stepped forward.

"Take me, sir!" they clamored. "Take me, sir. I ain't dived yet."

Young Mullinix saluted smartly. "Mr. Hunley, I claim the right to supplant Musgrove. It's over two weeks since I've been aboard."

"Very well, son, come along."

Horace Hunley's brow channeled itself into a V. One of the pectoral fins hadn't been operating too easily. Also, he'd been thinking about the slow rate of speed with which water ballast could be expelled. Perhaps an additional hand might speed up that operation? As if in answer to his problem, he heard feet hurrying along the dock above.

"Ah, there, Commander Seymour. Like the Good Samaritan, you appear in the nick of time."

"Do I?" Dabney clumped across the float. "Then, perhaps I can be of service?"

"Why, yes," the former cotton broker told him while stripping off a waistcoat of tabby velour. "While I intend navigating the torpedo boat myself, I wish to manipulate the diving fins during the first few moments."

Dabney Seymour smiled, glanced in the direction from which he had appeared. A squad of infantry was advancing at the double.

"I'll feel privileged to oblige, Mr. Hunley." Then he saw young

Mullinix and flushed. "What are you doing here, Drummond? You weren't posted for this practice dive."

Quickly, Donald Bryson explained about Musgrove's illness.

"I am certainly glad that you are to be aboard, sir," said Mullinix to Dabney. "That last dive we made together was a beauty. Mr. Seymour's really expert, isn't he, Mr. Hunley?"

"That he is," smiled the Alabaman. "Let's go aboard, gentlemen."

CHAPTER XX C.S.S. *Indian Chief*

IN accordance with their position along the crankshaft, the propelling crew lowered themselves through the after hatch and sought their seats in darkness dispelled only by a small lantern burning above the compass. Young Mullinix recognized the sounds of shoes rasping upon the iron skin and of the wavelets *lap-lapping* over the fish-boat's back.

Various muscular and often bearded crewmen called out greetings. They all liked the widow's son — so optimistic, so enthusiastic. He settled himself on the hard wooden bench, shoved his feet into broad leather loops and unbuttoned his shirt. Already the crew had begun to sweat.

"Shall we push off, Mr. Hunley?" Dabney demanded in a strained voice. "We're wasting air every instant we linger at the wharf." Mr. Hunley removed his cap and coat, left them in a little pile on the float and clambered down into the fish-boat's hull.

"We'll be back within half an hour," he called back, "so don't you reserve men go home. Pray take the wheel, Mr. Seymour."

"Aye, aye, sir," the Virginian complied, rigid of countenance. He alone had retained his coat.

In the distance sounded shouts of "Halt!"

"Secure hatch lids!" Dabney called sharply; then to the reserves on the float, "Let go all lines!"

The after manhole cover clanged hard shut, and Dabney himself secured the forward one. He hoped nobody within the fish-boat had heard the outcry or feet racing out along the wharf.

"Prepare to crank! Crank!" he snapped and sighed relief when he heard the propeller shaft begin to click against its braces. The craft trembled gently as it started away from the float.

"Halt! Stop that boat!" People were shouting. A faint singing noise became evident in Dabney's ears when, with eyes fixed on the binnacle, he manipulated the submarine's too small steering wheel. Long since he had found that a helmsman had to exert considerable strength to keep *Hunley* on course.

Mr. Hunley peered up from his position beside the starboard fin handle. "What's that yelling?"

"Why, sir, they are cheering us off." The commander's voice sounded odd, thought Hunley, but then almost everybody got tense whenever the fish-boat was preparing to dive.

"Depress fins five degrees, Mr. Hunley," he called. "Open Seacock Number Four. Slowly admit water to ballast tank." He himself opened Number One Seacock and heard the hiss of air escaping from the tank before him. Meanwhile he kept the wheel motionless, so, barring some trick of tide or current, the fish-boat should not veer from the course he had set.

Click-clack! Click-clack! Approximately forty revolutions to the minute, he judged, were pushing the *Hunley* ahead. When, gradually, water rose about the conning towers light faded beyond the heavy glass bull's-eye and soon darkness reigned, alleviated only by that tiny lamp which served to illuminate the compass. By it, Dabney could see the mercury gauge and the gunner's quadrant by which could be determined the depth, and the direction and the angle at which the fish-boat was proceeding.

"Open Seacock Number Three," Dabney directed. "Mr. Hunley, open Number Two, please."

A sibilant hiss of escaping air dominated the rhythmic sounds made by the propeller shaft and the quickened breath of the eight crankmen. Although a clock, hung level with Dabney's eyes, showed that *Hunley* had been proceeding submerged but three minutes the atmosphere grew hotter, more humid, and beads of moisture formed on the hull's interior.

The inventor arose and, bent over, read the mercury depth gauge. "We have sounded far enough, you can level off, Mr. Seymour."

If his calculations were correct the fish-boat must be traveling some thirty feet above the harbor's bottom, thus allowing plenty of room to pass safely under *Indian Chief*.

Silence ruled in the hull. Horace Hunley remarked, as if to himself: "Another time the seacocks should be opened more gradually. We descended at too sharp an angle. Might stick our nose in the mud."

"Aye, aye, sir." Dabney said. "And the tanks should be filled with exactly equal speed. That will permit us to submerge on almost an even keel."

The former cotton broker noticed the angular set of his helmsman's jaw and saw great drops of perspiration dripping from it. No wonder. The air already was growing foul. This was probably so because the crankmen, due to their exertions, were consuming oxygen at an amazing rate.

Hunley mused. Wonder how spare air could be stored? Perhaps it could be pumped into tanks under pressure, like air into a diver's helmet? If that were possible, where would I find room for them and what . . . His conjecturing remained incomplete. A gentle jar that hardly swayed the helmsman's long body had checked the fish-boat's progress.

"What's wrong?"

"What's happened?"

"We seem to have fouled something," came Seymour's calm announcement. "There's no cause for alarm."

"But there can *be* nothing to foul!" Hunley said sharply. "There's nothing in the harbor beyond the *Indian Chief*."

A grating noise over the fish-boat's back; she became slewed sharply to starboard.

"I'll take the wheel," Hunley said. "Prepare to back the propeller. Everybody stay calm. Wait until I count 'three,' then start cranking in reverse."

When he gave the word everyone heaved. Young Mullinix's back muscles crackled under power of his effort. The propeller revolved freely, but the scraping noise continued and the submarine boat did seem to be moving.

"Stop cranking!"

Peering down the length of the vessel, Dabney could discern, by the binnacle's dim glow, crankmen leaning, white-eyed, over their handles — panting like hard-run hounds and bright with sweat.

"We'll try going ahead," Hunley announced. A note of carefully stifled urgency had entered his tone. "Push as hard as you can on the word of command."

They turned the propeller faster and faster until spittle burst from the crankmen's lips.

"What says the mercury gauge?" cried Horace Hunley.

"As before," Dabney told him. A third and fourth time, the men alternately reversed and drove the propeller forward, but still the fishboat remained unable to move.

Young Mullinix said suddenly: "Sir, I reckon we've somehow fouled the *Indian Chief*'s anchor chain — that would account for those scraping noises."

"Yes, by God!" groaned Number Six man. "It must have got jammed between a fin and our side."

Mr. Hunley grabbed at the port pectoral fin's control handle and heaved frenziedly. Nothing happened, nothing. The ten men, crowded panting and wild-eyed within the iron skin, sensed that the midshipman's guess had been all too accurate.

"Flood tide must have carried us upstream faster than was calculated," Dabney said quietly. "Well, Mr. Hunley" — he turned, peered into those haggard features so dimly seen at his shoulder — "since it's evident we can't move in any direction, what do you suggest?"

The inventor could only stare, so utterly appalled by the prospects was he.

"Let's open the hatches," someone suggested. "Maybe water rushing in will shoot a few of us to the surface?"

With trembling hands they undid a series of butterfly nuts, but, because of the tower's circumference, only one man at a time could brace himself and attempt to force open the conning-tower lids; the efforts of the strongest proved futile. A few threads of water trickled coldly to spatter the anxious, upturned faces.

"The weight of the water above is keeping the lid shut," Hunley muttered as if to himself.

"Can't we somehow get out?" By the faint rays of the binnacle young Mullinix seemed to have aged a decade and kept swallowing spasmodically.

"No, Drummond," Dabney said. "About our only hope is that some-one aboard the *Indian Chief* felt us strike the anchor chain. Maybe they've heard and already have sent for the floating crane. They could get here in time," the Virginian continued, for all he knew that this was next to impossible.

"That's a lot of balls!" roared Number Two Crankman, a veritable giant. "I'll get that lid up." He braced massive shoulders and heaved.

"Stop that! Stop!" cried voices. "You're using up our air."

"Damn it, I ain't fixin' to suffocate. I'll drown first." So he continued to strain until, obtaining no results whatsoever, he dropped, gasping and sobbing, onto the *Hunley*'s floorboards.

"Let me out! I've *got* to get out!" Using bare fists Number Four com-menced to pound upon the sweating, rusty plates. "I've got to get home in time to milk the cows."

"Hush your fuss, Jed. Me, I was all fixed to tumble the prettiest gal south of Norfolk this evening." It was Number Three, a handsome young fellow with the cleanly chiseled features of a Greek statue, who spoke.

Then Mr. Hunley said: "Mr. Seymour, suppose you had better turn out that light while we wait for the crane. It's using up valuable air."

"No, no!" sobbed a voice from a stern seat. "It's bad enough to die, but to die in the dark . . ."

Said young Mullinix in a dull monotone: "Everybody ought to try to stay still and breath as shallow as possible."

The inventor said: "That's right. My next boat will have under-water searchlights or I'll develop some means of telling better where we are when submerged."

One by one, crankmen slumped against the clammy iron plates, mouths open and beginning to gasp like newly landed fish. Most of them closed their eyes.

Dabney Seymour, crouching below the wheel, tested the outline of that sweat-dampened letter in his coat. Curiously enough, he found that he could remember its contents as clearly as if he were in the act of composing it:

My Beloved and Respected Mother:
   Probably you will never read these lines, yet I feel that I must pen them. I must because I must explain to you,

and to my Maker, why I have done the terrible things I have done.

For some days now I have become convinced that Captain M. M. Gray has come to suspect me of espionage. At mess last Tuesday, he questioned me pointedly, and wanted to know why had I ordered a heavily laden ammunition wagon sent along the beach when the Federal fleet was passing. You see, that wagon's iron tires severed the electrical wires leading out to a great torpedo hidden in the channel as neatly as a pair of plyers, and prevented the blowing up of our magnificent *New Ironsides,* not to mention a heavy loss of life.

Dabney drew a labored breath, but felt no benefit. The hot air stank, lingered heavily in his lungs.

I had ready an explanation, but could tell that Captain Gray wasn't taken in. He put other queries, too, wondered if I'd any theory as to why so many blockade-runners were being intercepted; especially those carrying munitions of war. I cannot, even to you, reveal the source of my information.

Undoubtedly Posterity will brand me a traitor to the South, yet so dearly do I love our native State that I am willing to accept this stigma. Virginia ought never to have seceded and sought to perpetuate slavery. I console myself with the knowledge that my activities have preserved the lives of hundreds of brave men on both sides; that, by causing the loss of so many supply ships, I have definitely shortened the course of this war, so ruinous to Virginia's true interests. In conclusion, dear Mother, let me say that, with Nathan Hale, that other spy, "I regret I have but one life to give for my Country."

Several of the crew were whispering prayers and a Roman Catholic among them wearily was passing the beads of a rosary through his fingers. Dabney found it increasingly difficult to think clearly, the air he was gasping was so putrid, so devitalized, but he made a mighty effort when a half-formed thought occurred.

Should this letter to his mother, a Virginian by birth, be discovered? Let Captain Gray and the rest think and say what they would; they lacked concrete evidence of any description. When his quarters were searched nothing more damning would be discovered than a little heap of incinerated paper; nothing at all to implicate Elisha Peake. He wondered whether a similar sense of patriotism had motivated that curious character, the Vice-Consul? Certainly, Mr. Peake had never accepted one cent in payment for his information.

Now a tremendous effort was required even to find the letter. Most of the crew had slumped onto the fish-boat's bottom breathing with painful slowness. Only the midshipman opened his eyes at the sound of paper being torn. Because he had grown so weak and his head was swimming, Dabney had to destroy each sheet individually, reducing the paper to such minute shreds that they would become hopelessly separated and lost if *Hunley* was raised for a fourth time. Surely, even General Beauregard, stout advocate that he was, must lose faith in this ill-fated invention; thus far, it had claimed thirty-one Southern lives.

He sank back and dreamily watched little fiery spirals chase themselves about his eyeballs.

Mr. Hunley roused briefly, saying, "Must have air tanks — sufficient . . ." Then his voice dissolved into incoherent mumblings.

Midshipman Mullinix felt increasingly drowsy and lightheaded. His hands crept up to rub his throat, attempting to relieve a fearfully dry burning sensation. Why didn't I kiss Aurora the night I asked for that lock of her hair? I'm sure she wouldn't have been angry — not very, anyhow. She looked at me so steadily and seemed proud of my admiration. Looks like now I'll never get to wear a lieutenant's star. This is going to be awful hard on Mother — first Pa, now me. Dear Lord, is it right You should make her suffer so — she who's never been anything but good to everyone — a loving Christian, if ever there was one? How sleepy — getting, cold, too — won't have to get up, Mother — no school — no sch . . .

Barely drawing the poisonous atmosphere into his lungs, Dabney Seymour was visualizing a placid river in Virginia. He recognized every detail along its banks — he ought to. He'd played beside it so often in early childhood. The shining snowy slopes of New Hampshire, where he had grown to manhood . . . he saw himself studying under the magnificent elms of Dartmouth College; the day he got that scar . . . There he was after the first attack on Sumter as a young marine engineer volunteering and being sworn into the Naval Service of the

United States. Why had he been selected almost immediately for the Intelligence branch?

He was growing so weak and confused quite an effort was required to recall the English shipyard offices where he'd managed to see the plans for certain ironclads being built for the Confederacy.

More clearly, he remembered a certain Penelope — the Honorable Miss Something-or-other — and how they'd gone punting near Henley — had sat watching the sunset deepen over the Thames and the gentle English landscape — softly sweet her mouth . . . At a sound of a soft impact he groggily opened an eye; the last crankman had collapsed onto the floorboards.

The binnacle lamp's flame burned low, lower, then flared in farewell and went out. With it Dabney Seymour's consciousness faded and soon his life, as well.

CHAPTER XXI **Special Orders 297**

THE fall and winter of 1863–1864 proved wearisome in the extreme. It seemed that only bad news ever was reported by the magnetic telegraph. There were of course occasional sharp, minor battles in which the Yankees were routed as of yore; but there closed, inexorably, the jaws of a giant pincers devised by Generals Grant and Sherman — the only generals, apparently, who understood that the winning of a war depended upon comprehension of the overall problem. They alone appreciated that, sound if unspectacular, strategy, and not brilliant tactical successes, must determine the outcome. Therefore, down in Virginia and across Georgia, the jaws commenced to close upon weary, but still undaunted, Gray armies.

Every day came fresh reports of depredations committed by Sherman's well-trained, well-equipped forces, yet few of those standing before the bulletin boards appreciated that the casualty lists received from the Western Armies totaled not a fraction of those staggering losses reported from Northern Virginia.

"Here is a paradox," observed Alistair Bryson in his ramshackle hut near Railroad Wharf on the outskirts of town. "Everybody inveighs against Sherman and calls him a barbarian, yet most of our people admire Grant."

"I don't see your point," his brother said, extending hands towards a crude tin stove. He was thinner now. "What do you mean about a paradox?"

Alistair settled back on a bunk covered with a ragged quilt. "Suppose, Don, the Yankees offered you the choice of having your house burned down, or of seeing killed almost every male relative you have? What'd be your answer?"

"Naturally, I'd tell the bastards to go burn my house. After all, property can be replaced, lives can't — as I know all too well." The elder brother arose to toss a chunk of wood into the stove.

"There's your paradox. Grant unimaginatively slaughters Southerners by the tens of thousands; no battle is too bloody for him to fight. On the other hand, Sherman tries to win by outmaneuvering his enemies. I believe he has never fought a large-scale frontal battle."

"In other words," Donald said, "we tend to admire the man who destroys irreplaceable lives and hate him who burns replaceable property. Is that it?"

"Yes, that's it."

Donald fell to cleaning his spectacles. "Have you seen the new orders posted on the Navy bulletin board?"

"No. I don't venture into town except to see Rafe. Do you sawbones think he's going to pull through?"

"No telling. But for his amazing constitution he'd have been dead long ago. He's recovering from the amputation well enough — but" — the doctor hesitated — "that shell from *Housatonic* which blew him off the bridge caused serious internal injuries."

Alistair nodded and pulled a shawl blanket about him. Like everybody else in Charleston, speculators excepted, he had grown thin and hollow-eyed. "What about the orders you mentioned?"

"Orders Number 297, to be exact, were issued by Southeastern District Headquarters. General Beauregard directs that, under no circumstances, shall the fish-boat operate under water again. After all, he can't be blamed. On the way here I heard that poor Hunley's invention is to be refitted with a spar torpedo and operate like a *David*."

"Good!" Alistair jumped up, all animation. "That's what should have

414

been done after the first sinking. She'll prove a great success as a *David;* with no smoke to betray her approach, she'll be barely visible."

"Hold on! Hold on! Why are you getting so excited? You aren't crazy enough to think of volunteering, are you?"

Alistair nodded. "I've been thinking it's time I take an active part in this fight. Yes, high time." A chunk of pitch pine hit the coals, flared in the stove, bathing the hut's meager interior in a flattering, golden radiance and projecting the brothers' shadows against raw boards supporting the wall shingles.

"Has word come about India?"

"Only that she and Julia were reported to have sailed aboard the *Ella and Annie;* but, unluckily, she was chased back into Nassau."

CHAPTER XXII **News from Nassau**

ANOTHER war Christmas came to the blackened, bombarded and rapidly emptying city. Havoc wrought by that great gun emplaced on Morris Island daily was increasing the number of broken and tenant-less homes.

For some undeterminable reason, houses on the Ashley River side of Charleston seemed to bear a charmed existence. The ornamental iron-work on them, however, showed orange-red blemishes caused by rust, and paint peeled in great blisters from brick walls and woodwork. Glass, shattered by concussion of the Swamp Angel's shells, had been repaired any-which-way, or not replaced at all. The inner fortifications, which had yet to fire an effective shot, now were manned by Home Guards — invalids, boys and superannuated citizens who went about ragged as scarecrows.

A surprising number of new faces were to be noticed about town, Alistair noted, when, relying upon shoulder-long hair, abundant beard and mustaches for disguise, he ventured once again to prowl familiar streets. Although, since *Hunley's* fourth fatal dive, merchandise had commenced to reappear in the stores, very few people could find money enough to meet the exorbitant prices demanded.

Day after day dragged by in chill monotony, and long faces were worn about Naval Headquarters. Work on a new and more powerful ram, *Columbia,* had had to be abandoned. No longer were railroad rails anywhere procurable with which to contrive armor. Nor could any capable engine be found.

Charleston, having proved hopelessly sluggish, could only be utilized as a floating battery. Nowadays, she lay between Sumter and Pinckney, an ugly, rust-streaked and immobile outline.

One after another, freighters, damaged blockade-runners and coast-wise vessels, too long idle and neglected, sank at their moorings. At Eason's Boatyard there had been little or no activity until orders appeared directing that two more *Davids* should be completed and that the *Hunley* be converted to attack with a spar torpedo.

Since her fourth recovery in mid-October she had lain forlornly on the beach at Eason's. The men she had drowned reposed, side by side, in the same cemetery — including the body of Dabney Seymour, after a curious hesitation on the part of the authorities. There was but one exception; the remains of Horace L. Hunley had been conveyed back to Mobile by grief-stricken Lieutenant Dixon.

"I dread facing his widow," Dixon confided to Alistair. "She's always been dead set against the fish-boat. What with losing two sons at Vicksburg, the poor soul is left alone in the world."

Like too many other women, Alistair thought. Like Dorcas Mullinix, for instance.

Raphael Bryson found new strength, despite the Confederacy's fading fortunes. "I'll be up and around by the time mint sprouts," he laughed, "and buy a new runner. It's a two-to-one bet."

The Medical Officer described symptoms indicative of a stoppage in the intestines. This must, somehow, have become relieved sufficiently to permit Raphael Bryson's sitting up on New Year's Day in the bed-room devoted to his use by Dorcas Mullinix. He'd been glad to accept her suggestion that he should convalesce in her lonely home, so it was only natural that the widow should learn of Alistair's presence in Charleston.

When Rafe at last admitted the truth of that scene she'd witnessed, Dorcas Mullinix wept and declared she'd ever remain miserably ashamed of her suspicions.

For a considerable while the widow and her invalid guest debated whether Serena, because of Donald, should be included in the know, but they decided against it; St. George Lambkin was her father.

The widow had said, "There's no telling how a female's mind may react under stress, for all she's so happy planning her wedding. She and Donald are so deeply and beautifully in love — Cordelia, too, is mad for her Harry."

One January evening, the ex-journalist hastily admitted himself to the Widow Mullinix's back door because of a nasty moment he'd suffered through encountering Hugh Wasson. That the burly, young speculator had stopped to look back wasn't a bit reassuring.

A tiny fire glowed halfheartedly in a fireplace ample enough to have heated the bedroom well, but now all it was doing was to emphasize the mildewed state of wallpaper which, in many places, had loosened from the plaster to dangle in ugly little pennons.

"Well, dear Cousin, I was beginning to wonder if you'd ever get here," Rafe greeted. "I've been hoping you'd come early."

"Really?"

"Yes, really." The lively dark eyes actually sparkled. "I've received happy news — for both of us. George Hendricks, captain of the *Will o' the Wisp*, made port today."

"Yes, I hear she's made it once more."

Alistair sank to the foot of Rafe's bed and wished there weren't so much cold mud clinging to his shoes. Carefully, he studied the patient's face, noted how, in places, it had netted into a hundred little wrinkles.

"Don't tell me Hendricks brought news of . . . ?"

"Aye. Grand news. Pass me that cursed cough sirup, will you? My throat's sore again. What I need is shandygaff, but your damned brother won't allow it."

Alistair complied, offered the bottle with a wry smile. "Tell me more, will you?"

"Hendricks said Julia and your wife will leave on the *Banshee II*. She's an iron ship built along the same lines as my *Grey Ghost*, but vastly improved. Hendricks says she's faster than a scared fox, so she's been selected to import arms."

"I could wish they weren't booked on a munitions ship."

417

"So do I. All the same, I fancy their chances of running through may be good."

"Why?"

The haggard figure straightened. "Hendricks told me Commodore Tucker intends to attack and disconcert the enemy — don't ask me how — because there'll be three munitions carriers due to arrive the same night."

"Who told you this?"

"Lieutenant Bears."

Although he racked his brain, the nature of the attack eluded Alistair. Almost every form of onslaught upon the Federals had already been attempted: torpedo-bearing rafts, small-boat attacks, drifting mines, even pathetically ponderous sallies by the Palmetto Squadron.

CHAPTER XXIII *Sans Peur . . . Sans Reproche*

THAT, as usual, Raphael Bryson had been well and truly informed, swiftly became evident. He learned all details concerning the fresh attempt at departure by his wife and India from the Bahamas. News of the impending arrival of three runners bringing in arms, for a wonder, actually was kept secret and, if any of the general public noticed a sudden stepping up of activity at Jim Eason's Boatyard, they didn't speculate on the reason for it.

Cordelia, seated on a love seat in Uncle St. George's chilly drawing room, nestled closer within her fiancé's embrace. Despite a heavy mantle and several petticoats of fine flannel, the air kept nipping at her body like tiny sharp teeth.

"Betty Flood told me her uncle said you plan to re-fit that death-trap of a submarine boat. You're not going to, are you?"

"I — I really don't know," he lied uncomfortably. "I presume the commandant feels he must find something to occupy our time — we're just rusting away on this station, so we're to be set patching up some older *Davids* and trying to finish a new one."

The girl in his arms wriggled like an affectionate puppy and pressed the chill tip of her nose under his chin. "Oh, Harry, Harry, darlin', how in the world are we going to wait another long week to get married? I want you so — so — *terribly!*"

Convulsively, his arms tightened about her. "And I need — you, darling girl. You have no notion of how badly."

"Yes, I do," she objected through a cloud of breath vapor. "Besides, you can't begin to love me even half as much as I love you."

He stroked the softness of her hair until surprisingly she looked up into his face and said, "You haven't been telling me the truth, have you, Harry?"

"About what?"

"You *are* going to serve aboard the fish-boat. I feel it."

"I'm afraid so," said he gently. "You see it's my duty, darling."

"Kiss me, Harry." She raised wonderfully warm lips to meet his mouth. She smiled, looked him full in the eyes. "I'm glad you're going, because it's what you've been trained for, and it's what you've always wanted to do. It would be very wrong for me to whimper and protest any longer — after so many brave men like Mr. Hunley and Dabney Seymour have sacrificed their lives. Surely, it isn't possible for the *Hunley* to fail another time?"

"Oh, 'Delia, my precious!" A great gratitude warmed him, transformed his strong and handsome features. "You're right. This time we won't fail! We can't fail, because we plan to attack almost submerged, and after dark. The Yankees won't possibly see us coming, because we'll have no smoke stack sticking up, as in the *Davids*. As surely as we sit here, we're going to sink one or more of the enemy!"

"Or more? Surely that's a bit greedy, isn't it?"

"No. Two *Davids* are to attack at the same time."

He kissed her fervently until Cordelia demanded in a small voice, "When are you going to go — out?"

"When God wills it; likely a calm, dark night. Why do you inquire?"

"Because I mean to go to church and kneel until" — her voice quivered — "I hear that you, my Bayard, *mon chevalier sans peur et sans reproche,* are safe returned."

During the week preceding February fourth, the date upon which the munitions runners had agreed to make their attempt, work at Eason's mounted, approached a climax. Two complete crews were

trained to operate *Hunley,* others, the veteran *David Number Two.*
Both craft were maneuvered at night, at dawn, or whenever thick
weather afforded an opportunity.

Carpenters worked furiously on *David Number Four,* but she had
been constructed of unseasoned wood which so warped and twisted that
no amount of ingenious devices could induce her to proceed along a
straight course.

David Number Three, however, had been better built, and lay
ready for use *if* an engine could be found to propel her.

From Captain Gray's offices a series of increasingly desperate tele-
grams were dispatched to Wilmington. One read:

WHERE IS PROMISED LAUNCH ENGINE? IMPERATIVE IT ARRIVE
NO LATER THAN JANUARY THIRTY.

An answer came promising that the precious engine would be
shipped the very next day. Drays halted beside the freightyard's crane,
but when the Wilmington train rattled into Pocotazlio Yard, it was
pulling no platform car bearing anything like a marine engine.

Angry calls on the Northeastern Railroad's divisional superintendent
persuaded that harassed individual to send special agents in search of the
strayed flatcar. It probably, he explained, had been accidentally shunted
onto a siding. Nobody knew their job any more; the rolling stock was
about played out; in short, the railroad was just about done for. Why,
no one seemed to know where two locomotives recently had disappeared
to — or when.

Late on the afternoon of February seventh, a clerk strode into Captain Gray's office and presented a penciled message which stated that the
launch engine had been located. It lay, at present, on a rural siding
in the vicinity of Cerro Gordo, where the platform car upon which it
was being transported had broken an axle.

"Send a special for it, if you have to get P. G. T. Beauregard's own
signature! It must be brought here immediately."

Easier ordered than done. Although a locomotive towing a rolling
crane and a detail from the Submarine Defense did start northward,
they had travelled only a few miles when the Special was stopped. The
track ahead was blocked. A troop train had become derailed — no maintenance of the line these days — as the division superintendent had
said. It would be long hours before the track could be cleared.

"I reckon we will have to make do with two — *Number Two* and that God-damned fish-boat," Captain Gray admitted. "Even so, we ought to panic the Yankees enough to let the runners by."

CHAPTER XXIV **A Dash of Ipecac**

VOLUNTEERS serving in *David Number Two* and *Hunley* trooped into a bitter-cold mess hall. The air outside the shed was keen as a sickle, for all there was no wind to speak of — a matter which was easing several minds at Naval Headquarters. Another favorable factor: the barometer was standing high and steady. If only another twenty-four hours of such weather would prevail!

Each volunteer, as he appeared, sought a bulletin board upon which Captain Gray had caused to be posted the names of those selected for the attack. To Alistair's profound disappointment, his name appeared among those detailed to serve in *David Number Two*. His disgust lay in a discouraging familiarity with the torpedo boat's engine. It had never fully recovered from ill treatment suffered the night of her attack on *New Ironsides*.

Gloomily, the ex-journalist ran an eye over the roster of those posted to *Hunley*. It came as no surprise that Lieutenant George Dixon, recently returned from Alabama, should have been placed in command, for all that Henry Bears for weeks had conducted *Hunley's* trial runs. All the same, his name appeared. Apparently, he would go along to take over should any mischance befall terrierlike George Dixon.

Alistair knew all the crankmen — some of them very well indeed — Joe Patterson and Tom Clark, for instance. Also would go Corporal Carlsen, from Captain Wagener's Artillery Company, along with Arnold Becker, Robert Brockbank and Charlie Simpkins. He lingered before the list, listening to men kick mud from their boots before they entered the smoky little mess hall. Alistair did some rapid thinking. Could he induce Bob Brockbank to trade places? He might for he'd a wife and three small children and *Number Two* was much the safer proposition.

He crossed to a bench fixed to a long table and watched unappetizing food being ladled out into tin plates so battered as to suggest that horses had walked on them. Somehow, he must get aboard *Hunley* and help those munitions runners to bring in their cargoes — and India! But how?

Arnie Becker banged his tin cup on the table and sang out, "By Jesus, them boys at the front sure must be counting on us."

"Why?" A dozen shaggy heads swung in his direction.

"What for?"

Becker grinned and the gap left by missing front teeth showed black. "Heard tell two freights have come down from Richmond ready to haul rifles an' ammynition offen the runners."

"And food. Up in Virginny they're mighty hongry these days."

Alistair took care to broach the subject of a switch with subtlety. Brockbank, a large, beefy individual with a comical aspect because of a grotesquely broken nose, must have been hungrier than usual. He kept shovelling stringy pork stew between red-bearded lips.

"Well, what do you boys think?" Alistair made a pretense of eating. "Will we get us a couple of big cruisers, or maybe a monitor?"

"Sure will," remarked Corporal Carlsen. "It's been so quiet so long them God-damn Yanks ought to get caught with their pants down. Me, I'm shorely tickled to git aboard the fish-boat. Bet we sink a bigger Yankee than you mud-turkles in *Number Two*."

"Like hell you will!" snarled Jimmy Patterson. "Our boat's proved what she can do, and *she* ain't drowned a single man."

Hunley's crew shifted uncomfortably and looked at their plates. Not a man among their number but had watched at least one corpse taken out of the fish-boat.

"Well, Bob," Alistair asked in an undertone. "What say you swap places with me?"

"Naw. I ain't afeered, nohow."

"I want to go in the submarine boat. For fifty dollars will you swap?" The other's eyes narrowed. "Why you so keen?"

Alistair summoned a diffident smile. "I'd known young Mullinix since he was a tad. Well, I'd like to kind of avenge him from the same boat that killed him."

Brockbank elevated a suspicious red brow. "You wouldn't have no other reason?"

"Of course not. Will you swap?"

"Naw. I want to sink one of them boats been starving us all this while."

"Very well, I understand, but you're a good fellow, so drop in at my shack on the way to the dockyard." He winked. "I just happen to have a bottle of pine-top. We'll toast the work ahead."

At two of the afternoon of February seventeenth, the day remained cold and calm and clear. It was then Donald brought sad news concerning *David Number Two.* "It's a crying shame!" the physician informed his brother. "*Number Two*'s stripped her driving gears so badly she'll not go out tonight. Seems as if our Navy never plays in luck, except for the *Shenandoah, Florida, Alabama* and our other commerce-raiders."

The ex-journalist's eyes wandered to his brother's medicine satchel. It sagged open far enough to expose a bottle marked IPECAC.

"Don," said he after a little, "will you be a good fellow and go see whether there are any last-minute changes in the postings? I'd go myself, but there may be people out from town."

Once the doctor's chunky figure had disappeared, Alistair selected the ipecac and poised it over a tin cup, then hesitated. How large a dose would be right? Too much would certainly warn even the most unwary drinker that something was amiss — ipecac was so bitter and smelt so strong. Of course, these days, any kind of liquor one could find tasted so awful the dose might escape attention. He decided upon half a teaspoonful, and put the cup to heat on the stove.

He needn't have worried. When, a little later, Brockbank appeared, he tossed off the libation at a single gulp and did not even grimace. "Say, Andy, that's tol'able good. A bit rank, mebbe, but she spreads out fine and warms a man's guts."

Alistair raised his cup. "Well, Bob, here's death and damnation to the Yankees — and a safe trip in for the munition ships!"

Brockbank's gap teeth showed when he winked and grinned. "Say, ain't you the coony one?"

"What're you driving at?"

"Shucks! You knew all along that that damn' *David*'s engines hev quit."

"What!"

"Go look on the notice board iffen you don't believe me."

"I will. Honest, Bob, I hadn't heard. Wait here, I'll be back soon as I make sure you're not funning me."

It proved infinitely exasperating to see *Number Two*, to all intents and purposes ready for departure, even to smoke rising from her funnel.

"Ain't no use cursing," growled a member of *Number Two*'s crew. "We ain't goin' out, but ain't this the damnedest, blue-spangled luck you ever heared *tell* of?"

Lieutenant Dixon had begun calling *Hunley*'s muster roll when Alistair put foot to the wharf to which she lay tied up. A moment earlier, over his shoulder, he had seen Brockbank emerge from his shack, stagger over to the unfinished hull of a *David* and hang on as he commenced to throw up. He was arching his back like a frightened cat.

Lieutenant Dixon looked angry. "Where in hell is Seaman Brockbank?"

"He's suddenly — taken sick," panted the ex-journalist. "Sent me — take his place. I trust that will be all right?"

The Alabaman tugged briefly at a short, yellow goatee, then nodded. "You're not half so strong as Brockbank, Lieutenant, but I reckon you'll do. Take Number Eight seat."

One by one, yet another crew dropped into the fish-boat's cavernous interior, more than one wondering if he was not crowding in upon the ghosts of men who had looked upon this same mechanism, the same cramped, raw and ugly interior. It had been such a very cold day, the submarine boat's iron skin was covered with silvery frost scales.

The crankmen derived considerable satisfaction from seeing the pectoral fins locked in a horizontal position; especially since they acted as stabilizers. Black-painted and circular dodgers of waterproof canvas had been cleverly rigged about the conning towers to increase *Hunley*'s freeboard and preclude swamping, should the water grow rough.

While lowering himself through the after manhole, Alistair noted that the spare torpedo had not yet been rigged. The arming, he reckoned, would be accomplished at the Army Wharf at Sumter. Harry Bears, looking not a little disgruntled over having to serve as second in command, seated himself before the identical crank handle to which Midshipman Mullinix once had applied his boyish strength.

Crisply, George Dixon sang out, "Let go all lines!"

"Silence below decks.

"Prepare to crank." An indescribable exultation gripped Alistair when, after unbuttoning his jacket, he shoved his feet far under the toe-bands. Then, like the other crankmen, he bent forward, watching for Lieutenant Dixon's frayed gray sleeve to drop sharply as he commanded, "Crank!"

The round, use-polished handle before Alistair commenced smoothly to fall away from him when he applied his strength. Soon he was sweating, he realized, sweating as if it had been midsummer instead of midwinter. Amazing, how quickly it grew hot in this tubular limbo, for all that both hatch covers were up.

Before long C.S.S. *Hunley* — she had been purchased and duly commissioned at long last — felt the Cooper's current, so commenced to travel downstream at a good clip. She left behind a knot of anxious men standing forlornly above useless *Number Two*. They cheered themselves hoarse, all the same. Upon the fish-boat and her devoted company, now, depended the success of that attack intended to divert the enemy's attention from those three blockade-runners on their way from Nassau.

CHAPTER XXV **Off Beach Inlet**

TO the consternation of everyone connected with the projected torpedo attack, the barometer, towards sundown, commenced to fall at an alarming rate, and later, ominous white mare's-tails appeared to lash the sunset sky but the wind remained negligible.

As substitutes for the crippled *Davids*, a number of rafts, each carrying four spar torpedoes fixed at varying elevations, were towed into Swash Channel after dark, and sent drifting out on the ebb just before a dispatch boat dashed up and a gray-faced officer yelled: "Good God, don't you damned fools realize them torpedo rafts can sink an inbound runner just as easy as a Bluebelly?"

General Ripley, commanding the Harbor Defense, and Captain Gray, during the afternoon, had ascended to the crosstrees of Fort Sumter's flagstaff, from which point of vantage they studiously had observed ships forming the inner cordon.

Both officers had noted that, off Beach Inlet, lay U.S.S. *Housatonic,* that fast steam sloop which had captured or driven ashore a very considerable number of blockade runners. She now lay to her anchor, a trim, beautifully designed vessel.

Through their telescopes the observers could make out lookouts on duty at all three of the sloop's mastheads. Ever since the near-sinking of *New Ironsides,* the Federals had been most alert, suspicious even of drifting snags, and, more than once, had fired upon their own picket boats in the dark.

Finally, Captain Gray beckoned. "Mr. Dixon, I think you had best be getting under way. This wind may freshen."

"Yes, sir. We'll do that," the Alabaman glanced at his watch, noted that its hands indicated half after seven. It being February, darkness long since had settled, but was relieved by the light of a good many stars.

General Ripley's manner became gravely impressive. "I need not remind you, Mr. Dixon, of the vital necessity of sinking an enemy vessel, preferably the *Housatonic?*"

George Dixon nodded. He himself had seen those special trains from Richmond waiting in the freightyard.

"Rest assured, sir, that we will surely accomplish our mission, and return here before daylight." He spoke confidently, as well he might. Tonight there would be no blind attack, submerged; he'd be able to keep his target in sight until the moment of impact.

Henry Bears, just before lowering himself into the forward manhole, cast a final look at the sprinkling of yellow-gold lights that was Charleston and wondered whether Cordelia and Serena yet had repaired to St. Philip's.

"Proceed at your best speed, Mr. Dixon," Captain Gray called out. "The wind is beginning to rise."

A crankman who had served during several successful dives in the old days uttered a chuckle. "Say, boys, it's sure fine not to see them hatch covers battened down. There was sumpin' fierce about knowing you was bein' sealed in."

Henry Bears grinned boyishly, ran fingers through his long yellow hair. "And it's good, breathing fresh air. Those dodgers are a real help."

"They're helping already," Dixon called down from the wheel. "The sea is making up."

Someone called over the clacking of the propeller shaft, "Think it's going to storm, sir?"

"No. But looks like it'll blow a bit."

The captain, standing on a wooden box which permitted him to see over the dodger, could glimpse lights aboard Federal ships on watch near Morris Island, rising and falling beyond the slim torpedo boom and its angular supports.

Silently, Henry Bears asked himself just what happens when seventy pounds of gunpowder goes off at so short a range? All along, he'd wondered whether the torpedo spar shouldn't have been longer than a mere forty feet. He kept on cranking, left off worrying.

H. L. Hunley glided through the water with the rising waves slipping smoothly over her dully gleaming back. Suddenly, Dixon uttered a startled cry.

"What's wrong, George?"

"I just saw a big flash off to port; might mean one of our torpedo rafts has struck a Yankee ship."

"That's fine!" Bears called up.

But Alistair Bryson didn't agree. Such an explosion would serve to alert lookouts aboard *Housatonic* and the other blockaders. He said as much.

A crankman named Collins, long features gilded by the binnacle lantern's light, shook his head. "Naw, Lootenant, them Bluebellies won't take much fright. Our torpedoes is always fetchin' loose and bursting somewhere — like the one sunk the *Ettiwan.*"

Shaggy heads along the length of the propeller shaft nodded agreement; not only *Ettiwan,* but several blockade-runners had been sunk by these submarine menaces which, after a time, developed an unfortunate propensity for going adrift.

"What time is it, Mr. Bears?" asked Corporal Carlsen.

"Nine o'clock," Harry replied. He'd been conjecturing whether a new uniform would get down from Richmond in time. This morning, Cordelia had been prettily occupied with alterations to her mother's once magnificent but slightly faded wedding gown.

Thank God, only five more days! The dear girl ought to make the loveliest bride Charleston had beheld in many moons. Um-m. How many ushers could he count on? So many naval officers were being transferred to the Artillery for want of vessels in which to serve.

427

Fifteen minutes later, Lieutenant Dixon ordered the ballast tanks half filled, whereupon the men toiling at the crank handles felt a gradual increase of drag. Apparently the explosion *had* stirred up the Yankees because signal lights were blinking and winking beyond Charleston Bar like fireflies over a summer meadow.

When the command "Ballast enough!" was given, Alistair closed the port seacock promptly.

Dixon felt icy spray splashing against his face and running down inside his collar. The tide was practically at ebb and should turn in time to speed his command back to Sumter. How different from the fish-boat's first cruise across Mobile Bay! That had been made under a torrid sun and the water had been as warm as soup. To realize that at last, at long, long last, Horace Hunley's invention was about to attack! Briefly, he wondered: might not the cotton broker's shade be hovering overhead?

He now became able to discern the outline of a tall steam sloop, the tracery of her spars and rigging black and sharp against the stars. Then, over a whispering of water about the conning tower's base, he heard a disturbing sound. A drum was beating aboard *Housatonic*. Damn! The Bluebellies weren't to be caught drowsing, as they'd been aboard *Mercedita* and *New Ironsides*.

Using elbows, the Alabaman forced down the collapsible dodger; ordered the after protection lowered, too. No use giving the Federals anything more to notice than was unavoidable. Surely, sharp eyes would be required to sight the insignificant outlines presented by *Hunley*'s torpedo spar and conning towers.

Click-clack! Click-clack! Probably because the crankmen were breathing relatively fresh air the propeller was being turned over at a smart clip.

"We are closing in, men," he informed them. "Enemy's less than five hundred yards distant, so pick up the beat the best you can."

An odd, buzzing sensation manifested itself in the calves of Alistair's legs, then numbed his fingertips. The man next to him commenced to pant, and the air within the hull grew rank with the sweat of unwashed bodies. By looking directly upwards, he could see a circle of stars swaying, frostily gleaming. Faster sped the all but invisible fish-boat.

Another bright but brief explosion in the distance suggested that a second torpedo raft might have found some target. The flash threw *Housatonic* into sharp relief and, for an instant, penciled her masts and yards in gold.

The enemy was alert, all right. All manner of lights were springing into being aboard of her.

When the Federal cruiser's outline showed but a scant two hundred yards ahead, George Dixon felt his mouth go dry and his hands tighten over the steering wheel's spokes.

"Quickly, Mr. Bears! The enemy seems about to get underway!" Dixon called down excitedly. "Take the wheel and keep her as she goes. I'm about to lower the spar."

In the fetid depths, crankmen heard a sharp hail, followed by spatter of small-arms fire. Bears heaved himself erect and glued his eyes to the compass. Dixon, meanwhile, worked the pulleys until the torpedo spar shaft was cutting the water deep, deeper.

"Back your propeller!" the Alabaman yelled over a bawling of voices aboard the enemy. "Mr. Bears, steer one point to starboard. Sloop's begun to move."

Musket balls moaned past the forward conning tower and either went *splat* into the water or clanged against *Hunley*'s iron skin.

"Faster!" implored Dixon. "For God's sake crank faster! We're almost there." The men did their best; spittle foamed about their lips. Alistair Bryson braced himself. India! India!

To the only man who could see the target, it seemed as if *Housatonic*'s side was being magically elevated, so steep and black did it loom. George Dixon, sighting along the spar's shaft, heaved mightily on these lines depressing the torpedo until the lethal charge was forced as low as possible: maybe twenty feet below the surface. Now, only one of the ugly little detonating horns need scrape the sloop's bottom.

Amid a tumult of shouts and small-arms fire, *Hunley* closed in until foremast shrouds were right over Dixon's head, forming a sable geometric design almost within reach.

The Alabaman crouched down in the manhole, screaming, "Back harder! Back for your —"

A tremendous column of flame-lit water spouted high above *Housatonic*'s topmasts, then came cascading down and drained solidly into the manholes.

Too late, Dixon realized he should have ordered the conning towers' lids secured just before the torpedo could be expected to detonate. Smothering torrents of sea water beat upon his head and shoulders, knocked him down and projected him into a blind maelstrom of struggling men.

Aft, Alistair Bryson was pinned to his seat by the inrushing water, half-heard gurgling screams of animal terror. Corporal Carlsen grabbed the driving shaft, but was beaten flat.

All became hideous, nightmarish confusion; arms and legs clutched and beat; water boiled into Alistair's mouth and ears, all but extinguishing consciousness. He remembered the stars above him and lunged for the manhole's grips. He found them and made a supreme effort.

Water, gushing up his nostrils, was choking him, when, to his vast astonishment, the turmoil suddenly faded, as, ejected by air escaping the hull, he was propelled upwards with the force of a stone launched by a boy's catapult. Ice-cold salt water then blinded and deafened him, and he struggled frenziedly until his head popped above the surface.

The ex-journalist succeeded in coughing up quantities of oily-tasting water and recovered sufficiently to make feeble swimming motions.

Vaguely, he was aware of pandemonium reigning aboard the stricken vessel. Dreadful cries and orders given in unnaturally calm voices sounded over the black water. Furious clouds of steam, boiling from *Housatonic,* were so forceful they sounded like the shrieking of a blizzard. Then the man-of-war's boilers came in contact with the water and burst, causing a deafening explosion which sent her decks heaving upwards.

Must — must — what? Oh, yes. You must swim off — not get sucked under. On his back, Alistair swam numbly away, at once fascinated and horrified by the sight of men swarming into the foundering steam sloop's rigging. She settled fast, to a chorus of eerie groans and whistlings caused by air rushing from her hull. When *Housatonic* came to rest upon the bottom, only the top of her funnel and her rigging remained above water.

Rockets, fired by the blockaders raked the sky in all directions with jewel-bright parabolas. Alarm guns thundered and soon were joined by Confederate batteries, for all that their shot could not hope to range the inner cordon. Then, calcium searchlights commenced to converge upon the sunken cruiser, transfixing her in shimmering radiance. Far out to sea, the outer cordon's rockets flared as brief, bright pinpoints upon the horizon.

Alistair grew so cold he began to feel sleepy, but, realizing his peril, he refused to succumb.

"India! India!" he kept choking.

Resolution was all very fine, yet he knew his limbs were fast becoming so numbed no amount of will power could keep them moving much longer. In an effort to utilize a new set of muscles, he turned onto his side and saw a dim outline off to his right. He had no notion what that floating object might be, but struck out feebly towards what proved to be a torpedo raft. Slowly, it was drifting landwards, its deadly charges pointed at the harbor.

Somehow, Alistair pulled himself onto its slimy timbers and lay dazed, totally exhausted and only dimly aware that the tide should carry him towards safety.

Towards daybreak, a Confederate picket boat, patrolling off Castle Pinckney, sighted the drifting menace.

"There's another of 'em," someone said. "Give away smartly and we'll take her in tow, but for Christ's sake, keep clear o' them torpedoes."

They did just that. They lifted the ex-journalist into the launch and, after rubbing his wrists and ankles, urged some liquor down the throat of the only man surviving C.S.S. *Hunley*'s last plunge.

CHAPTER XXVI **Major Lambkin Reconnoiters**

THREE silent and preoccupied men occupied the President's richly appointed office in the Excalibur Trading Company's building and, for the moment, stared uneasily into a fire of cannel coal snapping in the grate. For once no papers, account books or cashboxes littered the shining Chippendale table separating them.

Mr. Archer Wasson finally shook his head, then sat up and, placing hands, palms down and fingers spread, on the table, gazed fixedly at the uniformed figure occupying the president's chair. "Then it's true the Judge has suffered a stroke?"

St. George Lambkin's narrow, dark head inclined. "Learned of it only an hour ago. Mr. Rigby, my lawyer, came to tell me."

From beneath knitted brows the younger Wasson asked sharply, "What brought it on?"

"As you no doubt suspect, two things: that infernal Rafe Bryson's deposition to his lawyer, and Alistair Bryson's reappearance." The diminutive figure's buttons glinted by the lamplight as he glared at Hugh Wasson. "And *I* counted on your having taken care of Bryson!"

"Thought I had, but seems I was mistaken. What else did your lawyer tell you?"

"Rigby's law partner is Job Wheelock, he who was retained by Rascal Rafe; he said certain manifests and invoices — we all can guess their nature — were brought in aboard the *Banshee*," St. George Lambkin said heavily, "and are ready to be published, together with an account of those bungled attempts on Alistair Bryson's life — and who was behind them." His breath came in slowly, shudderingly. "In short, gentlemen, those accusations Bryson printed in the *Argus* last year are about to be substantiated."

Archer Wasson heaved himself to his feet, took a series of quick turns before the fireplace. At last he halted, and shrugged. "Well, it was a profitable enterprise while it lasted — none of us can deny that. We've all become very rich."

The younger Wasson laughed unpleasantly as he stood staring at the fire, hands gripping lapels. "Seems a damned shame we've got to quit, but I suppose it isn't safe to keep on."

"No, it isn't," grunted his father. "The traffic's about played out, anyhow, what with so few runners making port. No, the game's no longer worth the candle."

The small figure in uniform raised his head; a stricken look was in his eyes. "Well, what are we going to do? Stay, and fight to clear ourselves — or what?"

Hugh Wasson snorted and a large diamond in his shirt's bosom sparkled as he scratched a long, blue chin. "Well, doesn't look as if the Judge is going to have much to say about it, even if he recovers consciousness. Is that likely?"

"No," said Major Lambkin. "The doctor says his stroke undoubtedly will prove fatal." He blinked, glanced nervously from son to father. "What do you think, Archer? Maybe we could reason with Rafe Bryson? A rogue of his ilk would likely listen to the rustling of sufficient greenbacks."

"Maybe, but I doubt it. And what about our durable ex-editor?"

"That newspaperman can be taken care of."

"We tried that before, and failed, when he wasn't well guarded," Hugh Wasson reminded him. "Now he's a popular hero — somehow, I don't think I'll stay around."

"Odd, isn't it? Only the other day, my doctor advised a change of climate," grunted Archer Wasson.

From the head of the table Major Lambkin grimly regarded his partners. "So that's what you intend? Running like whipped dogs."

"No call to get unpleasant, St. George; you're no lily, either," growled the elder Wasson, and produced a watch on a liberally be-jeweled fob. "Um-m. Well, Hugh, if we step lively, we still can catch the night train for Wilmington. There's a runner up there about ready to sail."

"You will never get away" — predicted he in the smart gray uniform — "not with all that money."

Archer Wasson laughed and smirked. "Really, Mr. President, you're being scarcely flattering. Don't you think that, for a long time, we have been building credit in France? You surprise me if you haven't been depositing any of your" — he sneered — "hard-earned profits abroad."

Lambkin looked absurdly indignant. "Why, it never occurred to me. I've invested my profits in the South!"

"How very patriotic of you."

"Don't sneer. At least I kept the money at home." In the big chair, St. George Lambkin seemed suddenly to shrink to half of his small size and his hands gripped its arms so hard the knuckles crackled.

"Let's not be so grim, or part on unpleasant terms, old friend," grinned Archer Wasson, and went over to pluck a tall hat and coat from the tree standing in the richly paneled room's far corner. "Surely, you must have foreseen that, sooner or later, this enterprise was too good to last?"

"Well, Major, what's your intention?" Hugh Wasson demanded. "Run, while the running's good?"

The ticking of a tall Dutch clock punctuated the Major's deliberation.

"No, I don't intend to run, although I could. I happen to have a modest sufficiency on deposit in Havana."

"Then what do you intend to do?"

"I know exactly." The trim little man stood very erect, and spoke succinctly. "But I shan't tell you, my dear ex-partners, because you wouldn't understand."

Private Nehemiah Benson, on picket duty some two hundred yards from the Swamp Angel's emplacement, noticed, through the deepening dusk, a covert movement amid a clump of palmettoes and beach bushes, so cautiously brought his Springfield to his shoulder. He was grinning with satisfaction. Venison for supper? He licked his lips. Yep, a sizzling piece of deer meat would afford a mighty welcome variation from hardtack, beans and bully beef.

Back home in Vermont he'd always been partial to venison chops, preferably off a young buck — does were too small. He settled lower behind the sandbag revetment of his post, pushed off his hat, then slipped his finger around the trigger.

The palmettoes threshed again, more violently this time; then, to his amazement he saw appear on the rosy sand not a deer but a man, a Rebel officer in full uniform. He was holding a revolver ready and advanced as stiffly and steadily as if crossing a parade ground.

Private Benson cursed his disappointment. He drew a deep breath, called, "Halt! Who goes there?" But the figure in the bright red sash and the black hat kept right on towards the emplacement.

"Halt, or I'll shoot!" Five — six more paces the enemy officer advanced, polished boots half losing themselves in the yielding sand. "Halt, where you are, you damned ijit! Don't want to take so easy a shot."

St. George Lambkin hesitated not at all, but marched on, eyes fixed, not on the Swamp Angel, but on Sumter. Out yonder, the Stars and Bars just could be discerned flapping briskly.

"Hi, Reb! You crazy? Take two more steps and —"

Evenly, the officer, a very short man, leveled his revolver at shoulder height.

Private Benson re-settled the Springfield's stock against his shoulder. "For the last time — *halt!*"

The lone figure's weapon swung in line with the sandbags. When he fired, his bullet sang by a good foot above the Vermonter's head.

"All right, you damn' Reb', you've asked for it!" he growled, and squeezed the trigger.

CHAPTER XXVII **Vengeance Is Mine . . .**

GIBED Rafe Bryson, angular and shawl-swathed, from his rocking chair, "And how does it feel, India, being married to so popular a hero?"

"No different than before," the girl smiled from her place on Alistair's lap. "He's always been a hero to me. It's a wonder it took the rest of you so long to appreciate him."

"It takes time for the unspectacular sort to win recognition — if they ever do. You never could say that about me, now could you, dear?"

Julia looked up from a small vest she was knitting. "What was that, Rafe?"

"I said there's nothing unspectacular about me." His brows joined above hollowed and lackluster eyes. "What were you thinking about?"

"Serena and her family. How terribly they must feel."

The gaze of the five persons in this sunny little bedroom flickered about.

Dorcas Mullinix put aside her sewing basket. "Poor souls; but no one can say St. George Lambkin didn't die bravely."

India drew a quick breath but, under warning pressure from Alistair's fingers, remained silent although her tawny cheeks flooded with color.

"Yes," the widow continued, "I expect St. George Lambkin will always be remembered among the most patriotic citizens Charleston has produced — and there have been so many."

"Well, now, Mrs. Mullinix, I don't —" Rafe drawled until a gesture from Alistair cut him short.

"Let Serena's father go to an honored grave," said Alistair softly. "Let only us remember him for what he was."

He glanced at Julia, heard her catch her breath and saw two small tears escape.

"But damn it, man, *why?*" Rafe burst out. "You know what he —"

"Right now, I only remember a passage from the Bible. Under the circumstances it seems wholly applicable."

"And that is . . . ?" India asked, her glorious dark eyes swimming.

" 'Vengeance is mine, saith the Lord!' " murmured Alistair Bryson.